THE BLACK-HORNED GRAVE

THE BLACK-HORNED GRAVE

THE DEMON-SLEUTH SCROLLS BOOK TWO

DAN JOLLEY

FALSTAFF
BOOKS
WWW.FALSTAFFBOOKS.COM

For Tracy — without her encouragement, brilliance and, above all, patience I would be lost.

PART I

THE FOREST

1

———————

Saltwater lapped at the hull, dark and patient and hungry.

Titus Binkovsky groaned and squeezed his eyes more tightly shut, but the morning sun forced its golden light relentlessly through each shutter of wrinkled skin. Titus's nose still hosted the scents of wine and girl and sweat from the night previous, competing now with ocean salt and whiffs of piss and vomit.

He threw out one hand, reaching for the nearest bottle of...it didn't matter what, he just needed something to wet his throat, but instead of cool glass he found himself with a handful of ample naked breast. *That's worth opening my eyes for*, he decided, and pried his lids up.

The breast in question belonged to—he knew her name, it would come to him—*Rayna*. One of the girls his brother Maki had brought with him. Titus couldn't remember if he'd sampled Rayna's charms the night before or not.

He sat up with some effort and, once his head had steadied, tried to take stock of the *Gray Stag's* situation. Empty bottles clinked and rolled around every square meter of the yacht's deck, animated by the motion of the waves. His friends lay on the bare wood, emptied of their strength and lust, every bit as drained as the wine bottles cast off among them.

Rayna shifted on the deck. A tiny, somewhat endearing snore escaped her lips. Her thick, black hair had fallen across her eyes, which Titus figured was what kept the sun from waking her up.

"I feel like Dragon's ball crust," Maki said from behind him, and Titus twisted around to see his brother sitting just inside one of the doors to the wheelhouse. "Also, quit groping my girlfriend."

Titus scooted the meter and a half it took to put him in a tiny measure of shade, leaning against the wheelhouse. Kirker lay right out at the prow, curled up with a brown-skinned, red-headed girl whose name Titus didn't think he'd ever learned. Saerg half-lay, half-sat, slumped against a rail post with Sheeli's head in his lap. Both of them were awake now. Saerg played with Sheeli's hair as she grinned up him.

"Look at those two," Titus said, softly enough that Saerg wouldn't hear him. "How long have they been together? Ten years?"

Maki grunted. "Since Saerg first grew fuzz on his balls."

"You're awfully ball-centered this morning."

Maki had found a mostly-full bottle of wine somewhere and took a long pull off of it. "I'll tell you what's true. Together ten years or not, you know who's been getting his cock wet on the regular? Like, whenever he wants it, no matter what?"

Titus shrugged. "Saerg."

"Yeah. Just remember that, the next time you're hard up for some tail."

"As if either one of us is ever going to be hard up for tail again."

Maki grinned. "Well. True."

Titus ran his hand along the deep, lustrous wood of the deck. Their father had accepted a new position in Caulspring the previous autumn—a position that brought with it prestige, respect, and more money than the Binkovsky family had ever dreamed of. "Wise to be in the Cathedral's favor, that's a fact."

Maki got unsteadily to his feet. "No shit, that's a fact. You think we'd have this fucking boat if Dad was still stacking numbers at that termite-infested sawmill? The answer is no." He turned in a slow circle. "Hey. Uh…"

Titus cranked his neck to look up at his brother. "Something wrong?"

Maki's voice lost its wine-fueled mellow. "Get everybody up. You'd better get everybody up."

Titus lurched to his feet, and when he saw the whites all the way around his brother's deep brown irises his stomach tightened. "What is it? What's wrong?"

Maki made a broad gesture with one trembling hand. "Where's the shore?"

4

Titus's world snapped into crystal focus as he peered in every direction.

There was nothing but water.

"Get them all up," Titus said, his words shaking as badly as his brother's hand. "*Get them all up now.*"

He could hear Maki shouting at their friends, but the sound of the voices grew muffled and distant, masked by the frantic roaring in his ears as he scrambled to the stern. The *Gray Stag's* anchor line disappeared into the water, exactly as he'd left it the previous evening at sunset, but when he took the great rope in his hands and tugged, it moved easily.

Titus Binkovsky came very close to losing control of his bowels.

They'd taken the *Gray Stag* out into the bay the night before, the lights of Caulspring watching over them from the northwest, nothing more than a couple of fortunate brothers wanting to show off their new yacht for a few friends.

Wanting to show off. The voice of Titus's father came to him, the chastising tone, the warnings against flaunting the family's newfound affluence. *I'm sorry, Papa,* Titus wished he could say. Fractured thoughts sought out the Great Silver Dragon, begging for help, begging for deliverance. *I'm sorry, I'm so sorry!*

He pulled and pulled, dragged the heavy line over the gunwale, and no more than three or four meters came up before it ended in a ragged, frayed mess. Titus was holding the end of the anchor line in both hands when Maki and Kirker and Saerg came back to the stern, Sheeli and Rayna and the other two girls trailing after them, and when Maki saw Titus's face, all the color drained out of his own features.

"I was supposed to get the anchor line changed out," Maki said, almost too softly to hear. "It needed—needed changing, it was on the schedule, I was supposed to do it, I—"

Titus tried to talk. It didn't work, and he had to swallow hard and get his breathing under control before he could make any sound at all. Finally, in a soft, tiny voice that chilled him even as he spoke the words, he said, "I think we're past the Buoys."

Sheeli screamed.

A girl whose name he didn't know burst into tears.

A fragment of a children's rhyme came to him as he blinked away tears of his own.

The deep, deep water will take your breath

The deep, deep water holds only death

Kirker said, "Get the sails, get the sails up, we've got to get the sails up," but Titus had already thought of that, and didn't make a move toward the mast because there was no wind.

It was Saerg who first went to the rail and looked over. Down at the water, down *into* the water, and when he turned his head and met Titus's eyes, Titus knew.

By then Kirker had also realized how still the air was, and he ran up and down the *Gray Stag*'s length, shouting, "Oars, there have to be oars, we can still get back to land! We can row, all of us, we can do it if we work together, we can't be *that* far out!"

Maki had joined Saerg at the railing. As Kirker passed him, Maki caught his arm and dragged him to a halt, and pointed at the water below. "Oars won't help," Maki said, and the cold, bleak words stopped Kirker cold.

Titus went to his brother's side. He didn't want to gaze down at the glassy water—at what might be lurking beneath the surface. Waiting. Watching. When he finally summoned the will to follow his friends, some dim, distant part of his mind obscenely grasped at the smallest shred of hope.

An elegant, streamlined head emerged from the waves, staring back up at the hapless humans on the yacht. Ivory in color, sleek and hairless, fashioned so as to knife elegantly and gracefully through the water, yet with a domed skull that left no doubt as to the intelligence lurking within. Larger than some of the river dolphins Titus had seen, yet...not *that* large. Not a...not a *monster*.

Despite the silver eyes that shimmered and flashed in the unforgiving sunlight.

"It's not doing anything," Sheeli whispered. "It's just watching us."

Rayna clutched Maki's arm. "Maybe it's not—not like—maybe it's not angry?"

Titus wanted to echo her. Desperately wanted to believe that the creature observing them felt nothing more than curiosity.

Then, below the creature at the surface, *something moved.*

Something immense.

Something that also bore eyes of silver.

A raucous chorus overhead made Titus look skyward, and when he saw the gulls and pelicans circling the *Gray Stag*, the hope that had struggled in his heart lost its strength and died.

Those Who Dwell Beneath the Waves had come.

Sheeli screamed again as the sea boiled around them, and the last thing Titus saw, rising up beneath the hull, was the gaping, tooth-filled maw of a vast ocean-born god.

2

Marshall Bendt remembered struggling to describe Caulspring to his parents the first year of his apprenticeship. Part of his lessons involved reading and writing—a skill required of the Empire's citizens, but to which he had never been exposed in his home village—and his instructor had encouraged him to write letters back to the tiny, mud-encrusted hamlet of his birth.

People call this city "the Bloody Forest," Marshall had written, a year into his new tutelage. *It's the oldest city in the Empire, and all the buildings are made of brick or stone or both. All of them! I haven't seen a single building inside the city walls made of wood, and all the roofs are stone, too. I know Maree's going to think I'm making up stories, but it's true, everything I'm telling you. The city walls are stone, but they've got red bricks built into them in patterns. I climbed up to the top of the tallest tower I could find, and that wasn't the tallest tower in the city, just the one they'd let me up in, and I couldn't count all the buildings. It really is like a whole forest of bricks and stone blocks, and even the streets are made of stone, and there's a waterfall right beside the Emperor's Palace, you can see that from anywhere, and the river goes through the city and all the bridges over it are stone and the bridges have roofs just like the houses and churches.*

Marshall had kept up writing letters back to his family for the first two years. Then, in the spring of the third year, a Cathedral soldier came and gave him back the latest letter he'd written, and told him that his family and the rest of the village had been slaughtered in a Skahna raid.

That was the last letter Marshall ever wrote. He fell out of love with the written word that day, but it didn't seem to matter much to the Imperial tailor's office. Numbers reigned there.

Forty-one years later, Marshall Bendt had become the Imperial Tailor himself, and as such had been charged with outfitting the latest group of visitors to Caulspring with proper clothing for an audience with the Emperor. The closest he'd come to writing anything of substance in four decades was the notes he always took on the chalk-slate he habitually carried with him. Marshall polished the slate as he walked along one of the glossy stone corridors of the Palace's south wing, preparing himself to jot down measurements and fabric requirements. He tapped the comforting shape of the coiled measuring twine in his pocket.

One of the two bronze-clad soldiers standing outside the door to the parlor bowed crisply and worked the latch. Marshall pushed the heavy door inward, drew a deep breath to introduce himself, and—

For a moment, just a heartbeat, as his voice clenched in his throat, he forgot to breathe. No, more than that—he forgot *how* to breathe.

Everything Marshall thought he knew about tailoring, about beauty, about the world itself, changed in a heartbeat.

A creature of breathtaking grace stood before him, the kind of grace that the coarse bronze-inlaid leather armor could not hide, the kind that a tailor longed to see.

One hundred ninety centims tall if she was a millim, though he'd have to measure to be certain. Broad shoulders, but not too broad. Modest curves at the bust and the hips, legs as long as dreams. Right behind those stunning proportions, crowding up in his head now that he'd taken a few seconds to think, were her deep violet skin, her eyes of brilliant yellow gold, and the tasteful, jet-black horns protruding from her forehead—he'd have to take those into account, of course, especially with a hood or a veil—

"You've struck the fucker speechless, Nysska," someone declared, and Marshall had to drag his attention away from the violet-skinned goddess to acknowledge that there were indeed other people in the room. He looked them over perfunctorily. All in the same unremarkable bronze-and-leather. All human, which just in the last few seconds he'd come to find terribly boring.

One dark-skinned, straight-backed man with a Commander's band around his head; another man, this one small and pale with long, snow-white hair and a forked white beard. A dark-skinned woman who, before today, would have taken every bit of his interest. Now he found her athletic build and shorn-off hair and high cheekbones ordinary, her ample bosom and full hips problematic, the gleaming silver runes embedded in her irises nothing more than a distraction.

The dark-skinned man said, "We are the Ninth Crucible, reporting as ordered. I'm Commander Raoul Cullen. This is Keeper Percy Bitters, Sensor Camble Delakroy, and—" He nodded toward the goddess. "—Enforcer Nysska Stonegate."

Marshall succeeded in clearing his throat. "I am, uh, if I may—pardon me—" He took a deep breath. His lungs felt creaky. "Please allow me to introduce myself. I am Imperial Master Tailor Marshall Bendt. I—"

Marshall broke off when he felt something touch his ankle. He looked down and found himself staring into a pair of silver eyes—not more glimmering argonium runes like Sensor Delakroy's, but pure, natural, true silver. The sight made his balls tighten. The eyes belonged to the biggest cat he'd ever seen, easily as big as many of the stray dogs that roamed the streets of Caulspring.

A seraphic animal. A seraphic *blood lynx.*

Marshall had been around seraphic animals before. They had made him intensely nervous then, and continued to do so now. He said, "Uh... good kitty?" and rummaged through his pockets. "I might have a treat in here somewhere...?"

The cat made a noise that sounded like *Hmph* and walked away from him. Marshall watched as it joined another large, silver-eyed cat at the other end of the room, and he realized the second animal had been there the whole time, sitting perfectly still.

"Look, Mister Bendt," said the small, pale man—*Keeper Percy Bitters,* Marshall reminded himself. "If you're going to do this measuring thing, could you please get the fuck on with it? We've been waiting here for half an hour, none of us have been fed yet, and if I don't get my kitties some meat here shortly they're going to make off with a small child."

Marshall fumbled the measuring twine out of his pocket. "Yes, of course!" He dropped the chalk, scrambled to pick it up, and then almost dropped the slate. "Please forgive me! With whom shall I start?" Marshall knew he should be directing questions like that to the Crucible's Commander, but simply could not take his eyes off Nysska Stonegate. *Nysska Stonegate.* He said the name silently a few more times.

"Let me guess," the goddess said, speaking for the first time as she shrugged off her heavy bronze-inlaid jacket. "I'm the first sethyd you've met."

She spoke Plainish with an accent he'd never heard before, a lilting, husky melody, and Marshall felt himself begin to sweat. *Sethyd*. He'd been aware of the term, of course, but had never heard it spoken by one of them. "True, I've not had the pleasure—er, not been tasked to—it's not been my duty before now, no. To fashion clothing for a, a sethyd."

Out of the jacket, Nysska Stonegate wore one of the Cathedral's standard-issue long-sleeved shirts, tucked into a pair of bronze-inlaid brown leather trousers. The trousers fit her snugly enough, but the shirt was too baggy, no doubt sewn for a man of her height but without her proportions.

Gathering his nerve, Marshall said, "Would you mind—Enforcer, if I may assume you have the standard undergarment—what I'm trying to ask is if you wouldn't mind, could you please remove your shirt, so that I may be as accurate as possible?"

Her flame-yellow eyes glittered and narrowed.

Raoul Cullen stepped up beside the towering sethyd woman. The top of his head reached her ears. "Just do what he wants so we can get this over with."

Nysska Stonegate sighed and said a word in a language Marshall had never heard before, though her tone made it obvious what she meant by it. He watched as she unbuttoned and stripped off the shirt, revealing the standard-issue camisole beneath it, and he tried to keep his breathing even as he took in the long, graceful lines of her perfectly toned arms. *My designs will fit this woman better than any clothing I've ever touched.*

"This won't take a minute," Marshall said, and grabbed a small wooden stool from beside the door, measuring twine stretched out and ready to go.

Ninety minutes later, after the Imperial tailor had taken all of their measurements and left—and after the members of the Ninth Crucible had been moved to a chamber adjacent to a small kitchen and fed a decent meal—Nysska Stonegate stood in a room with marble floors, stacked-stone walls, a waist-level trough with a stream of clear water running through it, and six narrow doors in a wall behind her. She had just finished washing her hands in the trough when one of the narrow doors opened and Cam Delakroy emerged, straightening her clothing.

Nysska didn't turn. A long, horizontal window above the wash-trough looked out over the roofs of Caulspring, and she kept her eyes focused on the most distant one.

Cam made her way to Nysska's side at the trough and washed her hands just as Nysska had.

"How happy are you to have indoor plumbing again?" Cam asked. "And how miserable were those last two villages? I don't mind so much when we're out on the trail, but the Empire's had, what, three hundred years? You'd think they would've made this kind of accommodation standard by now."

"Every home on Patrinamonto had indoor plumbing. It was the first thing I learned to do without when we had to flee." Nysska turned and leaned against the trough. Folded her arms across her chest and let her chin drop. "I don't want to talk about indoor plumbing."

Cam put her hand on Nysska's arm. "You can still change your mind. You can take it to Raoul—something like this should come from a Crucible's commander anyway."

Nysska pursed her lips. Exhaled softly. "No. No, we stick to what we discussed. You know nothing about it. None of you do." She turned her head, yellow-flame eyes meeting silver. "*None* of you. Promise me."

"I already promised you."

"Promise me again."

Cam moved in front of her and gently unfolded Nysska's arms. Moved into her embrace. "It's going to be all right."

"You don't know that. There's no way you can know that."

Cam traced the curve of Nysska's lips with a light fingertip. "Whatever happens, I'm here for you. You know that."

Nysska kissed Cam's fingers. "You're only saying that because there's a decent chance my headless body will hang from a fork in the city center tomorrow."

Cam's eyes narrowed. It made the silver of the argonium runes shine just a hair brighter. "You're bringing him valuable information. Information you're sharing of your own free will. You'll probably be rewarded."

"And if I weren't? If I'd decided to keep it to myself?"

Cam's body stiffened. "But you didn't."

"So pretend I had."

"What's the point?" Cam pushed away from her. "Why even bring that up?"

"What if I said, 'Yes, Cam, I'll tell the Emperor about the sethyd plot to overthrow the Empire—on the condition that you only use your runes when you have no other choice.'"

"I would say that's a really shitty thing to do."

"Cam..."

"You said you understood. I explained—"

"The runes are still poison. They're still killing you."

Cam jabbed a finger toward Nysska's nose. "Do *not* fucking cut me off. I told you why I made my decision, and you said you understood. I—" She made a quiet growling sound in her throat. "You want me defenseless, just so I might make it to forty before the runes take me?"

"You're hardly defenseless without them."

"I'm *blind* without them. Great fucking Dragon, how many times do I have to say this? It doesn't matter how well I've adapted if I can't see an archer twenty meters away! If I do what you ask—knowing what I know —" Cam sighed, a long, raspy, exasperated sound. "Ten or twelve years versus however long it is before we get ambushed again. Take your pick."

Nysska opened her mouth, but then closed it again. She had almost said the words she wanted to say.

I can protect you.

But she'd said that to Cam once before, and the conversation had gone poorly. Poorly enough that she didn't want to risk it again.

A knock sounded at the door, and Nysska did her best not to look relieved. Cam called out, "What do you want?"

An attendant's polite voice answered, muffled by the door's heavy wood. "Master Bendt's people have brought your clothes."

Cam peered up at her, and loaded up a single word with a barrage of emotion. "*Well?*"

"Well," Nysska answered quietly. "I suppose we should go get dressed."

3

Nysska wasn't sure how much time had passed when she and Cam walked into the Emperor's antechamber. Stripped of the armor to which she'd grown accustomed, as well as the weapons on which she'd been forced to rely, Nysska felt more than a little naked.

She caught sight of Raoul first. Abandoning the traditional bronze, Marshall Bendt had decided to dress them all in whites and soft grays, and as irritating as Nysska found the whole process, she could find no fault in the tailor's skills. Or rather, the skills of the dozens of junior tailors who'd no doubt scurried about in a frenzy of fabrics and leathers under Bendt's orders.

The expertly fitted clothing, and the speed with which it had been assembled, reminded her of a time when her mother had decided to hire a crew of builders to replace the roof on their house. Twelve sethyd men and women had shown up at the crack of dawn and swarmed over the house. First in one direction, like a cloud of locusts, stripping tiles away—then back over it in the other direction, leaving new roofing in their wake. The entire job had been finished by mid-afternoon.

The gray leather boots, immaculate white trousers and shirt, and gray leather jacket all fit Raoul's lean, muscular body perfectly. He touched his now-bare head in a motion like a nervous tic, fingers searching for the

Commander's band that had been whisked off to their as-yet-unseen quarters by Bendt's people.

The tailor's staff had done an equally skillful job putting Percy in an outfit similar to Raoul's, but where the Commander's new clothing seemed to accentuate him, Percy had diminished. His shoulders slumped, his eyes had lost their customary obscene, mischief-laden glimmer—and in the next moment she saw why. The black leather gloves he normally wore had been taken away as well, and as his trousers appeared to have no pockets, the pale little man had nowhere to hide the mangled ruin of his left hand. Nysska watched him fidget, holding his hands clasped behind him, dropping them to his sides, and finally folding his arms, so that he tucked the disfigured hand into one armpit.

"Cruel," she whispered.

At her side, Cam said, "What was that?"

Nysska glanced down at her. The tailor staff had brought Cam an elegant long-sleeved blouse, a gray suede skirt that hugged her hips and dropped to just above her knees, and a pair of soft white leather boots that laced up to mid-shin. She looked amazing, but as soon as the junior tailors had unveiled both women's outfits, it had become painfully clear which of them Marshall Bendt favored.

"I said, 'cruel.' They've taken Percy's glove. That's not fair."

Cam swept her gaze across the men. "Agreed." Then, after a pause, "I suppose the Emperor prefers truth to be exposed."

Nysska almost flinched at that. As Cam went to greet Raoul and Percy, Nysska caught sight of herself in one of the floor-to-ceiling mirrors lining the far wall.

Marshall Bendt had made good on his promise to dress her like a goddess. No blouses or skirts for her. She wore a long, slim sheath dress of snow-white silk with dove-gray panels on each side, ribs to hips, which served to create the illusion that her waist tapered even more than it already did. The dress left her arms bare, and plunged in both the front and the back, exposing more of her breasts' slim contours than she would've liked. At the same time, though, it was the softest, most comfortable garment she had ever worn, and that included the furs she'd stitched together herself.

Her night-black hair, which normally hung in a single long braid, now flowed loose around her shoulders, arranged so as to emphasize the cobalt-blue streak she'd had since girlhood. But the touch that drew her eyes the most, with its bespoke elegance, was the pair of diamond-accented silver wire sheaths that Bendt's people had fitted over her horns. With every movement of Nysska's head, the horns flashed and sparkled, and while a part of her wanted to reject the decoration as gaudy and ostentatious, a deeper part relished it in secret, silent delight.

Is this what a sethyd princess would look like?

If such a thing existed?

The only part of the outfit she didn't care for were the shoes. Bizarre, slanting affairs they were, with ridiculous tall heels that made her tower over the humans even more than usual. She hated the heels, and hated the way the shoes made her prance about on her toes, and so she stood and waited in bare feet, shoes dangling from one hand.

Nysska spotted the two blood lynxes, Flax and Jax, off in a corner. Flax was busy grooming her nether regions, while Jax crouched low, paws drawn up under him, hind end wiggling as he lined up a pounce on his sister. The pounce took Flax completely off-guard, and the two cats rolled around in a ball, wrestling and letting out the occasional hiss.

The motion made Percy glance up, and when he saw Cam and then Nysska behind her, his eyes and mouth sprang open all at once, three perfect circles in his face. "You two've missed your calling, you have," he said, mouth swiftly widening into his customary grin. "I don't know what that calling would be, exactly, but it's sure as fuck not serving in a Crucible."

Raoul saw them a second after Percy did, and Nysska tried her best to read the lightning-fast emotions that raced across his features like a volley of arrows.

Raoul had spent the better part of the last five years hopelessly in love with Cam. He'd never acted on it. Never even spoken about it, as the Thaumetallicon was quite clear about relationships between personnel. The worry lived in the back of Nysska's mind, small but ever-present, that her relationship with Cam would eventually prove unbearable for him. She wondered how much it must hurt to see Cam looking so radiant. And so very much not his.

Raoul's face had returned to its normal stoic condition by the time he'd taken the five steps across the marble floor to reach them. Percy followed after him, openly eyeing Nysska up and down, for which she decided to forgive him just this once.

"You both look...suitable for an audience with the Emperor," Raoul said, his tone neutral.

"Thanks," Cam said. "They did pretty well with you two, also."

At that moment the enormous stained-cherry double doors at the far end of the antechamber opened. Two men emerged who, at first glance, Nysska took for ordinary Cathedral soldiers—until she noticed the gleaming strips of tin, rather than bronze, laid into the leather.

Argonium Infantry.

Of *course* the Emperor would be attended by members of the Empire's deadly elite force. Nysska had witnessed the might of the Infantry herself twice before. Tonight, bearing no armor or weapons, she cautioned herself to do nothing to provoke their anger.

"The Emperor is ready for you," one of the soldiers called out.

"Here we go," Cam said.

Nodding, Raoul turned and led the way—until the same soldier who'd spoken held up a hand. "No. Not all of you. Only Enforcer Stonegate."

The team froze in place. With an edge to his words, Raoul said, "Our orders were to report to Emperor Valco. The entire Ninth Crucible. Not just our Enforcer."

The soldier didn't bother to look at them. "And now you have different orders. The Emperor will speak to Enforcer Stonegate alone. The rest of you may retire to your quarters, or wait here. Your choice."

Behind them, the door through which Nysska and Cam had entered swung open, and a couple of women in bronze-and-brown livery appeared, each bearing a practiced smile. One of them said, "If the rest of you will come with us, please?" She paused. "That includes your animals, as well."

Nysska could all but feel the tension radiating from Raoul. She turned and spoke to him directly. "We serve at the pleasure of the Emperor, don't we? If he says I go in alone, I go in alone."

Raoul stayed silent. Nysska knew he was thinking, analyzing, trying to come up with some way both to ensure her safety and determine what this meant for the Crucible as a whole.

"Yes, of course," Raoul finally said. "But the rest of us will stay here and wait for you."

One of the two liveried women shrugged, and they both turned to leave. "We'll be out here," the other woman said, and they disappeared, shutting the door behind them.

One of the Argonium Infantrymen said, "Enforcer Stonegate. Now." Nysska stooped to slip the ridiculous shoes back onto her feet, but the soldier spoke up again. "No time for that. Come on."

With the briefest of glances at her teammates, Nysska took a deep breath, smoothed down the silk of her dress, and padded barefoot past the soldiers and through the doorway. A short hallway ended in another set of doors, which the Infantrymen opened for her.

The room on the other side wasn't as large as she was expecting, though it was difficult to judge its size since most of it lay hidden in shadow. When Emperor Valco Overthorne the Twelfth stood up from one of the plush, fur-covered chairs and turned to face her, the room seemed to get smaller still.

Silhouetted against the roaring fire in the massive fireplace on the opposite wall, Emperor Valco seemed more like some kind of honorary statue than a man. He stood at least a head taller than Nysska, and though the multiple layers of silk, cotton, and leather that made up his suit must have added to his bulk, she had no doubt that underneath it all he was a *mountain* of bone and muscle.

One of the things that had struck Nysska most when she first ventured into human lands was the sheer diversity. She'd come to think of humans a bit like dogs. Take the biggest, most barrel-chested shepherd, or the most muscular pit-fighting dog. Put it next to a tiny short-haired roundhead, and one might legitimately wonder if they were even of the same species.

Humans, she'd observed, were much the same. Never mind the ridiculous difference in size between males and females. Even among the males alone, she had seen tall, slender, wiry men not too dissimilar to the sethyd build; wide-shouldered, bull-necked men, like human bison; and short, scrawny, reed-necked men who, for their sakes, she hoped were extremely good at writing or doing calculations, since they wouldn't have lasted ten seconds in either wilderness or battle.

Emperor Valco was very much in the wide-shouldered, bull-necked variety. And yet, as she watched him stride across the chamber toward her, he *moved* more like the slender wiry kind, with a limber, easy gait and graceful, economical motions.

Finally he drew close enough that the silhouette effect left him, and the light of one of the nearby lanterns shined full on his face.

Nysska stifled a gasp.

Emperor Valco Overthorne the Twelfth was *old.*

His long hair, swept straight back from his face and falling to between his shoulder blades, was a solid silver-gray, and though the rich blue-green of his eyes glittered with intelligence, deep lines crossed his face and crossed again. The ugly brown spots she'd seen on elderly humans blemished his forehead and his cheeks. When he spoke, his voice creaked and wavered like an unsteady shutter on a windy night.

"At long last," he said, and favored her with a smile full of perfect, straight white teeth. She wondered if they might have been false. "Enforcer Nysska Stonegate. Born Nysska Kaur, of the now-abandoned island nation of Patrinamonto. Please come and sit with me. Would you like something to drink? You have eaten, yes?"

So surprised was Nysska by the Emperor's unexpected physical presence, as well as by his knowledge of her birth name, that it took her long enough to answer for him to raise an eyebrow. A gesture of impatience? Amusement? She couldn't tell.

In the silence, she noticed another presence in the room. Out of the shadows stepped a tall, gaunt, pale-skinned, bald human in a long bronze-colored robe. He wore—Nysska squinted, making sure she understood what she was seeing—a sort of *desk*. A strap around his neck held up a writing board with two wooden spindles attached, one at the top, one pressed against the man's waist. A scroll ran between the two spindles, and a glass inkpot rested in a well at one of the desk's top corners. The Scribe—that had to be what he was—dipped a long quill pen in the ink and brought his hand back to the parchment, watching her and the Emperor. Poised.

"I require no sustenance, sir," she said at last, and Valco laughed. That brought with it ghosts of what his voice must have been like years ago—deep and booming and utterly unself-conscious. The scritch-scratch of the Scribe's pen against the parchment, recording her words, was almost lost against the crackle of the fire.

"How formal! And yet you mistake the proper attribution. I am to be addressed as 'Your Brilliance.'"

"Oh—my apologies, Your Br—"

He cut her off with a wave of his hand. "No, no, I think I like 'sir' from you better. Come, please, have a seat. There are matters I wish to discuss."

Valco led her closer to the fire, but not so close that the crackling flames might interfere with their conversation. As Nysska settled into a soft fur-upholstered chair, she noticed a series of horizontal slits in the walls at roughly chest height. She wondered how many of the crossbow-armed soldiers for which the slits were meant stood at the ready, prepared to turn her into a violet-skinned pincushion if she made any threatening moves toward their Emperor.

"What would you like to talk about, sir?" she asked, trying to figure out what to do with her hands and whether or not she should cross her legs. The dress fit snugly enough that she wasn't convinced crossing her legs was even possible.

The Scribe watched her with glittering light brown eyes. Pen at the ready.

Valco had taken the other chair, and now he leaned forward, elbows on his knees, and tented his fingers in front of his lips in a contemplative gesture. "I have read the official reports, and spoken with Governor Vachs, but I am interested in hearing directly from you an account of what occurred in the Green Needles Territory."

Nysska took a deep breath. "I would be happy to oblige, sir, but before I do, there is another matter that I need to bring to your attention. I—"

He cut her off again, but this time the air of friendly grandfather slipped, revealing beneath it the face of a man who had never, not once in his life, been disobeyed. "There will be time for other matters once my curiosity is satisfied, Enforcer. I asked you to give me your recollection of events. You may begin doing so now."

Nysska took a breath. She *hated* this. Hated showing deference to a human who, as far as she was concerned, had done not a fucking thing to earn it. And yet she sat in the heart of his seat of power, where his word commanded instant life or death. "Well…sir…what it boils down to is that a group of people hostile to the Empire have discovered a way to alloy argonium with some other, unknown kind of metal. That metal interferes with the traditional uses of argonium—which is to say, the runes used by the Thaumetallicon's Sensors—and it also appears that this alloy can be fashioned into a new kind of rune. Like the traditional argonium ones, these new runes imbue the recipient with thaumaturgical abilities when implanted under the skin. But they cause effects…um…." She wasn't used to talking so much all at once, and her Plainish threatened to fail her. "Effects not…seen before."

"These new runes. Fashioned with the alloy. You're saying they don't function the same as argonium ones."

Nysska wasn't sure whether that was a statement or a question. "Ah… no, sir. The traditional ones enhance one of the five senses in various ways—which you already know—but the new ones…" She cleared her throat. "We've seen them animate the dead. And in at least one case, they elevated a man's strength to tarn-like levels."

"Yes," Valco said. He seemed to be speaking to himself. "Yes. Runes implanted beneath the skin, yet not by Imperial runemasters. And not with the chaotic effects displayed by Tarnished Ones." His focus returned to her. "This…enhanced fellow you met. He was not, I am given to understand, what one might call a normal human?"

"No, sir. He, and another individual we encountered—the Ninth Crucible encountered them, I mean—they both had skin like…forgive the informal nature of the description. We called them 'cuttlefish.' They seemed able to control the pigmentation of their skin to such a degree that they could disguise themselves as other people."

"And these *cuttlefish*. They are the driving force behind this…whatever it turns out to be. Rebellion. Insurrection."

"Correct, sir. The one I killed in Tember—the one who called himself 'Lockridge'—indicated before he died that there were many more like him. I don't know if he was telling the truth or not."

The Scribe scratched furiously at the scroll.

Valco nodded. "Yes, yes, the one you killed by *screaming*, is that right? You screamed into his ear at such volume that, correct me if I misunderstood, it caused his *skull* to rupture?"

"I…was trained as a singer, sir. I never had the best technique, but my volume was unparalleled."

The Emperor sat back in his chair and drummed the fingers of his right hand on the armrest. "That was quite a surprise to us. And by 'us,' I believe I mean humanity as a whole. No one knew the sethyd voice could reach such heights."

"I cannot say for certain, sir, but it seemed to me that the alloyed runes he possessed were what reacted to the scream. Not his—his bones or his blood." Valco's eyes flashed firelight as he stared at her. Nysska took another deep breath. "Sir…if I may, the other matter I wanted to bring up to you?"

His profoundly creased face wore an unreadable expression. "Go on."

She leaned forward. Hands on her knees, mirroring his posture. "Sir, there exists a faction within the sethyds. It was much larger before the *Krizo* drove us from our home, but it's still there—a faction that believes the sethyds are the world's rightful rulers, and that intends to conquer the Empire and reduce humans to a race of servants."

Emperor Valco said, "Yes, yes, the Mountain Bulls. I already know about them."

Camble Delakroy pushed open the door that led back into the rest of the palace. Just as they'd said, the two women in livery lingered nearby, talking quietly. They both looked around at her, and the one who had spoken last said, "May we help you?"

"I was wondering where the nearest, ah, 'ladies' room' might be." Cam peered over to the right, where the hallway turned a sharp corner. "Around there, maybe?"

The other woman pushed away from the wall. "Good guess. Here, I'll show you."

Near as Cam could tell, the corridor down which the woman led her ran parallel to the short hallway Nysska had traversed to speak to the Emperor. Cam really did need to relieve her bladder, but when the woman showed her a door on the right-hand side of the hallway, she began to entertain another thought.

Leaving the woman outside, Cam entered the ladies' room. It was very much like the one in which she had spoken to Nysska earlier. Smaller. No window. But the dimensions looked promising. If her mental map of this wing of the palace proved accurate, maybe even ideal. After she had relieved herself and washed her hands, Cam went to the far wall and pressed her ear tight against it.

Yes.

Faintly, so faintly, she could hear voices. One of them might have been Nysska's.

Cam glanced back at the door to the hallway. It seemed to fit well enough in its frame, but to be safer, she stepped into the last stall and shut the door. With a deep breath and a flare of concentration she brought the power of her runes up, and the stall filled with soft silver light.

Cam used the runes to look through the stone wall.

Seconds later she gasped and clapped her hands over her eyes, shutting the runes down entirely, just as a knock sounded from outside. The door to the hall opened, and the liveried woman's voice called softly, "Is everything all right, miss?"

"Everything's fine," Cam said, carefully casual. "Just another moment."

As she washed her hands again, she prayed to the Dragon that the woman wouldn't notice her trembling.

Nysska's jaw fell open. Only briefly. "You—I'm sorry, you already know—?"

"The 'Mountain Bulls' *is* what they call themselves, correct? Yes, I've already taken care of it."

Nysska sputtered. She didn't think she'd ever sputtered before. "Sir—but—*how*? How do you know? And, and you've *taken care of it*? How could y—"

Valco cut her off again. "That is not for someone like you to worry about, Enforcer Stonegate. You are a subject of the Empire now, and more than that, you have proven yourself a valuable member of the Thaumetallicon. Some might say *invaluable*." The hint of a smile raised one corner of his mouth. "Some might have used that exact word, in fact."

Nysska couldn't decide which sensation was about to overrun her brain, relief or bafflement. She had gnawed at this revelation ever since that night on the slopes of Altamar. The night when she'd first revealed the Mountain Bulls' plan to invade the human lands to Cam in a moment of painful honesty. Worried over it. Chewed on it until it had left a bloody wound in her mind and on her conscience.

I've already taken care of it, she repeated silently. *What could that possibly mean?*

Emperor Valco went on. "You see, for twelve generations our system of justice has relied heavily on the use of Thaumetallicon Sensors, such as your teammate, Camble Delakroy. Perhaps too heavily. When your Crucible encountered this force which rendered Sensor Delakroy's talents impotent, well...that was where the Imperial training ended, wasn't it? No one in the field had any idea what to do. We were not equipped to deal with the problem. We still aren't." Valco stood and moved closer to the fire, staring into it. "But *you* are. You were ready."

Nysska didn't know if she was supposed to stand and join him or keep her seat. "Sir, I didn't—"

The fire threw the lines of his face into stark relief. "You gripped that lion by its mane and *forced* it to give up its secrets. You and the rest of the Ninth Crucible took all of the information, all of the details that the Empire would have overlooked, and saw the patterns of it. The depths. The *meaning*. I am deeply impressed, Enforcer. Here. Come to me."

Nysska rose. She tried not to look overtly suspicious, but the presence of the crossbow ports made that difficult. Moving slowly, deliberately, keeping her hands in plain view, Nysska went and stood a meter away from the Emperor, in front of the fire. She had to crane her neck to look up at him—a first for her.

"There is someone I would like you to meet." The Emperor made a tiny gesture with one hand, and a door in a shadow-laden corner behind her opened. "Allow me to introduce the Empire's first sethyd Ambassador and Liaison to the Throne." Nysska turned, putting her back to Emperor Valco just as he said, "Gerrit Longcrest."

That the Emperor couldn't see her face in that moment saved her life, and Nysska knew it.

Gerrit entered the light of the fire, moving past the furiously scribbling Scribe, and any words Nysska might have spoken or even thought locked up tight inside her. Gerrit wore splendid clothes of bronze-and-white leather and silk—more of the Imperial Tailor's handiwork, she felt sure, which made her whirling brain wonder how long Gerrit had been there at the palace—as well as a placid smile that made her want to strike him across the face as hard as she could.

That *perfect* face. Handsome even among other sethyds, now sporting a carefully-trimmed coal-black beard that complemented his boldly curving horns. The firelight turned his violet skin a ruddy sort of brown.

"It is a true pleasure to meet you, Nysska Stonegate," Gerrit said. He had never grown as comfortable with Plainish as she had, so his accent deeply colored his words. "I have heard many great things about the brave sethyd who killed the usurper and saved the Empire."

Nysska blinked. Blinked again. Summoning calm from…somewhere, she wasn't sure where, she said, "I saved the Green Needles Territory, at most. And yes, it is a pleasure to meet you as well, Gerrit Longcrest."

They clasped hands. Gerrit's face betrayed nothing, and by the time she turned back to the Emperor, neither did hers.

"The sethyds," Emperor Valco said, his tone mild. "You are a fascinating people. I never hesitated to offer you asylum, after your Crisis, did you know that? The first of you showed up on my shores, explained to me what had happened, and I welcomed you all with the proverbial open arms. With that amazing skin, and those exquisite horns, and the…the *uniformity* of your bodies. Just look at the two of you. Not a kilgram or a centim of difference. I told my Close Council, every sethyd woman I saw was beautiful, yet with just a touch of masculinity about her. And every sethyd man, handsome enough to make me envious, yet just a bit on the feminine side." He peered closely at her. "And your *eyes*. I could write sonnets about sethyd eyes."

Nysska had no idea how to respond to any of that. She kept still and waited for him, Gerrit's presence at her side as dangerous and oppressive as a swordpoint at her throat.

"Now I realize," the Emperor continued, "that I let your physical attributes distract me. You have proven that there are depths to the sethyd people of which I had no clue. And if one of those depths involves the solving of crimes *without* the use of argonium runes, well...invaluable indeed."

Something in his voice led her to say, "'*If*,' sir?"

Valco's eyes glittered. "Oh, I have yet to be fully convinced, Enforcer Stonegate. The Empire will make great use of your talents, assuming talents they are and not *luck*. If what I have heard proves to be the truth, and not the kind of embellishment that so often plagues a story told over kliks." He showed her his teeth. "I mean to *test* you, you see. You and your Crucible."

Nysska swallowed. "Test us how?"

His face hardened. "A crime has been committed. A crime that has stopped the Third Crucible in its tracks. You and Cullen and Bitters and Delakroy will go and perform an investigation of your own. If you can do for me there what you *claim* to have done in Green Needles, well...then we shall have a great deal more to discuss." He waved a dismissive hand as he turned from her. "My staff will provide you all the details. You may go now." His back to her, Valco went to a bronze-and-glass table in one corner of the room and poured himself a drink.

"Here," Gerrit purred beside her. "Let me walk you out."

"Your Brilliance," she called to the Emperor, because she could think of nothing else to say. Nysska moved with Gerrit out into the short hallway that led to the room where the rest of her Crucible waited. The Infantrymen, apparently every bit as done with her as was the Emperor, stepped back through the doorway and left the two of them alone.

As soon as they were alone, Nysska whirled on Gerrit and spoke in a quiet but forceful hiss. "What the *fuck* are you doing here? What *is* this?" She cast an anxious look in her teammates' direction, but the door at that end of the hall remained closed. "You told him about the Mountain Bulls? What're you trying to do?"

"What we've always done," he answered her with a tiny, smug smile. "We're taking advantage of a situation."

She got closer to him, almost nose to nose. "Where is Mother? How is she?"

His smile broadened into a grin, and he clapped her on the upper arm. "That *is* the question, isn't it? Well. Sounds to me as though you have an investigation to get to." After a tiny pause, he said, "The cat is out of the bag now, as the humans say, regarding the Mountain Bulls. But no one knows I'm your brother. No one knows you're reporting to me. Keep it that way."

Nysska couldn't help herself. "Or *what?*"

Gerrit favored her with a disapproving look. "You *know* what. Don't make Mother suffer needlessly."

Gerrit left her, vanishing through the door to the Emperor's chamber, and Nysska did her level best not to hyperventilate.

When she entered the room where the Ninth Crucible waited, Cam stood poised just inside the door, her body nearly vibrating with tension. Percy and Raoul hovered right behind her, looking equal parts irritated and confused. Nysska said, "What's wrong? What happened?"

"We need to get out of here," Cam said, words unsteady. "Right *now.*"

4

Two hours later, as the sun began to set, the members of the Ninth Crucible sat around a hastily constructed campfire in a clearing off the Mikhail Road. Nysska and Percy had made sure to set up the camp far enough off the road to be out of earshot of any passing soldiers.

"All right," Raoul said, hands on his hips. "Both of you look like you're about to have seizures. What's going on?"

Cam raised her eyebrows at Nysska. "You want to go first?"

Nysska hesitated. "Does yours involve an immediate threat to our lives?"

Cam's face creased. "Maybe?"

"Then you'd better go."

A ring of stones polished by generations of travelers' hind ends provided a ready enough place for a huddled conversation, but once they had all taken seats Cam motioned for them to lean in even closer.

"You all remember, when we were up at Altamar, and I said I could try to look through the stone and see what was around the corner, right? And Percy, you said something like, 'Why the fuck didn't we know you could look through fucking walls, that could've been fucking useful to us before now, fuck,' right? Remember that?"

The team affirmed the recollection with nods and grunts.

Cam went on. "So, the reason you didn't know about it—that I could look through things—is that it's *really severely frowned upon* among Sensors. I'm allowed to use the runes to see, and to Read a crime site. Anything else, if I get caught doing it, I get censured. Severely."

Frowning, Raoul said, "Then why were you so eager to do it at Altamar?"

"Because we were a long way from anybody who could've reported me, and I was afraid we were all about to get killed! Desperate times, desperate measures, all that shit. I should've said something about it once we got back—made sure none of you mentioned it to anyone—but then we got the summons to Caulspring, and I've had other shit to think about."

Percy seemed fascinated. "But why? Why's it such a big fucking deal?"

"For all the reasons that would come to you if you stopped and thought about it." Cam ticked off items on her fingers. "Invasion of privacy. Cheating at gambling. Espionage. Plus, who would ever let a Sensor anywhere near them if it got out we could do shit like this?"

Gently, Nysska asked, "What does this have to do with what happened today?"

Cam seemed to steady herself with some effort. "I thought it was weird and irritating that the Emperor only wanted to talk to you. So I found a toilet room that shared a wall with the room you were in, and...I took a look."

Raoul's brow wrinkled. "You *spied* on the *Emperor?*"

Cam threw her hands up. "I'd never seen him before! Aside from paintings and statues, I mean. Also, I wanted to know what he was talking to Nysska about."

Flax and Jax had sauntered into the conversation ring and flopped down at Percy's feet. He absently scratched Jax's head as he watched Cam. "So? Did you see him?"

"Did I ever." Cam hugged herself, and her voice dropped to a whisper. "The Emperor—Emperor Valco—*he's got runes.*"

No one responded to that.

A chill night breeze made the leaves in the surrounding trees rustle against each other, a sighing, wistful sound.

Nysska said, "What?"

"I know!" Cam's eyes had widened, letting the whites show all around the runed irises. "Believe me, I know how this sounds. It's impossible. But Valco's got runes, all up his arms and legs and in his chest. Kind of like the

Argonium Infantry, but I didn't recognize any of the designs. Also—they weren't silver."

"Great bleeding Dragon's ball sweat," Percy breathed. "He's a, a, a *fake*? Like what they did to Wendell Anwar? Somebody's killed the fucking Emperor?"

"No." Cam shook her head. "No, it's—it's weirder than that. Regular argonium runes are silver, and the ones we saw at Altamar were red."

Raoul's patience seemed to have run out. He all but shouted, "What the hell were these, then?"

"They were white." Cam shuddered. "White as snow." She looked from face to face. Plaintive. *Scared*, Nysska thought. "What does that mean?" Cam asked, her words shaky. *"What the fuck does that mean?"*

Another breeze made Nysska's restored braid shift against her back. "It means there are things about this situation we don't understand."

"Oh, well thanks," Percy snapped, springing to his feet. "Thanks for pointing out the absolute fucking obvious." When Nysska cocked an eyebrow at him, he put up one gloved hand. "Sorry, sorry. I just—I feel like I need a fucking target."

"You said they were white," Raoul said, moving closer to Cam. "You know what the red ones *feel* like. Were Valco's like those?"

Cam put her face in her hands. "No. Not at all. They felt like...like argonium, but not the same. I don't know how to explain it."

Percy returned to his seat. "So. All right. So what do we do with this information? It flies in the face of everything I've ever heard about the Empire. And runes. And...fuck. *Everything.*"

Carefully, deliberately, Nysska said, "It means we carry out the mission. Valco said he meant to test us with this investigation. Us, specifically—the Ninth Crucible. So until we understand what's going on behind the scenes...I think we have to play the hand we've been dealt."

Raoul groaned, but said nothing. When neither Percy nor Cam said anything either, he turned to Nysska. "So what did *you* have to tell us?"

Nysska shared a swift look with Cam. "It's, uh...not as immediate as what Cam saw. It's probably nothing, in fact, based on what Valco told me."

Percy picked up Flax and cradled her in his lap, stroking her head. Nysska thought it looked a bit like a child holding a security blanket. He said, "Fine. What the fuck is it, then?"

"It's...um. Well. It's that there's a faction within the sethyds called the Mountain Bulls, and before the *Krizo* killed most of us, they were putting together an army and were planning to invade the Imperial lands and conquer the humans. All the humans, I mean. All the humans everywhere. And I thought they were too weak to do anything after the *Krizo*, but it turns out they're still out there, and I was going to tell Emperor Valco about them, but he said he already knew about them and had taken care of the problem. He even had a sethyd ambassador there that he introduced to me."

After a long, strained moment, the campsite erupted into heated shouting.

"I'm just trying to understand it," Raoul said, for at least the fiftieth time.

Nysska sighed. She caught sight of Flax and Jax at the edge of the clearing, stalking something in the underbrush, and silently wished them good hunting.

"I didn't tell you because I wanted you and Percy to have plausible deniability."

"But you told Cam?"

"Cam figured it out. Put clues together. She's very smart, you know."

The fire had burned low, but the second moon rode high in the sky, so Nysska could see Raoul's eyes clearly as he glared at her. "And you knew this. All the time you were with us—all the time you were with the Forty-Seventh, you knew, and you didn't say anything."

Cam and Percy sat near the diminished fire. Cam had her eyes closed and her Imperial-issue cloak pulled tight around her. Percy had both cats in his lap now, and didn't seem bothered by the cold.

Nysska spoke loudly enough for all three of them to hear her. "I'm sorry. All I can do is apologize for betraying your trust. I—look, my time in the Forty-Seventh made it clear as crystal how much humans hated me. And *you* didn't want me in the Ninth yourself, Raoul, at least not to begin with. On top of that, if you'll recall, at least nine out of every ten sethyds *died* on Patrinamonto, and the rest of us were more concerned with growing and hunting enough food in the Crags not to starve. I didn't think any of the Mountain Bulls could pull their shit together well enough to organize any kind of army." She paused, trying to gauge whether any of her words were getting through to him. "I should have told you. I wish I had. I'm sorry."

Raoul stared at her for a good fifteen seconds before turning away and throwing his hands up with a disgusted grunt. "Shit. *Fuck.* Fucking *shit*, Nysska, this is—it's—how? How are we supposed to trust you now? How're we supposed to go back to just *functioning?*"

Nysska cleared her throat softly. "This may be a bad time to point it out, but we have no choice. The Ninth has to investigate this...this whatever it is. This crime. Raoul, I can only apologize so many times here, but if you're not going to accept an apology, can we at least call a truce?"

Raoul surprised Nysska by yawning. He said, "Part of me wants to laugh at all this. You've thrown us under a waterfall of information, Nysska, and my brain is soaking wet." He looked around at the campsite as if seeing it for the first time, and his eyes finally settled on his tent. "A truce. Yes. Fine. A truce, and some sleep, and once I've had a chance to think everything through, we'll talk. Yeah? How's that sound to you two?"

Cam and Percy both muttered variations of *Fine with me.* Raoul yawned again and stretched, but when he spoke again his voice held a note of dread. "Maybe Valco's got this potential sethyd uprising under control. Maybe he only *thinks* he does. But one way or another, sooner or later, we're going to be crotch-deep in shit. And I want to be prepared for how deep it is, how fast it's flowing, and from which direction." He headed for his tent, and over his shoulder said, "You should want the same thing."

Cam stood and brushed dust off her trousers. "Well, I'm going to bed." Her runed eyes flashed at Nysska. "You coming?"

Nysska held up a finger—*Be right there*—and spoke to Percy. "You taking first watch?"

He nodded. "I'll get you up in a few hours."

She paused next to him. "Are you angry with me, too?"

With no trace of his usual mischief, Percy said, "I just wish you'd told us sooner. Dragon's shit-caked bunghole, Nysska, this is fucking *huge.*"

"Do you...think you'll be able to forgive me?"

Percy let out a long, slow breath, and lifted one corner of his mouth as he glanced up at her. "Probably." He patted her hand. "Now get some fucking sleep, I don't want any *more* surprises tonight."

Nysska squeezed Percy's shoulder, and followed Cam into the tent they shared. Her last glance out at the fire showed her Percy, humming to himself with the two big cats curled up asleep on the rock where Nysska had been sitting. She closed the flap, wriggled free of her boots and leather armor, and stretched the considerable length of her body out on the bedroll, lying on her side. Cam joined her, but whereas normally she'd wriggle close and press her back and ass to Nysska's chest and groin, tonight she lay staring upward, with a couple of centims space between them.

After a silent half-minute, Cam rolled over and put them face to face, her brow furrowed. "What if Valco *has* been compromised in some way, and ends up putting the whole empire at risk?" Her hand closed on Nysska's arm. "Where would *we* fit in, if the Empire falls?"

"I think it would depend a great deal on who did the felling." When Cam seemed to be waiting for more, she added, "I don't know. We need more information. When we get more, we'll decide what to do then. But for tonight...if we're not going to fuck..."

Cam laughed quietly. "We are *not* going to fuck."

"Then we should probably get some sleep. One of us will have to relieve Percy. And by one of us, I mean me."

Cam kissed her, a tender but quick peck on the lips, and rolled over. A few minutes later her breathing deepened and evened out, and Nysska let herself drop off to sleep as well.

No one spoke the next morning as the Ninth gathered around a re-kindled fire and ate a cold, unsatisfying breakfast. Nysska caught Raoul looking at her a couple of times, but he didn't seem to be glaring at her. More as if he were trying to think of something to say.

Nysska had just finished eating and stood when the sound of hooves on the hard-packed road reached her ears. It wasn't uncommon. The Mikhail Road was one of the main highways into and out of Caulspring, and they'd passed at least two dozen travelers on their way to the campsite. Nysska had concluded there were two riders before she saw either of them.

The two horsemen came around a bend in the road, out from the obscuring veil of trees and underbrush, and immediately veered off into the grass and headed straight for the campsite. Nysska's hand didn't stray far from the hilt of her longsword, and out of the corners of her eyes she saw her teammates taking up similar stances.

They were both human, and neither of them were soldiers, that much was obvious at a glance. They looked more like farmers. Perhaps a father and a son, Nysska thought, taking in the similar shapes of the noses and cheekbones. They shared the same skin tone, an unremarkable brown, and wore plain, rough clothing and identical broad-brimmed hats. She might have dismissed them entirely if their mouths hadn't been set in such flat, determined lines.

"Good morning," the father called out. Nysska chose to think of him as "father," in any case. "Out on military business, I see?"

"That's right," Raoul called back. "Is there something we can help you with?"

The two riders slowed and came to a halt a few meters away. Neither of them made any move to dismount. Something about their demeanor made the skin on the back of Nysska's neck pucker, and she found herself glancing around the site's perimeter.

"Well, that depends," the father said. "Son, what could they do to help us?"

The younger man—Nysska put him at eighteen years, though that was no more than a guess—spoke casually, as if placing an order for a chicken skewer from a street vendor. "You could take the head off that filthy demon there and put her body on a fork where it belongs."

A dagger appeared in Percy's right hand, but Raoul gestured for him to stand down. "Excuse me?" Raoul said, and stepped closer to the pair. "It sounded to me as though you just threatened an Enforcer of the Thaumetallicon."

"Wa'n't no threat," the father shot back. "You asked what you could do to help us, and we told you. Well, my son told you. We ain't said a word makin' no threats, have we?"

The situation had veered into the bizarre so quickly that Nysska wasn't even sure how she felt about it. Neither of the two men appeared to be armed. They simply sat there on horseback, staring at her, as if from behind some kind of invisible armored wall.

"Gentlemen," Raoul began, hand resting on his longsword's pommel, "I don't know who you're supposed to be, or who you think you're speaking to, but the Cathedral follows a well-worn and time-honored tradition regarding civilians who can't keep civil tongues in their heads."

"Yes, intimidate us," the son said. "Or rather, *try* to intimidate us. I think you'll find we are protected by the Great Silver Dragon in all of His glory. We follow His will, and we have come to tell you, it is His will that that purple-skinned tower of blasphemy there be expunged from the land. Along with all her horned demon brethren."

"I can sink a blade into that loudmouth's temple from here no problem," Percy muttered.

The son went on. "A day of reckoning will come for you, Nysska Stonegate. A day when everyone sees through your lies to the true demon inside you. The Church of the Great Silver Dragon is rising up against you, and you shall suffer endless torment at the hands of the righteous."

A little louder, Percy said, "*Please* let me kill this dumb motherfucker," but Raoul held up a hand.

"We are investigators," Raoul said to the father and son. "As such, we are only empowered to act during or after the commission of a crime, and are expressly forbidden from bringing harm to any unarmed, non-violent citizen of the Empire." When the two men did nothing but stare at him, Raoul continued. "That is the *only* reason I don't drag you both from your mounts and take your heads off myself. Now get out of my sight before I forget to follow orders."

The two men tugged on their horses' reins just enough to turn them, and touched heels to sides just hard enough to send the horses away at a casual pace. The father called over his shoulder as they left, "Your day is coming soon, Nysska Stonegate. The fangs of the Dragon strike swift and true."

The Ninth Crucible stood and stared after the riders until they had disappeared around another bend in the road.

Percy said, "Did that just happen? Did I get really drunk last night and now I'm seeing things?"

Cam came to Nysska's side and took her hand. "I guess not everyone can love you as much as that tailor back at the palace."

"Or as much as all the humans whose lives you saved back in Tember," Raoul all but spat out. "Fucking ridiculous."

"The Church has never cared for me much," Nysska said, staring at the spot on the road where the two men had moved out of sight. "I once got rebuked by an innkeeper's son for similar reasons."

"That felt like more than a rebuke," Percy said as he re-sheathed his dagger.

Raoul turned his back to the road. "Come on. Let's break camp. We've got a job to do, religious bigots or no religious bigots."

Nysska didn't say anything else, but the way Raoul and Percy had immediately and without question stood beside her made her want to cry a little.

The sun had barely cleared the tops of the trees the next morning when they reached their destination. A narrow cleft in a ridge led them into a long valley running north and south between two snow-capped peaks.

It would have been a feast for the eyes if the smell hadn't reached them first.

"Dragon's fucking *bones*," Percy coughed out. "What is that? It smells like...the worst kitchen...in the world's worst inn."

Cam waved a hand in front of her face as if to fan away the stench. "Dragon curse it, I wish I could close my *nose*."

Nysska caught sight of the look on Raoul's face, and called out to him. "You've encountered this before, haven't you, Commander?"

Raoul cast a glance at her over his shoulder. Worlds lived in that glance. "You're smelling burnt flesh," Raoul said, simply. "A lot of it."

The rutted gravel road threaded down a steep hillside, switching back on itself, until they reached the valley floor, where it continued south alongside a broad stream. Signs of civilization appeared quickly, in the form of simple wooden footbridges across the stream and a couple of fishing sheds. Within minutes, Nysska spotted a hillside reduced to a graveyard of efficiently sawn stumps, while across the stream a broad pasture stretched out. A small herd of the long-haired cattle favored in this climate grazed placidly.

When the stream hooked around to the left, the Ninth Crucible followed the curve, and a village made itself visible through the trees. At first glance, Nysska thought it looked a lot like other villages they had seen this close to Caulspring: homes and businesses with stacked-stone foundations, topped by wood frame construction and thatched roofs.

"Dragon in the heavens," Cam breathed, her silver runes shining bright. "It's all *burnt*."

Cam was right, Nysska saw. Beyond the few buildings at the village's edge, a fire seemed to have torn through the place. The closer they got, the more damage they saw, such that at the village's center there was little left besides scorched stone and heaps of ash.

From off to their right, a horse neighed, and Nysska caught the flash of Imperial bronze as four riders came galloping out to meet them. The one in the lead, a lean, pale man with a commander's band around his salt-and-pepper hair, raised an arm in greeting. "Ninth Crucible, I would guess?"

Raoul raised his arm in return. "At your service. Commander Raoul

Cullen. This is Sensor Camble Delakroy, Keeper Percy Bitters, and Enforcer Nysska Stonegate."

The four riders came within a few meters and stopped, their Imperial mounts as obedient as highly-trained dogs. The man with salt-and-pepper hair touched his own chest.

"I'm Paul Olafsson, Commander of the Third Crucible. This is Sensor Mykal Tallinger, Keeper Nora Ambers, and Enforcer Roald Sykes."

The other members of the Third Crucible nodded perfunctorily, and Nysska gave each a thorough once-over.

Mykal Tallinger had skin even darker than Cam's, and either shaved his head regularly or was severely prematurely bald, though he seemed to be trying to make up for the lack of hair on his scalp by growing it out of his face. Nysska had never seen a thicker beard. Tallinger sat his mount in such a way that made her think he'd been raised on horseback, and when he smiled at some private interaction with the Third Crucible's keeper, he showed off big, white teeth with a glaring gap where the left upper incisor was supposed to have been. Silver runes flashed in his eyes, making him a Sight Sensor, just like Cam. She wondered what kind of animal he worked with to carry out his duties. Morrin James—the only other Sensor Nysska had ever worked with, back during her time with the Forty-Seventh Crucible—bore scent runes, and found the objects of their investigations with the help of a big, friendly dog named Greta. Nysska saw no such dog, or any other animal.

Nora Ambers, the Third Crucible's Keeper, at first reminded Nysska of Morrin. She had the same slight build, and the same shade of mousy brown hair. But whereas Morrin's weak eyes had always darted away, seeking out the least offensive place to rest—or the best place to hide—Nora Ambers sat in her saddle and boldly eyed Nysska not unlike the way Cam had when they'd first met. Fearless. Inquisitive. The similarities to Morrin dissolved completely when a full-grown gray timber wolf loped up and sat beside her horse.

The wolf was *huge*. No trace of silver gleamed from its eyes—this was no seraphic beast, just a natural one—but the way it responded to Nora Ambers made Nysska think its intelligence must have been above average for its species. She estimated the wolf's weight at ninety kilgrams, but thought that might have been conservative.

The wolf weighed a good bit more than the Third Crucible's Enforcer in any case. Roald Sykes was what one might call "compact." She didn't expect him to stand any taller than Percy, and his narrow shoulders and slender limbs were the opposite of intimidating—

If taken on their own. Roald Sykes wore the traditional leather-and-bronze armor of the Thaumetallicon, but he had modified it such that it *bristled* with knives. Leather bands encircled each calf and forearm, and two stretched across his chest, all of which were festooned with edged weapons of varying sizes and purposes. Throwing knives. Close-combat knives with short, hooked blades. A couple of long-bladed daggers that could have been called short swords.

Nysska had seen men before who felt the need to adorn themselves with sharp bronze. To let everyone around them know how dangerous they were, usually making up for some deep-seated weakness or insecurity. She didn't think Roald Sykes was like those men. He sat perfectly still, eyes raking over her with no greater or lesser attention than they gave every other member of the Ninth, and yet near-palpable waves of confidence washed off of him.

Nysska decided if a man that small, with that level of confidence in his own abilities, had been made Enforcer of a Crucible, he most likely deserved it.

"So this is the one we've all heard about," Commander Olafsson said, unapologetically gazing at Nysska. "The first-ever demon member of the Thaumetallicon."

"I am not a demon, Commander," Nysska said before Raoul could stop her. "I am a sethyd. We are no more creatures from hell than you are."

Olafsson maneuvered his horse over to Nysska and held out a hand. "Right, right. No offense meant. We all heard what you did in Tember. Guess it takes a non-human to beat a non-human, huh?"

Nysska shook his hand, trying not to curl her lip while she did it. "I think you'll find we bleed just as red as you do."

"Burn just as well, too," Nora Ambers said quietly.

"Excuse me?" Raoul nudged his horse forward. "What's that supposed to mean?"

A sort of ripple went through the Third Crucible. A moment of non-verbal communication, the fleetest of glances. Olafsson spoke to Raoul. "Were you not briefed on this?"

Raoul's face tightened. "We were not. The Emperor gave us a direct order to come here, and said we needed to investigate something that, and I'm quoting him, 'has stopped the Third Crucible in its tracks.'"

Nora Ambers muttered, "Bloody fucking ponce," which made Nysska wonder if the Keeper was talking about Raoul or about the Emperor.

"We should show them," Mykal Tallinger said. "Now."

Commander Olafsson nodded. "Come on. It's just up here. Close enough to walk—we might as well leave the horses."

The Third Crucible dismounted, and after a moment or two, Raoul signaled the Ninth to follow.

As soon as Nysska's feet touched the ground, the massive gray wolf padded over and peered up at her with clear, round, sky-blue eyes. Nysska knelt, which put her nose-to-muzzle with the beast, and held out a hand, fingers curled under, palm down. The wolf sniffed it—moved forward and sniffed its way up her arm—and ended by snuffling all around her face. Nysska laughed and scratched the animal under the chin. When it seemed to like that, she scratched up around the ears and stroked it along its back and sides.

After a few long moments, during which she thought the wolf might try to climb into her lap, she glanced up and saw every member of both Crucibles staring at her. Nora Ambers's jaw actually hung open a centim. Nysska stood. "What?"

Nora patted her thigh. "Sickle. Come."

The wolf glanced up at Nysska one last time before padding back over to its keeper. Nora said, "Good boy," but her inflection made the words sound more like, "What the *fuck?*"

Commander Olafsson cleared his throat. "If you'll all follow me?" As the group walked, he said, "I'm sure you know the name of this village. It's called Summergray, and for the last fifty years at least, it's been hotly contested by two larger towns—Nivenston, at the northernmost point of the valley, and Painter's Bluff at the south end."

As they walked, Nysska spotted a foot patrol of three regular Cathedral soldiers approaching from a narrow alleyway. Olafsson saw her watching the soldiers. "Caulspring dispatched a division. They're camped on the far side of town. Nothing wrong with securing the site, I hope?"

Nysska didn't respond, but shot a look at Raoul. Broken trust or not, she saw the same thing in his expression that she felt. *Just what a crime site needs. Dozens of soldiers stumbling through it.*

Olafsson picked up where he'd left off. "Legal disputes, border squabbles, feuds between families. If you can think of some way to have trouble here, it's been had. The Empire has spent much too much time trying to resolve it, and finally they decided to punish both towns for not being able to come to a reasonable solution. Six months ago, Emperor Valco—yes, he got personally involved—declared that *neither* Nivenston nor Painter's Bluff had any claim to Summergray, and as soon as word got out, a new group swept in and set up shop. Promised the Empire they'd improve the land, and signed contracts that they'd pay double the tax rate for the privilege."

As Olafsson talked, the group of eight people, one wolf and, trailing along at the edge of the village, two blood lynxes, passed burnt-out house after burnt-out house. Scraps of charred wood littered the dirt streets. The smell of scorched flesh grew more and more overpowering. Most of the soldiers in the three additional patrols they saw had wrapped cloths around their faces to try to block out the stench.

"Nobody in either town was happy about this turn of events. They said this land, this valley, should belong to either one town or the other, and sure they'd squabble over it, but it was *theirs*. No damn outsiders had any business trying to take it for their own. Threats started flying. Both towns talking big. We had a few people in place, keeping an ear on things, as it were. Nobody thought anyone would take real action."

Olafsson stopped outside the blackened ruins of what had been the town hall. Nysska thought it looked like a converted barn.

"Then we got reports of the fire. Some regular Cathedral soldiers came in as fast as they could, but everything was done by the time they arrived."

Percy had been looking around as they walked, and now he spoke up. "Hey, uh, Commander Olafsson. I'm seeing plenty of fucked-up buildings, but I'm not seeing any fucked-up *people*. Fire as bad as this, where's all the corpses?"

Olafsson's face, which Nysska suspected never made it all the way to happy, grew even more somber. "In here," he said, and moved aside from what had once been the town hall's main entrance.

Nysska pushed forward, side by side with the rest of the Ninth. When she saw what lay inside the building her lungs locked up tight in icy cages.

Raoul's words sounded hollow. "There must be thirty corpses."

From behind them, Commander Olafsson said, "Thirty-two."

Charred, twisted, soot-covered bodies lay in the middle of the ruined floor, and from every single blackened skull, a pair of horns sprouted.

Someone had slaughtered an entire village of sethyds.

5

Nysska's head swam as she fought down a wave of nausea. She wasn't sure for a moment whether the world was spinning or if her mind had come untethered from her body and, lacking a connection to the real, begun to spin off course like a boat caught in a swift current.

"Is this what it looks like?" Raoul said, and the sound of his voice cracking through the stench-filled air snapped Nysska back to the present. "Is this a bunch of dead sethyds? Or has someone stuck animal horns on human bodies as a sick prank?"

Commander Olafsson turned solemn eyes on the members of the Ninth. "Here's what we know. The Empire cleared this settlement with the demon leaders in Slocum—oh, beg your pardon. With the *sethyds*. Told the people of Nivenston and Painter's Bluff to keep it quiet. It was a..." He seemed to develop a foul taste in his mouth. "An experiment. See if a third party could keep the two towns from going at each other's throats."

Nysska hadn't been able to tear her eyes from the sight of the shriveled, blackened cadavers. "Did it work?"

"From what I understand, your people farmed the land and raised the livestock *better* than anyone in Summergray ever did. The Emperor had plans to announce Summergray's 'new management,' as it were. Point to it as proof that sethyds and humans can get along." He spat on the wood plank floor. "Little premature, I'd say."

Cam spoke up, words directed at Mykal Tallinger. "All right, but politics aside, you've got a Sensor here. Who did this? How, and when?"

Tallinger's sparkling silver eyes flared, but the easy-going smile on his face never wavered. "I tried to read the site as soon as I got here, sweetheart." The smile seemed to fix in place. "Something went wrong. Couldn't see shit. I hear you're an old hand with runes fucking up, though."

A tiny, frosty smile graced Cam's lips. "Oh, I've seen some things," she said quietly. Tallinger didn't seem to know what to do with that.

Nysska closed her eyes and scrubbed her face with both hands. As far as she knew—despite how far the story had reached of her defeating a tarn in the Tember city center—the public didn't know about what she and the rest of the team had started calling "blood runes." Nysska moved closer to Tallinger. "You couldn't read the site, you say. Describe what happened, please. In great detail."

Tallinger glanced at Olafsson for approval, and when the Commander returned a subtle nod, Tallinger said, "I started here, with the bodies. The way my runes work, I see a series of still images, like—all right, don't give me shit about it, it's just how the talent functions—"

Cam had moved closer. "No need to apologize. We're all different."

Tallinger inclined his head. "I see *oil paintings*. A series of oil paintings, like an artist had watched the crime being committed and painted what was happening, a different image every two seconds or so. Then, uh... then the scent of the scene comes through in my, uh...in my sweat."

Cam frowned, just a tiny bit. "Sensor Tallinger, I weep the blood of the perpetrator. Literally. Blood flows out of my eyes. Please stop being embarrassed and tell us what fucking happened."

Tallinger's eyebrows raised. He shot quick glances around at Raoul, Percy, and Nysska, as if to make sure Cam wasn't having him on. "All right. All right, I turned the runes up, but instead of seeing the paintings, it was like—" He took a breath. "It was like I went blind again. Not the darkness I used to see, before I got my runes, it was like...everything went *gray*. No, wait, I'm not explaining it properly. It wasn't like I *saw* gray everywhere. It was like...not being...*aware of sight*. Like my brain just suddenly forgot what vision was."

Nysska watched the other members of the Third Crucible. She decided they had all heard this account before.

41

Cam's frown deepened. "You said you started here at the bodies. Did you try to read anywhere else?"

Tallinger opened his arms wide. "All over the place. I kept trying, again and again, moving each time, which is how I figured out there's a sort of perimeter. About halfway from here to the edge of town. Soon as I got farther away than that, the runes started working again, but at that distance there was nothing to see."

Raoul said, "Sensor Delakroy, do you feel comfortable making your own attempt?"

Cam's shoulders lifted and dropped. "I don't think I have much choice."

Percy turned away from Cam and made big shoving motions with both arms. "Everyone step back, please, she needs room to work." Nysska and Raoul immediately gave Cam the amount of space she always requested when surveying the site of a crime, but the Third Crucible lagged. Percy's pale blue eyes hardened. "No disrespect, Commander Olafsson, but if you want her to do her job, you all need to get the fuck out of her field of vision."

Olafsson narrowed his eyes at Percy, but gestured with his chin, and joined Tallinger, Ambers, and Sykes as they withdrew from the barn.

Cam stood directly in the burnt-out doorway, staring at the bodies inside. Silver flames started at the outer corners of her eyes, flickering, dancing. The flames brightened, surrounding her head with an eldritch icy glow—

And went out.

Cam took an uncertain step backwards and turned, eyes squeezed shut, runes dark. One hand went to her temple, and as her knees buckled Nysska took a swift stride forward and caught her.

Raoul and Percy were there almost as fast, and Raoul said, "Are you all right? Do you need to lie down?"

Using Nysska's arm to steady herself, Cam got her legs back under her, but kept her eyes closed. She still wore her sounding rings, and clicked them together a couple of times as she got her bearings. "I'm fine. I'm fine. But—Tallinger's not wrong. Dragon's scaly balls...that was...*weird*." With another click of the rings, she faced the Third's Sensor. "Can you show us this perimeter?"

No one in the Third Crucible moved until Olafsson gave them another subtle nod. It made Nysska wonder if they had to ask him permission to masturbate.

Tallinger beckoned. "Of course. Follow me."

Half an hour later, after being shown exactly how far from the cadaver-filled barn both Tallinger's and, as it turned out, Cam's runes abruptly started functioning again, Raoul pulled the Ninth Crucible aside. Offering a perfunctory apology to Commander Olafsson, he led the team to a mostly unburnt building that appeared to have once housed stockpiles of grain. The floor crunched underfoot in a way that set Nysska's teeth on edge.

Raoul pitched his voice low. "Cam, is this the same thing we went up against at Altamar?"

Cam shuddered. Nysska didn't blame her. The memory of the re-animated corpses, blood runes glowing beneath their skin, made her own insides clench.

"Not exactly. The thing that shook me up so badly in Altamar was the...we never settled on what to call them. The blood-rune corpses." She had activated her runes again, just enough to allow normal vision, and the painful memory haunted her eyes. "And let me just say, if I never, *ever* have rotten corpse juice squeezing out of my tear ducts again, that'll be fine with me. But no—there's none of that here. I mean, there's *something*. Obviously. But it's not the same."

Raoul turned to Nysska. "So you didn't know anything about a few dozen sethyd farmers moving in this far to the southeast?"

Nysska shook her head. "I've been cut off from my people, if you'll recall." That made her guts tighten for a wholly different reason, as the lie she was still maintaining struck her like a secret fist. "But even before Mother and I were exiled, I heard nothing about any kind of...settlement. Everyone was too busy trying not to starve to death."

Raoul blew a long breath out between his teeth. "And here I was hoping the whole 'collapse of established procedure' was something we'd only have to deal with once." He gave Percy and Cam plaintive looks. "Anyone have any ideas about...anything?" The effort of it plain on his face, he turned to Nysska. "Suggestions? *Anything?*"

Nysska hesitated. In the silence, Percy said, "We could do what we did in the runemaster's quarters, back at Taurus Hill—ask the kitties to sniff around. See if they dig up anything out of the ordinary." He glanced over at the two blood lynxes, who were both crouched at a crack in one of the baseboards, staring intently at some small, unseen creature. "Though I'll admit, there's a big fucking difference between one man's rooms and an entire town. Might be too vague for them."

Nysska cleared her throat. "We need to find something. Anything. Some kind of, of *evidence* that points to who or what killed everyone. Something tangible. I know it won't be this easy, but if one of the sethyds had a knife stuck in his back with 'property of Raoul Cullen' stamped in it, that would lead us in a definite direction. Right?"

Raoul smiled thinly.

She went on. "So we look for tangible evidence. And we try to figure out what's causing this blank spot that's keeping runes from working. Percy, maybe that would be finite enough for the cats? Take them to the perimeter, and explain that something from that point to the barn is different. See what they can turn up?"

Percy nodded.

A mouse burst out of the crevice Flax and Jax had been watching and bolted straight across the floor, out the door and into the street. Both lynxes spun and dashed after it, leaving a wispy wake of tawny fur in the air. Everyone looked at Percy, who put both hands up, palms out. "They are still *cats*, y'know."

Raoul gestured back toward the cadaver barn. "The Third can help us look. Maybe a few soldiers, too. What do you think, start at the barn and go building by building?"

Nysska considered the question. "The bodies should be first. See if there *is* anything on them that points to the killer. Then, I don't know, maybe move in a spiral? The barn's the center, widen out from there?"

Raoul shrugged with his eyebrows. "Yeah, that'd probably be more efficient than just house to house. We're not looking for a fugitive. Let me go talk to Olafsson."

Raoul led the way back out onto the hard-packed dirt street. Percy jogged ahead, calling out for the blood lynxes, but Nysska lagged behind. When Cam fell in beside her, Nysska asked, "Are you all right?" Her yellow eyes scanned the town ahead of them. "Or have you just learned to hide trauma more effectively?"

Cam let a tiny smile curl her lips. "You mean, am I willing myself to hold it together? Am I in danger of going to pieces, screaming and crying, so that my big, beautiful woman can hold me in her arms and give me comfort?"

Nysska sighed. "That is not...exactly...what I was asking."

Cam chuckled. "I meant what I said earlier about it not being the same as it was before. I don't *think* there are any glowing red corpses shambling around out here. This feels...colder. Drier. Devoid of...well, everything. Devoid of life."

They turned a corner, putting them a dozen meters away from the cadaver barn, and Nysska slowed at the sight of a mounted Cathedral soldier talking to the gathered members of the Third Crucible. Even Sickle, the wolf, was there, sitting patiently and staring at the rider's horse. Nysska watched as the rider handed Commander Olafsson a slender bronze tube, saluted, and rode away at a canter. She recognized the type of tube. It contained an official Imperial message—usually orders.

Raoul reached Olafsson, and Nysska heard him say, "What's going on?"

Olafsson's face remained impassive as he unfurled the scroll and read the text. He spoke to Raoul, but looked at his team as he did. "We've been given another assignment. Effective immediately." Olafsson handed the scroll to Raoul. "Summergray and everything in it is now officially the Ninth Crucible's problem." He gave his team the tiny, subtle nod that Nysska had come to find unbearable, and without a word all four of them walked away, headed for their horses.

Sickle turned as they went and gave Nysska a long look, but he never broke pace with Nora Ambers.

Raoul seemed to be working hard to keep his expression neutral as he faced the rest of the Ninth. "I suppose we should've been expecting this, what with the Emperor telling Nysska he was going to test us. And I don't think it changes anything. Percy, gather up the cats and start searching the perimeter. Nysska, you still want to get some of the regular troops to help us look the bodies over?"

Nysska eyed a dark line on the horizon. "Yes. But I'm afraid we're going to get rained on before the day's out, and if we're to be examining charred corpses, I'd rather they not be *soggy* charred corpses. Not to mention, the faster we can do this, the better. Those cadavers already smell horrible, and the longer we take, the more they're going to rot." She frowned, and looked around until she spotted one of the soldiers on patrol. Raising an arm, she signaled to him.

The young man in bronze who came hurrying over couldn't have been older than eighteen. A patchy beard did little to cover his unlined face. When he reached them, his attention kept flitting between Nysska and

Raoul. Finally settling on Raoul, the soldier said, "How can I help, Commander?"

Raoul simply gestured to Nysska, and the soldier faced her with visible reluctance. "Uh...yes, ma'am?"

"Do any of these buildings have basements? Root cellars? Anything that will keep the rain off?"

He screwed up his face in thought. "I think so, ma'am. What used to be the inn—that one, right over there—" The soldier pointed at a ruin that had been left as little more than low stone walls, all the wooden construction burned away. "That's got a place belowground, I think where they stored food."

Nysska nodded in appreciation. "Very good. Now, would you call over eight or ten of your fellows?"

The young man hesitated. "May I ask why, ma'am?"

"Because you're going to help us carry all these bodies into the cellar. And we're going to need lanterns. As many as you can get your hands on."

Nysska couldn't help but think of the empty ale cellar back in Tember where she'd been ambushed. That place was a good bit larger than this, but the stone floor had been laid out in much the same way, and the same style of sconces were hammered into the walls. Lanterns now hung from those sconces. Not as many as Nysska would have liked, but enough to see the bodies clearly.

They all lay, shoulder to shoulder, twisted limbs touching, in three lines along the north wall. Raoul had noticed a long table in one of the inn's back rooms that had mostly escaped the fire, and now it took up space along the south wall, lanterns hung from the ceiling above it, the first of the cadavers resting on it. Waiting.

Cam's eyes glowed silver as she drew closer to the corpse. The cellar seemed like a cave now. Or some kind of oubliette. An Exemplar-forsaken place where inconsequential flesh and bones had been unceremoniously dumped, the refuse of lives cut short. Radiance from the runes implanted in Cam's irises cut through the yellow lantern light and cast long, strange shadows as it fell across the victim's horns.

"I don't know what I'm looking for," Cam said quietly. Reverently. As if, on some level, afraid to disturb the lifeless bodies. "I can't even tell if these are men or women. They're all built so...so similarly."

"I had always thought of that as a good thing," Nysska said, matching Cam's volume. "Especially after arriving in human lands. Seeing the advantage human men took of the smaller, weaker women. I never would have guessed our physical equality might cause us trouble." She took down one of the lanterns and held it close to the corpse's face.

Raoul grabbed another lantern. "For the purposes of this investigation, I don't see it making that much difference. At least, not at this stage. We're not trying to figure out *who* was killed. We're trying to figure out *how* and, Dragon willing, *why*."

Nysska nodded. She slowly moved the lantern down the body's length. "From the scraps I can see, this one's wearing typical sethyd clothing."

Cam stepped closer. "How can you tell?"

Nysska pointed. "This bit of stitching. And…though most of the fabric has either burned away or…become fused with the flesh…this hemline, here. It's a style I've seen more than once among farmers outside Fajrosxtono." She reached the body's feet. "I don't see anything obvious. Raoul, will you please help me turn the body over?"

Raoul grimaced. "I suppose that's unavoidable."

In an attempt to lighten the mood, Nysska said, "I understand your reluctance. Especially if your knife actually is sticking out of this poor fellow's back."

Raoul's lips didn't curve, but Nysska thought she caught a glint of amusement in his eyes. He said, "Glad the uniform comes with gloves," and carefully took hold of the blackened shoulders. He and Nysska rolled the body and re-centered it on the table, and she moved from the feet back up to the head, looking over every centim.

Nysska sighed. "I see nothing unusual here, apart from the fire damage. Cam? Are your runes working any better?"

Cam gestured vaguely toward her eyes. "As far as simply letting me see, they're fine. Using them to read a crime site…shit, who knows? I'm willing to give it another try."

Nysska moved around the table to stand next to Raoul. "You need us out of the way, yes?"

Cam shook her head. "Don't bother yet. This might not—hang on—" She squinted, and bit her lower lip, and Nysska wanted to say, *No, no, don't try it, we shouldn't risk it, you're far too important and this might hurt you,* but instead she clenched her teeth and said nothing.

Cam's eyes flickered, flared, tiny tongues of silver flame dancing around the outer corners—but then she shuddered and staggered backward, runes going dark. Nysska started toward her, but Cam held up her hands and steadied herself. "No, no, not necessary. I'm fine. I cut everything off as soon as I felt it going wrong." The silver glow came back up to normal vision levels. "Sorry."

Raoul glanced from one woman to the other and back. "Suggestions?"

Nysska had begun steeling herself for more corpse-handling when Cam said, "Maybe."

Raoul folded his arms. "I'm listening."

Cam made a vague gesture, out toward the rest of town. "The Sensor from the Third—Tallinger—he said there was a perimeter, yes? Inside it, his runes didn't work, and it seems as if mine are behaving the same way. So what if we take one of the corpses *out* of the perimeter? Maybe I could read it then?"

Nysska was going to say, *Can't hurt to try,* but then realized it very much *could* hurt.

Raoul went to the doorway of the cellar and called out for the Cathedral soldiers.

Ten minutes later, two nose-wrinkled, mouth-breathing boys in bronze set down the corpse from the examination table on a wooden walkway ten meters beyond where Tallinger had marked the perimeter. One of them spoke to Raoul.

"We return to our posts now, Commander?"

Raoul gave them a mildly sympathetic look. "Yeah, go ahead. We'll haul it back ourselves if we need to." When Nysska raised an eyebrow at him—the soldiers already in full retreat—he said, "It's never a bad time to boost morale."

"All right," Cam said, approaching the cadaver. "Step back, please. This might actually work."

Nysska watched carefully as Cam brought up the power of the runes. This time, instead of shutting them down immediately, she stared, the silver light shining steadily. After what felt like a solid minute, the light flickered and vanished, and Cam turned to face her teammates.

"Something else I can't explain." A bitter note had crept into her voice. "I'm not getting the same kind of interference here that I did back in the cellar, but it's...like...it feels—reading this body is like reading a, a *rock.* Or a tree stump. You know I mentioned the psychic energy that crimes generate? This has *none* of that. Like it's been...I don't know. *Scrubbed.* I'm sorry. I don't know that I'm going to be any help at all on this investigation."

"Not true," Raoul shot back, smiling a little. "You can help us look over the rest of the bodies. Get your gloves on, and let's haul this one back to the inn."

After returning to the cellar with the body, one by one they carried the other flame-ravaged sethyd corpses to the table and examined them. Centim by charred, stinking centim. Every so often they found some feature still whole enough to tell them something about the deceased— usually a piece of plain jewelry—but never anything that provided even the tiniest hint of how they were killed.

Overhead, the thunder grew steadily closer. Nysska kept waiting for the rain to come crashing down. She feared it would find its way through whatever seams or cracks the fire had caused, and that they might end up ankle-deep in foul, trapped rainwater.

When the last examination was finished, they laid the final body back down with the others, and Nysska leaned against the edge of the table and folded her arms. Staring at nothing.

Raoul said, "Thirty-two dead bodies, and *nothing*. No limbs hacked off. No blades embedded in bone. No skulls crushed. It's as if they all just went to that barn, huddled up on the floor, and waited for the fire to take them." He pulled his gloves off and tucked them into his belt. "And what in the name of the Great Silver Dragon does this have to do with whatever's interfering with Imperial runes?"

With a massive crack of thunder, the rain finally fell, and with it Percy and the two blood lynxes came bounding down the steps into the cellar. "Whooo! We just barely fucking made it, didn't we, kitties?" Percy crossed to the table and slapped a leather pouch down onto it.

Nysska watched as Flax and Jax immediately went to the dead bodies. Jax took a few sniffs and abruptly lost interest; he turned, went to the middle of the unobstructed area of the stone floor, and began vigorously grooming. Flax took several sniffs as well, backed up half a pace, and stared at the corpses with her mouth hanging open. She lifted one paw off the floor and made a quick fanning motion, as if to swat away the odor. Then she joined Jax, flopped down onto her side on the floor, and appeared to go to sleep.

No water seeped through the ceiling. A trickle rolled down the cellar stairs, but disappeared into a floor drain Nysska hadn't noticed before. She thought, *Maybe we won't have to deal with dead body soup after all*, and made a mental note—*We need to establish some dry, secure place to store bodies. With cool temperatures if possible.*

Percy said, "Well? Figure out what happened yet?"

Raoul snorted. "Hardly. What about you? Any luck?"

Percy's mouth stretched into his typical twinkle-eyed grin. "Maybe. But before I show you and take a chance at looking like a giant fucking asshole...have we thought about the bigger picture here?"

Nysska said, "What bigger picture would that be?"

Percy twirled one half of his forked beard around two fingers. "Well, I did some thinking while the kitties were busy. I know we've got to figure out how three dozen sethyds got killed, but more than that—who in their right fucking minds would even *try* it? The whole Empire knows what Nysska did by now, taking on that tarn. Then somebody's going to wipe out an entire fucking village? Who's got that big a death wish?"

Her yellow eyes boring holes through the floor, Nysska murmured, "It's a question of who benefits."

Cam said, "Sorry, what was that?"

Nysska raised her head. "I remember that much. From hearing my grandfather's friend talk, back home. He said the first question he always asked, whenever there was a crime, was 'Who benefits?'" She looked around at Raoul, Percy, and Cam. "Who's going to come out better because thirty-two sethyds died?"

After a few moments Raoul broke the silence. "Well, we've got the two towns. Nivenston and Painter's Bluff. They're the ones who've always wanted this land, and neither one of them was about to get it while your people were here."

Cam spoke up. "That goes back to what Percy was saying, though. Are there any humans around here brave enough to try it? What if they'd screwed it up? Can you imagine thirty-two pissed-off sethyds coming at you?"

Flax got to her feet and walked over to Percy. He scooped her up and held her in his arms on her side, her feet against his chest, and stroked her head. "Well, that's the thing," he said. "Was it somebody from one of those towns? Maybe. Maybe even *probably*, because who knows this territory better? But was it somebody from one of those towns *acting alone*? I don't think so."

Raoul looked from the leather pouch on the table to Percy and back. "Does that mean you're finally going to show us what you found?"

Percy kissed Flax on the muzzle and set her down. "Bet your bronze ass it does." He undid the leather thong at the pouch's neck and dumped its contents on the table.

Nysska had turned to watch, and Cam came to stand beside her. "Um…" Cam said. "Is that…dirt?"

Still grinning, Percy smoothed the dirt out on the table. "For the most part, yes. But let me ask you to cast your minds back to the encounters we had with those glowing red fuckers up at Altamar. And Nysska's legendary fight with the tarn. This whole thing revolves around some fucking wise-ass coming up with a new kind of thaumaturgical metal, right? They've alloyed argonium with something new, and instead of silver, it's red, right?"

Raoul said, "Percy. Please. Get to the point."

Percy kept spreading the dirt out on the table, flicking some tiny bits of it left and right as he went. Nysska realized he was sorting it in some particular way, but couldn't guess what that way might be. "The point, Commander, is that the kitties figured out what was causing everything inside a certain area to go bearshit for Cam and that Third Crucible fuck-stick." He gathered up a pinch of matter from the table. "Nysska, hold out your hand, would you?" Only a tiny bit hesitant, Nysska extended her right hand, and Percy sifted something onto her palm. "Now. Shine one of those lanterns real close there, and tell me what you see."

Cam grabbed the nearest lantern, held it as close as she could without burning Nysska's skin—and gasped.

"The whole center of town is seeded with that shit," Percy said.

Raoul groaned.

Nysska didn't say a word. She found she couldn't, thanks to the breath locked in her chest, and could only stare in silence at the sparkling flakes of red metal gleaming against her violet skin.

6

The members of the Ninth Crucible reached the town of Painter's Bluff just before sunset. It looked remarkably like Summergray —stacked-stone foundations, wooden frames, thatched roofs. Nysska couldn't help thinking of it as a "before" image, with Summergray's charred ruin as the "after."

Percy squinted. "I don't see a bluff anywhere. Painted or otherwise."

Indeed, the land beyond the town stretched out, sloping gently upward and narrowing until it disappeared into a pass between two converging mountainsides.

"I don't give a shit about bluffs," Raoul said. He'd been in a foul mood all day. "We've got a bunch of pieces on the board. There's the Empire, and these rebel sethyds we just found out about..."

Nysska winced, but said nothing.

"...and those Dragon-damn cuttlefish and their Dragon-damn blood runes, and fuck me up the nose if I can figure out how it all fits together. And now that mess at Summergray." He turned in his saddle to look directly at Nysska. "Are all those dead sethyds back there Mountain Bulls? If they were, who'd want them dead? Or were they all *against* the Mountain Bulls, and that's who killed them?"

Nysska shrugged slowly. "I can't know how sethyds I've never met before—of whose existence I was, in fact, unaware—might or might not have felt. For that matter, I can't speak with confidence for *any* other sethyd. Any more than you can speak for Percy. Or Cam."

Raoul scoffed softly. "That's very helpful, thanks."

The team had gotten close enough to the town to spot more and more of the citizens. They passed a few mule-drawn carts filled with crops, a couple of traders with saddlebags crammed full of trinkets and other goods, and a flock of sheep in a field with three sheep-herders. All of the townsfolk stopped what they were doing and stared as the Ninth Crucible passed by. Nysska felt sure they were all staring at her, specifically, but chose not to react.

Cam's silver eyes flashed as she looked around. "Does anyone else find it bloody miraculous that there was an entire sethyd settlement here, and word didn't get out about it?"

Percy had been twisted around in his saddle, looking for the blood lynxes. He spotted them, prowling along in the tall grass on the side of the road, and beckoned. Jax came out of the grass and bounded up into the saddle, but Flax stayed where she was, keeping pace with the horses. Percy said, "Not really. Send in a company of boys in bronze, threaten to do something horrible if the people don't keep their mouths shut, and suddenly six months goes by without anybody saying a fucking word. That's the Empire for you. *Bronze is law. Bronze is peace.*" He snorted. "Bronze is fucking *terror.*"

"There's the mayor's house," Raoul said, in a tone that meant *Everybody shut up now.*

The mayor of Painter's Bluff had tried very hard to turn his house into a provincial version of a governor's mansion, but had succeeded only in making it loud and gaudy. No amount of bronze-colored paint could disguise the house's origin as a small-scale sawmill.

Leaving their horses outside, the team nodded to the two Cathedral soldiers stationed at the mayor's front door and walked into what was meant to be a grand audience hall. Long tables on either side of a broad flagstone-floored room led to a small dais with a large, ornate chair at the far end. Flanked by two more soldiers, the mayor of Painter's Bluff sat, sipping a cup of wine. Nysska got the impression that he had alighted in the chair only seconds before, and that the wine cup in his hand and his casual posture were meant to convey a sense of nonchalant authority. *Yes, I'm entertaining one of the Thaumetallicon's Crucibles, but this happens all the time in my line of work, nothing to get excited over.*

Nysska saw the cup tremble ever so slightly. Cam spotted it as well, and she and Nysska shared a brief, subtle smirk.

"Welcome to Painter's Bluff," the mayor said, once everyone had gathered before what Nysska was sure he thought of as his throne. "I am Mayor Klaudio Turk. How can I be of assistance to the Thaumetallicon?"

"We want to talk to you about the massacre at Summergray," Raoul said without preamble. "We need to find out what you know, what any of the people in your town know, and determine exactly who or what was responsible."

Mayor Turk couldn't have been more than forty, Nysska didn't think, and had the kind of pale, waxy skin, washed-out eyes, and scrawny build that indicated a severe lack of physical activity, or severe inbreeding, or both. She pegged him as someone whose family had been in power in this part of the land for decades, maybe centuries. Someone who delegated every important decision and simply sat back and collected tax revenue. Someone who would grovel at Emperor Valco's feet every chance he got. Nysska saw a flicker of what might have been panic in Turk's watery blue-gray eyes, but that panic swiftly gave way to a bluster that bordered on comical.

"I see," Turk said. "Well, Commander, I will of course help you in any way possible. But I am sure you've been traveling all day, and could benefit from a hot meal, a hot bath, and a warm bed for the night. Why don't you follow one of my people over to the inn, and we can attend to all your questions first thing in the morning?" Turk's pale eyes tracked down to where Flax and Jax sat, uncharacteristically formal, right behind Percy. "Your animals will have to sleep outside, of course."

Percy muttered something so quietly that not even Nysska could pick out the actual words, but his tone was unmistakable. Raoul said, "Mr. Mayor, time is of the essence. If we could speak to you now, in private, your cooperation would be most appreciated."

A note of petulance crept into Turk's voice. "And I want to be as cooperative as possible, Commander, which is why I believe everyone will benefit from a good night's rest. No one wants to try to answer important questions with a fatigued mind. I insist that you accompany my steward across the way. We can begin as early as sunrise, if you like, but not before then. Oh, and don't worry, my people have already taken your horses to our stables."

A young man in brown livery appeared at a side door leading off of the audience chamber. He looked terrified as he stared at Nysska. To her own quiet dismay, she found that she had finally become accustomed to that reaction from humans.

Raoul sighed. "Fine. First thing in the morning, then."

Mayor Turk favored them with a placid smile as they filed out of the chamber.

The sun had set as they spoke to the mayor, and what light reached the narrow, hard-packed street came from guttering torches affixed to poles set every ten meters or so along the street's length. The page guided them directly across the way to a two-story building. A sign swinging above its door declared it to be the "Turk Public House."

Cam groaned. "Of course the mayor owns the inn. Can't miss a chance to weight his own pockets with Imperial coin."

Percy moved up to the page and put his arm around the young man's shoulders, which made him yelp. "So tell me, my boy, why exactly is this place called Painter's Bluff if there's no bluff here?"

The page's voice cracked as he answered. "It's not that kind of b-bluff, sir."

Percy didn't move his arm. "No? What kind is it?"

"M-Mayor Turk's great-grandfather won the town in a c-card game, sir. He c-called Alphonso Painter's b-bluff."

"Fascinating. Fascinating. Now, tell me, exactly where does the mayor expect my kitties to sleep tonight?"

The page pointed with his free arm, indicating a long, low building on the inn's far side. "The stable's right there, sir. Lots of nice, warm hay. Probably, uh, probably a good selection of mice, sir, if I had to g-guess."

Flax and Jax, padding along behind Percy, exchanged glances. Nysska wondered what kind of communication passed between them. She knew full well that they both understood Plainish, and that they were at least as smart as the average human. The argonium in their blood, shining in the silver of their eyes, testified to that. She had no idea what kind of sleeping arrangements they'd prefer for themselves, though—a warm bed and a fireplace? A barn full of mice? A burrow in a hillside, lined with cotton and old rags?

Percy seemed satisfied with the page's answer. He clapped the young man on the shoulder and let him scuttle out a few paces ahead of the team.

Raoul shot the rest of them a look. "Food, and then bed, people. Don't go wandering off tonight."

Cam leaned closer to Nysska and murmured, "I think he was talking to you."

With a smile in her voice, Nysska murmured back, "Where would I go?"

"Where would you go *this time.*"

Fair, Nysska said to herself, though she had only ever ditched the rest of the team to run off on an infiltration and espionage mission once. Even then, Flax had gone with her.

Keeping her tone light, Nysska said, "Hush, you," and Cam chuckled.

The same brown-liveried young man he'd talked to before showed Percy and the blood lynxes to the stables. Percy had never known nor cared that much about horses. He knew enough to ride one, of course, and enough of the basic care and feeding to keep whichever one the Empire assigned him alive while in the field. What constituted a good or bad stable, on the other hand, he wouldn't have sworn to. This one was large, and more or less clean, and none of the horses housed there seemed to be actively complaining, including the one on which he'd ridden into town. He figured that was good enough.

The young man gestured at an empty stall. "H-h-here you go, sir. I'm sure the three of you will be c-comfortable here."

Percy's snow-white eyebrows shot up. "The *three* of us?"

"Uh...y-yes, sir?"

"What's your name, young'un?"

"B-Brian, sir. Brian Henstall."

"Hen-stall? Your family raise chickens, Brian?"

"Uh...n-n-no, sir...?"

"Never mind, Brian. There seems to have been some sort of miscommunication. This is for the kitties to sleep. I'll be taking a room in the inn along with my teammates."

Brian Henstall began sweating, despite the cool of the night air. "B-but, sir, the mayor said K-Keepers usually stay with their animals, sir."

Percy put his arm around Brian's shoulders again, and couldn't help laughing to himself when the young man started trembling. "You see the bronze in their harnesses? You see the silver in their eyes? You think *anyone's* going to fuck with them?"

"W-w-well, s-sir, I suppose the mayor figured b-better safe than sorry...?"

"I'm going to say goodnight to my kitties. You run over to the inn and make sure I have a room, why don't you. And make sure it's alongside my teammates' rooms, too. I don't want to get stuck behind the kitchen or some shit like that."

"Of course, sir, right away, sir!" Brian ducked out of Percy's single-armed grasp and all but sprinted to the inn.

Percy turned to Jax and Flax, who sat in the middle of the stall, watching him. He gave them a wink, and whispered, "We'll just give him a minute."

"Now this is some luck," Cam said softly as she closed the door behind her.

Whatever clerk was in charge of arrangements in Mayor Turk's inn had put Nysska and Cam in adjoining rooms, eliminating the need for either of them to go sneaking out into the hallway.

Nysska lay in the bed she'd been assigned and watched as Cam crossed the floor to her, already out of her bronze-inlaid leather jacket, trousers, and boots. The soft silver shine of Cam's eyes lit the room with a glow like moonlight.

"You know you don't have to use your runes now," Nysska said as Cam slipped under the sheets.

"What, you don't want me to look at you?"

Whereas Cam still wore her Cathedral-issue undergarments, Nysska had not a stitch on, and she lifted the sheet with a not-terribly-coy smile. "You can look all you want." She released the sheet and let it settle down onto her long, lean frame. "I'm just saying you don't *have* to."

Cam rose up to one elbow and sighed. "Are we really going to have this conversation? *Again?*"

Nysska slid one hand up along Cam's arm, and traced a delicate line across her cheekbone, down to the tip of her nose. "No. Not tonight."

Voices came to them from outside Nysska's door—directly across the hall, she thought. One of them spoke up, and she recognized Percy, though she couldn't make out what he was saying. The voices died down and went quiet.

Cam slithered closer. Her hand trailed down Nysska's ribs to her hip, then slid around and cupped a cheek of her ass. She kissed Nysska's collarbone, hot breath intoxicating against Nysska's throat.

Nysska groaned. *"Mia karulino..."* *My darling.*

Cam leaned far enough back for the silver of her eyes to reflect like icy fire in the yellow of Nysska's. "Nysska..."

"Yes?"

"Mi amas vin."

Nysska gasped. Blood roared in her ears and her heart.

Mi amas vin.

I love you.

Cam grinned. "Did I get that right?"

Nysska pulled her close and found Cam's lips with her own and did her best to show her how right that was.

Across the hall, Percy wasted little time in opening his window. Mayor Turk had put them on the second floor, but Percy knew that wouldn't make any difference, and as soon as he made a soft kissing noise both blood lynxes came bounding out of the darkness. Jax took a running start and leaped all the way up to the window pane, sinking his front claws in and digging with his back ones until he scrambled into the room. Flax took a more measured approach, scaling the side of the building, and arrived half a minute later with much less drama than her brother.

"You two just make yourselves at home," Percy said, closing the window. "I'm going to get a fire started." He dug a chunk of meat out of his pocket. "Also, this is from dinner. *Share* it." He dropped the meat on the floor between the two cats. They seemed to have a brief discussion about it before Jax pinned it to the floor with one broad foot and Flax sliced it in half with a heavy, wickedly curved claw.

A few minutes later, Jax lay curled up right in front of the pleasantly crackling fire. Flax had molded herself into the angle made by the backs of Percy's knees as he lay on his side in bed.

Later, when the fire had burned low, Flax and Jax both raised their heads at the same moment.

Nysska came up out of her dream in a heartbeat, but wondered if she might have still been asleep, because the shrill, rasping, ear-splitting sound that filled every cubic centim of her room sounded like nothing she had ever heard before.

Cam sprang upright next to her, runes blazing, and the sudden silver glare made Nysska flinch and shut one eye—which made it all the more disorienting when the door to her room smashed inward and a man she didn't recognize staggered screaming across the floor. The unearthly noise tripled, and she understood that she was looking at its source: Jax, attached to the strange man's face, jaws clamped into the ridge of one of his eye sockets, back feet shredding his neck, all the while yowling at the top of his feline lungs.

The man stumbled across Nysska's room, screaming and flailing at the big cat, and crashed through the window in an explosion of shattered glass and splintering wood.

Nysska turned to see if Cam was all right—

And saw *another man in their room*, emerging from a shadow-cloaked corner.

He gripped a long, broad-bladed knife in one hand, raised and about to plunge between Cam's shoulder blades. The fire already lit in Nysska's blood became a roaring inferno.

Nysska grabbed Cam's shoulder and yanked her down and sideways across the bed, pulling her out of the man's reach, and before the man could react she picked up the heavy wooden end table and smashed it into his face.

The table's flat top crunched into his nose and the tip of his chin. As blood sprayed across the bedclothes and the nearest wall, Nysska vaulted over Cam and, with an unearthly shriek of her own, drove the heel of her right foot into the center of the man's chest.

The man's sternum and ribs all but turned to powder under the force of the blow. Nysska thought she might have felt the actual beating of his heart against the sole of her foot for a split second before he collapsed in a bloody, gurgling heap in the corner.

Cam had made it up to her knees on the bed, eyes wide. "What the fuck is happening? *Where did that man come from?*"

Nysska might have tried to formulate an answer, but a panel in the wall behind the dying man's crushed body swung open on concealed hinges, and two more men rushed into the room, knives flashing.

The presence of the secret door caught Nysska off-guard just enough for the first man to close the distance between them. He was big, almost as tall as she was, packed solid with muscle, and though she caught the wrist of his knife hand and squeezed hard enough to make him howl, his sheer mass bowled her over and they crashed to the floor together.

Nysska screamed, "Cam!" and was going to follow that with "Run!" until she heard a thick, wet *crack*. The second man—who had barged past Nysska and gone straight for Cam—fell to the floor on his side and started screaming, clutching his knee.

Nysska worked one foot up and found purchase against a hipbone. With a grunt she shoved the man off of her, and the strength of the move sent him slamming ass-first into the wall beside the secret door.

Voices bellowed from the hall outside, followed by more grunts and impacts, and she clearly heard Percy scream, *"That's for picking on my cats, you spider-fucker!"*

The beefy man had recovered himself by then, but Nysska scrambled up to her feet as well, and when he came at her again—knife somehow still in his hand—she took the knife away from him and let his own speed send him shoulder-first into the broken window frame hard enough to shatter more bones.

The man turned toward her, glaring—and surprised her a second time by throwing himself out the window.

Percy came rushing into the room and shouted, "Where's Jax? Where'd he go?" He stopped for a second, blue eyes going wide, and Nysska realized she was still stark naked. She pulled a sheet off the bed and wrapped it around herself as Percy went to the window and peered out. "Jax! Jax, are you all right? Are you hurt? Just stay there! I'll come get you!" He turned and rushed back out of the room.

The man on the floor, writhing and groaning and holding his knee, went quiet when Nysska kicked him in the face. "Cam?" She looked around. "Cam! Where'd you go?"

Cam emerged from her room through the adjoining door, all her armor on and longsword in hand. The two women stared at each for two seconds before they said, in unison, "Where's Raoul?"

Nysska heard a faint thump and a muffled cry, and abandoned both modesty and her bedsheet as she sprinted through the doorway, down the hall, and slammed open the door to Raoul's room.

Raoul lay on the floor, flat on his back, struggling and spitting as two men held him down. One had his knee on Raoul's neck, pinning one of his arms with both hands, while the other actively tried to stab him with another broad-bladed knife. Raoul's free hand was clamped around the second man's wrist, but the second man was using his own free hand to drive hammer-fist blows into Raoul's face, and Nysska could tell Raoul only had a few seconds' resistance left in him.

She crossed the floor in one stride and drove her foot straight up into the second man's crotch hard enough that he flipped ass-over-feet off of Raoul and landed on the bed.

The man with his knee on Raoul's neck had just enough time to turn his head. That was how long it took Nysska to whirl around, extending the momentum of her first kick, and connect her shinbone to the man's jaw. His head snapped sideways, and his body fell in the same direction, landing at the foot of the bed in a nerveless heap—just in time for the first man to flop to the bed's edge and puke all over him.

Coughing, doing his best to suck air into his lungs, Raoul let Nysska help him up to a seated position. When he seemed to have filled his lungs again, he gasped out, "Why are you naked?"

Cam had followed Nysska to Raoul's room, the discarded bedsheet in her hands, and wordlessly handed it over. Nysska wrapped up in it, and didn't bother to keep the edge off her words. "You're welcome, *Raoul*. Happy to save your life, *Raoul*."

He got unsteadily to his feet, eyeing the two men who'd tried to kill him. The one on the bed vomited blood and collapsed, his eyes open and glassy. Nysska checked the one on the floor and found no heartbeat. Raoul favored Nysska and Cam with bloodshot eyes and asked, "Where's Percy?"

From the doorway, Flax meowed at them, and moved her fuzzy head in an unmistakable gesture: *Follow me.* The big cat led them back to Nysska's room and over to the window.

Nysska glanced outside. The man Jax had been attached to lay on the ground below, with Percy standing next to him, holding Jax in his arms. Nysska thought the big cat might have looked a little bit proud of himself. The beefy one who'd thrown himself out the window had vanished.

She turned to see Raoul kneeling next to the man who'd been clutching his knee.

"What happened with this one?" Raoul asked.

Cam had been standing near the foot of the bed and hadn't said much. Nysska swept over to her, sheet dragging on the floor. "Yes—what *did* happen with him? I was busy with the other one, and suddenly this one was down a knee."

Cam hugged herself. "Strangest thing…when the yowling woke me up, I thought we were under attack—which we were—and I sort of…I *would* say accidentally, but I think I meant to do it, it was like instinct—I turned the runes up all the way. And as he was coming toward me, I saw through his clothes and his skin and his muscles, and I saw that his knee was damaged, so I…well, I kicked it as hard as I could."

"But *you're* not hurt?"

Cam shook her head. "I'm fine."

Nysska looked over at Raoul. "Commander? You're all right?"

Raoul stood. "Nothing a few bandages won't take care of. You did good work, Cam. We can question this one—find out who sent him and his friends."

"Like fuck you will," the man with the ruined knee said, and before Nysska could get there, before she'd even fully realized he'd regained consciousness, he slit his own throat with a tiny, thin blade.

Raoul pounced on the man, knocked the blade away and clamped his hand over the wound. "Get a doctor! *Somebody get a doctor!*"

A small crowd of people had gathered outside the door, including the young page from earlier, and several of them broke away to run off down the hall. Judging from the amount of blood pouring between Raoul's fingers, though, Nysska didn't think it would make any difference whether a doctor came or not.

Raoul seemed to come to the same conclusion. He let his hands relax and sat back, scowling.

Nysska shut the room's door, blocking out the remaining onlookers, and began getting dressed. Quietly, she said, "I know who I'd very much like to question."

Cam said, "Who?"

Nysska gestured at the secret door, which still hung open. "The man who owns the inn with passageways built for assassins."

Seven minutes later, fully armed and armored, the members of the Ninth Crucible walked out of the inn and across the street to the house of Mayor Klaudio Turk, the two blood lynxes following just behind them.

Raoul touched Nysska's arm, and spoke with a quiet voice rendered hoarse and gravelly from the would-be assassin's attack. "Nysska."

She looked down at him. "Yes?"

"Thank you. If you—if you hadn't—"

"Think nothing of it."

His grip tightened on her arm. "I owe you my life. I want you to know that *I* know. It's not nothing."

"We look out for each other. Right?"

He nodded, and dropped his hand. "Damn straight we do."

Some weight lifted from Nysska's heart in that moment. Not all of it. But the little bit helped.

Both of the Cathedral soldiers stationed outside the door saluted and got out of their way, and Raoul's voice rang and echoed through the audience chamber despite his hoarseness, bouncing off the polished wood of Turk's throne.

"Mr. Mayor! By the authority granted to the Ninth Crucible of the Thaumetallicon, you are to present yourself for questioning immediately!"

They got no answer. Concentrating as hard as she could, Nysska said, "I hear something upstairs."

Raoul led the way with his sword drawn. "There has to be a staircase somewhere—"

Cam cut him off sharply. *"Look!"*

Nysska turned to see Cam pointing upward and followed her line of sight. Out among the rafters, at the very top of the peaked roof, Mayor Klaudio Turk crouched—with a noose around his neck.

Nysska traced the rope to a sturdy-looking knot secured to the rafter just behind him. Turk sniffled, tears running down his face, and before Raoul or anyone else could speak, he threw himself out into the empty air.

Nysska had seen hangings before. She knew there was a measure of mathematics involved, depending on the height and weight of the person being hanged. Too little rope and the neck wouldn't break, leaving the one sentenced to dangle until they suffocated.

Too much rope over too great a distance...

She could tell what was going to happen, and tried to move Cam out of the way, but bodies fall very quickly. Mayor Turk had used far too much rope, and when it snapped taut at the bottom of the drop, Turk's head tore completely free from his body, spraying blood in every direction as the decapitated corpse collapsed twitching to the floor.

7

C am had felt no trace of what they decided, for the moment, to call "blood rune dust" anywhere around Painter's Bluff, and her runes functioned perfectly when she used them to establish the identity of the muscular individual who had disappeared after heaving himself out the window of Nysska's room. Once she "read" his blood, reproducing it from her own tear ducts, Flax and Jax tasted that blood and led the Ninth Crucible out of town, through a nearby plowed field and a cattle pasture, and into a line of trees that followed the course of a swift-moving stream.

The man in question lay face-down in the stream. He appeared to have been there for at least an hour—long enough for small fish to begin nibbling at him. No one could tell whether he had succumbed to the injuries sustained during the fight and collapsed, or simply slipped on a wet stone, but either way he had landed on a sharp rock headfirst. Nysska and Raoul hauled his body out of the stream.

By the time they returned to Painter's Bluff, the sun had decided to peek over the eastern horizon, and they gathered in the inn's kitchen, first to clean off as much of Mayor Turk's blood as they could from their faces and armor, and second to drink several pots of coffee. Nysska's eyes lit up when one of the thoroughly cowed serving staff offered her several pieces of ham on a plate.

After they had all been served as much breakfast food as the inn had to offer, Raoul shooed the staff out of the kitchen and closed the door. He came back to the makeshift cluster of chairs and crates on which everyone had perched and sank down into his seat. "What the hell happened last night?"

Nysska got the impression that he knew full well each and every beat of the previous night's action, but hadn't fully processed it all. She said, "Who's ready to submit the after-action report?"

No one said anything for a few moments. Finally, Raoul rubbed his eyes and spoke. "Number one, this wasn't an officially sanctioned Thaumetallicon operation. This was an assignment given directly by the Emperor himself. Did he inform our superiors of what we were doing? Maybe. We don't know."

"Right," Percy said. "This was supposed to be some kind of fucking test, yeah? I don't know about the rest of you, but I feel like so far we're getting really shitty marks."

Raoul inclined his head toward Percy in acknowledgement. "Number two, whatever kind of shitfest we've gotten ourselves stuck in the middle of, it's obviously connected to the...y'know what, I'm not calling them 'cuttlefish' anymore. They're *skinshifters*. Unless someone else has a better name?" He looked around. Neither Percy nor Cam said a word, and Nysska made a point of sipping her coffee. "Done. All right, this has something to do with the skinshifters, because they're tied up with the blood runes, and it's looking like they've learned to use that Dragon-damned blood rune metal to taint entire crime sites. Any comments so far? Am I missing anything?"

Quietly, Cam said, "Not that I can tell."

Raoul went on. "Third, the skinshifters and whoever else they might be working with really, *really* want us dead. They want it bad enough to get the mayor of an Imperial town to cooperate with an assassination attempt on a Crucible. That's...that's *unthinkable*. Or at least it used to be. And they're terrifying enough that two men took their own lives rather than talk to us. Are we all still marching in the same direction here?"

The group mumbled assent.

Raoul said, "So what do we do now? Report to the Emperor?"

Nysska chewed and swallowed a bit of ham before she spoke. "That might not be the wisest thing."

Raoul lifted his head and looked her in the eye. No hostility. Just an even gaze. "Why?"

"Because we still haven't established who benefits from all this. A land dispute like Summergray is the kind of thing that can destabilize an entire territory. Old alliances, treaties, feuds—something horrible like this massacre happens, things can get ugly in a hurry." She paused. "Maybe even start a war."

Percy frowned. "Hang on. Are you saying Emperor Valco might benefit from having one of the Empire's own territories destabilized?"

Nysska shrugged. "We don't know what part he's playing in all this. We don't know what kinds of *new* alliances have been struck. Have the, ah, the skinshifters started using different kinds of runes? Is that what Cam saw under Valco's skin? For that matter, what if Valco himself is a skinshifter? We don't know. We don't know *anything*. On the other hand, wouldn't a village full of dead sethyds be a perfect excuse for the sethyd government in Slocum to get involved? When I left with my mother, the Mountain Bulls were not in control, but I've been gone for a while. What if they use Summergray to say, 'Look, this is how the humans treat us, we should take the fight to them.'"

Cam let out a long breath. "Well *that's* fucking terrifying."

Raoul rubbed the back of his neck. "I still don't see how that could benefit Valco. Unless, as you said, he's not human, which I find a little difficult to believe. No offense. It's not like he's playing from a weak position here. He's got the entire *Empire*. He's got the Argonium Infantry at his beck and call."

"Unless he doesn't," Percy said, his face screwing into a sour expression. "We talked about that kind of shit back in Tember. If a little fucker like Sergei Benitoff can get an Argonium Infantryman working for him, who's to say others wouldn't follow?"

"We can't trust anyone," Cam murmured. "*Anyone.*"

Raoul groaned. "All right. So we don't go back to the Emperor. Yet. But we don't have any other leads! Maybe find out if Turk had a Conversation Stone? Use it to speak to Governor Vachs?"

Nysska's eyebrows climbed up until they crowded her horns. "Wait, what? A *Conversation Stone*? What are you talking about?"

Raoul tapped the faceted white gem decorating the pommel of his longsword. "Same general idea as using this to summon the Tribunal once we've captured a perpetrator, except it's just the stone's owners communicating. The Runemasters just came out with them about a year ago. Not available to the public. They're still pretty rare, and expensive as shit, but I think I heard someone back in Tember say that Wendell Anwar had one. And since Galena Vachs took over from him, she might have one, too—

which won't matter at all if Mayor Turk was too cheap to get one for himself."

Nysska sat silent, letting that thought percolate. If messages could be sent instantly…instead of via rider on horseback, or tied to the leg of a carrier bird…the ramifications of that were difficult to comprehend.

Cam cleared her throat. "I don't see what Governor Vachs would have to offer, honestly. I know she's been an ally in the past, but she's five days' ride west of here and has nothing to do with Summergray." Her glimmering eyes settled on Raoul. "Or are you—and I mean no disrespect here, Commander—are you just looking to get some kind of official guidance for what we do next?"

Raoul took a breath to answer, but a knock sounded at the kitchen door before he could. He snapped his mouth shut, then opened it again to say, "What?"

Percy's favorite liveried servant opened the door just far enough to poke his head in. "Uh, sirs? And ladies? I thought you would want to know—there's someone here who claims to have seen one of the men who, ah, who died last night—he says the man tied up his horse in back of his field, and—um, the horse is still there? I think is what he's saying?"

With cold dew still heavy on the grass, the Ninth Crucible found themselves standing in a farmer's field, arrayed in a half-circle around a nervous horse tied to a sturdy young sapling. The farmer himself, a wiry man in his forties with skin like aged, dark brown leather and a pair of startling green eyes, stood with them, gaze twitching back and forth from the horse to Nysska.

Raoul seemed to have talked himself out back in the kitchen, so Nysska spoke to the farmer directly. Part of her wanted to assure him that she wasn't going to bite his head off. Another part was too sleep-deprived to offer humans any extra patience, and enjoyed the thought of seeing him squirm a little. "What was your name again, sir?"

The farmer had one of the deepest voices she'd ever heard from a human. The tremble of fear in it came out incongruous and unsettling. "Walters, ma'am, Patch Walters."

"All right, Patch. You say you saw one of the men who attacked us riding this horse?"

"Yes ma'am, he showed up last night, tied the horse here and headed toward town."

"And you didn't think to report that?"

"Well, it happens sometimes, ma'am, people got business in town but they don't want to pay the stable fee, Mayor Turk's...Mayor Turk *was*... kind of greedy about that, if you don't mind me saying so. The fellow this horse belonged to, he wasn't messing with my farm, I figured, no harm done, no alarm raised." Walters seemed to realize at that moment how his words might have sounded. "I know he did plenty of harm, ma'am! I'd've told somebody if I'd known what he set out to do!"

Nysska kept her tone patient. "And you said you didn't recognize him?"

"No, ma'am. Never seen him before."

Cam turned to Nysska and spoke softly. "Doesn't this just put us right back where we were?"

Figuring it was worth a try, Nysska said, "Mr. Walters, do you recognize anything about the horse?"

Walters moved closer to the animal. It stamped its feet at him and shook its head, and he held up both hands. "Whoa, whoa there, girl, I'm not about to hurt you." He moved around the horse slowly, and came back to Nysska. "I don't recognize anything about the horse, ma'am, but I can tell you where that saddle's from."

Raoul almost choked on his own spit. Percy let out a loud bark of laughter.

Nysska said, "How?"

Walters pointed. "Saddlemaker's mark. Right there. It's from Yang's, up in Nivenston."

The Ninth Crucible spent the day on horseback, traveling from one end of the long valley to the other. They stopped briefly in Summergray to check in with the Cathedral commander there, but the only change he had to report was that the burnt sethyd bodies smelled even worse than before.

"Could've told him that myself," Percy muttered as they rode north out of the village. "Nothing wrong with any of our noses."

The afternoon shadows had begun to grow long when they arrived at Yang's Saddlery and Smith.

Lydia Yang had skin the same rich brown as Cam's, eyes as pure black as Raoul's, and thick, wavy auburn hair. Nysska thought that combination might have made her beautiful if she hadn't quite so much resembled a bulldog otherwise. Her tiny nose, heavy jowls, and thick neck matched her wide torso and brawny arms. Nysska chuckled to herself, imagining the woman barking instead of speaking, but then felt bad about it.

Yang's business sat beside her small, modest cottage, and consisted of a simple four-walled structure chock-a-block with leatherworking tools, forms, and a massive, coal-black anvil. A heavy odor hung in the air, a bit like smoked pork, but with a sharp edge to it.

Cam's nose wrinkled as she spoke quietly to Nysska. "What is that? Do you smell that?"

"I do. It's brain oil."

"I'm sorry...did you say *brain oil?*"

"You haven't spent much time tanning hides, have you?"

Cam turned so that Lydia Yang couldn't see her face and stuck her tongue out at Nysska.

Yang wore a heavy wool shirt and matching trousers, with thick leather boots and a leather apron from her collarbones to her knees. She put her hands on her hips and eyed the team critically. "Can I help you folks with something?"

Raoul dismounted, took the reins of the horse Walters had found from Percy, and led it up to her. "I'm Commander Raoul Cullen of the Ninth Crucible. This horse was found down in Painter's Bluff, and its saddle bears your mark. We're wondering if you could tell us anything about the man it belonged to."

As utterly unimpressed, unintimidated, and unconcerned as Nysska had ever seen a human in the presence of a Crucible, Lydia Yang moved on stubby legs to the horse's side and peered up at the saddle. "Yup. Sold it last week." Her eyes traveled around to the other members of the team, and spent exactly as much time on Nysska as on Percy and Cam. Nysska decided she liked the woman, and felt even worse about mentally comparing her with a bulldog. "Sold five last week—been a good month." Yang's fingers glided along the lines of the saddle. "Yeah. All right. I believe I recall. Stout fellow, it was. Rode in here bareback on this proud beast." She reached out and stroked the horse's nose. "About your height, Commander. Sandy hair."

Nysska gave a soft grunt. That description matched the man they'd found dead in the creek.

Raoul traded glances with the team. "Do you remember anything else about him? Where he was coming from? His name?"

"Man paid me full price. Didn't even try to haggle. I'm not about to ask questions if he's not offering answers."

Raoul took a deep breath and let it out slowly. "All right. Thank you. We may be back later to ask more questions, so please don't leave the vicinity."

Lydia Yang snorted. "If I'm not here, I'm at the tavern, so you've got pretty good odds of tracking me down." Still eyeballing the saddle, she asked, "What happened to the fellow? My nameless customer?"

Raoul said, "He's dead, I'm afraid."

"Well. That's a shame. So…what's to become of the saddle now?"

"The horse and the saddle are both parts of a Thaumetallicon investigation. They're Imperial property."

Lydia Yang scoffed, which turned into a hacking cough, and resulted in her spitting something brown and horrible on the ground. "Figures," she said, and stomped back into her shop.

Raoul came over and looked up at Cam in her saddle. "Do you think you could trace his movements? Find out where he came from?"

Cam's forehead wrinkled. "*Oh.* Uh. I don't know. The runes let me read crime sites—you know? This wasn't a crime. This was just a man buying a saddle. For a fair price, even."

Percy had been twisting around on his horse, trying to spot Flax and Jax, but he abandoned that search to ask, "Yeah, but have you ever *tried* to use the runes for something like this?"

Cam put her hands up and dropped her voice. "Whoa. Hey. Can we not talk about this where a civilian can hear us?"

A few minutes later, a quarter of a klik from Yang's place, the Ninth Crucible dismounted in an unoccupied meadow. Nysska and Percy had gotten into the food they'd packed—salted meats and dried fruits and nuts—and they both chewed and listened while Cam talked. Raoul had taken a seat on a stump, and for once, both blood lynxes had decided to grace him with their affection, so he listened with a double armful of purring cats.

"We already went over how Sensors aren't supposed to use our runes for anything except basic getting around and reading crime sites. Well, the way they explained it, the reason we *can* read sites is that a crime like murder releases a lot of energy. Psychic energy, they call it."

"Yeah, you've told us that before," Percy said, but not unkindly.

Cam nodded. "You just need to understand. The act itself, it…charges the world around it, in that particular location. That energy is what the runes pick up on. So there's no point in trying to read sites where mundane shit takes place, because there'd be nothing there to read."

Raoul scratched Jax's belly as he spoke. "If you don't think it's going to do any good, then we're not going to pressure you. But right now we're pretty much looking at a dead end. We could try to call in some backup, just start asking everyone we can find if they know anything about that fistful of assholes who jumped us, but Dragon only knows how long that would take."

"I don't *know* if it's going to do any good or not, is the thing. Look at it like this: you've got a blacksmith. Lydia Yang—why not. Lydia's been taught how to use a blacksmith hammer. It's good for one thing. Smithing. And she's good at smithing, good at using the hammer, she *has* to be good, because that's how she makes her living, so she uses her hammer in the smithy all day, every day. Then someone comes along and says, 'Hey, you know what you should do? Try using that hammer to play the piano.'"

Percy laughed, a deep, free sound from his belly, and the thought of Lydia Yang performing a concerto with her smithing tools almost made Nysska chuckle as well.

Cam went on. "How many blacksmiths have ever tried to play piano with their hammers? Somewhere between zero and...zero, I'm guessing? That's what you're suggesting I do here. Trying to pick something up from this horse, who wasn't around when any crimes were committed—"

"That we know of," Raoul broke in.

"Be that as it may. This is not what the runes were designed for. Not what we were trained to do with them."

"Understood," Raoul said. "But are you willing to give it a try?"

Cam heaved a great sigh—one big enough that Nysska thought it might have been mostly for show—and walked over to the dead man's horse. Over her shoulder, she threw out, "Probably the only thing that'll happen is that I cry that dead asshole's blood, and the kitties take off back toward Painter's Bluff."

"I'll make sure they don't get too far, then," Percy said, around another mouthful of food.

Nysska watched closely as Cam put her back to the team and brought up the power of her runes. The silver flames licked out, dancing on either side of her head, and Cam said, "Come on...come on...show me where you've been..." Her head tilted a few degrees to one side. "If I—if I push a little—I think there's something...something...ooh, this feels really strange..."

The flames flared.

The sudden burst of light spooked the horse. It reared, screaming, and bolted away from her across the meadow. Cam didn't move, didn't react at all, and Nysska realized she had gone rigid, caught in some kind of seizure. She rushed to Cam's side just as she lost her balance—caught her and lowered her gently to the ground as the silver fire faded and went out.

Tears of blood streamed down Cam's face.

She let out a long, shuddering breath and clung to Nysska. "Dragon's scaly cock," she said, barely above a whisper. "That was a *terrible* idea."

Flax and Jax had bounded over as well, with Raoul and Percy right behind them, but whereas the blood lynxes normally reared up and stretched to get a taste of their target's blood, this time they no more than sniffed before they lost interest.

Raoul's and Percy's words tumbled over each other as they knelt on Cam's other side. It sounded to Nysska as though Raoul said, "Are you all right?" as Percy said, "What's wrong with the cats?"

Cam waved them all away and slowly, carefully got to her feet. "I'm fine, I'm fine. I think. There's nothing wrong with the cats, Percy." She pointed at her face. "This is *my* blood."

"How?" Raoul asked. "Why? What happened? Did you see anything? Or was that just something we shouldn't ever ask you to do again?"

"Yes, and yes," Cam shot back. She took the handkerchief Percy was offering her and wiped the blood off her cheeks. "Well, more like yes and maybe. Feels like I burned a hole in my brain trying it."

"Then you're definitely *not* ever doing it again," Nysska said, yellow eyes flashing at Raoul.

Cam put a comforting hand on Nysska's arm. "Calm down. Please. I think...this might just be the kind of thing you have to practice to get better at. Like...well, like everything, I suppose." She turned to Raoul. "I saw a *lot* just then. Not really so much from the dead asshole, but—this is an experience I never expected to have—more from the *horse*."

Raoul hesitated. "Uh...all right? So—you could tell where the horse has been?"

"Yeah. The mayor's house. In Nivenston."

While Raoul groaned, Percy said, "What is it with these fucking *mayors?*"

8

I t makes sense, I suppose," Cam said. It was her turn to hold the reins of the dead man's horse, and she kept twisting in the saddle to look at it. The horse was acting twitchier than it had when either Percy or Raoul had been the one to lead it, and Nysska suspected it was because of the silver in Cam's eyes flashing every time she turned to peer at it. She smiled at the animal every time, too, though, and Nysska didn't have the heart to tell her she was frightening the horse instead of making friends with it.

Cam went on, "If I was going to try to pull off something as crazy as killing a bunch of sethyds in a place like this, I guess I'd want the leaders of both towns in on it. If the heads of Painter's Bluff *and* Nivenston want to make it so that a secret's kept a secret? That'd be the way to do it, wouldn't it?"

Raoul's face had taken on a shade of bitterness that seemed extreme even for him. "It's rotten. What we're talking about doing. It's not just against procedure. It's against the *law*. We could get court-martialed for this."

Percy said, "Dragon's teeth, Raoul, all we're going to do is question the little fucker. It's not like we're arresting him and summoning the Tribunal or any shit like that. We're not even accusing him of anything. We're just going to...encourage him to talk."

Raoul spat. The blood lynxes were trotting along beside the horses, and one of them—Nysska thought it was Jax—leapt out of the way with a grumpy hiss as the spittle hit the ground. "But we've got no *proof*. No Sensor saw him committing any kind of crime. No tracking animal led the way to him. We're not even sure if that dead asshole in the creek has any real connection to him. So we go and brace the man in his home and barrage him with questions based on...on what? On nothing!"

Nysska guided her horse up next to Raoul's. "Commander. If I may. Barraging someone with questions, as you put it, is what we did with the prisoner back in Taurus Hill. Remember that? We had no evidence, but we questioned him, and he gave us a crucial name. That's all we're talking about here."

Raoul shot her an irritated look. "Three hundred years. *Three hundred years.* The Empire has solved crimes a certain way, according to certain procedures, for as long as there's *been* an Empire."

She nodded. "But now circumstances have changed. And unless the Empire changes along with them...well, what would you have the alternative be? The, ah...what did you call them?"

Raoul muttered, "Skinshifters."

"The skinshifters are going to use their new kind of thaumaturgy to shatter the Empire—from within, if they can get away with it. No one has ever done *any* of this before. We have to figure out new ways. New practices."

He theatrically let his shoulders rise and fall, but in a voice that might have held traces of apology, he said, "I don't think you can blame me for being resistant to it. That's all."

Mirroring his tone, Nysska asked, "How're you feeling? Your face looks less swollen."

Raoul snorted. She saw one corner of his mouth raise as he did it. "Yes, and I'm free of stab wounds, too. You're not going to let me forget that you saved my life, are you?"

"Well...does this mean I'm forgiven?"

He turned and looked her in both eyes. After a couple of silent false starts, he said, "No more secrets. Agreed?"

Nysska had only recently learned, to her own satisfaction, how to read all of the emotions conveyed by a human's face. She had also prided herself, though she admitted it was a petty thing, in being able to keep her own face so stony that no human would ever be able to tell what she was thinking or feeling unless she wanted them to.

But...

Atiina curse her for a fool, the Ninth Crucible had become something very like a family to her. Much more so than she'd expected. Much more so than she'd even *wanted*, and yet her relationships with Raoul and Percy, and especially with Cam, felt warmer, more solid, more *real* than anything back in Fajrosxtono.

That sense of family, of fellowship, of…love…abruptly felt more like a weakness, because Raoul saw something in her eyes. Something that almost made him recoil. He said, "Nysska? *Is* there something else you want to tell me?"

From behind them, Cam called out, "Hey—there's the town. We're here."

Looking ahead, sure enough, the village of Nivenston came into view, more and more as they crested a low hill.

Insistent now, Raoul said, "Nysska?"

She reached across the gap between them and put a hand on his forearm. "No. I'm just happy to have your forgiveness."

Raoul gazed back at her. Unreadable. He nodded once. "Don't mention it."

Nysska felt guilt crush her heart—and yet the prospect of coming clean, of telling her newfound family every single bit of the truth, made that heart flutter with something that felt like hope. She examined that hope as though it were a caged bird. Wondering how to take care of it. How not to let it die.

As they rode into town, Nysska decided that Nivenston looked as if someone had taken Painter's Bluff, turned it sideways, and mushed it into a cliffside. The buildings, at least the visible parts, all seemed to follow the same general construction as Painter's Bluff. Low stone foundations, wood-frame walls, thatched roofs. But almost every building, homes and businesses alike, appeared to have been built onto a series of caves dotting a rock face that, while not vertical, was *extremely* steep. As near as Nysska could tell, instead of streets, Nivenston had broad staircases, ramps and, in a few instances, actual ladders leading from one building to another.

The sun had begun to set, and as they approached the town, Nysska saw torch after torch being lit. In a reverse of what she would have expected, the more affluent parts of the village seemed to be at the bottom, with the tiniest, poorest dwellings situated at the top. She wondered if that was because they would be the most difficult to get to, or the least safe to live in, or—watching the smoke from the torches—because at the top the air would be most polluted.

On the bottom-most level of the village, seated firmly on solid bedrock, was a Church of the Great Silver Dragon. One of the church's brilliantly-polished dragon-shaped kites flew from the spire, the color of flames in the setting sun.

Not at all surprising to Nysska was how everyone in Nivenston went out of their way to stare at her as the Ninth Crucible rode past on the way to the mayor's house. The heroic subject of songs or not, no one in the village appeared to hold her in any kind of high esteem, and she heard at least a dozen voices use the word "demon" as she passed. Gray-haired men spat on the stony ground. Mothers hid their children.

Nysska noticed that most of the townsfolk sported Dragon amulets—winged shapes made of hammered tin—around their necks or pinned to their clothes.

"I'm sorry," Cam said quietly.

"For what?"

"For the way they stare at you."

Nysska shrugged. "Not hard to believe they would have wanted a sethyd settlement dead and gone."

One of the broad stone ramps that took the place of streets led straight to what had to be the mayor's house. It was the largest home in the village and, much like the one in Painter's Bluff, decorated with bronze paint in a halfway successful bid to look official. Arriving outside the front door, Raoul greeted the two Cathedral soldiers standing guard.

"Evening. I'm Commander Raoul Cullen of the Ninth Crucible. Can you get someone to take our horses to the stable? We need to speak with your mayor."

One of the soldiers didn't quite openly sneer, but his words held only contempt. "I don't recall the mayor saying a Dragon-damned word about having visitors tonight." To the other soldier, he said, "You?"

The second man shook his head. "'Fraid not. Reckon you folks need to make an appointment. Come back in the morning, see if he's available then."

Raoul took a moment to think about that. "Boys, I don't think you're understanding the situation here. We're on official Thaumetallicon business, and we need to speak to the Mayor of Nivenston. Immediately."

The first soldier laughed. "Fuck your official business. We take our orders from the mayor and nobody else. Now gather up your mangy cats and your shiny-eyed bitch and your filthy fucking demon and fuck off."

Nysska saw Percy bristling, but Raoul seemed more bemused than anything else. He said, "Let me give this one more try. We're here on the specific orders of the Emperor. You might have heard of him. You're in his army. Now, you can either bring the mayor out here so we can have a pleasant word with him, or—"

The second soldier cut him off. "Or *what*, you piece of shit? This is Nivenston. We're under the protection of the Great Silver Dragon Himself. You don't like it, you can go crying back to your fucking Emperor."

Raoul wheeled his horse around to face the rest of the team. "Either they know a *lot* we don't, or they're both brain damaged. You all ready to do this the hard way?"

Nysska gave him a tight smile. "Define 'hard.'"

The rest of the Crucible followed as Raoul dismounted. He went to the first of the five stone steps leading from the ramp-street up to the mayor's house, and when he was sure he had the two soldiers' attention, he said, "Boys, you may not realize what the different positions in a Thaumetallicon Crucible are. I'm the Commander. I coordinate, make decisions, do the talking. Cam over here is our Sensor. She uses argonium runes to read the sites of crimes. Then you've got the Keeper. That's Percy. He handles the tracking animals we use to run down the suspects. Now *this*— this is Nysska Stonegate. She's our Enforcer. You know what Enforcers do?"

Before either of the soldiers could answer, Nysska picked up a rock the size of a ripe lemon and whipped it around sidearm. The rock struck the first soldier directly between the eyes, which rolled up as he sank to the stone stoop, blood pouring from the bloody divot in his forehead.

The second soldier's face registered shock, then a near-comical indignation, and settled on unbridled rage as he drew his sword and charged, screaming, straight at Nysska.

She didn't bother drawing a weapon of her own. Instead, she slapped the flat of his blade sideways with the heel of her hand and punched him in the larynx. He sagged to his knees, weapon forgotten and clanging on the street as both hands flew to his throat, and Nysska pushed him over backward with her foot and stepped on his chest as she led the Ninth Crucible up the steps and into the mayor's house.

As they walked through the door, Percy said, "What's this guy's name, again?"

Nivenston Mayor Hallum Penn's house wasn't set up to present quite as grandiose an image as the one in Painter's Bluff. Rather than walking into an audience chamber with a chair like a throne, the front door simply opened onto a hallway, multiple doors leading off of it, with a stairway to one side climbing to the second floor. The Ninth Crucible had found Mayor Penn sitting alone in the large, tastefully appointed dining room. After a terse exchange that swiftly escalated in both volume and profanity, Raoul had escorted the mayor to a small parlor down the hall for further conversation, away from the curious ears of his household servants.

Now Penn sat in the middle of the parlor's floor, straight-backed in a plush leather chair, arms folded and one leg bouncing up and down in peevish impatience. Since, like most structures in Nivenston, the house had been built in front of a cave, the parlor walls were natural stone and the room had no windows. Percy and Cam had stayed in the dining room, helping themselves to some of the mayor's dinner, but Nysska hovered outside the parlor in the shadows, watching and listening.

"Look, Commander," Mayor Penn said, "I don't see what any of this has got to do with me. Did I want Summergray's lands? Yes, of course. No one in their right mind wouldn't, they're the most fertile part of this whole valley. But I had nothing whatsoever to do with what happened to those demons that came in and took the place over. Not to mention, I've complied with the soldiers' edicts that we not let word of the demon settlement out of the valley. I don't even know what you're doing here."

Raoul put his hands on the back of another plush, leather-bound chair. "I'm here, my Crucible is here, to figure out who's responsible for those *sethyds'* deaths. And we think you might know something about it."

Penn smirked. "'Sethyds,' you call them. How polite. They're fucking demons, no matter how you dress them up."

Hallum Penn reminded Nysska strongly of another young man they'd met. Sergei Benitoff—a member of one of the High Noble families. Penn looked to be roughly the same age, and had the same spoiled man-child demeanor, the same unlined face. He seemed smarter than Benitoff, more disciplined, maybe, but just as clad in the same bronze-hard shell of entitlement.

Raoul tried a different approach. "We encountered a man in Painter's Bluff—a burly, pale-skinned, sandy-haired man, seen very recently here at your house. What can you tell me about him?"

Penn laughed. It had a nasty edge to it. "That's all you have to give me?

Burly, pale, and sandy-haired? One in every ten people in Nivenston has pale skin, Commander. You could be describing anyone."

"This man was using a saddle that had been sold to you. Also recently."

Penn spread his hands. "I provide for the townsfolk. That's my *job*, Commander. You see, I understand what it is that I'm supposed to do. Don't know that I could say the same about you. *Sir*."

Nysska found her eyes wandering around Penn's house.

Preoccupied by the conversation between the Mayor and Raoul, it took her a couple of minutes to notice the abundance of Dragon-themed art. Paintings. Sculptures.

As Raoul and Penn continued talking, Nysska stole away down the hall to the kitchen, where Percy was feeding the blood lynxes bits of chicken while Cam sipped a glass of what looked like tea. Cam seemed to recognize the urgency on Nysska's face. "What's going on?"

Nysska beckoned them close. "I have an idea."

Hallum Penn sat, fuming, as the idiotic Thaumetallicon goon babbled at him. Penn had stopped listening, and only made non-committal grunts whenever Cullen paused for breath.

The commander broke off at the sound of a knock on the parlor door, and the woman he had introduced as Sensor Camble Delakroy popped her head in.

"Sorry, Commander, but we just received a message you need to see."

Cullen frowned, but turned to Penn. "Pardon me. We'll continue this discussion in a few minutes."

Penn, busy examining the fingernails of his right hand, didn't even look up. "Whatever. You want to keep wasting time, we'll keep wasting time."

Cullen left, closing the door after him, and Penn heard a few low voices speaking in the hallway. They retreated, heading toward the back of the house. He spent the next couple of minutes composing the letter he planned to send to the territorial governor, complaining in the most stringent tone about the incompetence of the Ninth Crucible. If his influence extended as far as he thought it did, he'd have all four of them decommissioned and court-martialed.

The door cracked open. He expected Raoul Cullen to walk back in, but when that didn't happen, Penn looked up—

And saw, in the crack of the door, a yellow eye watching him.

Penn's brow furrowed. "What're you doing?"

When the demon simply stood there, staring at him, he said, "What do you want?"

The door opened a few more centims. The demon had taken off the leather-and-bronze Thaumetallicon jacket, and a long, sinewy, violet-skinned arm reached into the room—to the table where one of the parlor's two lamps burned—and snuffed out the flame.

Penn's skin contracted into gooseflesh. Fingers digging into the wooden armrests of his chair, he said, "What the *fuck* are you doing?"

The door creaked farther open. Slowly, agonizingly, the demon now silhouetted against the lamps from the hallway. The only other light source in the parlor, a lamp on a table in the far corner, provided just enough illumination to make her hellish yellow eyes shine in the gloom.

Still having said not a word, the demon slipped inside. Pressed her back to the door until it quietly latched.

Dropped to a crouch.

Penn couldn't decide whether or not to stand up. He stayed where he was—this was his house, Dragon damn it, he was in control here—but as the demon crept noiselessly across the floor toward him, he began to feel *trapped*.

"I knew you were the one as soon as I saw you," the demon breathed, her words icy, and his skin clenched even further.

"Wh-what are you talking about?" Penn managed, pressing himself deeper into the chair's cushions.

"My people said I was sick." The demon's voice dropped to a hoarse whisper. "They said they had to keep me locked up. But then the *Krizo* came, and I ran and ran. Away from the cells and the shackles." Black horns caught the lamplight, gleaming onyx ridges. Her body stretched out, so low to the floor that she seemed more like some kind of panther than anything that walked upright, and silently she slithered closer.

The situation had descended from merely annoying into whatever kind of surreal nightmare this was *so quickly* that Penn's mind couldn't cope. Part of him wanted to insist that this wasn't happening, that he was dreaming, that the demon slinking toward him was no more than a figment of some icy, fanged nightmare.

He wanted to scream. Knew he *should* scream. *Needed* to scream—and yet Penn realized he no longer had the ability to move. His lips quivering, he made a sound like, "Wh-wh-wh-wh—"

The demon's head rose, unholy hell-flame-yellow eyes no more than a meter away from his and drawing closer.

"They said it was wrong to do what I did," she whispered. "They wanted to keep me away from everyone." Her husky voice took on a sing-song quality. "Eh-ver-y-one. *Eh-ver-y-one.*"

The demon reached him. Traced lines up his legs with her fingertips. Moved closer until he could feel her breath on his skin. "But then I found out a secret."

"Y-y-you can't do this," Penn gasped. "You're in a Crucible—you work for the Emperor!"

The demon continued as if he hadn't spoken. "Do you want to know what the secret was?" She stroked the inside of his right forearm with a sharp black fingernail.

Penn started crying.

The demon moved her lips to his ear. *"Humans taste better."*

Penn's throat seized and struggled. No sound came out.

The demon slid a long-bladed knife out of a sheath on her thigh. "I'm going to spirit you out of this house." She spoke in a whisper, sultry and raw, as if to a lover in the throes of passion. "No one will see us. No one. I'm going to take you somewhere nice and safe and quiet, because…" She licked his earlobe. "You're one of the *tasty* ones."

The dam blocking Penn's throat gave way, and he screamed at the top of his lungs, *"Get away from me, get away, somebody help me, somebody help!"* and the door to the parlor burst open.

Raoul Cullen and the Keeper and the Sensor all rushed in, and Cullen bellowed, "Nysska, no!" It took all three of them, but they wrestled the demon away and out of the room, and she screeched and flailed and gnashed her teeth until the door slammed again and he was alone.

Penn slumped forward in the chair and sobbed, and then nearly jumped out of his own hair when Raoul Cullen reappeared in the doorway.

Cullen looked mussed but otherwise unhurt. Penn had blinked his tears away, but they started again when the Commander said, "Sorry about that. We've got her mostly under control, these days, but every now and then…well. Someone takes her fancy."

Penn got to his feet, found his knees weak, and sat down again. "Takes her *fancy*? She wanted to fucking kill me and *eat* me!"

Cullen shoved the other leather chair closer and sat down, facing him. "True." He leaned forward, features going stony. "Which means you, sir, are left with a choice. Either you tell me what I want to know, or the Ninth Crucible will...how can I word it so it looks good on the report... we'll let our Enforcer take you to a more private, secure location. For *questioning.*" Cullen stretched and yawned. "Who can say what might happen after that?"

Penn was afraid a blood vessel might have burst in his eye, his heart thundered so hard in his ribcage. "No! *No, please!* I'll tell you, I'll tell you, just *keep her away from me!*"

Fifteen minutes later, Raoul walked out of the parlor, his face unreadable. Silent, he gestured to everyone else—who'd been standing around outside the door, listening—and led them to the kitchen. Keeping his voice low, he said, "Nysska, next time you want to put on a show like that, can you *please* give me some warning?"

Nysska gave him her best and least threatening smile. "Sorry, Commander. It was a spur-of-the-moment thing."

Percy's grin held every bit of his normal gleeful mischief. "*That* should be in the songs about you. That shit right there." He gave Nysska an appreciative bump to the shoulder.

Cam twined her fingers through Nysska's and squeezed, but spoke to Raoul. "Did it work?"

"Oh, it worked like a charm. But the person Penn's been taking orders from, and this is verbatim, 'Changes his face every time I see him, so I don't ever know who he's going to look like, or how to find him.'"

The members of the Ninth Crucible let that information sink in for a few moments.

Percy said, "Well, fuck."

9

Cam rubbed her eyes. It made the silver light of the runes shine through her eyelids. "I'd like to echo Percy, here."

Nysska stared up at the ceiling. "This puts us in an incredibly precarious position."

Raoul nodded. "I know."

Nysska went on. "The town's hostile to us. We don't know how many people here are more loyal to the mayor—and therefore to the skinshifters—than to the Emperor. We could get overrun."

Raoul put his hands up. "I *know*."

"What we are," Percy said, "is in so fucking far over our heads that we can't see the surface. What if this is our worst fears? What if that Lockridge asshole and his skinshifter fuck-buddies already *have* struck an alliance with the sethyds? Or with the Argonium Infantry? What if they were just waiting for us to tip over this particular barrel of week-old fish to come charging down on top of us?"

Raoul paced back and forth, the length of the kitchen. "We don't know the bigger picture. We *can't* know the bigger picture, because..."

Into the pause, Nysska quietly said, "Because we don't know where Emperor Valco stands. Or what those white runes mean."

Raoul kicked the floor. "Shit."

Cam perched on a stool next to a marble-topped bar. "There's also the fact that Valco himself, *himself*, charged us with solving the massacre at

Summergray. If we don't do that, we still face the Crucible getting broken up. Or worse."

Percy grunted. "Does it feel like Valco sent us there as some kind of trap? Or is that just me?"

Nysska leaned back against a heavy teak breakfast table and folded her arms. "We need help. But I don't think it would be wise to go straight back to the Emperor. Not yet." She spoke directly to Raoul. "How fast can we get word to Galena Vachs?"

In the far corner of the kitchen, where Flax and Jax had been stretched out on the cool stone floor, Flax sat up, yawned, and popped Jax on the top of his head with one big, furry paw. Jax started upright, swatted at Flax, and both cats bolted out of the room.

Raoul had stopped pacing. Now he stared at Nysska, brow furrowed. "What could Galena Vachs do? She's all the way over in Green Needles."

Nysska said, "Yes, but she's Territorial Governor in Green Needles, and has some pull. She might be able to get us at least a little bit of protection."

Raoul drummed the fingers of one hand on his biceps. "Maybe. Maybe. We talked about reaching out to her back in Painter's Bluff, before we got distracted with people trying to kill us. The question is *how*, though."

The two blood lynxes came back into the kitchen. Clamped in her mouth, Flax carried an ornately-carved, seventeen-centim-long wooden rod, affixed to the end of which was a globe-shaped, multi-faceted white quartz stone roughly ten centims across. Flax took the object straight to Raoul, placed it at his feet, and sat primly, looking up at him. Jax joined her a second later.

As Percy started laughing, Cam said, "Holy shit."

Nysska asked, "Is that…?"

Raoul knelt and scratched both cats along their jawlines, which caused them to purr loudly enough to echo around the kitchen. He said, "Yes, that's a Conversation Stone. And you two are very, very good kitties."

Mayor Penn, who had been left in the parlor, bound to the plush leather chair and with a gag in his mouth, proved quite willing to explain how the Conversation Stone worked, on the condition that "that fucking crazy demon bitch" stay far away from him. Raoul took careful notes on the

Stone's use, retrieved the activation ring from the table beside Penn's bed, and replaced the gag.

The Ninth Crucible gathered in Penn's study, a room on the house's second floor outfitted in more teak furniture—a desk big enough for the Emperor himself, Nysska thought, and four matching chairs—and thick, luxurious rugs dyed in rich reds and purples. Nysska murmured to Cam, "I think this is the first time I've actually agreed with one of these Imperial assholes' taste in furnishings."

Making sure that neither Percy nor Raoul was in earshot, Cam went up onto her toes and whispered in Nysska's ear. "Plenty of things I'd like to do to you on this rug, that's for sure."

Nysska's heart sped up, and she gave Cam's ass a surreptitious squeeze.

On the far side of the room stood a bronze-inlaid teak tripod. Raoul hefted it, carried it over and set it down in the center of the floor, and carefully slid the Conversation Stone's rod into the socket at the tripod's apex.

Percy watched with keen interest. "So, it's like your Tribunal stone?"

Raoul patted the white quartz stone that decorated the pommel of his longsword. "A lot like it, yeah, if Penn's telling the truth. Except the Tribunal stones are all linked to the Tribunal Hall in Caulspring. This is more...uh, far-reaching."

Cam and Nysska had walked over so that the four of them stood in a circle around the tripod. Cam said, "But you activate it the same way?"

Raoul nodded. "It's supposed to be pretty simple. So here goes." He picked a large, gaudy ring up from Penn's desk. In its lumpy gold band was set a much smaller version of the Conversation Stone. Raoul slipped it on his ring finger, reached out, and tentatively tapped the larger stone three times.

A familiar, argonium-fueled silver radiance sprang to life deep within the quartz. It grew brighter and brighter, and just before Nysska thought it might become too painful to look at—

A burst of light sprang out of the Conversation Stone, sharpened, and to Nysska's astonishment, resolved into a silvery, translucent *globe*. The world, the *entire world*, spun slowly half a meter above the Stone. Nysska gasped louder than she'd meant to when she realized that, hanging several meters out in space from the world's surface, all three moons were there as well.

She had seen maps before. In school, she had learned the topography of Patrinomonto to a greater degree of detail than she'd thought strictly necessary. Since fleeing to the Empire, Nysska had seen maps of Kainos, the single great continent emerging from the world-spanning sea, with islands both large and small dotting its coastlines. As the colossal landmass came back around in its slow, elegant rotation, she spotted Patrinomonto, there off Kainos's northeastern shore, separated from the mainland by the Scyllan Channel. She didn't think whatever mapmakers were responsible for this display had gotten her homeland's contours quite right.

"Great Dragon's oily taint," Percy said, staring open-mouthed. "They've even got the territorial borders in place!"

Nysska looked more closely, and saw he was right; thin, sparkling silver threads lay across the continent, marking out the Empire's northern and southern borders. Between those, other threads outlined the Fifteen Territories. In fact, as she looked closer—

Cam beat her to the observation. "It's not just the borders. They've got the capitals marked, too."

"That's what we've got to focus on," Raoul said. "As long as I've got this ring on, I'm supposed to be able to touch one of the capitals—well, it's not that the capitals are marked. Each of those dots is the location of another Conversation Stone. Look there—down in Red Sky. Nothing. I guess no one's bought one there yet."

Nysska said, "So we need Tember, then. For the Conversation Stone in Galena Vachs's mansion."

Raoul raised his arm. "Right. And I think...that's it right there." He stepped forward and, as the tiny dot slid past him, reached out and touched it—and recoiled with a sharp cry of pain, shaking his hand.

Percy said, "You all right, boss?"

Raoul clenched and unclenched the hand that bore the ring. "I don't know. Wasn't expecting it to *hurt*. I—"

He broke off as the revolving world shimmered, burst into a cloud of shining silver motes, and re-formed...into a monochromatic image of a small but tastefully appointed room, in which a balding male servant in Tember's livery peered at Raoul. "Who addresses Governor Galena Vachs?" the servant demanded, a good bit more haughtily than Nysska thought appropriate.

Clutching the ring hand with his other one, Raoul used his Crucible voice. "This is Commander Raoul Cullen of the Ninth Crucible. I need to speak to Governor Vachs at once."

The servant peered at him suspiciously. "The Governor is otherwise occupied. May I have her return this courtesy at a later time?"

Raoul barked, "You'll get her right now, or I'll have you on a fork, you bald piece of shit!"

The servant flinched and scurried away. Cam went to Raoul's side, frowning. "Are you all right? That was a little testy, even for you."

Raoul held up the ring. "Sorry. It's just—it hurts more than I was ready for. I'm fine. I'll be fine." He tried for a smile. "I'll do my best not to yell at Governor Vachs."

"I should hope not," a rich, clear, feminine voice said, and the silvery representation of Galena Vachs slid into view above the Conversation Stone. "Also, I think the four of you can safely call me 'Galena.' At least when no one else is listening." She squinted, looking past Raoul. "Where are you? And are you alone? Everybody get where I can see you."

In person, Galena Vachs was easily the most physically perfect human female Nysska had ever seen. Wise beyond her years at only eighteen, she looked more like some sort of earthbound goddess than a young woman, with crystalline eyes of blue and hair of gold and skin like rose-touched snow. Now, displayed in different shades of silver, the unearthly quality of her beauty was only magnified. Nysska realized she was staring, even as Percy and Cam crowded closer to Raoul, so she moved into the rear of the group and gazed at Galena over everyone else's heads.

Galena Vachs smiled, which ramped up her magnificence even more. "Hello, everyone! Cam, Percy—Nysska. Dragon's chin, has your horn grown back already?"

Nysska smiled politely, reached up and tugged the false horn loose. "Not yet, I'm afraid. Broken horns are not unheard of among my people. I carved myself a replacement while the new one comes in."

Galena's smile took on a mischievous nature that mirrored Percy's frequent grins. "Good to see humans aren't the only ones to make occasional concessions to vanity. Now. I know this isn't free, so what can I do for you?"

Raoul cleared his throat, and everyone else let him speak. This was, after all, part of his official duties. Clearly, concisely, and with an impressive economy of language, Raoul laid out everything they had learned and been through, from Emperor Valco's initial assignment—and the shocking, strange white runes Cam had seen beneath his skin—to the gruesome discovery at Summergray and the escalating conflicts at Painter's Bluff and Nivenston.

"This is the Nivenston mayor's Conversation Stone, by the way," he said, finishing up. "So we've got to complete this investigation but, not to put too fine a point on it, our asses are hanging out in the wind. Is there any way you could arrange some sort of security for us while we try to see this through?"

The silvery image of Galena Vachs drummed immaculate fingertips on its chin. "Yes. Yes, I think so. Not immediate, I'm sorry to say, but soon. Do you think you can get back to Summergray unscathed?"

Raoul stammered as he answered. Nysska noticed his hands trembling for a moment, but the tremors stopped. "Y-yes, I think so. If we leave now, travel by moonlight—probably. I think we're most likely safer on the road than if we stay here."

She nodded. "All right then, go. Get there as soon as you can, and if I'm thinking straight, I can have some reinforcements waiting for you by morning." Pausing, with a disbelieving shake of her head, she muttered, "*White runes?* What the *fuck?*"

"Thank you, Galena," Raoul said—and his knees buckled. Nysska moved faster than Percy or Cam, and caught him before he hit the floor, but even as she held him upright he resisted her and fought back to his feet.

"Yes, I'd say it was time to end this conversation," Galena said, frowning. "You know how to reach me. Dragon keep you all safe."

The image above the Conversation Stone burst into a storm of silver motes again and vanished, the light from within the Stone abruptly gone. Nysska guided a shaky Raoul into a nearby chair—and when she got a good look at his face, she grabbed a nearby lamp and held it closer.

Raoul looked sick. Dark hollows had appeared under his eyes, and his skin had tightened against the bones of his skull. He tugged the quartz-and-gold ring off and shoved it into Nysska's hands. "I think...I understand...what Galena meant about this not being...free." His eyes slid closed. "Could you see if there's maybe some fruit juice or something around here?" He held his hand up, and Cam gasped at the sight of a band of withered flesh where the ring had touched his skin. Raoul squinted at it. "Hope that plumps back up."

Nysska growled. She turned and almost ran down the hallway to the parlor, burst through the door, grabbed Hallum Penn by his lapels and hoisted him up and off of his feet. "You explain how the Stone works, but don't bother to mention it saps your fucking *life* while you use it?"

Penn screamed as best he could with the gag in his mouth, and when

Nysska looked down, she saw that he had pissed himself. She threw him back in the chair with a cry of disgust, spun the entire chair around with him in it to avoid standing in the puddle, and put her face a centim from his. He whimpered as her yellow eyes narrowed. "Just for that, you mangy little turd, your Conversation Stone is coming with us. And *so are you.*"

10

Only the first moon had risen when they set out for Summergray. They rode in a square—Raoul and Percy at the front, Nysska and Cam at the back, with Mayor Penn in the center, gagged and bound to his horse. Nysska's head stayed on a near-constant swivel, watching for assailants in the woods whenever the road passed through a forested area, checking for archers behind bales of hay as they moved through pastures and meadows.

By the time the second moon rose, bathing the cloudless night in silver-blue moonglow nearly as bright as sunlight, she began to think that maybe, possibly, they weren't all about to be slaughtered.

By third moonrise, and still with no pursuit, she thought they could relax a tiny bit. She'd been watching Penn, tracking his body language—judging whether or not he was about to try something stupid. Only after the third or fourth hour of the ride did she noticed that he was stealing hateful little glances at her.

"Something you'd like to say to me, Mr. Mayor?"

Penn worked his chin until the gag wriggled out of his mouth and fell down around his neck, his mouth set in a hard, bitter line. "You were *lying* to me."

The other members of the Crucible began listening to the exchange as Nysska said, "What makes you think so?"

He all but spat. "You're all laughing at me, aren't you? Let's scare the poor bumpkin. Get him to confess. Let's put on a show, so we can get information and mean-spirited amusement at the same time. You should be ashamed of yourselves. All of you. And *you*, demon. I'll never trust one of you again. Ever. I'll make sure *no one* does."

Raoul said, "If you don't shut up, I'll gag you again," and Penn fell silent.

Nysska and Cam exchanged quiet, amused glances. Cam frowned, thoughtful, and after a second's hesitation, carefully and slowly said, "*Li estas tiel kolera, cxu ne?*" *He's very angry, isn't he?*

Nysska's eyes sparkled in the moonlight as she laughed. "*Tre bona!* Very good!"

Percy turned in his saddle. "Whoa, whoa, the fuck was *that*? Cam, since when do you speak sethyd?"

Cam grinned. "Nysska's been teaching me. Honestly—and I mean this as no slight to the language—it's *really* easy. Much easier than Plainish."

Percy laughed. "That's fucking great! Hey, you know what this *means*? If we all learned it, we could have our own secret language!"

Cam chuckled, and with a smile Nysska said, "Yes, the Ninth Crucible and several hundred thousand sethyds."

Raoul spoke up. "Tell you what—why don't we all pretend there's still the possibility that a bunch of Mayor Penn's goons are going to pop out and try to stab us a lot, so maybe we shut the hell up and keep watch?"

Percy winked at Nysska, and flashed his grin at Cam, but turned back around in his saddle and fell silent. Cam and Nysska followed Percy's example. Penn let out a quiet but unmistakably disgusted groan.

For a long time only the sound of the horses' hooves on the road rang out.

After another hour, Raoul dropped his horse back to ride beside Nysska. Quietly, he said, "There are hundreds of thousands of sethyds up in the Crags?"

"Roughly four hundred thousand, yes."

Raoul appeared to consider that for several moments. "That's more than I realized."

Nysska said, "It's not that many. Before the *Krizo*, there were something like eight million of us."

Raoul's eyes widened, but he said nothing. A moment later he spurred his horse back up to the front of the formation.

When they rode into Summergray, visible in the weak light of pre-dawn, it was a place transformed. Instead of the two or three dozen Cathedral soldiers stationed in the valley, now at least three hundred human men and women swarmed around the village, and a broad meadow to the town's immediate west had become a low forest of military-issue brown tents. Not only were the soldiers present in shocking numbers, but they had also set about rebuilding Summergray at large. Piles of charred, ruined lumber steadily grew in the center of each intersection as hundreds of hands pulled them down from the fire-damaged structures; likewise, wagonloads of fresh timber sat at the village's southern end, waiting as brown-clad soldiers set up carpentry stations bristling with hammers and saws.

"Dragon fuck me," Percy said, "when the Cathedral decides to do something, they don't waste any fucking time, do they?"

"They do not," Raoul replied, gazing toward the center of the town. "I wonder if they've moved the corpses."

Nysska's whole body had clenched at the sight of what she couldn't help but think of as an occupying force. "I hope they haven't. They're the only solid evidence we have at this point."

"I'll expect a full debriefing on that."

The deep, booming voice carried across the length of the entire village. Nysska snapped her head around, and saw the voice's owner step out of a mid-demolition home to their left.

A painful sort of choking noise escaped Raoul.

Cam sucked in a quick, sharp breath, and Percy whispered, "Dragon fuck me harder."

Nysska recognized the man, though in truth she'd never seen him before. One of the skinshifters had impersonated him, back in Tember—a man named Lockridge, whom she had personally bested and killed in front of a crowd in the city center despite the hellish strength granted to him by those infernal red runes.

In person, General Boris Cullen was taller, even more gaunt, and at least twice as intimidating as his doppelgänger had been.

Raoul brought his horse to a sudden halt, dismounted, snapped to attention, and gave his father the crispest, most flawless salute she'd ever seen executed by a human. She whispered to Cam, *"Should we dismount, too?"*

Cam made a barely verbal sound—*I don't know.*

General Cullen, gleaming polished bronze in his full field armor, his tight cap of snow-white hair shining in the sun peering through the trees, moved to within arm's reach of his son, who still stood arrow-straight at attention. The General's ink-black eyes raked over Raoul from head to toe, then speared Percy, Nysska, and Cam in turn.

"So, this is the Ninth Crucible," he said. His voice, now that Nysska could hear more of it, sounded a *lot* like Raoul's, just deeper and huskier. He walked slowly around Raoul, who had begun to tremble just the tiniest bit. "Do you realize, Commander, that this is the first time I have seen your unit as a whole in four years?"

Raoul stood, quivering, still at rigid attention. Long enough for it to become clear to everyone present that the question was not rhetorical. "I apologize, General," he said, voice strained. "I—have done my best to— that is, sir, I've tried to take my duties as seriously as possible—"

Nysska had heard a lot about General Boris Cullen. How incredibly strict and demanding a parent he'd been, how unswerving in his own loyalty to the Empire. How he had instilled in Raoul a desire—no, a *need*— to seek his father's approval in such a way that that approval could never be fully attained.

Another silence fell. Stretched.

Nysska couldn't see Raoul's face, but she studied the General's as he stood there, stonelike. Giving as much away as an Exemplar statue.

General Cullen bellowed, "Major Raines!" A tall, rake-thin woman with ash-blond hair emerged from the same building the General had. Cullen said, "Get these horses brushed and fed, and show the rest of the Ninth here to their tents. I'm assuming the man tied to his saddle is a prisoner?"

"Yes, sir," Raoul snapped out.

"Take that man into custody until the Commander here decides what to do with him." Cullen moved back around until he stood facing Raoul. "But right now...I need some time to talk to my son..." He got even closer, and Nysska saw every centim of Raoul's frame seize up tight—

Until General Boris Cullen's mouth stretched wide in a dazzling, perfect smile.

"...so I can tell him exactly how *proud* I am."

Raoul gasped, but before he could react any further, his father flung his arms wide and embraced his son. Raoul seemed to be stunned beyond the capacity for speech, and only stood there, unmoving, until Cullen released him. "My son! My boy! Saving the life of a Territorial Governor!

Routing a threat to the Empire itself!" Cullen put his arm around Raoul's shoulders and steered him away.

Raoul cast one dazed glance back in the team's direction before his father led him around a corner and out of sight.

Major Raines's face stayed completely neutral as she approached the rest of the Ninth. "If you'll dismount and come with me, please," she said, and five soldiers wordlessly moved in to take their mounts' reins. Nysska made sure the Conversation Stone was safe in her saddle bag as she and Percy and Cam followed the Major. Percy made a kissing sound, and Flax and Jax scampered out of another half-destroyed building and fell in right behind him.

"If I may ask, Major," Nysska said, "how long have you been here? Governor Vachs couldn't have gotten the message to you before last night."

Major Raines answered without turning her head or slowing down. "Our division wasn't far from here. We arrived a couple of hours before dawn and got to work."

"The bodies we stored in the cellar—you haven't moved those, have you?"

"I wanted to, because they stink like dead skunks in August, but no, we haven't." She led them into the field of brown tents. Closer up, Nysska saw that each one was designed to sleep two people comfortably. Major Raines pointed at one. "Keeper Bitters, you're in that one. Commander Cullen will bunk with you." She pointed at another one across the aisle. "Sensor Delakroy, Enforcer Stonegate, the two of you are in there. I'm sure you could use some rest after riding all night. Just flag down anyone in bronze if you need anything and I'll see that you get it."

Raines turned on her heel and walked swiftly back toward the village.

Nysska, Percy, and Cam moved in close right outside Percy's tent and waited till they were sure no soldiers were within earshot. Cam spoke first. "What'd we just see back there? Wasn't Raoul's father supposed to be some kind of ball-crushing ogre?"

"That's all I ever heard," Percy said. "Couple years ago—I know you remember this, Cam—we were on our way to South Boryon, and passed a field full of tents like these, and Raoul saw his father's division flag flying? You know the day I'm talking about?"

Cam nodded. "You'd have thought someone had cursed him. He started sweating really bad, and his voice got kind of high-pitched, and he made us all break into a gallop till we couldn't see the flag anymore."

Nysska glanced back toward the town. "So what changed?" A horrible thought occurred to her, and she said, "Fuck," and dropped into a whisper. "What if Raoul's father is like Wendell Anwar was—dead and stuffed with red runes and working for the skinshifters?"

Cam coughed softly. "No. I, uh...I snuck a peek. I'm getting pretty good at that. You didn't even notice, did you?"

Nysska's eyes narrowed. "Did I notice you using your runes in an expressly forbidden way, *in front of a Cathedral general?* No, Cam, I did not."

"I waited till his back was turned! Anyway, he's clean. No runes of any kind, red or otherwise." She spread her hands. "Maybe...maybe he's just decided to be...nice?"

Percy yawned hugely. "As fucking fascinating as Raoul's home life might be, that Raines woman was right about us needing rest. Well, right about me, anyway, you girls can do as you like." He held the flap of the tent open. "All right," he said to the blood lynxes. "In you go." As the cats padded into the tent, he flashed a grin at Nysska and Cam. "Just like back at the inn! Except with fewer assassins. Probably. Wake me whenever." He disappeared inside and shut the flap.

Cathedral-issue tents had a ground layer that was supposed to be padded and waterproof, but Nysska thought the one in the tent she shared with Cam felt more like a thin blanket. Still, the ground on which the tent had been pitched was more or less level, which combined with her lack of sleep to render her dead to the world seconds after her head went horizontal.

She woke to Cam's gentle touch on her shoulder, and when she stirred, Cam followed that with a tender kiss on her lips.

"Careful," Nysska said, blinking at the fully laced-up tent flap. "They might not be able to see us, but we're still in the middle of a military camp."

"I'll be good if you will," Cam said, but then ducked her head and very lightly bit Nysska's left nipple. When Nysska gasped, Cam sat back, laughing. "All right, *now* I'll be good. I promise."

Nysska sat up, giving Cam a baleful glare with zero force behind it. "What time is it, anyway? Have we slept the day through?"

Cam pulled on her Thaumetallicon jacket and undid the first few laces on the tent flap. Peering outside, she said, "No, I think it's just mid-afternoon. Want to go see what kind of unholy shitshow we're in because of Mayor Penn?"

Nysska quickly dressed. "Food first. Then shitshow."

The two women left the tent, and found Percy sitting outside his on a folding three-legged stool, eating what appeared to be a ham sandwich. Every couple of bites, he picked a tiny shred of meat off and fed it to the blood lynxes, who sat at attention in front of him, patiently waiting their turns.

"What's going on?" Cam asked as they walked over to him. "Where's Raoul?"

Percy grinned around a mouthful of food. "Haven't seen him."

Nysska had been eyeing the sandwich. "Where did you get that?"

Percy gestured toward town. "There's a tent. Just go ask for something. They have a great selection, as long as you want a ham sandwich."

The silver in Cam's eyes grew brighter as she peered down the long aisle of uniform brown tents. "Do they have coffee?"

"I believe they do."

To Cam, Nysska said, "Once we get some food, I'd like to go take a look at the bodies again, and I'd like you to come with me. I have an idea."

Cam's nose wrinkled. "Can we let the food settle for at least a few minutes before we stick our faces into a bunch of rotting burn victims?"

Nysska shrugged, and turned to Percy. "Want to come with us?"

Percy fed Flax another bit of ham. "No offense, ladies, but this is the first time I've felt relaxed in...yeah, I literally cannot fucking remember when. So until Raoul comes through with some sort of official orders, I'm going to sit here and calmly eat my food, and calmly feed my kitties, and just try to be fucking *calm* for once."

Cam grinned. "That's fair."

Nysska nodded. "So, if we need you, this is where you'll be?"

"Here, or in the tent asleep." As they headed toward the village, he called after them, "Try not to need me, yeah?"

Upon their arrival early that morning, Nysska had been exhausted enough that she hadn't really paid attention to the reaction her presence provoked from the rank-and-file human soldiers. Now she did, and discovered something that unsettled her. Almost every soldier they passed—young, old, male, female—watched her carefully.

Yet she registered no fear in any of them.

None of them recoiled from her violet skin, her yellow eyes, her jet-black horns.

None of them recoiled at all, in fact.

It was more as if they had silently begun to *study* her.

She let that percolate.

The young man in attendance at the food tent was not a soldier at all, but a civilian, a thoroughly ordinary-looking human with brown skin and dark brown eyes and dark brown curly hair, but it seemed that the soldiers' aplomb had rubbed off on him. His face stayed expressionless as he handed Cam and Nysska heavy sandwiches and metal cups filled with not-quite-boiling coffee. The only thing he said was, "Please bring those cups back when you're done."

"I want to bounce an idea off you as we go," Nysska mumbled to Cam around a bite. "Let's walk slowly."

As they made their way through the town, dodging the crews of efficient soldiers tearing down and rebuilding the fire damage, Cam said, "What's on your mind?"

"I was thinking about how you knew where to kick that sneaky piece of shit who came out of the secret door at the inn. How you looked *through* his skin and muscles, and saw his damaged knee."

Cam chewed and swallowed, and followed it with a sip of coffee before answering. "Yeah. We talked about that already, didn't we? Same as how I knew General Cullen was rune-free."

Nysska nodded. "We did, yes. And I know trying to read the crime site here is pointless, because of the blood rune dust scattered all over the place."

"Also true, yeah. I can still feel it. Trying to use Ruby Tears in Summergray is a dead end."

Nysska smiled as she chewed and swallowed another bite. "Have I ever told you how charming it is that you named your talent?"

Cam shot her a sidelong glance. "Are you making fun of me?"

"What? No! No, I'm completely serious."

"Well, thanks, I guess, but it wasn't my idea. The talents are varied enough from Sensor to Sensor that it just sort of became a thing we do." She chewed and downed another bite. "But what's that got to do with your idea?"

"Well, your use of the runes has different levels. Yes? But the level of power it took to see through flesh—or stone—that's not as high as when you use Ruby Tears, is it?"

"Well...no..."

They arrived at the burnt-out foundation housing the cellar. Nysska could smell the decaying bodies with painful clarity. Cam said, "Oh! You want me to look through the burned bodies' flesh and see if I can spot anything that could tell us how they were killed."

"Exactly."

Cam finished her sandwich, frowning, and licked her fingers. Took a long sip of coffee. "Yeah, I can try that. I was serious about letting my food settle first, though."

"You can try what?" Raoul asked from a couple of meters behind them, which caused both women to jump.

Nysska said, "Where's your father?" at the same time that Cam asked, "How did it go with the General?"

Raoul was still in uniform. Nysska couldn't tell if he'd slept, but as she watched, his face creased into a fascinating study in cautious bafflement. "It went...*really well.* I swear, I'd think he was still a skinshifter *impersonating* my dad, but it's him. No doubt. I recognize his scars. That's my father, but..." He massaged the back of his neck. "I don't know. He's different. *Really* different."

Nysska imagined that if Percy were there, he might say something like, *Not crawling up your ass all the time, huh?* Instead, she said, "Has something happened to make him behave this way? Some incident?"

Raoul shrugged elaborately. "Maybe? I mean...I just...I don't know." He shook his head, and pointed at the burnt-out inn. "What were you going to try? Something about the bodies?"

Nysska cleared her throat, about to launch into an explanation, but Cam beat her to it. "I'm going to look inside the bodies. Not read the site, just...see what's in there."

Raoul's eyebrows rose. "What, looking for—what, exactly?"

"Don't know," Cam said. "That's the point, I guess? See if it turns up anything new?"

Nysska said, "We're hoping she'll know it when she sees it."

Raoul made a sound like *pffff* with his lips. "Shit. It's better than any idea I've had. Let's go for it." He led the way past a couple of soldiers with cloths tied over their mouths and noses, down into the cellar, and Nysska and Cam followed after him.

The bodies hadn't been moved since the Ninth Crucible had last been there, and they didn't look any different, but they smelled a good bit worse. Instead of wafting throughout the town, as their stench had when they were still in the barn, now something about the cellar seemed to have contained the odor and concentrated it. The ham sandwich rolling in her stomach, Nysska said, "Do you need us to put them up on the table again?"

Cam waved a hand in front of her face and spoke through a grimace. "No. They're fine where they are. Besides, I'm afraid if we touched one it might rupture." She made a familiar gesture, and Nysska and Raoul dropped back, giving her room to work.

Cam took a deep breath, and Nysska saw the silver radiance grow brighter, glimmering around her face—but it stopped just short of the blue-white flames that meant she was reading a site. Or attempting to.

Cam walked slowly forward, and the tilt of her head and orientation of her eyes cast a faint, moonlight glow on the first body, shining on its head and torso. The glow flickered and moved as she examined it, all the way down to its feet.

"Anything?" Nysska called out.

Cam shook her head. "Let me try another one."

Body after body Cam stared at, stared *through*. One after another, until she had peered into the deepest marrows of every one of them. Her eyes dimmed back down as she turned and approached Nysska and Raoul. "I'm sorry. I really am. There's just *nothing*. I found a few old breaks that had healed, but other than that…they're just corpses. No knife points. No blade marks we missed before. Just…nothing."

Nysska said, "Maybe we could discuss that up in the fresh air?" to which Cam and Raoul hastily agreed.

Back on the street, in a cool, dry breeze that tasted sweeter to Nysska than any wine, Raoul seemed to be voicing his thoughts to no one in particular. "So we've got thirty-two sethyds, otherwise healthy as far as we know, who either gathered in a barn and died of unexplained causes, or died of unexplained causes and were then carried to the barn." He frowned. "Nysska—sethyds don't catch human diseases, correct?"

"None that I know of, no."

"All right—could it be poison, then? Are there any poisons that work on sethyds?"

Nysska's eyes narrowed in thought. "There are, yes, but poisoning in my homeland was vanishingly rare. If one sethyd wants to hurt another— in a way that can't be settled legally—we usually do it with bladed weapons. And once Patrinomonto was rendered uninhabitable…since coming here, I haven't heard of any poisonings at all." A thought had been bouncing around in Nysska's forebrain for several moments, spurred by Raoul's questions. "Cam, you couldn't *see* anything out of the ordinary with the bodies."

Cam gave her a quizzical look. "We established that, yeah?"

Nysska said, "What if we tried another Sense?"

11

In mid-morning of the following day, as Nysska sat in an uncomfortable camp chair outside her tent eating another ham sandwich, a distant baying made her pause in mid-chew. She stood and peered off into the distance. "I think they're here."

Cam grunted assent from inside, slipped on her boots, and stepped out just as a big, barrel-chested, brindle-coated dog with very floppy ears tore around the corner at the far end of the aisle and came charging straight at Nysska.

She shoved the remainder of her sandwich into Cam's hands and knelt and opened her arms wide, and the dog threw itself into them. Nysska let its momentum carry her over onto her back.

Percy had stepped out of his own tent, as well, and he and Cam stood there wide-eyed as Nysska laughed wildly and rolled on the ground, letting the big dog lick every bit of her face.

"Did you miss me?" Nysska asked between laughs. "Did you miss me? I missed you! Yes I did! Yes I did!" She scratched the dog all over its head and played with its jowls and thumped its ribs as if it were a ripe melon, and the dog ate up every bit of it.

"Um. Nysska?" Cam ventured. "Who or what is this thing?"

Nysska shot her a reproachful look from her prone position. "What do you mean, 'what is this thing?' I know you love dogs! Perhaps not as much as I do—my sweet girl, you're just the most lovable hound in the world, yes you are!"

A small crowd of soldiers had gathered, gaping at the spectacle. Nysska didn't care that they were watching, but she did finally make a small concession to dignity and sat up. The dog licked her face one more time and then curled up in her lap like an animal a third its size, gazing up at Nysska with the kind of unqualified devotion only dogs can muster.

Nysska noticed Flax and Jax, peering out from inside Percy's tent, their silver eyes as wide as Cam's. She got to her feet, gently depositing the dog on the ground, and said, "Do you still follow orders, girl? Sit. Sit!" The dog obediently sat, tail thumping the earth and a prodigious tongue lolling out the side of its mouth.

Percy had wandered over—leaving the blood lynxes where they were, still staring skeptically—and to him and Cam together, Nysska said, "This is Greta. I worked with her in the Forty-Seventh Crucible."

"Her name isn't Greta anymore," a thin, hesitant voice called out. "It's Rosie now."

Nysska looked up and saw Raoul escorting a small, thin, pale-skinned girl with straight, mousey hair and weak eyes that weren't quite interesting or memorable enough to be considered brown. More like beige.

Slim argonium runes inlaid along either side of her over-large nose gave off a flash or two in the morning sunlight. Dressed in standard Thaumetallicon-issue bronze-inlaid leather armor, she looked not so much like a Crucible member as a child playing an ambitious sort of dress-up. The hint of a smile tried but failed to curve her lips when she met Nysska's eyes.

As soon as they came within easy conversational range, Raoul said, "Members of the Ninth Crucible, allow me to introduce Sensor Morrin James of the Thirty-Fourth. Sensor James, this is Sensor Camble Delakroy, Keeper Percy Bitters..." He had spotted the blood lynxes, and pointed them out. "...and his tracking animals, Flax and Jax. You already know Enforcer Nysska Stonegate."

As Raoul spoke, Morrin seemed to grow smaller and smaller. She lifted one hand in a tiny, faltering wave and said, "*Hello*," barely loud enough to hear.

"You get more than a wave." Nysska swept Morrin completely up off the ground in a hug and spun her in a circle. Rosie the dog, formerly Greta, barked once and panted. A happy sound.

When Nysska set Morrin back down, the tiny woman had gone red in the face and uttered a desperate, embarrassed sort of giggle. Nysska said, "It is so good to see you! And so good to see you kept Gr—Rosie with you! How have you been?"

Eyes darting from one member of the Ninth to another, Morrin murmured, "I've been all right..."

Nysska turned to Raoul. "We don't have to get started right this instant, do we? Could I catch up with my former teammate for a few minutes?"

Raoul seemed awfully amused by Nysska's display and Morrin's petrified reaction, but he kept his tone professional. "That should be fine, yes, but we need to get this resolved as soon as possible. If it can *be* resolved. Orders from the Emperor, remember?"

Nysska gave him a grateful smile, and asked Morrin, "Are you hungry? Can we offer you a sandwich? Some coffee?"

Appearing dazed, Morrin said, "Sure...that would be fine..."

Nysska put her hand on Morrin's arm and steered her toward the food tent. Over her shoulder, she said, "Cam, would you join us?"

Cam looked as if she couldn't decide what to think of the last several minutes, but she said, "Of course," and fell in beside Morrin.

Nysska heard Percy mutter, "Girl talk?" to Raoul, and heard Raoul's armor shift in what was most likely a shrug.

Morrin stopped in her tracks. "What about Rosie?"

Nysska looked around, and saw that Flax and Jax had emerged from Percy's tent and approached the dog. The big scent hound sat, docile, panting, as the cats—each of which was about two-thirds the dog's size—circled her, sniffing. The blood lynxes traded a long, silent, silver-eyed glance, after which Jax walked up and rubbed his face all over Rosie's ear and muzzle. Flax immediately did the same on the dog's other side, prompting another single bark, and then all three of them bounded away down the aisle of tents and out into the meadow.

Morrin looked stunned. "They're not going to kill her, are they?"

Nysska laughed. "No, no. I think your dog just made the best friends she'll ever have. Outside you, of course."

Morrin followed Nysska and Cam toward the food tent, casting regular glances back at the meadow where the two cats and the dog chased each other through the tall grass.

Twenty minutes later, the three women sat under a tree at the edge of the village, sipping mugs of coffee. Nysska touched Morrin's hand. "How have things been in the Thirty-Fourth? Better than the Forty-Seventh?"

Morrin's eyes glimmered. "I can't—there are no words, Nysska—you wouldn't *believe* me if I told you how much better." She covered Nysska's hand with her own. "Was that you? I know you had a lot of influence with Governor Anwar...before..."

Nysska finished the sentence silently. *Before he was killed and re-animated with blood runes, and I had to lop his head off.*

She nodded. "That was my condition for joining the Ninth. Getting you and the dog out of there. Away from Brux."

Morrin shuddered at her former Commander's name. "Dragon shred the skin from that man's bones." To Cam, Morrin said, "Did Nysska ever tell you about Brux?"

Cam favored Nysska with a thoughtful expression. "Can't say she ever did."

"He's not worth talking about," Nysska said, but Morrin kept on.

"He beat me. He...violated me."

Cam's mouth dropped open. "Your *Commander*? Your *Crucible* Commander. Holy *shit.*"

Morrin dropped her eyes to her lap. "I should have let you kill him, Nysska."

Nysska made a low, rumbling sound in her chest. "Yes, well. Men like Brux Haller are non-viable. Sooner or later he will encounter someone with no fear of him and no constraints, and then the world will see the last of him." In what she hoped was a brighter tone, she said, "But enough about Brux. What did your new Commander say when the message arrived for you?"

Morrin let out a long exhale. "She didn't know *what* to say, I don't think. The rider showed up with the scroll, and four Cathedral soldiers with him, along with a brand-new Sensor, straight from the Imperial College in Waring. Next thing I know, I'm ordered to some place I've never heard of called Summergray."

Nysska said, "Well, boiling everything down, we need to ask you a question. And you should know, nothing you say goes anywhere beyond the three of us. All right?"

Morrin had grown slightly paler as Nysska spoke. "What question?" she whispered.

Cam asked it. "Have you spent any time using your runes for anything other than reading crime sites?"

Morrin's light brown eyes widened. "You know we're not supposed to! *You know* that, Ms. Delakroy, you're just as much a Sensor as I am!"

Cam let a friendly, disarming smile warm her face. "For Dragon's sake, girl, call me Cam, all right? And yes, I know. The Empire owns us. They have entrusted us with a precious gift, and we are to use it exactly, and *only*, as instructed." She leaned closer. "But *you* know Sensors experiment sometimes." Her words took on an even more conspiratorial timbre. "I figured out how to see *through* things."

Morrin gasped. "See...see through *what?*"

Cam described how she'd picked out the assassin's weakness and exploited it. "I'm talking about using the runes, not for reading crime sites, and not for just ordinary sight or smell, but something in-between."

Morrin crunched up her face. "Well...I've always been afraid to, though. And, and even if I could, the scent runes aren't the same as sight runes. I can't *smell* through walls or anything."

Quietly, Nysska said, "But have you ever used them to scent something ordinary humans couldn't?"

Morrin shook her head. "That's not procedure! That's why we have the tracking animals—once I give them the scent, *they* can move faster than any human, *they* go and run down the target. Not me."

In her best placating tone, Nysska said, "I know it's not procedure. But we're dealing with a situation that isn't covered in any kind of training. And the reason I asked that you be brought here is that you might be able to help us." She leaned close enough for her right horn to graze Morrin's forehead. "You might be able to help the *Empire*."

Morrin swallowed hard. "How?"

All four members of the Ninth Crucible—along with Flax, Jax, and Rosie —accompanied Morrin to the cellar. There they found General Boris Cullen waiting on them, flanked by five of the most intimidating Cathedral soldiers Nysska had ever seen. The General eyeballed Morrin.

"So this is the Sensor for whom I pulled a great many strings," he said, and Nysska heard Morrin gulp. To the girl's credit, however, she stepped forward and gave the General a passable salute.

"Sensor Morrin James of the Thirty-Fourth Crucible, at your service, sir."

Nysska pulled Raoul aside and dropped her voice. "Is your father all right with this?"

Raoul matched her volume. "You mean with the highly-frowned-upon non-Thaumetallicon way of using runes?" His eyes flicked toward General Cullen. "He is, yes. I broached the subject very *very* carefully, and he didn't seem to have a problem with it." In response to Nysska's raised eyebrow, he said, "I can't figure out what's going on with him. But we'd better take advantage of it while we can."

The set of the General's jaw might have relaxed a tiny bit. "I've not met very many Scent Sensors before. It occurred to me while we awaited your arrival that the smell of this place alone might knock your head from your shoulders."

Morrin faltered. As if speaking to him in a coherent manner for the length of a single sentence had sapped all of her confidence. "Oh, sir, that's n-not a problem. F-f-filtering out strong odors is one of the f-first things we learned at the Imperial College, sir."

As if waiting to make a point, the breeze shifted at that moment, and the smell of burnt, decaying corpses washed over them like a putrid tide. Both blood lynxes hissed, and Rosie moaned mournfully.

"That's a talent I envy," the General said. "Let us do this thing if we're going to do it, because that aroma won't get any better." He pulled a scarf up over his nose and mouth and led the way down through the ruined foundation and into the cellar, where even more lanterns had been gathered.

Morrin's runes lit up. They cast bizarre patterns of light and dark across her face, making her look, for the moment, even less human than Nysska. She turned to Cam, worry evident in her words though her face remained unreadable.

"You're *sure* about this?" Morrin's pecan-shell eyes cut toward General Cullen. "We won't get in trouble? *I* won't?"

Cam put her hands on Morrin's shoulders. "You're still a Sensor. You're still doing work in the Empire's service. It's not as though you're down at the local tavern, winning bets by picking out which man let out which fart."

Morrin giggled, an abrupt, surprised sound, and she immediately covered her mouth with one hand. When she'd recovered her composure she turned to the General again. "Sir, before I try this—I don't want to disappoint you—but you should be made aware, sir, I can't identify anything I've never smelled before."

General Cullen cocked his head slightly to one side, and his eyes narrowed, but Nysska thought it looked more like the expression of someone who's just seen a puppy pull an amusing trick than of someone growing angry or impatient. "I would never have expected anything different, Sensor James."

Percy sidled up to Nysska and spoke softly out the side of his mouth. "Raoul's old man won't throw us in prison for this?"

Nysska dipped her head toward him. "Apparently not."

"So at least one thing's gone right." He watched Morrin move slowly closer to the corpses. "Talk about getting thrown into the deep end of the lake. Especially at her age—I'd've been pissing my pants, stuck in this position."

"These days you save that for when you're drunk, right?"

His eyes flashed at her as he grinned. "Oh, you're funny now? Sethyds got jokes?"

General Cullen turned a genuinely stern glare on them, and they both straightened up and fell silent.

From right behind Nysska, Raoul whispered, "The look he just gave you? *That's* the Boris Cullen I grew up with."

Morrin took several deep breaths. With each breath the runes alongside her nose grew a shade brighter, and when she moved over to the nearest body, they glowed with such radiance that it was hard to make out any of her features at all.

"Sethyds, no doubt," Morrin said to the room at large. "Not that the horns aren't instant giveaways. I learned your scent well during our time in the Forty-Seventh, Nysska. These were definitely your countrymen." Her speech paused every so often as she took in more deep, exploratory breaths. "Equal number of men and women. All full-grown. Were they sent here as couples? Expected to reproduce?"

Nysska grew conscious of several pairs of eyes turning to her. "It's possible," she said evenly.

Raoul took a step closer to Morrin. "I'd like you to concentrate, if you can, on whatever it was that killed them."

Morrin nodded. "I understand, sir. Cam and Nysska said it might have been poison." After another deep breath— "There's something…"

Raoul said, "Yes?"

"I'm…not sure…" Morrin turned to face the group. The effect of the shining runes was unearthly. As if she had become some kind of super-natural messenger, sent by the Great Silver Dragon Himself to move among mortals. "If it really is poison—and I hate to ask this—but it might make it easier if I could get at the contents of their stomachs."

General Cullen didn't hesitate. Breaking out a tone that fit him like a well-worn glove, he barked, "Enforcer Stonegate. Open up one of those bodies."

"Dragon above," Cam breathed, but Nysska met Raoul's eyes, and wordlessly the two of them went to the nearest corpse and hoisted it onto the table. Nysska unsheathed the dagger she wore on her thigh—the same one she'd used to threaten Mayor Penn—and, as efficiently as she could, carved away the charred flesh from its midsection.

Halfway through removing the cooked, leathery muscle, she noticed that Morrin had come to stand on the other side of the table. "You realize, whatever's in here is going to be cooked almost as thoroughly as the outside."

"Sorry," Morrin said meekly.

Finally, Nysska reached the stomach. She made a cross-shaped inci-sion and used the dagger's tip to peel back the organ's walls, exposing a ghastly mush that looked for all the world like wet cornbread. She saw what might have been bits of vegetables and shreds of meat threaded in here and there.

"Dragon help us," Percy muttered. "That is *foul.*"

Morrin didn't get any closer. The runes on either side of her nose shimmering, she simply took a deep breath. Then another—

And sagged, staggering sideways, runes going dark.

Her hands flailed, grasping, and latched onto the end of the table, where she slumped forward over the cadaver's feet and sucked in desperate breaths. "Found your poison," she wheezed.

By then Nysska had dashed around the table and grabbed her, supporting her as everyone else moved in.

"Are you all right?" Nysska asked, as Morrin coughed wetly. "Are you hurt? How can we help?"

Morrin clung to Nysska, but got her legs back after a few more seconds. "I'm fine. I'm fine. I just..." She gestured toward the corpse's opened mid-section. "There's something there. Definitely. Some kind of... it's *got* to be poison. But..." She looked up at the General, the beginnings of tears in her eyes. "It's nothing I've ever encountered before. So I can't tell you exactly what it is. Just that it tried to shut my lungs down. I'm sorry, sir."

General Cullen folded his arms across his chest and exhaled through his nose. "The Empire does have its own poison masters. I'll have my men collect this...*sample*...and see if one of our people can tell us what it might be. Or who concocted it. Or both." He paused. "Were you able to discern anything else?"

Morrin closed her eyes and shook her head, as if resetting her brain in her skull. "Um, first of all, nobody put your face near whatever's in that corpse's stomach. All right, uh...yes. Yes, I think the poison must have been in some kind of...baked goods? I'm thinking? Something like a meat pie."

Percy grumbled something, which Raoul then put into words. "Could you be more specific? Meat pies are pretty common."

Morrin blinked. "Well, the meat is bison."

Cam said, "Seriously?" but then got out of the way as General Cullen moved closer.

"Bison? You're sure?"

Morrin frowned. "Yes, sir. It was bison...corn flower...peas and carrots, no surprise there, I wouldn't think. And the poison, of course." She paused. Her frown deepened.

Nysska said, "Is there something else?"

Morrin hadn't moved from near the foot of the table, where the corpse's charred, booted feet lay. "Maybe. Give me just a moment here— when I was hugging the table, I thought..." She closed her eyes and took another deep breath, and her runes flared again. After a few seconds, she said, "Nysska, would you mind bringing over one of those lanterns?"

Nysska grabbed one hanging from a joist overhead and handed it to Morrin, who set it on the end of the table and put her face right down next to one of the corpse's feet. The dead sethyd had been wearing leather-and-fur boots, just as many of the others had, and Morrin seemed to be sniffing the scorched fur around the boot's cuff. Slowly and carefully, she picked something out of the fur and, straightening, held it right under her nose, runes shining bright silver.

"What is that?" General Cullen all but demanded. "What have you found?"

Morrin turned to face him. "I don't know if it's anything, sir..."

The General said, "Why don't you report what you've found, Sensor James, and allow *me* to decide if it's something or not?"

"Sorry! Sorry, sir. Um. Yes." She held up a thread a few centims long. "This is linen. Nysska, is it common for sethyds to wear linen?"

Nysska didn't have to think about it. "Unheard of. Sethyds favor sturdier clothing, suited for harsher climates."

Morrin absorbed that. "All right. Well, this is linen, and you can't tell from looking at it because of the fire, but when this was part of a larger piece of fabric, it was dyed purple."

General Cullen's jaw clenched so hard Nysska thought his teeth might crack. He turned and stalked away, up and out of the cellar, leaving everyone else standing there staring after him. To Raoul, Nysska said, "Do you know what just happened?"

"At least partly." Raoul started toward the stairs, beckoning the rest of them to follow. "He's taking a minute to put his thoughts together. We'd better be there to hear them when he's done."

Aboveground, they found General Cullen pacing back and forth in the dusty street. In that moment, the General's body language and movements bore an almost comically strong resemblance to his son's.

Raoul approached him. "Sir?"

The General stopped pacing. Turned and faced them, his expression stony. "First. The kind of meat in those poisoned 'baked goods,' as you called them, puts the source firmly in the Flat Rocks Territory. Second. Flat Rocks is even colder than Green Needles. Linen clothing up there is scarce as fish milk. Third. The only people who *would* wear it—dyed purple, to boot—are those who never have to set foot outside a keep if they don't want to."

Percy breathed, "More fucking royals."

General Cullen went on. "Fourth. I've seen exactly one person from Flat Rocks in purple linen." His hand closed around the pommel of his longsword. "And we're about to pay that person a visit."

12

Flames crackled in uneasy parallel with the chatter of cicadas, filling the woods with echoes and writhing shadows. Nysska stood next to Cam, surreptitiously holding her hand in the darkness, with Raoul, Percy, and the blood lynxes rooted to the spot in front of them. Morrin and Rosie hovered off to one side. Morrin had her face averted.

In the center of the clearing, a young man in a cream-colored silk suit with a brilliant purple linen vest stood on a hastily-constructed gallows. The people of the Flat Rocks Territory performed hangings in a way Nysska had never seen. The noose around the man's neck looked familiar enough, but there was no slack in the rope as it rose to a horizontal beam above him. Another rope bound his ankles, and connected to the ankle rope was a carefully measured stack of lead plates. Nysska had heard the Plainish term *Tied top and bottom* before, and knew it meant "doomed," but she'd never seen it in action.

The young man's name was Nikolai Petrovich. Like Sergei Benitoff, he was part of one of the Empire's most favored noble families. That hadn't seemed to matter to his father. Nikolai's head turned, hollow eyes searching through the shadows, until he found Nysska. Firelight glimmered in his irises as his voice rose, trembling and high-pitched but staunch with conviction. "Everything I did, I did for the people of Kainos."

Nikolai Petrovich's father, Leonid, stood on the far side of the gallows, talking quietly with General Cullen. Leonid turned away from the General and, though he didn't look at him, spoke to his son. "Is that to be your final statement?"

Nikolai spat, or tried to. He didn't seem to have much saliva left.

Leonid nodded once to an armored knight on the far side of the gallows. The knight kicked a bracing strut loose, so that the platform on which Nikolai stood swung down and away from him. The lead plates fell, the noose held his head in position, and Nysska heard his neck snap.

Leonid Petrovich swung up into the saddle of the huge, night-black stallion he had ridden to his son's execution and, with a touch of his heels to the great animal's flank, cantered away into the darkness. Two more armored knights cut Nikolai's body down from the gallows, slung it across a spare horse, and followed after Leonid. General Cullen came and rejoined the Ninth Crucible, his face even more gaunt than usual.

Raoul spoke first. "I wasn't...none of us...were expecting this. A Tribunal, for certain, but to do this to his own son..."

General Cullen looked fatigued. It was the first time that Nysska had seen him project anything other than perfect poise. "Baron Petrovich takes his loyalty to the Empire seriously. And his son has been...less than impressive, one could say."

"So he had it coming," Percy offered. "But we've been in the dark since we left Petrovich's keep. What happened back there?" He bent and picked up Jax, who'd been pawing at his leg. "And what did the dead kid have to say, anyhow? Do we know who killed everybody in Summergray now?"

The General let a faintly amused smile curl one side of his mouth. "Nikolai Petrovich admitted to providing the poisoned food, which was apparently presented to the settlers at Summergray as a welcoming gift. The kinds of poisons that affect sethyds seem to be difficult to come by in human lands—for which I am grateful—but Nikolai had access to one of them as a by-product from a mining operation his family owns." Cullen's eyes raked over the group. "To the best of our knowledge, based on what Nikolai had to say under...pressure...the people we're looking for are using one such mine, abandoned for decades, as some kind of base of operations. People who can change their faces, he said. People who go from one identity to another in a matter of seconds." Cullen's gaze shifted out into the darkness, unfocused. "He said he thought they were just disguises. Performers, like the kind you see at a carnival. The boy might have been dim enough to have believed that."

Raoul opened his mouth to speak, but seemed to think better of it, so Nysska moved into the gap. "If we know where the people—the skin-shifters—are, then forgive me, but why are we standing here? Why isn't the Cathedral moving on it? Why not send in the Argonium Infantry and have them tear the place apart?"

General Cullen let out a long breath. "According to Nikolai, the mine is serving two purposes. First, they're setting it up to be able to produce more of that red alloy you lot discovered in Altamar." His gaze flashed toward Morrin. "The same substance that interfered with Imperial College runes in Summergray. We cannot allow that to happen. Second, and perhaps more important, they're storing something there. Not the metal—something fragile. Valuable. I suspect it's some kind of device that makes this alloying possible, some new kind of smelter, perhaps. What-ever it is, it sounds as though it's one of a kind, and if the skinshifters lose it, it deals their cause a major blow. Maybe a fatal one." His lips tightened. "Which is why the Cathedral doesn't want to risk a frontal assault. If the device, or whatever it is, can be moved, and we attack openly, they could make off with it via some hidden escape route. Or destroy it."

Cam had let go of Nysska's hand when the General came over, and now had her arms folded under her breasts. "All right, but, wouldn't that be a good thing, sir? You just said it could cripple them."

Flatly, Raoul said, "The Cathedral wants it, don't they? It's not enough to make sure the skinshifters can't produce any more blood runes. The Cathedral wants to make blood runes for themselves."

General Cullen had his back to the flames, and though Nysska could see a few lines of his face, his eyes remained hidden in deep pools of black. "It would give us a military advantage, yes." General Cullen pulled a scroll from inside his jacket. "From here on out, this mission is to be conducted with the utmost stealth. You are to rendezvous with another team at the location I have marked—" He unfurled the scroll, revealing a Cathedral-standard map of the Flat Rocks Territory. "Here." One gloved finger traced a short distance over the map. "The mine is here. Recon-noiter the site and meet me back at the rendezvous point."

Morrin spoke up, surprising Nysska. "Where are you going to be, sir?"

General Cullen turned to face her. At her feet, Rosie panted and thumped her tail on the ground. "I have to return to Coalgarden. It's going to take every bit of political capital I have to make sure the Ninth Crucible's stealth mission *stays* a stealth mission. And you, Sensor James, are coming with me."

Morrin actually squeaked. "Sorry! Beg your pardon, sir, but—sorry? Uh—what I mean is—why me?"

"Your contribution to this effort has been significant, Sensor James, and it's started me thinking. There are matters I wish to discuss with you."

Raoul had turned back to the group by that point, and General Cullen handed him the map scroll. "Get moving. I've already sent word to the team you'll be working with—you can meet them by tomorrow at sunset if you don't dawdle." Before Raoul could say anything in response, the General reached out and put his hand on Nysska's upper arm. "Enforcer Stonegate—a word?"

Exchanging the briefest of surprised glances with Cam, Nysska allowed herself to be guided away, out of earshot of the rest of the group. Cullen pitched his voice low nevertheless. "You continue to impress, Nysska. May I call you Nysska?"

"Uh...sure?"

"Don't think for a moment that I'm unaware of *your* contributions in all this. Without you, Naveed Olkoff's murder would have gone unsolved, leaving these Dragon-forsaken face-changers free to do who knows what. The Empire might have already fallen by now, if they'd been able to get their animated corpses into enough positions of power. Or simply impersonated Imperial officials themselves. We have a whole new set of security protocols in place now because of you."

Nysska didn't know what to say. "You're too kind, sir."

"Like hell I am. You're also the one who thought of bringing in Morrin James." He stepped slightly closer. "*And* you're the one who saved my son's life at the inn in Painter's Bluff. Yes, I heard about that, no need to look surprised. I think you'll find there isn't much I don't know." He frowned. "Except for what's in that fucking mine. In any case, I wanted to make you aware...you are much appreciated. And I intend to see to it that you are appropriately rewarded."

"I..." Whatever she might have been expecting the General to say to her, this wasn't it. "Thank you, sir."

"You're more than welcome. Now go and join your team. They can't do this without you."

The next eighteen hours passed in a blur for Nysska. She remembered stopping in a well-used campground alongside the narrow forest road on which the General had set them. She vaguely recalled eating, and trying to catch a few minutes of sleep with Cam snuggled up against her, and hearing Percy speaking in hushed tones with Raoul for what seemed like hours on end.

Finally, back on the road and watching Raoul and Percy continue their conversation, she said, "What're you two mumbling about?"

"Wasn't mumbling," Percy shot back. "I've just been trying to figure out whether it's me or the whole world that's gone completely squirrel-fucking insane."

Nysska glanced over at Cam, who gave her a look that said, *It's not a bad question.* Nysska urged her horse up to ride abreast of Percy, with Raoul ahead of them and Cam right behind. She said, "Care to elaborate?"

Percy made a face as if he'd just bitten into something with worms in it. "Remember what we used to point out with, may I say, appropriate regularity—that we're a fucking investigative unit? Not a combat unit? Well, we're sure as *fuck* not any kind of stealthy-abandoned-mine unit. Why is Raoul's dad acting like we are?"

Raoul spoke over his shoulder. "I've been telling him it's because my father trusts us."

Percy made a rude sound with his lips. "Trusts us to go and get killed?"

"No," Cam said from the rear. "Trusts us to keep our Dragon-damned mouths shut."

Percy threw his arms up in an exaggerated gesture. The blood lynxes, following along in the grass beside the road, both flinched and looked around for a threat, so Percy called out to them. "You're fine, nothing's wrong, we're good." He turned to Nysska. "Plenty *is* wrong, and we're *not* good. I'm looking at it every which way I know how, and not a damn bit of this makes any sense."

Percy's frustration seemed to have galvanized Nysska's thoughts, bringing her back into focus. "Cam's right. We need to think in larger terms. Biggest picture possible. The skinshifters sent someone to poison the sethyds in Summergray. Nivenston and Painter's Bluff have been feuding over the land there forever, but they've never resorted to anything like *this*. Not mass murder. The skinshifters must have known the massacre would lead to both sides accusing each other, and eventually to an all-out war between the two towns."

"Which could have escalated," Raoul said, morose. "If word of it got outside that valley."

"Exactly." Nysska mimed a fire raging out of control with her hands. "Both towns call in all their favors. All the treaties they've signed for the last two or three centuries. All the alliances they've made. What starts out as two towns squabbling over a patch of fertile land escalates into a Territory-wide conflict. Before you know it, the Empire's expending a lot of time and resources trying to quash it."

Cam said, "Which would leave it vulnerable to an outside attack."

"Or an inside one," Raoul added. "Since we know the skinshifters like to infiltrate shit. Get the Cathedral busy putting down a budding civil war, security measures get lax, all of a sudden half the noble families are either re-animated blood rune corpses or skinshifters in disguise."

"Fine," Percy grumbled. "I suppose that all makes a little sense." He spat off to one side. "So it's just *me* going squirrel-fuck crazy."

"It still leaves one glaring question, though," Nysska said. "At least, it's glaring in my mind. *Why* would Emperor Valco have approved the sethyd settlement in the first place? Why *there*, of all possible locations? The Empire has more unoccupied space than it knows what to do with. Why put an already divisive populace in such a politically treacherous place? What does he have to gain by it?"

Cam quietly said, "Unless he wants the Empire destabilized."

Those words disappeared into the wind, vanishing without the tiniest trace, and the Ninth Crucible rode on wordlessly.

The sun had dipped below the horizon when they reached the rendezvous point General Cullen had indicated on the map scroll. Once it had been a windmill, but the wide, proud blades had long since broken or rotted away along with most of the roof, leaving the skeleton of a pyramidal structure atop what might have passed for a small, boxy house. The mill sat at the peak of a gentle rise, and though tall grass surrounded it, the trees had yet to encroach, making it an unmistakable landmark in the middle of a wide clearing.

"Well this is in the middle of fucking nowhere," Percy said as they approached. "How close is the nearest town?"

Raoul looked at the map. "Place called Dugglass...about five kliks to the southeast."

"And what's between Dugglass and here?"

"Trees."

"Four horses at the mill," Cam said, eyes shining as she peered ahead of them. "You think General Cullen assigned another Crucible?"

Nysska pursed her lips for a second. "Don't see what the purpose would be. As Percy has amply stated, Crucibles aren't really suited for reconnaissance."

"No point in speculating," Raoul said. "Let's just go see who they are."

The Ninth Crucible dismounted outside the defunct mill, and Raoul led the way inside. It was still more than light enough to see clearly without the aid of lanterns or torches, and when he saw the compact man lounging against a broken table, he muttered, "Oh, Dragon fuck me in the eye."

Roald Sykes stood up straight, which put the top of his head at Raoul's collarbone. Nysska thought the cocky smile on Sykes's face must have been stolen from some much, much larger human. She noticed his normal Thaumetallicon-issue armor had been replaced with soft, all-black leather, and that he'd swapped out all his shiny knives for matte black duplicates. "We get to work with the demon-fuckers again?" Sykes said, eyes glittering. "How grand."

Beyond Sykes stood two men and a woman, all of them in unmarked, coal-black leather armor. They came forward, faces neutral, and as Nysska watched them move she decided they should be treated with utmost caution.

"I'm Gower," the taller of the men said. Pointing to the other man: "This is Lasko. And she's Boggs."

Raoul quickly introduced the members of the Ninth Crucible. Sykes stayed to one side, not quite openly sneering.

As soon as Raoul had finished, a soft sound of realization escaped Cam. "I knew I recognized that armor," she said. "You're Argonium Infantry! You've just turned your uniforms black!"

By way of response, Gower, Lasko, and Boggs stared at her. Silent. Motionless. Sykes said, "They're Infantry. I'm just on loan."

Gower and Lasko looked remarkably alike. Their skin tone wasn't the same—Lasko was every bit as dark brown as Cam, while Gower had lighter skin that appeared to be covered completely in freckles—but they both had smooth-shaven heads, square jaws, and...Nysska realized what the real similarity was. They both had the same look in their eyes. A look that went beyond confidence into something more like a foregone conclusion.

Boggs had short, curly brown hair, slightly lighter skin than Lasko, and might have been classically beautiful if she weren't missing her left nostril. Judging by the faint scar that began between her eyes and ended on one side of her upper lip, her nose had been diminished by the very tip of a swiftly-swung blade. Nysska imagined Boggs jerking backward, avoiding almost all of a stroke meant to split her skull in half, leaving her with a merely inconvenient hole in her face. From her bearing and inter-action with everyone else in the mill, Boggs had either forgotten the nostril was gone, or gave not one oily eel shit about its absence.

Percy made noises of protest. "Since when does the Infantry have a stealth unit? I thought you were supposed to be all shock and awe—roll in and fucking flatten whatever's in your way."

Gower said, "I imagine there is a great deal you don't know about us."

Percy huffed and went quiet.

Boggs addressed Raoul. "General Cullen gave you a map scroll, yes?" She pulled out an identical one and unrolled it on the table. Tapping a spot on it due north of the windmill, she said, "The abandoned mine is here. Gower?"

Gower had folded his arms across his chest, and spoke in a way that left no question as to whether or not he expected to be obeyed. "On approach will be me, Lasko, Boggs, Sykes, Cullen, and Stonegate. Delakroy and Bitters, you are to stay here and make sure nothing happens to our horses. Cullen and Stonegate, you'll leave your armor here. We have some non-reflective clothing you can change into."

Percy said, "Why the fuck do we have to stay behind? This is recon-naissance, right?" He pointed to Flax and Jax, both of whom were lying on the mill's dirt floor just inside the doorway. "They're seraphic—we can send them in to look around and *nobody's* going to spot them." He gestured to Cam. "And she's a Sight Sensor! Talk about gathering some fucking intelligence!"

Gower didn't move so much as a millim when he spoke. "Number one, we're not about to trust a Cathedral mission to a couple of cats, seraphic or not. They don't speak Plainish, they're out." Percy tried to object, but Gower talked over him. "Number two, correct me if I'm wrong, Sensor Delakroy, but your eyes glow in the dark, do they not?"

"I don't have to use the runes," Cam said, a bit defensively. "I was blind my whole life before I got them."

Gower's left eyebrow raised just a hair. "I'm sure that's true, but it would be difficult to *sneak up* on a place with glowing eyes. And if you're not using them—no offense—what would be the point of you going?"

Cam's mouth tightened. She said nothing.

Gower nodded once and pointed to a duffel leaning against a wall. "Stonegate, Cullen, your gear's in there. Get changed. We're leaving now."

13

I t didn't take the six of them long to cover the ground between the
mill and the abandoned mine. They didn't dare use any light
sources, and since only the first moon had risen, Nysska found
herself picking her way through the dark woods at a slower pace than she
would have liked. Raoul followed right behind her, acknowledging that
her night vision was a good bit better than his. None of the other four
seemed to have any trouble finding their way through the underbrush
and low-hanging branches. It made Nysska wonder how.

They reached the edge of a broad, shallow canyon just as the second
moon glided up over the horizon, bathing the landscape in its soft, blue-
white shine. The mine—as much as they could see of it—was built on the
far side of the canyon's floor, digging into the wall and, Nysska assumed,
down into the rock and earth below. There was no yawning, cave-like
opening. Instead a two-story wooden structure with corroded bronze
tracks leading out of it had been built over the entrance, broken-down
mining carts piled in a heap nearby.

Gower beckoned them back, away from the canyon's edge and out of
line of sight of anyone who might be in or around the mine. Silently, he
handed Nysska a round, flat piece of white quartz a couple of centims
across, with a thin bronze hoop affixed to one edge. She watched as Lasko
gave one to Sykes, and Boggs passed another to Raoul. Quietly, locking

eyes with Nysska, Gower said, "Put the loop around your ear, so that the stone lies flush against your skull."

Nysska eyed the stone critically. "Why? What is it?"

"We don't have time for questions." He took it out of her hand and, before she could object, set the stone in place so that it rested just behind her ear.

The stone's surface was warm. Almost uncomfortably so.

Gower stepped back. His mouth never moved, but a deep, buzzing voice filled Nysska's head. "Can you understand me?"

She came very close to yelping, and snatched the stone off of her ear. "What the *fuck* was that?" She looked over and saw that, while Raoul hadn't taken his stone off, he did look as if he'd just been kicked by a medium-sized mule.

Sykes had either used one of the stones in the past, or was more in command of himself than she'd given him credit for.

Gower gestured for Nysska to put the stone back on. She did, albeit reluctantly, and when it rested against her skull, Gower's bizarrely altered voice came to her once more. "This is an offshoot of our touch runes. Lasko and Boggs and I can communicate with each other, but it's one-way with you and Sykes and Cullen. Don't try to talk back, it won't work—but that's fine, since all you three need to do is listen, and do what we fucking tell you."

Raoul, Sykes, and Nysska all glanced at each other. Sykes seemed to be enjoying Nysska's discomfort to a degree that made her want to smash his face in.

Gower said, "We're traveling in pairs. Stonegate and me, Lasko and Sykes, Boggs and Cullen. Stay low, move quiet, and don't do anything till we say. I didn't see any obvious guards around the mine's exterior, which makes sense if the place is supposed to be abandoned, but I'd bet my left ass cheek there'll be some resistance once we get inside."

Raoul scowled. "What are you talking about, once we get inside? The General's orders were to reconnoiter. He specifically did not want us to engage."

Gower spoke normally as well. "We're not going to engage, Commander. We're going to infiltrate, get a good look at whatever's inside there, and exfiltrate before anyone even knows we're there. Or would you rather go back to your father and report that there is indeed an abandoned mine where everyone already knew there was? Exactly how useful do you think that information would be?"

Raoul kept scowling, but didn't answer.

Gower's stone-carried voice—*stone-voice*, Nysska thought, *I like that*—reappeared in her head. "There looked to be plenty of cover. We'll make our way to the canyon floor and approach from three different directions. Everyone ready? Let's go."

Nysska had grown truly accustomed to her Thaumetallicon armor. She felt naked in the soft black leather tunic and trousers the Infantrymen had given her, but couldn't deny that it allowed for quiet movement. She let Gower set the pace, and followed him to a narrow trail that zig-zagged down the cliff face behind a covering of thorn bushes.

A thorn pierced the skin on the back of her hand, and she caught Gower watching her, as if waiting to see whether or not she would hiss in pain or make some other kind of exclamation. Nysska clenched her fist and kept her lips sealed.

By the time they had reached the canyon floor, she had completely lost track of the other two pairs, but every so often Gower paused as if listening to an unheard voice. Moving carefully, he led her to the deep shadow behind a boulder, then across a ten-meter gap to a discarded mining cart.

"Hold up here," the stone-voice rasped into her skull. "We're waiting for the others to get close enough."

She wanted to ask, *Close enough for what?* but didn't think it was worth it to draw Gower's ire. At least not yet.

The stone-voice came again. "We've got two sentries." He inclined his head, and she followed his line of sight to a rickety-looking balcony that divided the top and bottom floors of the wooden entrance building. When a cloud skidded away from the second moon, she saw one man at each end of the balcony, crossbows in their arms.

"Almost there," the stone-voice said. "We're going to cross to that stand of brush, then come in from the side, underneath their position."

Nysska nodded acknowledgement—and froze. Staring.

A third man had joined the first two on the balcony, and she thought she'd caught a familiar glow...*yes. There.* Nysska grabbed Gower's shoulder, and when he snapped his head around to glare at her, she did her best to make him understand with hand signals.

Too little, it turned out, and too late.

The rune-enhanced eyes of the third man on the balcony flared a blazing silver, shining like stars, and when those unflinching eyes turned and fixed on their position, Nysska growled, *"They've got a Sight Sensor! He can see us! He can see all of us!"*

The Sight Sensor on the balcony let out a short, sharp cry as one of Sykes's knives thunked into his left eye socket, but by then it was too late. All hell broke loose inside the mine.

From somewhere within, a great bloody bell began clanging. The sentries rolled tripods to the edge of the balcony topped by lanterns mounted in front of huge, round, concave mirrors. The lanterns flared, and broad beams of light swept across the front of the mine—more and more appearing as additional lantern-lights arrived at the balcony's edge —and feet pounded on wood as at least three dozen men poured out of the entrance.

"Fire at will!" a voice cried from the balcony, and both arrows and crossbow bolts whistled through the air and smashed into the ground on all sides of their woefully inadequate mining cart. One arrow grazed the heel of Nysska's boot, and she pulled her legs in tighter beneath herself.

Beside her, Gower looked intensely aggravated, but not shaken. Nysska saw silver light gleaming through the seams in his armor as the argonium runes under his skin powered up, and he said, "Fine. They can all eat Dragon shit and die."

Abruptly Gower wasn't next to her anymore.

In the following heartbeat she heard a horrible cracking impact.

Men began screaming.

Nysska risked a look over the pile of rocks, and in the instant before an arrow glanced off her unbroken horn and made her duck down again, she saw three black shapes weaving in and out among the archers and crossbowmen. Flickering like unholy specters, movements punctuated by the whispering of matte-black blades and hot sprays of bright blood and scream after scream after scream.

"Fuck every bit of this," Nysska muttered and, rolling away from her cover, sprinted to another of the trashed mining carts littering the area. She wrenched one of its walls away, held it in front of her like a shield, and charged into the melee.

By the time she reached the wooden decking that served as a low porch for the building's ground floor, the arrows and bolts had stopped flying, but the screams and impacts kept increasing in both frequency and volume. Nysska set the mine cart wall down and drew her longsword.

She knew she'd seen three dozen or better men emerge from the building, but half that many must have retreated, because Gower, Lasko, and Boggs were taking on three opponents each in front of the heavy wooden double doors of the main entrance. Another ten men lay dead or maimed on the ground around them.

Nysska had seen the Argonium Infantry in action twice before. Once when a company of them had put down a Tarnished One—a crazed, chaotic man who'd killed a runebearer, torn out their runes, and implanted them under his own skin, granting him near-godlike strength at the cost of his sanity. Then the second time when the nobleman Sergei Benitoff had an Infantryman on his payroll—a brute named Darlo— whom Nysska had been forced to kill in unarmed combat.

Gower and Lasko and Boggs appeared to be Argonium Infantrymen of a different stripe. They had the strength and speed that Touch Runes granted, but she recognized long-time, dedicated practitioners of combat arts when she saw them. Not a one of them had been touched by arrows or blades at all. She watched as their own swords and knives swatted aside incoming blades as easily as knocking down cobwebs. One man fell, Gower's swordpoint in his throat, and another toppled less than a second later as Boggs sank a dagger into his temple up to the hilt before jerking it back out in a geyser of blood and gray matter. *Thud...thud...thud...*the men dropped, nerveless, boneless.

Sykes and Raoul emerged from the shadows and joined Nysska as what could only have been called a bloodbath continued. Raoul said, "Did I see that right? These assholes had a Sight Sensor working for them?"

Sykes grew even more smug. "Not anymore, they don't."

"Yes, yes, nice throw," Nysska said. "But I don't know what this mission is now."

Raoul grimaced. "Sure you do. The Cathedral wants this mystery prize —this secret new smelter, or whatever it is. So the Three Headsmen up there are going to go in and take it, no matter what."

Gower crossed the deck to them, shaking blood off his sword. "Come on. We've got no choice now, so move your asses."

Nysska and Raoul exchanged uncertain glances, but when Sykes bulled past them and followed after the Infantrymen, Nysska said, "It's either this or abandon the mission."

Raoul's face soured further. He and Nysska watched as Gower and Boggs kicked the heavy, locked main entrance doors into kindling. One lucky random cut had sliced through the lower part of Boggs's trouser leg, and though it hadn't touched any flesh, the leather now flapped open and exposed the long, gleaming silver runes flashing underneath her skin.

Immediately inside the building were what appeared to be a mess hall, a small barracks lined with dusty, rotting bunk beds, and an office, all lined up on the left. On the right, a broad hall with corroded tracks in the floor led to a huge, dark opening—the mine entrance proper.

Six men sprang out at them from the mess hall, swords raised and shrieks on their lips, but they might as well have been tiny children wielding sticks. Nysska began to think of the three stealth-unit Infantrymen less as people and more like some irresistible force of nature. Something absolute and inarguable, like bolts of ebon lightning, that reached out and killed with the most graceful of touches.

No wonder the Empire has such a stranglehold on its citizens, she thought, watching as the Infantry dropped body after body to the dirty wooden planks.

As the last two of the six fell, another ten men fanned out from the barracks with cocked crossbows, and Nysska found herself wishing for the wall of the half-rotted mining cart back. This wasn't like the wild volleys that had gone spraying into the night outside—this was like fish in a barrel. A killing floor.

Except two of the crossbowmen fell before they could pull their triggers, both with black knives hilt-deep in their eyes, and in that split-second of realization—the kind of hesitation that both granted and destroyed life—Gower grabbed up a long table and threw it straight into the crowd, his runes blazing so bright Nysska thought they might burn through the stitching of his armor.

The table smashed into the eight men left, knocking them flat, but the Infantrymen had already leapt before they hit the ground. A few crossbows twanged as bolts thudded harmlessly into walls and ceilings. Gower and Lasko's swords flashed, as did Boggs's knives.

In seconds, the only sound was the gurgling breath of the last dying man, and that noise soon faded—

To reveal something else. Nysska walked past the carnage and used the tip of her sword to push open the door of the small office, exposing one last man frantically trying to open a metal strongbox. He shot a terrified glance at her, and his hands started shaking in an even more pronounced way, but he kept at it. The box had three locks. Two keys stuck out of the top two, and the man was trying so hard to open the third lock that Nysska thought he might start crying. "Pretty sure this is something worth seeing," she called over her shoulder, and the three Infantrymen came into the office, followed by Sykes and Raoul. All six of them stood there, watching the panic-stricken man with varying degrees of curiosity as he kept desperately trying to work the last lock.

The man didn't look like much. Average human appearance, well-fed, somewhere between twenty and thirty years old, dressed in clothes just a shade nicer than one would expect from a farmer. Or a miner. The only thing that stuck out to Nysska was a conspicuous ring on the middle finger of his left hand, made of bronze but with a large, gaudy red stone set in it.

The man groaned in pained frustration. Tears had started from his eyes, as Nysska had anticipated, and he blinked furiously as he tried once more to fit a key into the third lock, dropped it, grabbed it back up as it bounced at his feet, and dropped it again.

Nysska stepped forward and covered the key with her booted foot.

The man sagged. He sank to the floor, sitting with his back to the strong box, and covered his face with his hands. Gower said, "What's your name, brother?"

The man didn't look up. "K-K-Kress. It's Kress."

Nysska bent and picked up the key. Kress didn't try to stop her. Gower moved closer to him and asked, "What're you trying to do there, Kress?"

He sobbed once, but clamped down on his tears. "It's, it's, it's imp-important."

Gower crouched, putting his head on a level with Kress's. "The contents of this strong box. Is this the thing you were all guarding?" He softened his tone a degree or two. "Were you going to offer it to us in exchange for your life?"

Kress dropped his hands and stared at Gower, his eyes wild. "Yes! Yes! Take it, it's yours, just don't kill me!"

Gower stood and offered Kress his hand, and after a few seconds' hesitation, Kress took it and let Gower pull him to his feet. Gower said, "Go stand by the door and don't move. Boggs, Lasko, make sure he doesn't go anywhere."

"Thank you, thank you," Kress said, over and over, wiping tears and snot away with his shirt sleeve. Perfectly cooperative, he stood between Boggs and Lasko and clasped his hands silently.

Gower turned to Nysska and held out his hand. "If I may have that key, Enforcer?"

Nysska traded a glance with Raoul. "Something's not right," she said quietly. "The box might be trapped."

Gower reached out and took the key from her hand. "If you're uncomfortable, you can go wait outside." When she didn't respond, he fitted the key into the third lock, turned it until it produced a loud, clear click, and swung the strong box's door open. Nysska took a step backward, tensing, but nothing happened.

Inside the strong box, resting on a plain gray piece of cloth, was a round red stone a little smaller than a grapefruit. Gower looked from the stone to Kress and back. "This is it? This is what your employers care about so much?" He unsheathed a dagger and tapped the stone with its hilt. When it simply sat there, inert, he put the dagger away, reached in, and picked it up.

A knot had formed in the pit of Nysska's stomach. She said, "Gower, I don't think you should touch that—"

Gower turned to her, his lips thinned into an unattractive smile. "What? This? This stone that I'm holding?"

"We don't know what it is. Or what it does. Or why it's here."

Raoul watched the stone with tight eyes. "She's right. We should secure this location and get somebody from an Imperial College to come and figure out why that thing's so valuable."

"I can show you," Kress said, and lunged forward.

He did not move fast enough to prevent Lasko's sword from plunging through his back and into his heart—but he *did* move fast enough to fling out one hand.

Nysska's brain made a flashing, horrible connection.

The touch of the Commander's ring Raoul wore activated the Summoning Stone on the hilt of his longsword. Just as the touch of Mayor Penn's ring had activated the Conversation Stone back in Nivenston.

As Kress died, the stone set in his ring tapped the larger one in Gower's hands.

A blood-red light like the eye of some malevolent god flared to life inside the bigger stone, and Gower and Lasko and Boggs screamed as every rune in their bodies burst into silver flame.

Nysska tore the stone out of Gower's burning hands, sprang clear of the office, and heaved it as hard as she could through the entrance, out into the dark. She saw the ghastly red light flicker and die as the stone soared away, but it didn't matter. By the time Nysska came back all three of the Argonium Infantrymen were unrecognizable lumps of still-burning flesh, and as she watched silently, the silver fires burned through the wooden floor and dropped the corpses into unknown darkness below.

Nysska stood there with Raoul and Sykes, searching for something to say, for some way to react. Nothing came to her. Nothing seemed to come to the men, either, and the three of them spent several long moments in silence.

That silence ended when, from somewhere far, far down in the mine beneath their feet, they heard a faint, muffled roar.

14

I t had only been ten minutes, but Nysska was already heartily sick of
arguing.

"It's as plain as the fucking horns on your fucking head," Sykes
all but shouted. "That thing destroys runes! It could take out the whole
fucking Argonium Infantry! Of *course* that's what the skinshifters wanted
to hide from us! We need to march our happy asses out there, find wher-
ever you threw it, and take it back to the General!"

Raoul sighed. He had already made his case, but since Nysska agreed
with Raoul and Sykes was being a gigantic piece of shit, she tried again.
"We don't know for certain that…that *rune trap* was the objective. It might
have just been a safeguard. Kress was probably meant to activate the thing
as soon as the alarm went off. If he hadn't screwed up, this fight might
have gone in a whole different direction."

Sykes puffed his chest out and put his hands on his hips. "Did that
stone destroy runes?"

Nysska rolled her eyes. "Yes."

"Is that the most devastating weapon you've ever heard of?"

"I guess you could look at it that way."

"Then we get it and get the fuck out of here!"

From the doorway, Cam said, "Is this what you're arguing about?"

Nysska's head snapped around, and when she saw Cam, Percy, and the
two blood lynxes standing there in the ruined doorway—the blood-red

stone in Cam's hands—she thought her heart might stop dead in her chest.

It did not stop, though, and before she realized she was moving, Nysska had crossed the distance between them and grabbed the stone away fast enough for Cam to jerk her hands back. "Hey! Ow!"

Nysska ripped a cloak off a dead man, wrapped the stone in it, and set it carefully in a corner. The activation ring, which she had slipped off Kress's cooling finger while Sykes wasn't looking, rested in her pocket.

Raoul fixed Percy with an irritated glare. "The hell are you two doing here, anyway? What happened to 'stay at the mill, don't come and endanger yourselves'?"

Percy opened his mouth to answer, but Cam stepped in. "I climbed up to the top of the mill, and was trying to use my runes to see what was going on. It didn't work—try as I might, I can't get them to function like looking-glasses—but I did see the flare. It was pretty hard to miss. There was a Sight Sensor here?"

Raoul groaned, and in clipped, concise words, explained to Cam and Percy exactly what had happened.

Percy let out a long, low whistle at the sight of the gaping, char-edged hole where the immolated Infantrymen had fallen through.

Cam said, "Dragon above, that's *horrible.*"

Nysska nodded. "So now Mr. Sykes here—"

"That's Enforcer Sykes, demon," Sykes said. He looked as if he were about to start literally tapping his foot with impatience.

"Sykes thinks that rune-trap stone thing is the reason we're here, but Raoul and I think we should take a look farther into the mine."

"Only because I'm obviously right." Sykes soaked each word with contempt. "And because there may be hundreds or thousands of reinforcements on their way to our location *right this fucking second,* and I don't know if you noticed, but the people who could have *maybe* gotten us out of that have been turned into charcoal."

Flax and Jax had moved slowly past the office, approaching the proper entrance to the mine's subterranean area. They stood there, sniffing, and Flax turned and stared at Percy, her silver eyes wide and her mouth hanging open. Jax took a tentative step onto the broad slope that led down into the dark.

Percy quietly said, "The kitties think there's something interesting down there."

"Hello!" Sykes got in Percy's face. "Were you not paying attention about the *roaring*? Of course there's something down there! It's probably some fucking bear trying to hibernate. Which is another excellent fucking reason for us *not* to go down there!"

Raoul turned to the group. "He's right about the possibility of reinforcements. If we stay—especially if we take a look around down there—we might find ourselves boxed in."

Nysska stared at the floor, her brow knit. "I don't see some huge band of fighters making their way across the countryside to a location that's supposed to be secret." She peered up from under her brows at Sykes. "You haven't found a Conversation Stone here, have you?"

Sykes grunted and rolled his eyes. "No."

Nysska went on. "So, I don't see how they could've sent for help, since the late Gower, Boggs, and Sykes killed everyone."

Sykes grunted again, but said nothing.

"Also, that trap stone…whatever you want to call it, I'm sorry, it feels like something that was supposed to *prevent* us from exploring further." Her eyes darted to Cam. "The greater the distance we put between you and it, the better, by the way. We don't know if it was a single-use thing, or if it might spark back up again."

Cam said, "I'm fine leaving it right where it is."

Raoul stretched, his back popping. "All right, we put it to a vote, because standing here jawing accomplishes not a Dragon-damned thing. Who's for seeing what's down there?"

Nysska's hand went up, followed by Raoul's, Percy's, and Cam's. Sykes made a sound of disgust and exasperation, but when Raoul fixed him with a pointed look, he threw up his hands. "Fine! Fine. I'm not about to ride back to the General on my own and explain how I left his idiot son to die. Lead the way, you dumb shit."

The broken, corroded tracks led down the center of the slope and stopped at a once-sturdy wooden platform, meant to be raised and lowered by means of massive ropes fitted to equally massive pulleys. One pulley still hung from a piton driven into the rock wall, but the others had fallen, and only scant fibrous remnants of the ropes remained. The platform itself still looked sturdy enough, chocks in place beneath it, but Nysska felt zero desire to set foot on it.

That turned out not to matter, because a set of steep wooden stairs off to the left plunged down the side of the broad, vertical shaft dug into the heart of the earth. A series of lit lanterns and burning torches indicated it had recently been used. Nysska took tentative steps to the edge and peered over.

"I count seven flights," she said to the group. "Then it looks like the shaft takes a dog-leg and turns horizontal. The torches stop at the dog-leg."

Everyone else had gathered at the head of the stairs. Raoul said, "All right, I'll go first to make sure the stairs are steady. These shitheads may have booby-trapped them for all we know. Everybody just walk where I walk."

Nysska softly cleared her throat. "Not to second-guess you, Commander, but I weigh more than you do. If anyone's going to test the stairs, I should."

"Damn fine idea," Sykes said. "Let the demon be the one to fall."

Nysska turned to the small man, who stood barely a centim taller than Percy, though Percy tended to slump. She towered over him, and though he didn't back down or show any fear, she couldn't help thinking he looked a little ridiculous, craning his neck that far to peer into her eyes.

"You know, Sykes, there was a time when hearing a human call me 'demon' didn't sit very well."

His lip curled. "Is that right?"

She bent down so that her face was on a level with his, and gave him her best, most disarming smile. "But hearing you say it? Damned if I don't think I'm starting to like it." Sykes's jaw clenched, and Nysska decided to make it worse by playfully tapping him on the end of his nose with one fingertip. "Don't worry, I'll keep you safe, you poor little thing."

Without waiting to get any reaction from the rest of her team—though she thought she saw Percy half-assedly stifling laughter—Nysska pivoted and, grabbing the nearest torch out of its sconce, began making her way carefully down the stairs.

Behind her, she heard Sykes say, "Oh, shut the *fuck* up," but she couldn't tell at whom it was directed.

The stairs held up under her weight surprisingly well—well enough that she decided they had been re-built, and not very long ago. Halfway to the landing, over to her left, she noticed an abandoned tunnel that led in from the direction of the entrance. Nysska took two more steps, which allowed her to see along its length, and froze in her tracks.

Ten meters in lay three smoldering lumps, faint flames still dancing here and there on the charred flesh and exposed bones. Nysska couldn't tell whether the three Argonium Infantrymen had fallen down an air shaft, or had actually burned through stone to get where they were. The sight of the corpses made her wish she had gotten rid of the trap-stone completely. Or maybe shattered it. Even the most fleeting thought of it causing Cam's runes to ignite made Nysska's insides clench and turn icy.

"Something wrong?" Raoul asked from above her.

Nysska twisted around and spoke to Sykes. "The Infantry will want to recover the bodies, yes?"

Sykes came and peered into the tunnel entrance. His face clouded. "I'll put it in my report."

Nysska nodded and continued her descent. At the seventh landing, wooden planks gave way to a smooth stone floor. Off to the right, the floor ended at a sheer drop. To the left, a hand-hewn tunnel had been gouged into the rock, easily large enough for her to stand upright in.

Nysska cautiously approached the drop-off to the right. As she got closer, the light from her torch revealed a gaping, natural chasm at least five meters across and twice that wide. She couldn't see the bottom. With the toe of her boot, Nysska kicked a pebble the size of her thumb off into the darkness. Even listening closely, she never heard it hit.

Backing away from the edge, Nysska turned and saw everyone watching her. She hooked a thumb toward the precipice and spoke just loud enough for the group to hear her. "Anyone need a bottomless pit?"

Cam came and took her elbow. "Let's not get that close to it, what do you say?"

Wordlessly, Raoul pointed down the length of the tunnel, at the far end of which stood a massive wooden door. Torchlight flickered from beneath the door and around its frame.

Ignoring Sykes, Nysska addressed Raoul, Cam, and Percy, as Flax and Jax twined nervously around her feet. "Well? What do we want to do?"

Cam said, "I could creep down there and try to look through the door."

Raoul nodded. "You and Nysska go. Watch for traps along the way."

Nysska flashed Cam a grim smile and drew her longsword. "Anything comes through that door, you get behind me."

One corner of Cam's mouth curled up. "*Pfff.* Anything comes through that door, I'll know it before you do."

As the two women crept slowly down the length of the tunnel, Cam's silver eyes shining on every square centim, Nysska heard Sykes mutter, "Dragon's eyeballs, are those two *fucking*?"

Even more faintly, she heard Percy say, "See, it's remarks like that one that make me think, 'Sykes has to go to sleep at some point.'"

They found no traps in the tunnel. Just a fifteen-meter stretch of unbroken rock. Cam brought the power in her runes up when they reached the door, and though Nysska worried that anyone on the other side might spot the glow of the silver flames, she couldn't think of any way around it. Cam turned her head left and right, then signaled to Nysska to head back. They returned just as quietly as they'd made their approach.

"It's a big round room," Cam said without preamble. "Wide enough that I can't see the walls on either side of the door, but straight across there's another door, with a man sitting in a chair beside it. Can't see through it, sorry, it's too far away, but I think I saw something moving underneath it. Oh, and this big one's not locked, just latched."

Raoul digested that. "All right. We keep going. Everybody be really *fucking* careful. Heads on swivels. No talking, no noise till we get to the door—then we go through fast and take out the jailer before he can sound some other alarm. Percy? You good with that?"

Percy grinned and slid a knife out of its sheath at his belt.

With Nysska in the lead, the group moved silently to the huge wooden door, and at Raoul's signal she slowly, carefully lifted the latch.

The door swung quietly inward on well-oiled hinges. Percy darted through, and Nysska saw the man on the chair beside the far door lift his head, no surprise registering yet. Percy's knife spun across the room and sank into his neck just beside the Adam's apple. The man crumpled and slid to the floor as, one by one, they filed into what was indeed a large round chamber—a dome, in fact, as the sloped ceiling above them rose to a central point. Nysska estimated the chamber to be ten meters across, with torches set every few meters around its perimeter.

Cam and the blood lynxes, bringing up the rear, had just cleared the door when it slammed shut with a thunderous boom.

Nysska whirled and sprang toward the door, but even as she moved, two massive, bronze-reinforced wooden beams dropped out of the ceiling and crashed into the stone directly in front of it.

Sykes snapped, "Oh, fucking typical. *Let's go see what's down there, it'll—*"

His sneering words broke off at the sound of heavy, clanking footsteps.

Out of an alcove a few meters from the door stepped a figure clad head to heel in gray, segmented metal armor, clutching a war hammer longer than Raoul was tall.

Nysska's brain bucked and shook, refusing to acknowledge what her eyes were seeing.

Nothing about the armored figure made sense.

The giant—she could think of it no other way—stood a full three meters tall, the limbs and torso thick as tree trunks, and Nysska blinked, breathing quickly, guts clenching.

It was neither human nor sethyd.

The proportions of the helmet were all askew. The face plate bizarrely elongated. The curve of the skull too flat.

The giant took another step forward. It didn't move quickly, but Nysska felt the vibration in the stone with each horrendous footfall. She hissed, "Cam, what the fuck *is* that thing?"

Cam's eyes blazed—grew wide—and tears started in them. "I—" Her voice faltered. "I don't know...!"

"Impressed," the giant said in a voice that seemed to emanate from somewhere deep within the earth, the words weighed down by an accent unlike anything Nysska had ever heard. "Feel pride as you die."

Nysska realized too late that the giant's measured movements had been all for show. With a roar—*the same roar they had heard just after the Infantrymen died*—the giant swung the hammer over its head and brought it around in a devastating arc that caught a stunned, gaping Sykes squarely in the ribcage.

Sykes came apart.

Like a squirrel beneath a speeding wagon wheel, the impact of the hammer ripped through Sykes's torso, and what was left of his body splattered against the nearest wall, knives clattering to the floor around him.

"*Get away from it!*" Nysska bellowed. "Don't let it near you!"

The giant roared again and lined up on Cam, and as that dread-filled hammer swung back to the pinnacle of its lethal arc, Nysska filled her lungs and unleashed a scream of her own.

She had used that scream in battle twice before—once to stun a group of twenty men who had ambushed her, and once to kill the skinshifter who had called himself Lockridge. She knew she couldn't expend as much energy as she had on Lockridge, or she'd wear herself out and get crushed, but she hoped to at least hurt the giant a little.

The scream had an effect: instead of targeting Cam, the giant shifted and came straight for Nysska. It seemed otherwise unbothered.

She heard Raoul and Percy both shouting something but had no idea what, since it took every bit of skill and concentration Nysska had to get out of the way as the hammer smashed into the floor where she had just been standing. A half-formed thought flashed through her mind, something about keeping the giant distracted long enough for everyone else to get behind it and maybe stab it in its back, but that thought shredded the second Nysska finally comprehended another detail about the armored giant.

Out of the tips of its armored gauntlets—as well as the tips of its metal-covered boots—protruded *claws*.

Long, black, curved, knife-sharp claws.

A voice in Nysska's head shrieked *What is this thing what is this thing what is this thing*, and she blinked tears of near-panic from her eyes.

The hammer came at her again. She ducked beneath its lethal arc only to be half-blinded by stone shrapnel as it smashed into the wall, and in the fraction of a second it took her to recover, the weapon's massive metal head jerked back and caught her on the shoulder.

She tried to roll with it. If she'd still been wearing her bronze-inlaid Thaumetallicon armor, she might have pulled it off, but since she only wore the coal-black leather that Gower had given her, the blow spun her like a top and filled her with splintering, wrecking pain.

An immense clawed hand reached down and gripped her by the head, and Nysska knew her neck was about to break—

Until an ear-splitting feline screech filled the domed chamber.

Looking up from between the massive armored fingers Nysska saw Flax clinging to the giant's head, blocking its eyes and digging with every claw she had at the seams in the helmet. The giant kept its grip on Nysska, but dropped the hammer and reached up with its other hand, and Nysska knew it would crush the blood lynx in less than a heartbeat.

The dagger sheathed on Nysska's thigh sprang into her grasp, and she forced the tip of the blade into a seam over the giant's wrist and pounded it in with the heel of her hand like a bronze nail.

The giant roared again, pitched higher this time, and staggered backward, flinging away both Nysska and Flax. Nysska slammed against the wall and fell, and when she tried to spring back up to her feet she couldn't. Red tinged her vision as it blurred and doubled.

The giant yanked her dagger out of the armor's seam. Bright red blood poured after it, spattering and spraying across the floor. Raoul and Percy darted in, their own swords seeking other seams, but the giant flailed about with clawed hands like scythes, and neither of them could get close enough.

The giant spun, crouching, and Nysska realized it was about to charge her. It huffed, blowing breath like a great demonic bull, and Nysska wondered what it would feel like to be crushed to death—

With a dull *clank*, something bounced off the giant's helmet. Raoul screamed, "Cam, *don't!*"

Clank! One of Sykes's throwing knives caromed off the side of the helmet, and a third found its way half a centim into one of the holes in the bizarrely elongated visor. The giant's growl shook Nysska's breastbone as it spun around and targeted Cam, who stood over Sykes's ruined body, his knives in her hands and tears streaming down her face.

"That's right!" Cam shouted. "I'm not afraid of you! Come get me! *Come get me!*"

The giant roared again—and Nysska landed on its back, a torch in one fist.

With her other hand she found the seam where helmet met shoulder, wrenched it upward, and shoved the burning torch through the gap.

The floor came up and hit her hard, drove the air from her lungs, and Nysska gasped and wheezed as the giant spun in circles. Its roars transformed to screams as flames filled the helmet, and as the screams grew more and more frantic, the giant reached up and tore the helmet loose from its head.

A near-hysterical sob filled Nysska's throat.

Horribly, impossibly, the head of an immense grizzly bear sat on the giant's shoulders, eyes bulging in pain and panic.

Silver eyes.

The silver of argonium. *Like the blood lynxes'.*

Nysska stared, hyperventilating.

Its fur burning, the great muzzle gaping wide, the giant slapped at the flames with clawed, armored hands. *Hands*, Nysska saw, sucking lungful after lungful of air into her aching lungs. *Not paws. Hands.*

The flames finally extinguished, the giant bear-headed creature fell to its knees with a sound like a sledge striking an anvil, panting, crazed with agony and fury.

Nysska brought the giant's hammer down squarely on its skull with every shred of strength she had left.

The blow didn't demolish the giant the way the giant had demolished Sykes, but the great sloped skull cracked nonetheless, and Nysska saw all the intelligence and malice flicker out as it slumped over sideways onto the cold stone floor.

Nysska let the hammer slide out of her hands. Cam ran to her and embraced her, and Nysska leaned on Cam to keep from falling over.

"How bad are you hurt?" Cam asked, fear obvious in the trembling of her body.

"Not too bad, I don't think," Nysska managed. "Don't let go of me just yet, though, yeah?"

Raoul and Percy and the blood lynxes came to stand beside them, and everyone simply stared at the hulking corpse for a couple of minutes.

Percy said, "Can someone tell me what the fuck we're looking at?"

Raoul sounded very tired. "This is...some kind of skinshifter thing?" He groped for words. "Can they turn themselves into...big... animal...people?"

Nysska remembered what Galena Vachs had said to her, upon learning of the existence of skinshifters. *"There are supposed to be three kinds of intelligent creatures in this world! Humans, sethyds, and seraphic animals. That's it. Do you know what kind of nightmare this is going to cause? A fourth kind of intelligence?"*

She wondered how Galena would react if she could see this...whatever this was.

A gurgling sound drew her attention. She went and knelt by the side of the man Percy had nailed with his throwing knife, who lay in a pool of blood spreading around his head and shoulders. As she watched, the skin of his face rippled and changed, patches and waves of light and dark pigmentation chasing themselves across his features.

"Imperial trash," he said. His voice was very weak, but steady, and Nysska thought the knife blade must have missed his windpipe entirely. Cam, Raoul, and Percy came and stood around the man, and his eyes flicked between them. His breath grew shallower and shallower, and beads of sweat dotted his chameleon-changing skin. "We'll kill you all."

"Why?" Raoul asked him, kneeling on his other side. "What does your kind have against the Empire?"

"Ask your fucking Emperor." His words came out as a harsh whisper. "Ask him why. Ask him what he did five years ago." The larynx hitched next to the knife blade, and the eyes went out of focus. "Where he—where he found us—he knows. He knows." The skin of the man's face settled on an unremarkable brown as the life finished slipping out of his body. Nysska thought about reaching out and closing his eyes, but decided she didn't want to touch him.

"Veetay?"

The team traded glances, and slowly turned to look at the door beside which the dead skinshifter had been sitting. The tiny, feminine voice had come from the other side.

Growing a bit bolder, the voice called out again. *"Veetay? Kos tam est?"*

Wordlessly, the members of the Ninth Crucible filled their hands with bronze and silently approached the door. Nysska left the bear-headed giant's hammer where it was, preferring her own sword, and the four of them took up positions on either side of the door.

At Raoul's nod, Percy threw the latch and swung the door wide. Nysska risked a peek around the doorframe—then lowered her sword and moved to get a better look. Raoul followed her, as did Percy and Cam, so that all four of them stared at the occupants of the cell.

Standing in the doorway, dressed in filthy rags, her feet chained together and her hands shackled to a chain around her waist, was a slender human girl of nineteen or twenty. She had deep golden skin, black hair as straight as a sethyd's, and eyes the same ink-black as Raoul's. She might have been beautiful if not for the coating of smeared dirt and dried blood. A disgusting rag hung around her neck. Nysska figured it had been a gag, since it appeared to have chew marks in it, and since the other girl sitting with her back against the far wall still had a similar gag in her mouth.

The second girl looked more like the humans Nysska had grown accustomed to, with brown skin a shade or two lighter than Cam's, a cap of curly black hair, and—

Nysska's breath left her when the second girl raised her head and peered up at them.

Her eyes were silver.

Silver like Flax and Jax's eyes. Silver like a seraphic animal's eyes.

Silver like the bear-giant's eyes.

Nysska's brain did somersaults, trying to understand what she was seeing. *Could this be...*

A seraphic human?

Could such a thing even exist?

A third figure, dressed in a long, coarse, black fur coat, sat in a shadow-filled corner, his head lowered.

The slender girl with the golden skin, Nysska realized, was staring at the team in much the same way they'd been staring at her.

No—she was staring at Nysska in particular.

Black eyes drawn to her own yellow ones, to her horns. To her face. Nysska read fear in the girl's expression, yes, but it seemed to share space with unabashed wonderment. Even awe. The girl spoke again in the tongue Nysska didn't recognize.

"Does anyone understand what she's saying?" Nysska asked.

The girl repeated the words with greater urgency, and the figure in the corner stirred.

"It's sure as hell not Plainish," Percy said.

"No," Raoul agreed. "I can get by in Estmani, and I've heard some of the Southern languages. Mainly Skahna. But this is new to me."

Cam's hand tightened on Nysska's arm as the figure on the floor leaned forward, emerging into the light. Its feet were bound, just like the other two prisoners, its hands likewise shackled to a waist chain, but instead of a gag…

It had been fitted with a muzzle.

That's no fur coat, Nysska realized with a dull thud in her gut.

The creature gazed at them with argonium-silver eyes set in the skull of a great black timber wolf.

PART II

THE JUNGLE

15

The shrieking scrape of metal on stone set Nysska's teeth violently on edge. She had her back to the bear-giant's vast bulk, heels dug in as best she could, and with Percy, Cam, and Raoul all helping they had managed to shove the armor-encased body about a third of the way down the hall toward the stairs. Nysska tried to feel thankful that Cam had found the release switch for the great bronze-clad beams blocking the door, rather than resentful that they had to put in this much effort and make this big a racket to get rid of the giant's body.

"I need a minute," Cam said, gasping, and the Ninth Crucible sagged against the giant's corpse. The thing smelled horrible. The stench of burnt bear fur filled the tunnel, and Nysska was pretty sure it had at least partially voided its bowels.

As they sat there, Nysska eyed the three prisoners they'd released. The trio hung back a few meters, watching with what she judged to be equal measures trepidation and confusion. None of them had spoken once they'd confirmed the quite solid language barrier, but Raoul had done a fair job of conveying with hand signals that the prisoners were in no danger, and that they should accompany the Ninth out of the makeshift prison.

Breathing hard, Percy said, "Tell me again why we have to do this shit?"

Nysska had already recovered her breath. "Because we don't know if we can trust the Emperor. White runes, remember? No idea whose side he's on?"

Raoul added, "Keeping that long-snouted gentleman at the end of the hall out of sight is one thing. But if Imperial troops do show up—or unfriendly sethyds, for that matter—do you want them knowing Mr. Bear Pants here exists?"

Percy shrugged and got to his feet. "Fair point, I guess. Come on, let's get this over with and get the fuck out of h—"

He broke off as the "long-snouted gentleman" walked up to them. Nysska stood, as did Raoul and Cam, and they faced the lupine creature in an awkward silence. He was at least half a head taller than Nysska, with thick, heavy arms and a broad chest that tapered to a narrow waist. She tried not to stare at the way his paw-tipped legs seemed to have one too many joints.

"Kagan," the wolf-man said in a deep, rumbling, raspy voice. He tapped his chest with one long, clawed finger, then pointed at the two young women—first the fully human one, then the one with argonium-colored eyes. "Aschling. Laula."

Aschling waved to them with a sunny grin. Laula's silver eyes narrowed, and she folded her arms under her breasts.

Raoul pointed at his own chest just as Kagan had. "Raoul." He named off the others. "Nysska. Cam. Percy." The two blood lynxes had moved ahead of the bear-giant relocation effort, but now they hopped up onto the corpse, peering at Kagan with eyes that matched his. Percy pointed to them exactly as he had the other members of the Crucible. "Flax. Jax."

Kagan jabbed a finger at the dead bear-giant, pointed down the hall toward the stairs, and used both hands to make an unmistakable "move aside" gesture. Nysska glanced at her teammates, then moved a pace to her right. Kagan stepped forward, braced his feet, put his hands on the giant's waistline, and looked up at Nysska. A short motion of his head could not have been clearer: *We moving this thing or not?*

Percy grinned and took up his own position, and after a second's hesitation, so did Nysska, followed by Raoul and Cam. Nysska cried, "Heave!" and, to her intense but pleasant surprise, the giant corpse *rolled over*.

Kagan's strength was astonishing. She thought it must have matched hers. Maybe even surpassed it.

Working together, the five of them rolled the giant the rest of the way down the hall, past the wooded stairs, and to the edge of the black chasm beyond them. "Over the edge," Nysska said, along with an arcing gesture with her hand.

Kagan nodded. He licked his muzzle with a long, dark red tongue and set to alongside the rest of them, and with a last grinding, scraping squeal, the giant slid over the lip of the chasm and plummeted into the darkness below.

Nysska turned to see that Aschling and Laula had joined them. Laula walked to the edge, peered over, and spat into the void. Aschling favored Nysska with another brilliant grin and pointed up, her eyebrows lifting to ask the question.

"Up," Nysska said. "Definitely."

When Nysska walked out of the woods and looked up at the windmill, she wasn't surprised to see two dozen soldiers surrounding the place. For once, she was glad of her non-human-at-a-glance appearance, as all she had to do was hold her head high and make sure the soldiers could see she held no weapons, and they let her walk right up to the dilapidated mill's entrance. The General waited just inside, and when he saw she was alone, his face clouded over.

"Where is everyone else? Where is my son?"

"Raoul is fine, sir." Nysska tried not to sound as tired as she felt. "And we have a great deal to tell you. But considering our circumstances, I fear I'm going to have to ask you to do something first."

General Cullen's eyes narrowed in suspicion. "Do what?"

Twenty minutes later, after General Cullen had spoken to one of his captains and sent all the soldiers riding away from the mill, Nysska walked out and waved to Raoul at the tree line. Raoul, Percy, and Cam walked up the hill, surrounding the three prisoners from the mine. Kagan had Nysska's cloak covering him and walked hunched over. Laula wore Cam's cloak with the hood pulled down, covering her eyes.

"All right," Cullen said, once everyone was gathered in the mill. "What exactly happened down there? Where are the Argonium Infantrymen, and who are these three? Did you find what these skinshifters were so dead-set on protecting?"

Raoul spoke up. "Sir, it wasn't any kind of device they were guarding. It was these people."

The General looked the prisoners over. "Fine, then. What's so special about them? Who are they?"

Raoul glanced at Nysska. She said, "We don't know who they are yet, sir. But as far as what's special about them...I'm afraid you're in for a shock. We all certainly were."

The golden-skinned girl—Aschling—had been watching and listening to this exchange closely, and Nysska got the impression that she understood most of it, language barrier or not.

General Cullen's frown had darkened to a scowl. "What shock? What is this? Out with it!"

Nysska mimed lifting Laula's hood, and the golden-skinned girl said something in the unknown language. Laula reached up, pushed the hood back, and turned her silver eyes calmly on the General.

Cullen's scowl vanished. His mouth dropped open half a centim. Nysska thought she could see the mental dominoes falling in his mind, as all the implications of an actual seraphic human struck him one after another. Quietly he said, *"Dragon fuck my wife."*

Percy made a sound like *snerk*, and Nysska heard him whisper, "That's a new one."

"How?" the General managed, followed by, "Does this—is this—are her —is she like those blood lynxes? Is that what I'm seeing? Those aren't runes? She's not a Sight Sensor—" He took a step closer to the girl, who displayed not even the tiniest shred of anxiety or fear and gazed back at him calmly. "Great fucking silver-plated dragon shit."

Raoul said, "That's not all, sir. And please, bear in mind, he's not hostile."

Cullen tore his attention away from the silver-eyed girl and focused on the last prisoner, who had stayed hunched and covered in the cloak. "Not hostile? All right?"

"Just prepare yourself, sir," Nysska said. "No need to draw any weapons."

The General blew out an agitated puff of air. "I don't know what's going to shock me more than the existence of—of—a *seraphic human*."

Nysska grinned.

The General went on. "But go ahead. Show me."

The golden-skinned girl once again seemed to be up to speed, and said something else. To Nysska, the language sounded...*dense*. Packed with sound and meaning.

The cloak slid to the ground, and Kagan rose up to his full height. He stretched mightily, back and neck cracking, and swung his arms as if to restore full circulation in a gesture which seemed to Nysska so fully, naturally human that it came off as disarming. Kagan said something to Aschling, and she gave him a warm, trusting smile as she responded.

General Cullen had taken a quick step backward, his hand flying to the hilt of his sword, but Nysska saw him deliberately move the hand away. Cullen and the wolf-man stared at each other—black eyes locked on large, luminous silver—until Kagan took a slow, careful step forward and held out his right hand. His voice reminded Nysska of the crackling flames of a fire in the dead of winter. *"Veetay. Menya zavud Kagan."* With his other hand, he tapped his chest. "Kagan."

Cullen swallowed hard. Looked from the outstretched hand to Kagan's face and back. Then he stepped forward and clasped Kagan's forearm. Kagan looked down at the grip, momentarily surprised, but quickly mirrored it, his massive, clawed, black-furred hand all but swallowing Cullen's arm.

The General touched his own chest. "Boris Cullen. Cullen."

Kagan waited for the General to release the grip and stepped back. "Cullen." He repeated it. "Cullen." Pointing at the golden-skinned woman, he said, "Aschling."

Aschling grinned at the General and said, "Asch." It sounded exactly like *ash*. She put her arm around the other young woman's shoulders— who looked unenthusiastic to the point of being bored—and said, "Laula."

"These three are what the skinshifters were protecting," Raoul said. "But we have no idea who they are, *what* they are, or why they were there."

Cullen seemed to have made a mental rally. "Well, obviously we're going to have to keep their existence a secret." He appeared to turn his thought process inward, mumbling, "Travel by night to reduce the chance of discovery...though defense would be easier by day..."

Asch gently cleared her throat. She said something that sounded apologetic, and put her hand flat against her belly. With her other hand she mimed bringing something to her mouth and took a bite of some imaginary food. When they saw her do this, both Laula and Kagan nodded, touching their own stomachs.

Cam said, "Well *that's* pretty clear. Who's got some food?"

"This isn't going to be any kind of gourmet fare," the General said. "Salted meat and some dry biscuits and..." He poked through the contents of a burlap sack. "Some jars of what I believe is apple sauce. But it should fill bellies just fine."

Nysska's own stomach had begun growling as soon as Cam had mentioned food, and as the rations got passed out, she and Cam took seats on either side of an upside-down, sawn-in-half barrel that might have once been used as a planter. Neither of them said much for several minutes. Nysska was fine with that, gnawing on salted ham and scooping up apple sauce with hunks of biscuit. Between bites she stole looks at the former prisoners.

Kagan, the giant, ebon-furred wolf-man, ate more like a human than an animal. She wouldn't have been surprised if he'd lowered his face to his battered tin plate, gobbled his food, and licked the plate clean. Instead, he used the same wooden utensils as everyone else. In fact, she thought he ate with more poise and grace than most sethyds she'd known, and more than almost all humans. He carried about him an air of quiet dignity she found appealing.

With a mixture of horror and delight, she realized she both wanted to have deep conversations with him and to stroke his head and scratch him between the ears.

Deep in such reflection, she caught Laula watching *her*, and had to wonder whether any of the three prisoners had ever seen a sethyd before. If they hadn't, she had to admire their restraint.

"Did you catch any individual words in their language?" Cam asked. "I've been listening hard every time they've talked, but haven't been able to pick anything out."

Nysska shook her head. "No. And I like to think I've got a pretty good ear for that sort of thing."

Cam had taken a bite of food, but she flashed the closed-lipped, lop-sided smile that Nysska loved so. She chewed and swallowed, and carefully said, "*Vi ankaux estas bona instruisto.*" *You're also a good teacher.*

Nysska dipped her head graciously. "*Gxi helpas havi bonan studenton.*" *It helps to have a good student.*

Four meters away, Asch's sudden, violent coughing fit sprayed bits of half-chewed biscuit across the mill's floor.

She dragged in a ragged breath and coughed again, and as another spasm wracked her body she started waving one hand—then both hands —at Nysska and Cam.

Flax and Jax crept closer to Asch, watching her with wide round eyes, and as everyone in the mill looked on with concern, Percy said, "Does she need help? Should we help her?"

After a couple of smaller, calmer coughs, Asch lifted her head, stared straight at Nysska, and with gleeful, almost manic eyes, said, "*Kiel estas ke vi parolas Esperanto?*"

How are you speaking Esperanto?

16

A minute later, after a flurry of simultaneous questions had escalated into overlapping gibberish, Nysska cleared her throat loudly enough to get everyone's attention.

"Look, we all want to know a great many things, but let's take this a step at a time, all right? I'll ask her questions and tell you what her answers are, but her accent is very nearly impenetrable, and it may take some time to understand her. So please bear with me. With us. Sound good?"

"Who are they?" Raoul barked, as if it were important to get the first question in.

"How does that girl have eyes like my kitties?" Percy all but shouted, then looked chagrined that his voice had come out that loud. In a more moderate volume, he added, "And how did that big hairy fucker get that way?"

General Cullen said, "We need to know why the skinshifters were holding them."

Nysska sighed and looked at Cam. "Anything you want to know?"

Cam shook her head, though she looked eager to listen. "No, no, I think those are all good to start with."

Switching to the sethyd tongue, which Asch had called "Esperanto," Nysska asked the young human woman, "Are you ready to answer some questions?"

Fully recovered from her coughing fit now, Asch all but bounced up and down where she was seated on the mill's floor. "Answer questions?" she shot back. "*Us* answer questions? *We* have questions! I never see woman with purple skin before! And—I do not know word for..." She mimed Nysska's horns. "Who are you? What do you call yourself? How are you—as you are?" Asch grunted. "I apologize for—not to know words. I do not—*ugh.* I think I never speak Esperanto. So I do not learn it well. Now I—" She frowned and thumped the heel of her hand against her forehead. "Now I regret."

Nysska turned to her team, where General Cullen sat beside his son, everyone looking at her expectantly. "She's got questions of her own. This may take a little while."

"We're not the ones who were being held prisoner," the General said curtly. "Get the information as fast as possible, Enforcer."

Nysska turned back to Asch. "First things first. My name is Nysska Stonegate."

Asch grinned at her. It was such an open, sincere, *wholesome* expression, it made Nysska want to take the girl home and feed her and give her a warm bed to sleep in. "It is pleasure to meet you, Nysska Stonegate. I am Princess Aschling Summerglory of Hawk's Nest. But everyone calls me Asch."

Nysska blinked. "Princess?...You were political prisoners?"

Asch's face screwed up. "Political...? I get to that." She pointed at Laula. "This is...in her language, her full name means Sings From Shadow, but she like to be called 'Singer.' You also meet Captain Kagan."

Nysska's eyebrows twitched upward. "Captain? He's in the—so you have a military?"

Asch nodded. "You do also, yes? And—I do not remember names for friends. Tell me who are friends again, please?"

Nysska pointed them out, one by one. "General Boris Cullen. His son, Commander Raoul Cullen. This is Sensor Camble Delakroy, Keeper Percy Bitters, and I'm Enforcer Nysska Stonegate. The two blood lynxes are Flax and Jax. They work with us."

Asch turned to Singer and Kagan, and all three of them chattered away in their consonant-heavy tongue. Nysska quickly understood: of the three, only Asch spoke the sethyds' Language of Truth. Coming back to Nysska, she said, "They want to know about the silver-eyed animals—and how Camble Delakroy sees with pieces of metal in her eyes."

"We'll come back to that. All of it. We have *worlds* of knowledge to exchange, I'm thinking. But please, if you would, first tell us why the three of you were being held prisoner?"

Asch's expression dimmed. "My husband. Chrysaor. He is governor of place where—metal—men take metal out of ground. Metal that is call *chervoxite*. Other men come and want chervoxite. All of metal we have. But—they do not—" She closed her eyes and gestured in the air. "They say they pay money. But not enough money. My husband tell them 'no.' Seven days pass, and..." Asch's eyes went glossy. "People I know. Their faces —*change*—I think they are friends, but they are not." She focused on Nysska. "I know what I say sounds—like—my head is wrong. But I tell you truth."

Nysska leaned forward and put her hand on Asch's forearm. "I believe you. We all believe you. We've been calling them 'skinshifters.' They're the ones who were keeping you prisoner, yes?"

Asch nodded. "*Skin—shifters*...yes. I understand. Yes, is good name. Skinshifters and *shvenyaskurval* Wukash and Barto." At Nysska's quizzical look, she said, "Giant one. Wukash. Like bear. Who wore..." She mimed a suit of armor. "And skinshifter, Barto. They take money. Put us in tiny room. We are happy they are dead."

Carefully, Nysska asked, "Is Wukash...was he like Kagan...?"

Asch blinked a couple of times. "Oh! No. But yes. I tell you. I think you do not see people like Kagan and Singer and Wukash here. Yes?" When Nysska nodded, Asch went on. "Wukash and Kagan are both—I try to say —God touch them. They have God-Touch."

Nysska could hear the capital letters in Asch's voice. "We'll talk more about...the God-Touched? I can call them that?"

Asch's grin came back. "God-Touched! Yes. I am sorry, Nysska, I never learn to say things happen—" Her mouth skewed to one side for a moment. "Before now. Things happen yesterday. I do not know how to say it."

Nysska said, "Past tense. I understand. We can work on that. Are you saying the skinshifters kidnapped you, and now they're forcing your husband—Chrysaor?—to give them this ore? This chervoxite?"

"They tell Chrysaor, 'You give us metal, or we kill your wife.'"

Nysska held up a finger and, turning back to the eagerly-awaiting Plainish-speakers, told them everything Asch had told her.

"Political ransom," Raoul said. "Human, God-Touched, greed's always the same, isn't it?"

General Cullen brushed aside the philosophy. "I've never heard of anything like chervoxite, and I've sure as the Dragon's in the sky never seen anything like the God-Touched. Not as far north as the Estmani polar outposts, nor down in the Skahna wilderness. Where exactly do these people come from?"

Nysska put the question to Asch, and she didn't hesitate with her answer. "From across ocean."

Nysska blinked. "What?"

Asch nodded emphatically. "You have same—uh, trouble. You have same trouble we have? Go out on water too far—away from land—bad things come. Bad ocean things come up and kill you. Yes?"

Frowning, Nysska said, "Right—we don't go far from the shore because Those Who Dwell Beneath the Waves take any ship that does." *Across the ocean.* She felt as disoriented as if someone had just told her the world was cube-shaped.

Asch's face wrinkled in sympathy. "Same with us. Also. Say who they are? The ones who kill us? Say what you call them again?"

Nysska repeated the name. "Those Who Dwell Beneath the Waves."

Asch said it back to her. "That is good name. We call them—I do not get this right, I am sorry—'hungry ones.' We never go out onto water because they kill us. But when skinshifters take us, they put us on boat and…" She mimed a ship traveling straight. "Away from land. And we *hear* them. We hear skinshifters and hungry ones *talking*. We do not think that is—that is—that it can be. But we hear them. And skinshifter ship go and go and go, and bring us here."

Nysska heard a note of hysteria creeping into her own voice, and did her best to fight it down. "You're saying there are other lands *across the ocean?*"

Asch laughed, a high, crystalline sound. "We do not think is true also. But is true! Sun comes up behind us and sets in front of us for…I do not know how many days. I am sorry. Then skinshifters bring us here, and we stay in tiny room and eat bad food and…Wukash smells very bad for many days." Her brow furrowed. "I think maybe Chrysaor thinks I die. He does not know." Asch's eyes darted around from Nysska to the other members of the Ninth and back. "Thank you. Thank you very much. I think if we stay in tiny room we die for true." Her anguish began shading into anger. "Skinshifters. If my husband does not give to them chervoxite, they say they kill me. Kill us. I think Chrysaor sends metal across ocean now, to—" She paused. "How do you call this place?"

"The entire continent—all of the land—we call it *Kainos*. There are different peoples throughout—but you're currently in one part of the Valconian Empire. We—" She made a collective gesture, including her group and herself. "We all work for Emperor Valco."

Asch nodded. "All right. I understand. I think. Understand Esperanto better than I speak. Our home is called Borealis."

Nysska sensed a hesitation. "And who rules Borealis?"

Asch let her eyes close for a moment and exhaled softly. "Chrysaor's mother."

The questions and answers went on for another hour before Cullen called the session over. "We all need to get some sleep," he said, sounding for a moment more like a father than a general. "We can pick back up in the morning, and decide how to proceed."

Percy quietly said, "Oh, sure, now that it turns out everything we were ever taught about the world is a big fucking pile of lies. I'll sleep like a baby."

When Nysska woke, she wasn't sure how much time had passed. The second moon was gone, leaving the night air thick and murky, like the water at the bottom of a silt-filled river. Her feet were cold, but she considered shifting under her blanket and trying to get back to sleep.

Instead she opened her eyes, and saw the matching pair of yellow gazing down at her from high in the rafters overhead.

Nysska stole outside the mill, cloak pulled tight around her against the chill of the night, and as she tugged her boots on she saw her brother drop silently to the ground in the deepest of the shadows next to the building. He beckoned to her and, gritting her teeth, she followed him down the hill and into the woods.

"Are you *mad?*" she hissed. "You're all but begging to get caught!"

Gerrit shook his head, condescending as always, and kept walking through the trees, forcing Nysska to keep up with him. "You're dealing with humans, sister. They are *staggeringly* unobservant." Growing more serious, he said, "So. Tell me what you've found."

The enormity of it yawned before Nysska like the widest of canyons, but a tiny voice in one corner of her brain acknowledged one truth: Gerrit wasn't aware of Asch, Singer, and Kagan. The shadows inside the mill had kept them hidden.

"I can't."

Gerrit's eyes narrowed to hard flame-yellow slits. "Excuse me?"

"I don't know where the Mountain Bulls stand. I don't know what dealings you've had with the skinshifters."

"Oh, is that what we're calling them now?"

"I don't know what you do with the information I give you. And—most important—I don't know if it's even necessary anymore."

Gerrit tilted his head back, looking down his nose at her. "Ohhh, you think Mother might be dead? That I'm holding you hostage with a corpse's welfare." He gave her the familiar grin that, while it made his striking face even more beautiful, never lost its cruelty. "But you have no other option, do you? Look, Nysska, Mother made a choice. A choice that betrayed our people. A choice you made right alongside her. Well, you're both dealing with the consequences now."

Gerrit led them out onto a narrow, nearly overgrown trail, where a sleek black stallion was tethered.

"I'm dealing with the consequences of my brother having his head filled with lies," Nysska said, low and firm, surprised at the words even as they left her lips.

Something in her voice made Gerrit pause. "Don't even *think* of defying me. You know what will happen."

"It's *all* lies," Nysska shot back, her blood heating up. "Our people were meant for peace. For knowledge—for ever greater understanding. For Atiina's *wisdom*, not this conquest bearshit. You and all your kind. You're worse than cowards. You've betrayed every sethyd everywhere. You've betrayed our very *purpose*."

"So you *want* me to start sending you pieces of our mother, is that it? You're like a two-year-old, testing her limits. You need me to spank you, just so you'll understand what I'm saying is true."

"Like the way you punished the sethyds at Summergray? That was you, wasn't it? No skinshifter would've known how to poison one of us. I'm damn sure no human knows, either. What was the point? What did they ever do to you—a bunch of farmers?"

His eyes glittered in the moonlight. "So confident. So undeservedly sure of yourself. Let me disabuse you of that thought right now: the Mountain Bulls had nothing to do with the deaths at Summergray. But *you* are going to find out for us who *is* responsible. Consider it your highest priority."

Something flashed in the moonlight. Something around his neck.

Nysska struck faster than a rattlesnake. Not fast enough to avoid damage—Gerrit's reflexive counter blow to her sternum sent her staggering backward, gasping with pain—but she still held a bronze chain in her hand. From that chain dangled a piece of jewelry she hadn't seen in years.

"Why?"

Gerrit had entered a defensive pose, but relaxed when he saw she wasn't going to come at him again. At least not immediately. He smirked. "Why what?"

"*Why do you have Mother's favorite horn ring?*"

Gerrit's smirk grew into a nasty grin. "Well, she hardly needs it anymore, does she?"

Nysska became aware of a decision coalescing inside her. It didn't seem to involve her conscious mind much at all, and she wondered if it had to do with her entire understanding of the world getting pulverized and blown away earlier in the night. She felt as if the walls of her own world—walls she had only just realized were even there—had been demolished, revealing a vast, wild existence surrounding her, that had *always* surrounded her, and now demanded all of her heart and her mind as sacrifice.

"I think our mother is long dead, Gerrit. You've used me. You've forced me to lie to those I've come to cherish, but I'm done with it. With the lies. With *you.*"

Gerrit closed the distance between them, faster than Nysska could react. A handful of her hair gripped in one fist, he cranked her head back and down, growling in her ear. "You're done with this when *I* decide. *I* decide. Do you understand?"

Nysska drove an elbow into his ribs and spun away, one leg set and ready to throw a stone-shattering kick straight to his jaw—but he moved again, fast, *so fast*, and the ground came up and struck her hard. Nysska's head rang with the impact and Gerrit leapt on top of her, hands around her throat.

"Stupid," he said, wheezing. "*Stupid*, you're a *priest-singer*, do you know how many times I could've killed you if I'd wanted t—"

Nysska drove two stiffened fingers into the hollow between her brother's collarbones. He sprang away from her, coughing, gagging, eyes ablaze with startled pain. A dagger appeared in his right hand, and his tortured voice grated out, "You've overestimated your usefulness, sister, but now you've helped me see—"

Something huge and black rammed into Gerrit's side and took him completely off his feet. He spun like a child's doll and crashed into a massive tree trunk, yet surged back up in an instant, knife flashing in the moonlight as blood dripped from his nose and mouth—

An arrow caught him in the right shoulder, smashed him back against the tree, and the dagger fell from nerveless fingers. Before he could take another action, Kagan came from behind the tree and clamped one immense black-furred hand around Gerrit's neck and slammed him face-first into the dirt, the shaft of the arrow splintering in the impact.

From the corner of her eye Nysska saw General Cullen come sprinting onto the trail, a heavy bow in one hand. Raoul, Cam, and Percy followed him, with Asch and Singer close behind.

In the Tongue of Truth, Nysska bellowed, "Kagan, don't let him see you! Don't let him see your face!"

Asch translated for Kagan, and the great black head nodded, silent as he pressed Gerrit's nose even more firmly into the dirt. Cullen, Raoul, and Nysska moved in and pinned Gerrit in place while Kagan faded into the shadows.

Gerrit spoke in the Tongue of Truth as well, his voice muffled by the ground. "So you've got secrets as well, do you, sister? I'll enjoy ripping them away from you."

Gerrit twisted, explosive, and threw the General and Raoul off of him. His foot came up and caught Nysska alongside her head, and as she toppled, vision flashing, he bolted to the black stallion, leapt into the saddle, and disappeared down the trail in a storm of hoofbeats.

Back at the mill, slumped to the floor and rubbing her head where Gerrit had kicked her, Nysska was painfully aware in the rawest way of how everyone's eyes bored holes in her. She felt her guts contract when General Cullen sat down facing her.

"Nysska, who was that?"

She found it difficult to look at him. To look at any of them. When she finally spoke, her words dropped to the floor. "That was my brother. Gerrit." She raised her head a few millims. "How much of all that did you hear?"

Cam's voice held a distant tone that sent thorns into Nysska's heart. "You said your brother died. That you lost him in the *Krizo*. Nysska, that's the sethyd I saw talking with you and the Emperor."

Nysska considered saying, "I never said he was dead, just that I lost him," but knew that would serve no purpose, so she glanced up at Cam, and in turn at Raoul and Percy and the General. "My brother Gerrit is a member of the Mountain Bulls."

General Cullen said, "The sethyd faction that wants to conquer all of humankind."

Nysska nodded, miserable. "So you know about them."

"The Emperor has assured the Cathedral that he's dealing with them diplomatically. That they pose no threat."

Nysska sighed. "I hope to Atiina that's true. What I *know* to be true is that my brother is the reason I accepted Wendell Anwar's offer in the first place. The reason I joined the Thaumetallicon." She made eye contact with Cam, because she needed Cam to believe her most of all. "Gerrit and a group of Mountain Bulls found my mother and me, where we were living in exile in the wilderness. They abducted my mother, and Gerrit told me if I didn't take Wendell's offer, he'd send me pieces of her until I did."

Cam gasped. Raoul and Percy looked openly horrified, but General Cullen's face had gone stony. He said, "That would not have been the end of his demands."

Nysska shook her head. "No. He wanted me to tell him what the Ninth Crucible was doing."

Raoul groaned. The General said, "He wanted you to *spy* for him."

"Yes."

"And that's what you've been doing."

Nysska put her face in her hands. "I've been lying to you all. For months. I've told you my mother and brother were dead. And when Gerrit came to me, I told him what we had done, yes." She looked up. "But I never told him anything that the public would not have known soon enough. I never told him anything that would have *hurt* anyone. And tonight...he wanted to know what we had found at the mine. And—"

General Cullen held up a hand. "We heard you defy him. As well as his response."

Nysska brought her knees up, folded her arms on top of them, and rested her forehead on her arms, horns pressing into the skin. "I'm sorry. I know I've failed you all. I know there's no trust anymore, and I hold no hope that you'll forgive me. I can only ask that you believe me when I tell you how sorry I am."

Cam came and sat down next to her, and put a hand on her shoulder.

"Nysska, if I'd been in the same situation, I don't know that I would've done anything different."

The General's voice stayed flat. Cold. "That doesn't change the fact that you've been a willing spy for an enemy power. Damage done or not, Nysska Stonegate, you have committed an act of treason against the Empire."

Raoul said, "*Dad...*"

The General said, "Nysska. Look at me."

She raised her head, ashamed at the tears spilling from her eyes. Ashamed of what caused them.

General Cullen went on. "However, we are faced with a set of circumstances that...no one in the history of the Empire has faced before. And given the delicate nature of...whatever one might call this situation... putting you in a cell would *not* serve the Empire." He paused. "It seems to me that if the skinshifters get their hands on a shipment of this new kind of ore—a shipment that Miss Aschling described as, I believe you said, 'all the metal'..."

Nysska blinked a couple of times before she realized he was waiting for her to jump in. "...*Oh.* Um. Then they'll be able to forge as many blood runes as they want. Re-animate as many corpses as they want. Create as many tarns as they want."

"We sure as fuck can't have that," Percy said, and Nysska let out a tiny sound, half-laugh, half-sob.

Raoul came and knelt next to his father, facing her. "Nysska, we can talk about coercion and mitigating circumstances and how horrible your piece-of-shit brother is. Later. And at great length, I'm thinking. But right now we need you with us. Will you help us stop these people?" He took a deep breath. "Even if it means you might lose your mother?"

Nysska's eyes hardened into flame-yellow diamonds as she swiped the tears from her cheeks with the back of her hand. The image of the moonlit horn ring danced in front of her. "My mother is already dead."

17

Nysska wasn't sure how long they'd been riding. The sun was threatening to come up, so…four hours? Maybe?

Someone—she couldn't remember who—had pointed out that they had no reason not to expect Gerrit to show back up, most likely with a dozen more sethyds, and kill them all. Following that observation and several minutes of hasty packing, the eight of them had made their way off the hill and struck out across country, shunning roads and hiding their tracks as best they could. Kagan helped that effort along by urinating over a broad area behind them.

"He does that when animals follow," Asch had said, with a gleam in her eyes reminiscent of Percy's mischievous twinkle. "Animals that follow by nose—they smell that and run to hills."

Flax and Jax had fallen in beside Percy's horse, and Nysska thought she heard one of them make a noise like *Pssh*. A feline-flavored expression of contempt for lesser trackers. Or at least, that was how Nysska interpreted it.

Having only five horses for eight people, they had decided to double up the heaviest with the lightest, so now Kagan and Asch shared a mount, while the taciturn, silver-eyed young woman called Singer sat in front of Raoul. Cam had wordlessly slid up onto the saddle in front of Nysska. To the comment of no one.

Now, with the eastern sky a luminous gray shading more and more toward blue, General Cullen called a halt. A dry creek bed ahead of them dipped down between two tree-covered hillocks, getting them out of line of sight of anyone passing by. "One hour," he said, the order unmistakable in his voice. "No fire. Break out what food you've got—we all need our strength." After a pause: "And we need to have a conversation."

A few minutes later, after helping Raoul and Percy arrange a few flat rocks in an uneven circle, Nysska took a seat. Cam sat down next to her, and one by one everyone else joined the circle, except for Kagan, who seemed to prefer pacing nearby. Nysska paid attention to his footfalls until her first impression was confirmed: he made no noise when he moved. Periodically Kagan raised his head and sniffed the wind.

General Cullen cleared his throat. "I have given my entire adult life to the Cathedral. The Emperor's army lives by laws. By *rules*." His brow furrowed. "Yet we find ourselves treading ground upon which no one has ever walked. And—as much as it pains me to say it—I fear *new* rules must be made." He looked around at the members of the Ninth, and shook his head. "Just as much as I fear I'm not the man to make them. The Cathedral drills imagination *out* of its soldiers. Therefore...son? Enforcer Stonegate?" He opened his mouth to speak, shut it, and tried again. "What do you suggest we do?"

Raoul looked over at Nysska. "Up to this point we were just dealing with skinshifters." He snorted softly. "Listen to me. *Just* skinshifters. But now we've got sethyds directly involved, and I'm not about to try to predict what the Mountain Bulls are going to do. Nysska?"

The sudden weight of everyone's stares—which seemed to come especially heavily from Kagan and Singer—felt like the proverbial millstone around Nysska's neck. She found herself faintly surprised she wasn't sinking into the ground with the weight. "Look, I was never part of the Mountain Bulls. Cam knows this already—I was a priest-singer, back in Patrinomonto. Sethyds who do what I did were supposed to remain strictly neutral."

General Cullen's face had begun forming interesting new wrinkles. "Excuse me—you were a 'priest-singer'? Not a, a fighter? Not a soldier?"

Nysska shook her head. "All sethyds receive what you'd call combat training in school. It's as common as arithmetic or writing. I'm no more skilled a fighter than any sethyd miner or tailor or chef."

Percy had scooted back until his shoulders rested against a fallen log, so that Flax and Jax could curl up on his chest and belly in a big, tawny, purring pile. Contented cats notwithstanding, he said, "Nysska, I don't say this lightly. That is fucking *terrifying*." Percy blinked at the group. "But, hang on—you said your brother was, what, some kind of elite fighter? Elite among the sethyds, I mean?"

She nodded. "I joined the priest-singers. He continued in the military. His unit would have been...I suppose equivalent, among our people, to what the Argonium Infantry is for the Empire. They were not peacekeepers, or builders. When they were called, it was to make sure none of their targets got back up again."

In the Tongue of Truth, Asch said, "I am sorry, Nysska, but we three do not understand any of your words. And I think you talk about us? Please tell us what you all say?"

Nysska held up a finger to her, and addressed the group in Plainish. "I'm going to have to translate for the—" She switched languages. "What do you call yourselves? Collectively?"

"Borealans," Asch replied, with a smile that Nysska could only think of as "perky."

"I'm going to have to translate for the Borealans as we go. They have a right to know what's being said."

"That's fine," Raoul said. "We're going to need some input from them, as well, since the fact that they're here, alive and—and *existing*—stands a good chance of dropping a dead rat in the soup."

Nysska quickly caught the Borealans up on what had been said so far. Kagan growled softly when she explained about Gerrit's training, and how he wasn't alone in possessing such lethal skills. Asch looked openly frightened. Singer appeared unimpressed. "The only reason he didn't kill me," Nysska said, meeting Kagan's eyes, "is that you tackled him when you did. I don't know if I've said it before, but thank you."

Asch translated quickly for Kagan. He made a sort of *chuff* and nodded.

Percy's face screwed up further. "Speaking of dropping rats in soup— what do we *do* with these people? These—Borealans, you said? Everyone in *this* distinguished company is, of course, erudite and open-minded, and it still almost sent our brains pouring out our ears when we got a good look at the Captain over there."

Kagan appeared to understand enough from Percy's tone to fix him with a baleful silver stare.

Percy went on, "But the typical citizen of the Empire still thinks Nysska's a demon from hell, come up from the steel caves to eat our souls. If we let any one of them get a glimpse of Kagan—or, for that matter, if anybody sees the young lady's eyes here and realizes they're natural—they'll get burned and hung on forks. At *best*."

Nysska translated. Kagan made a rumbling sound from deep in his chest, and Singer scowled. Asch hugged herself. Nysska saw gooseflesh rise on her forearms.

"All we want to do is go back to Borealis," Asch said. "We do not ask to come here. We want no trouble for anyone. You help us go home, we do what you say. We trust you, Nysska. *I* trust you."

Nysska cocked one eyebrow. "Your home across the ocean, you mean?"

"Well...yes..."

"Do you know how to cross the deep waters without getting killed?"

Asch changed from hugging herself to folding her arms defiantly. With her chin jutting, she said, "Give to us *skinshifter*." She didn't spit when she said it, but her inflection made it clear that she wanted to. "We make him tell how to cross ocean."

Returning to the Plainish-speakers, Nysska told them what Asch had said. "I agree with Percy. We can't let them be seen. But hiding them will take resources, which leads us to the question..."

General Cullen finished the sentence. "Do we tell the Emperor."

"Exactly."

The General steepled his fingers. "We're talking about the discovery of *another continent*. Of an entire new *species* of people. Multiple species."

"Who got here thanks to the skinshifters," Nysska said quietly. "And that dying one at the mine surely made it sound as if Valco has history with them. History of which he's claiming ignorance."

Raoul looked around at the group. "There are too many gaps. Too much we don't know. What are the Mountain Bulls trying to accomplish? Where do the skinshifters fit in with it all? ...How much shit is Valco keeping secret?"

Nysska translated. Asch said, "People here stab people in back. Just like in Borealis."

General Cullen rose and began pacing on the opposite side of the circle from Kagan. "I think, whatever we do, we need to keep the Borealans secret. No traveling by road, no stopping in town, and we take them somewhere and hide them. At least Singer and Captain Kagan. Until we can figure out how to get them back where they belong."

"That leaves a matter we have yet to discuss," Nysska said, and the General gestured for her to continue. "This shipment of chervoxite. The skinshifters seem to be everywhere. They sure as fuck *can* be everywhere. And if they get as much of that ore as Asch was talking about, and forge that many blood runes, then we could have hundreds or even thousands of people like Lockridge on our hands. And the Empire can kiss its ass goodbye."

"True. It's still a giant missing puzzle piece." Cullen exhaled, long and slowly. "One thing we *can* agree on, though, is that we've got to get the Borealans somewhere safe. Somewhere they won't be found."

Raoul raised his head. "Sounds as if you've got somewhere in mind."

The General didn't look happy about it. "It'll be at least a four-day ride, since we have to cut straight through the wilderness. But yes. Cliffside."

Raoul's eyebrows almost shot off his forehead. "Huh. *Wow*…yeah. That would work."

"What the fuck is Cliffside?" Percy said, sitting up so the cats jumped off of him.

The faintest trace of smile danced on Raoul's lips. "My childhood home."

18

According to the typically crude, hastily painted sign pegged to a tree trunk at the village border, the tiny hamlet into which the members of the Ninth Crucible rode was called Norwalk. Nysska's stomach growled loudly enough to make her horse react.

When they'd run out of food, she had suggested that she and Kagan could probably catch enough game in the woods to feed everyone, but General Cullen had insisted on a different plan. "That would take too long, and we need to keep moving. I have to get word to my men, also, before they think I've gone AWOL. You four get us some supplies, I'll make contact with the nearest Cathedral unit, and we'll meet back here."

"What about them?" Nysska had asked, gesturing at the Borealans.

"They stay here out of sight. You need to tell them that." Cullen had unrolled a map, and tapped two locations with a fingertip. "There's a village here, and a Cathedral encampment here. We'll only be gone a couple of hours each."

Nysska hadn't liked the arrangement then, and still didn't like it now, but Asch, Singer, and Kagan had all agreed to stay hidden in the woods. Nysska wanted to get in and out of this village as fast as possible.

The two blood lynxes had appeared to have a discussion about who should accompany whom and to where, which ended when Flax lifted a paw and popped Jax on the top of his head. Now Flax perched on the horse right in front of Percy, peering about her as if looking for assassins along the road, while Jax remained with the General and the Borealans. Both of the cats appeared to have developed a fascination with Kagan, and when the Ninth Crucible rode away, Nysska spotted Jax curled up against the wolf-man's flank.

"Not much to look at," Cam said, runes glowing as she peered ahead of them along the narrow, rutted road. "About as ramshackle as Robin Valley, but not even half as charming." She cut her eyes toward Nysska. "Remember Robin Valley?"

Nysska suppressed a shudder. "I'm not likely to forget the first place I ever saw a tarn."

Cam said, "How do you think it felt? For Lockridge? Having runes implanted? You said he didn't *act* like a tarn."

Nysska noticed Raoul and Percy both listening for her answer. "I don't know. They were blood runes. Not black—not tarnished. I don't know if some traitor Imperial runemaster put those runes in for him, or if the skinshifters have their *own* runemasters. As for how it felt...he was in command of his faculties. Strong as a damn ox." She thought about how she'd thrown him through a wall. "And he took punishment that would've killed any human. Would've killed most sethyds, for that matter."

"Here we go," said Percy, as they entered the village.

Their first stop was the Norwalk stables, where Raoul paid to have the horses fed. With Flax on his shoulders, curled around his neck, Percy led the way into the village proper, which wasn't much more than eight or ten buildings and a row of stalls manned by tired-looking, brown-skinned people, their complexions made even darker by countless hours toiling in the sun.

At the far end of the village, hidden around a curve in the road until now, stood a small, modest Church of the Great Silver Dragon. Their polished-tin-adorned kite had gotten hung up at the top of the steeple, so that the Dragon now dangled upside down, wings pointed at the earth. Nysska nudged Cam and indicated the church with her chin.

"Grand," Cam muttered. She moved closer to Raoul. "Let's get the food and get out of here."

Raoul nodded and pointed at the village's single inn, a squat, unap-pealing pile of stacked stone and weathered wood with a sign above the door that read, "The Hog's Egg."

Inside the Hog's Egg they saw one room, outfitted with two long bench-equipped tables and three smaller round ones flanked by three-legged stools. Nysska had seen an awful lot of places like this during her time with the Forty-Seventh Crucible. Frequented by travelers anxious to eat a hot meal, shit somewhere besides the woods, and get back on the road. Often as not polluted by local drunks. Usually staffed by a single family that may or may not have supplemented their income by selling the sexual favors of a halfway-attractive teenage child. If they had one. The sexual favors of the wife if they didn't.

A short, squat woman with skin the same color as her deep brown eyes and a head covered in tight, iron-gray springs stood behind the warped wooden plank that served as a bar, scrubbing a pot in a wash basin. Three men occupied the far end of one of the long tables, all of them drinking whatever served as ale in Norwalk. All four sets of eyes fixed on the Ninth as they came through the door.

Raoul put a more-or-less friendly smile on his face as he addressed the woman. "Good afternoon, ma'am. I'm Raoul Cullen, Commander of the Ninth Crucible, and I'm wondering who we might pay to collect about a week's worth of trail food for us?"

One of the men at the table gulped down his drink, stood, and wobbled out the door, deliberately staring at the floor as he went.

The woman behind the bar seemed roughly as impressed with Raoul and the Ninth as Singer was with...everything, Nysska thought. "Reckon we'd be happy to sell you what you want. There's vendor stalls just across the way. You good folks could just go pick out what tickles yer fancy. They'll cut you a good price. *Bronze is peace* and all that."

Raoul increased the charm in his smile. "*Bronze is law*, no doubt. But I've bought enough goods in enough small towns to know there's an advantage to getting a local perspective. Maybe you could collect the best pickings from the best vendors for us? There would be a commission for your services, of course."

The woman set down the pot she'd been scrubbing and dried her hands on a stained towel. "Oh, well, when you say it like that," she said, and Nysska couldn't tell whether the sarcastic edge to her words was put there on purpose or came through involuntarily. "Rascoe! Get your ass over here and make sure nothing walks off while I'm doing my part for the Empire."

Another of the men at the end of the table got to his feet. He looked a little steadier than the first one had, and didn't spill any of his ale as he crossed to the bar. "You got it, Delia," he said. "I'll turn a profit while you're gone, see if I don't."

"Yes, I'll see," Delia said. She bustled out from behind the bar and beckoned to Raoul. "Come on. It's a little late in the day to get the best picks, but you're in the middle of farm country. Even the bad carrots are still pretty good."

"Something's wrong," Nysska murmured to Raoul as Delia headed for the door. Her hackles had begun to raise as soon as the first drunk left the inn, and now they stood up straight.

Raoul's hand drifted to the hilt of his longsword. "What?"

"The way they were talking...it's an act."

Delia confirmed Nysska's suspicions when she paused two steps out from the inn's doorway and glanced to her right before continuing across the street. Raoul murmured, "Fill your hands." The four of them drew their swords as Flax jumped down from Percy's shoulders. Nysska led the way as they exited the inn.

Two dozen men, teenage boys, and children had gathered in the street, halfway between the inn and the Church, and stood there, staring at them. Some of the men were visibly, quakingly furious. Several more appeared to be in the throes of something more like righteous indignation. Quite a few were scared, but Nysska knew what fear inevitably became among packs of human males.

At the head of the crowd stood a priest of the Church of the Great Silver Dragon.

In cities like Tember or Caulspring, where the Church dripped with money and prestige and power, their priests wore elaborate harnesses over their white robes. Tin-plated bronze, polished until it gleamed. Mirror-finish bat-like wings sprang from their shoulders in a breath-taking display.

The Norwalk priest's wings hung from an ill-fitting harness, dull and gray, tips almost touching the ground—yet he seemed determined to make up for any lack of grandeur with the purest, most pious rage.

"Is there some sort of problem, Brother Priest?" Raoul called out in an admirably diplomatic tone.

"I should say there is," the priest snapped back at once. "Look at you. Weapons drawn, and in defense of what? Of *that*." He jabbed an arthritic, grimy-nailed index finger at Nysska. "Oh, how the Empire has stooped low! Consorting with beasts from hell! We know better than to believe your lies, demon! You didn't save the Empire at Tember! You were *in league* with that monster, and all his face-changing brethren!"

Nysska felt her jaw drop open.

"Don't argue with him," Cam murmured at her elbow. "Anything you say will only further convince him he's right."

Raoul either didn't hear Cam or didn't agree with her. He said, "Brother Priest, you have been misinformed. I was there that day. I saw what Nysska Stonegate did. Were you there, Brother Priest? Did you see it with your own eyes?"

Nysska wanted to tell Raoul to stop. He *hadn't* been there that day, and had seen nothing of the fight between her and Lockridge.

The priest sneered. He was a well-fed man, pale-skinned and heavy-jowled, with white hair worn too long for a man his age and red blotches on his cheeks and nose. "I didn't have to witness it myself," he said, as if explaining something to a dim child. "The Great Silver Dragon has *told* me what the truth is. And the likes of you, Commander, cannot hide the truth!"

Raoul let go of a breathy, raspy sigh that Nysska had come to recognize. It meant, *I am rapidly losing patience.* "Look, all we want to do is buy some food and be on our way. You can think what you want, I suppose, but we both know it's not wise to interfere with official Thaumetallicon business." His voice grew cooler. "Unless you want the Argonium Infantry to pay Norwalk a visit?"

Several of the men in the crowd blanched at that, and Nysska heard a few gasps, but it only fueled whatever perverse fire burned in the priest's heart. "Do you hear that, my brethren?" he called, his voice ringing out through village. "The Commander threatens us! He threatens us, to protect that purple-skinned demon! What kind of *man* protects a *demon?* One who's not a man at all! I say he's a skinshifter himself! Did you kill the *real* commander and take his place, monster?"

A ripple traveled through the crowd. They knew the priest. Almost certainly listened to him every Sunday. Had invested years into accepting his word as the absolute truth. *The tide has turned,* Nysska realized.

The man with the sad wings took a step forward and jabbed his finger at Nysska again. "I say they're *both* monsters! I say that demon is cursed—cursed to bear blasphemous horns and poison skin! Cursed to spit in the Great Silver Dragon's eye with every breath!"

Percy said, "All right, that doesn't even make any fucking sense," and Nysska spent about a tenth of a second hoping some kind of calming wind might smooth the confrontation over—

Until the two children jumped off the roof of the inn and landed on her back and shoulders.

Taken completely off-guard and startled enough to cry out, Nysska twisted and whirled, batting and grabbing at the two little boys who clung to her. She got a hand on one of them, pulled him free, and sent him rolling in the dirt with a relatively gentle under-hand toss. The other one leapt off of her shoulders, planting a foot in her cheek as he did, and a *pop* sounded out through the street as loud as a hammer strike.

The boy landed on his feet, stumbled, and held up his prize for everyone to see.

Nysska's false horn.

Her hand flew to the stump before she could stop herself.

The priest's eyes bulged. His entire head turned a reddish-purple as he bellowed, "*The demon wears a disguise! She's one of them for certain! Monster! Monster! The monster must be slain in the name of the Great Silver Dragon!*"

"Don't kill any of these morons!" Raoul screamed. "Just get to the horses and go!"

In the three or four seconds it took him to say those words, half a dozen men had charged forward, and Nysska had just enough time to register that the shabby-winged priest hadn't moved, content to let his faithful masses do the fighting for him. Her lip curling in a contemptuous sneer of her own, Nysska grabbed the first villager to reach her, picked him completely up and off his feet, spun him sideways, and threw him back into the crowd, bowling over the next four men.

That gave her the opening she needed. With a split-second glance over her shoulder to make sure everyone else was hauling ass toward the stables, she filled her lungs, focused on the priest in the center of the mob, and screamed.

None of these men had whatever protection had let the giant bear-warrior withstand such an assault in the mine. None of these men were even trained fighters, she didn't think. They were farmers. They were not prepared.

Nysska's scream built and built as all three levels of her voice took on a shrill, grinding edge, and as the unbridled sonic assault filled the street, it clawed its way inside the mob's heads and took every last bit of the fight out of them.

The sound of shattering glass rang out from inside the inn, and the closest men clutched their ears and squeezed their eyes shut and shrieked in pain. Everyone else—including the priest of the Great Silver Dragon—turned and ran away in panic. Nysska saw the ill-fitting wings flapping and slapping against the priest's ass as he disappeared inside his church.

Nysska let the scream die and sprinted down to the stables. Everyone else was already mounted, her horse ready and waiting. Too loud, Percy said, "Dragon's scaly balls, Nysska, you could warn us before you do that!"

Raoul barked, "Ride now, complain later!" and the Ninth Crucible took their still-empty stomachs and galloped away from Norwalk.

19

I s that him?"

Cam opened her mouth to speak, runes shining brilliantly as she stared off into the darkness, but before she could put voice to words the blood lynxes trotted into the campsite and flopped down on their sides.

Percy said, "Whoever it is, they're friendly."

The rustling in the underbrush grew steadily louder, until General Cullen guided his horse down a gently sloping section of the creekbank. He came alone, but his saddlebags were stuffed to bursting.

"This wasn't easy," he said, dismounting. "But no one's going to be asking any questions." The General unbuckled one set of saddlebags and handed them to Nysska. "If you're judicious with this, it should get you there."

Nysska allowed herself a thin smile. "I survived in the wilderness for better than a year while taking care of my invalid mother. I think I can look after this lot." Kagan had come up beside her while she spoke. Towering over her, he bent his great shaggy head and sniffed the saddle-bags' contents, and Nysska once again fought down the urge to scratch his ears. Kagan said something, and Nysska looked around at Asch for a translation.

Asch flashed an impish grin. "He says he travel farther on worse."

"Nysska?"

Cam's voice made her turn. "Yes?"

"May I have a word with you? Privately?"

Nysska ducked her head in assent. As she followed Cam a short way down the creek bed, she heard Percy murmur in sing-song, *"Somebody's in trouble..."*

Once out of both sight and earshot of the group—*well, out of earshot of the humans, anyway,* Nysska thought—Cam gestured toward a large flat rock, and the two women sat side by side.

Nysska took Cam's hand in hers. Brought it to her lips and kissed her knuckles. "Is this another attempt at talking me out of going?"

"It's another attempt at convincing you to let me come with you."

"I thought we had agreed."

Cam's eyes flashed, but she brought the runes' radiance back under control. "I don't recall agreeing to anything. I recall being outvoted."

Nysska sighed and put her arm around Cam's shoulders. Cam let her head tilt until it rested in the hollow of Nysska's neck. "I'm not saying it's perfect. I'm only saying it's the best any of us could come up with." When Cam started to protest, Nysska spoke quickly. "You saw the crowd in Norwalk."

"Not everyone feels that way about sethyds," Cam said, in a tone mingling misery and resignation. "About you."

"True enough. But put the Church aside. If anyone got even a glimpse of our Borealan...associates...they'd most likely kill them on sight." She shifted just far enough away to look down into Cam's eyes. "A Crucible on the move doesn't attract much attention. The rest of you can meet us at this Cliffside place, and I'll get Asch and Singer and Kagan there without ever coming within a klik of civilization."

Cam's features wrinkled and bunched, but Nysska watched as she smoothed them out with a clear effort of will. "If you'd told me you were going to travel through the wilderness right after you joined the Crucible, I wouldn't have worried at all," Cam said, eyes fixed on some distant point in the sky. "But now—now that we know what's really out there—shit, worse than that. Now that we *know* we *don't know* what's really out there..." She moved quickly, darting in for a kiss, and took Nysska's face in her hands. "Just promise me you won't get tangled up with anyone or anything you don't have to. All right? Discretion before valor. Yes?"

Nysska gently took Cam's hands in her own. "I promise." She kissed Cam's cheekbone, and then the place right beside her mouth, and then her lips. "Although, between Kagan and me, what*ever* might be out there, I like our chances."

"Don't say that! Just don't. Don't say anything to tempt fate, and come back to me in one piece. Promise me."

"Promise you what?"

"That you'll be careful."

Nysska gave Cam a tender, lingering kiss. "I promise."

"Is there some sort of sethyd thing that's stronger than a promise?"

"A promise is a promise, I'm afraid. But we would call it *promeso.*"

"And do you…um…*promesas?*"

"*Mi promesas, jes.*"

"All right. I don't like it, but all right." Cam paused, and laid a hand over Nysska's heart. "I love you. Come back to me."

Her stomach fluttering, Nysska mirrored the action, placing her much larger hand flush against Cam's breastbone. "I love you too. And I will."

After less intimate but just as heartfelt calls for safety from Raoul and Percy, a firm handshake and a good luck wish from General Cullen, and what amounted to an argument with Flax about why she shouldn't come along, Nysska led the way out of the campsite and into the wilderness—Nysska on one horse with Asch, Singer on the second one in front of Kagan.

"As the land gets rougher—and it will—Kagan and I will walk when we can. We need to save the horses as much as possible."

Nysska spoke in the Tongue of Truth, which Asch translated for Singer and Kagan. Asch asked, "How long is journey? How many days?"

Nysska gazed ahead of them. A cool, dry breeze made its way through the forest, sighing between the trunks of hickory and ash and pine. Their mounts' hooves made little noise as they pressed into the thick softness of the forest floor, and Nysska took a deep breath, savoring the dark, sweet scent of the wilderness. "The route we're taking…I would say a week, if nothing goes wrong."

"And…things that go wrong are what…?"

Nysska chuckled. "I'm afraid we don't have time for a comprehensive list. But the most likely candidates would include storms, impassable rivers, grumpy wild animals, and grumpier humans." She hesitated, but decided to ask the question anyway. "You are human, are you not?"

Now Asch laughed, a light array of notes that struck Nysska as optimistic. "I am human. Yes. Same as Raoul and Percy and Cam. But human is different in Borealis."

With the horses settled into a comfortable gait, reins held loose in her hands, Nysska said, "How so?"

Asch twisted around to look at her. "Empire. Valconian Empire—yes?" At Nysska's nod, Asch went on. "I think—you say if I am right—all of Kainos. Humans control Kainos. Yes?"

"Not all of Kainos is the Empire, but yes, these are human lands."

"Humans are in control."

Nysska weighed her words. "The sethyds—my people—kept to themselves until very recently."

Asch seemed to pick up on Nysska's careful turn of phrase, but didn't comment on it. "In Borealis are not many humans. Maybe we are like sethyds. Humans here—there, is God-Touched." She nodded toward Kagan. "His people are in control."

Nysska gently urged their horse around a massive, splintered tree stump. "All right, I've been meaning to ask more questions about them. The giant bear-man. Wukash. He and Kagan are both God-Touched?"

Asch grimaced. "I wish I study more. I do not have good words for this. I say 'yes,' both are God-Touched, but—not same. No one knows—how many years before now. Is God-Touched...book. Very important book. Tells story of how they are...how they are. *Ugh.* I sound stupid." She shook her head. "In Borealis, I use my own language, and people say, 'She speak very well, she is very smart.'"

"You're doing fine," Nysska said. "Please keep going."

"Story is that, many many years before now—how do I say this... One God...Into...Many. One God Into Many touches world—touches Borealis —and gives gift to people. Makes them like animals. Big, strong, fast. Gift —um. Hmm. Gift lifts them up. Makes them *better.*"

Nysska thought about that. "But not everyone became God-Touched, obviously."

"I talk about that. Near to now?" She rolled her eyes and tapped her forehead. "Soon! I talk about that soon. There are different kinds of God-Touched. Some are much like animals. Shaggy—claws, fangs, tails. Like Kagan."

"And like Wukash."

"Yes. Others are not like that. Some look much like us—like humans. Singer is like this."

Nysska's eyebrows bounced up to just below her horns. "Singer is a God-Touched?"

"Eyes like mine," Singer said from behind and to one side of them, and Nysska almost pulled a knot in her neck whipping her head around. "Can tell by that."

"You speak my tongue, too?"

Singer grunted.

"I make her help me with words," Asch said very softly to Nysska. "She does not want to."

Singer made a noise like *hmph* in response.

"This is all…a lot to take in," Nysska said.

Asch bobbed her head up and down. "Yes! Big. Huge. I know. We all know. Maybe—maybe bigger for me. Biggest for me. Here in land of *all humans?* Oh—I say more." She cleared her throat. "In Borealis, God-Touched are—at top. They are top of—of everything. Humans are at bottom. God-Touched think we are…um." She growled softly, as if at herself. "We are in dirt."

Without inflection, Singer said, "Filth."

"Filth," Asch went on. "Yes. But more bad than that. They think we are against One God Into Many. We do not get same gift. We are…" She trailed off.

"Profane," Nysska said softly.

"Profane?" Asch sounded the word out. "Profane. Yes."

"Then how did you come to be so close to Singer and Kagan?"

Asch's hands clenched into fists, but quickly relaxed. "I—am—force to marry God-Touched prince. Bear man, like Wukash? That is called *Irsan*. Wukash is Irsan. Bigger Irsan—huge, white Irsan—force me to marry Chrysaor."

"You're married to an Irsan?"

"No! No, Chrysaor is different. He is—"

Nysska waited for Asch to go on, but instead the young woman changed the subject. "I tell you how to call them. Different God-Touched. Irsans, bear-men, bear-women. They live in place called Serrenvahr. Most north part of Borealis. Huge white Irsan is Yustinian. He is like Emperor. Emperor of Borealis. Over everyone—even over Chrysaor's mother. She is…like king, but woman?"

"Queen."

"Yes. She is queen. But not over Yustinian." Asch screwed up her face.

"There is Serrenvahr, with Irsans. And Makenza—full of Timbrons. Kagan is Timbron. He protect me—with other military."

Kagan said something. Asch translated for him, speaking her native language as rapidly as storm-rain striking a roof. "Makenza is where I live," she said, switching back. Nysska noticed her speech had grown less halting, and wondered if whatever lessons she'd taken in the Language of Truth had begun to come back to her. "South of Makenza is Katorran. Full of Kogari. They are...hmm. Like little friends—Jax and Flax? Like them. But taller. Bigger. More like Kagan."

"And the humans? Is there some place they control? Or are they scattered around your Empire?"

"Humans have place. In north—past Serrenvahr, beside ocean. Cold there. Very cold."

Nysska thought about the Crags, and the sethyds dumped unceremoniously in Slocum by Cathedral troops. "I understand." When Asch didn't start up again, Nysska said, "Here's another question, then. Do all the God-Touched have silver eyes, like Singer and Kagan?"

Asch nodded. "It lets you see gift. No getting wrong." She squirmed a little. "But I see eyes in Flax and Jax...and light from Cam's metal—"

"Runes. In Cam's eyes—pieces of shaped metal, called runes. Made of argonium."

Asch said, "Argonium..." She seemed to explore the word with her tongue. "Argonium comes from...where...?"

"Argonium mines. It's dug up and refined, and the runemasters of the Imperial Colleges forge it into runes."

"But—it is in Flax and Jax."

"Right. There's argonium in their blood. No one's sure how that happens—some animals just turn up with argonium in their blood, and have silver eyes, and are at least as smart as people." At the unreadable expression on Asch's face, she finished with, "We call them 'seraphic' animals. Some poachers try to trap them and strain the argonium out of them to sell on the black market."

"So...is metal. Metal is in creatures, or *put* in creatures. And they use *magio*? Argonium lets them do that."

"Yes. In different ways. But here *magio* is called 'thaumaturgy.'"

Asch seemed to be trying to steady her breathing. "So Touch—thing that *makes* God-Touched...this argonium. Is *metal*." She chewed on her lower lip. "It is...against One Faith. Against One God Into Many. I do not know word—Nysska, in Borealis, to say those things—make God-Touched angry. Very very angry. In Borealis are many God-Touched. We do not tell them about argonium. Yes? You understand? We never tell them. Never."

Singer and Kagan had gotten slightly closer. Neutrally, barely moving her lips, Singer said, "I always think One Faith is bullshit anyway."

The conversation had trailed off after Singer's flatly stated pronouncement. Half an hour later, while the group had stopped to relieve themselves, Nysska spotted a couple of rabbits through the trees. She whispered, "Wait here, I'll be right back," and darted off after them.

Nysska had become accomplished at setting snares while living with her mother Simana in exile. With a bit of preparation and patience she knew she could've gathered up both rabbits, but at the moment she had neither, so she slid her dagger out of its sheath on her uninjured thigh.

She'd never been particularly good at knife-throwing. Her dagger wasn't weighted properly for throwing, either, but Percy had given her a few tips and a couple of lessons, and the whickering blade pinned the first rabbit to the ground. The second rabbit squealed and bolted away, as she'd expected it to, so after she'd snapped the first one's neck and cleaned her blade she went after it.

The sky had started out overcast. Deep among the trees, the white clouds turned dark, and a chill wind did its best to get inside her cloak. Nysska had never been overly bothered by extremes of temperature. She found this particular wind annoying, but only because it might make it harder for her to track the rabbit.

Nysska stepped around one broad-trunked oak tree and spotted the rabbit, ten meters away—just far enough to make her unsure she could hit it with the knife. She took a step forward—

And threw her weight back toward the oak as the ground gave way beneath her lead foot.

Nysska twisted and landed hard, teetering on the edge of a broad, deep pit. She scrambled for a grip, digging her fingers into the earth as the rest of the thin covering of leaves and twigs that had concealed the pit collapsed. Grunting and heaving, Nysska righted herself and turned, peering into its depths.

Two and a half meters down, a dozen sturdy, sharply-pointed stakes aimed up at her.

"Bear trap," she whispered, as a low roll of distant thunder sounded from the west.

Nysska studied the trap for most of a minute, circled to a spot halfway around its perimeter, and lowered herself into it. The stakes weren't that hard to uproot, and she pulled them out of the ground one by one, tossing them up onto the forest floor. Scrambling back out of the pit, she used one of the stakes to brush as much of the loose leaves and undergrowth away from the edge as she could.

Growing up, Nysska had always been taught to have respect for one creature above all others in the natural world: the bear. The great gray bear, especially, since that was the one land animal that struck fear in every sethyd's heart. She had asked her mother once, around the age of four, if the gray bears were so dangerous, why didn't the sethyds gather and go hunt them down?

"Because life is not about death," Simana had told her. "Life is about respect. How many times have you heard of a bear killing a sethyd?"

"Never," Nysska had said, yellow eyes wide.

"That's because they respect us and stay out of our towns and off our farms. And we respect them by staying out of their territory."

Nysska had taken that to heart. She had seen a great gray bear a handful of times when she and Simana lived in the wilderness, but only at a distance, and only for a moment each time. The thought of a creature that powerful, that majestic, writhing and screaming and dying in a pit turned her stomach.

Twenty minutes later, Nysska came back to the group, both rabbits dead and strung from her belt. Asch said, "Why are you gone for long time?"

"Just being a good neighbor," Nysska told her, and swung up into the saddle.

Shortly after that, the ground began to slope at a noticeably sharper pace, and Nysska and Kagan dismounted to give the horses a reprieve. The group traveled mostly in silence until the sun began to set.

In a hastily constructed campsite in the cavity left by the roots of a massive tree blown down in a storm, Nysska sat on a not terribly comfortable rock and gutted and dressed the rabbits. She caught Kagan watching her do it, and when he realized she'd spotted him, he ran a long red tongue down one side of his muzzle and up the other, followed by a wolfish grin that would have been unsettling had he not given her a playful wink at the same time.

Singer had gone off to relieve herself, and Asch came and crouched beside Nysska. "Some Esperanto comes back to me. I try to say proper sentence. Ready?"

"Sure."

"What religion do your people follow?"

"We don't," Nysska said simply. "The sethyds have never subscribed to any sort of belief in invisible omnipotent beings. As I have explained to Cam in the past, sethyds are taught that we have only one life, and that we are obliged to make the most of it." She threw Asch a quick look, expecting the girl to be some degree of horrified—but paused in her knifework to see an expression of delight on Asch's face. "Why do you look like that?"

Asch plopped down on the leaf-covered earth. "That is—that is what we—not all humans—some humans have religion, but my family—everyone who studies..." She stopped herself, catching her breath. "That was *bad* sentence. Let me try again." Asch spoke slowly and carefully. "We —my family, royal family—we believe to try to understand god, any god, is..." She cast about for the word, staring up into the trees until it came to her. "Pointless." Popping her hands up, palms out, she went on. "We do not say there cannot be god. Maybe there is? We do not know. But that is point of what we call—I think this is how you say it—Great Mystery. We do not know. There is no way *to* know. And so we..." She trailed off again, and stayed quiet long enough for Nysska to prompt her.

"Yes? You what?"

"Word is hard. Hard for *me*. When you try to know something. And you find things...about things..." Asch groaned. "I hate sounding stupid."

"You don't sound stupid. It's just a matter of vocabulary. You try to find things about things, so you can know something. That sounds like... study? Research?"

"*Tahk!*" Asch clapped her hands. "That is word! Research! My family, we research!"

Nysska had lowered her knife. "Research what?"

"Well...anything. Everything. My father, Aleksandr, he says we keep knowledge—when you get something, and...and you like it, and you want more like it, and you...um. Hmmm. Like you stack it up. On shelf. Together."

Nysska couldn't help grinning. "He's saying you collect knowledge?"

"Yes! He says we are knowledge collectors. My family is—" Another groan. "We are on top of humans. Wait. *At* top. Not *on* top."

"Your family is in charge of the humans in Borealis?"

Asch nodded. "My family is in power...*ugh*, I never learn numbers that big. Many years. Many...tens? Seven tens. And eight."

Nysska said, "Seventy-eight years."

"Seventy-eight? Is true? That is easy! Yes. For seventy-eight years, my father and his father send humans out to find more knowledge. Lost knowledge. They bring knowledge home, and learn it, and keep it."

Frowning, Nysska said, "And where does one go to find this 'lost knowledge'?"

Asch took a breath to speak, but Kagan said something that sounded awfully insistent, and Asch laughed. "Kagan says his stomach thinks his throat is cut, and please hurry with rabbits?" She stood, and put a hand on Nysska's shoulder. "I tell you more later."

They waited for the sun to set to cook the rabbits, which they ate along with a few flavorless, dry carrots and some biscuits that could have passed for dogs' chew toys. Nysska made sure the fire was out by the time the second moon rose, as the last thing she wanted was for anyone to spot a thin ribbon of smoke rising above the trees. It was bad enough worrying about wild animals that might be drawn by the scent of food.

She was about to tell Asch and Singer, so that they could let Kagan know, that she was taking the first watch when Kagan spoke up again. Asch tilted an eyebrow at him, but translated for Nysska. "Kagan says he keeps watch first. You know path we take, so you need most rest."

In the weak light of the first moon Kagan had become more like a hulking, monstrous silhouette than a real person. Nysska asked Asch, "I don't speak your language. How will he alert me if something happens?"

Asch relayed that message, and raised her eyebrows at Kagan's low, rumbling reply. "He says to sleep with your sword in your hand, because if he wakes you up, you know you have to use it."

Nysska considered that. Finally, she said, "All right, but tell him to keep an eye on the horses, too. If we lose them, we're looking at a good bit more than a week's journey."

Asch dutifully told him. Then, as Kagan settled down with his broad back to the now-doused campfire, Asch spread her bedroll out next to Singer's. Nysska heard the two young women talking softly in the language she couldn't understand. She wasn't sure what did it—the way the moonlight caught Singer's silver eyes as she looked at Asch, or the tone of her words—but lying there in the middle of the forest, Nysska realized that Singer was deeply, profoundly in love with the princess. She wondered if Asch was even aware.

The murmuring of their voices lulled her to sleep.

Nysska lurched into pained wakefulness at the sound of a mountainside collapsing, boulders scraping rock and shattering trees, and only after a couple of near-panicked seconds did she realize the sound was no landslide.

Kagan was *roaring*.

The second moon hung near the end of its arc across the sky, but clear silver light still slanted through the trees, glinting off knife blades and axe heads as the first of the men came streaming into the campsite, his sword swung back and ready to come down in an executioner's stroke.

Kagan sprang forward before the sword could fall and bit the man's face off his skull.

On her feet with longsword in hand, Nysska took a broad sideways step to place herself beside Singer and Asch and realized two things at once. First, whoever these men were, whatever their goal, they had the campsite surrounded.

Second, while Asch was now awake, Singer had vanished.

The faceless man Kagan had mauled slumped to the ground with a gurgle as screams and battle cries echoed through the forest, and chaos itself splashed across the camp.

"Stay behind me!" Nysska shouted to Asch, but when she spared a tenth of a second to make sure the young woman was still there, all she saw was an empty bedroll. "Fuck! Kagan, Asch is g—" Her words broke off when she realized Kagan couldn't understand her. "Fuck! *Fuck!* All right, then, you filthy shits, come and get it!"

The men rushed in, all around her, and Nysska caught no more than glimpses—a deep brown eye here, a lock of dark, curly hair there, a stained, badly-stitched shirt—only as much as she needed to confirm they were humans. A shallow part of her brain, a part not taken up with surviving, labeled them *brigands*. Some gang of robbers, dwelling in the wilderness, venturing out to a highway every so often to attack and loot travelers. How had they found the camp? Dumb luck? Some lice-infested asshole gone out to take a piss, who might have spotted something far away through the trees?

It didn't matter, not in that heartbeat or the next. What Nysska knew for certain was Kagan's location, looming like a great black tree, and she put her back to his and gritted her teeth.

Swords and knives reached out for her from the dark, and she knocked them aside or slipped them so that flew past, and in the immeasurable split-second that followed, her longsword found its way. The swordpoint sought out armpits and throats and ribcages and opened them up. These were no trained fighters. These were men who relied on darkness and surprise to overwhelm unsuspecting passersby, and under the waning light of the second moon they had neither.

A knife spun out of the shadows. Nysska felt an impact in her chest, but she had buckled the Thaumetallicon armor closed already and the knife that had sought her heart barely scratched her skin. She yanked the blade free, parried a brigand's short sword, buried the knife in his throat, then kicked him back the way he'd come so that he slammed into two men behind him and sent them all sprawling.

More blades thrust in, stained and dull and bristling in their numbers —how many, Nysska couldn't begin to guess—and her sword sheared through the closest one and bit deep into a threadbare knee, just as she caught another man's wrist in her vise-like grip and snapped it. A cry of agony scraped the air as her sword wrenched free and danced higher, carving a valley up the inside of a thigh, and a hot wave of blood drenched her left foot. She snapped her head forward, shattering an eye socket with her right horn, and a kick to a gut sent another man flailing backward. He crashed into two other brigands, sent all three to the ground in a screaming tangle, and Nysska lunged forward and nailed the trio to the ground. A tiny geyser of blood, turned black in the moonlight, shot skyward as she wrenched the blade free.

A lumpy, bloody berm of mangled bodies had begun to form two meters ahead of her. Yet another man charged her, misjudged the berm's height and tripped and fell forward with long knife flailing, so that his throat came down on the longsword's waiting edge.

The screams that filled the dark woods had stopped registering on Nysska's brain, but she saw an immense shape barreling toward her—a huge, bearded, axe-wielding man—and she readied herself to slip aside when his axe split the air—

An incandescent pain lanced into her upper thigh.

Nysska staggered, and saw a greasy, black-toothed man grinning up at her, both hands still on the hilt of the dagger he'd lodged in her leg, and she brought the longsword's hilt down straight into the bridge of his nose. The bone collapsed with a wet crunch and his eyes rolled back in his head as he died and his hands slid away, but he'd done his job, he'd distracted her, leaving her an easy target for the bull-necked human's axe—

Something sprang from a nearby tree and slammed into the axeman's head.

Whatever it was wrapped itself around him, covering his face, covering his eyes, tangling itself on his shoulders and under his arms, and the axeman screamed and staggered to his right, flailing at the thing with his fists, the axe forgotten.

Nysska struggled through the pain in her leg to make sense of what her eyes were seeing in the near-horizontal silver moonlight. The thing attacking the axeman seemed to have fangs, two enormous fangs—which Nysska then realized were knives—

Knives in Singer's hands, *it was Singer*—

The axeman fell to his knees as the knives tore at him, bit into him again and again, blood spraying from the raw gashes in his neck and chest, and as he slumped backward Singer's jaws gaped wide, *actual fangs* glittering in the moonlight. Nysska watched as Singer buried those fangs in the man's already-perforated throat and tore it the rest of the way free from the bones of his neck.

Somehow Nysska had sat down on the ground. She didn't remember doing so, but there she was, legs curled under her, and Kagan was beside her—hot, blood-scented breath flowing over her skin—as he packed cloth torn from his own shirt around the knife in Nysska's thigh.

Singer stepped away from the very very dead axeman and turned in a slow circle, breathing fast, eyes darting to every shadow.

"Is that—is that all of them?" Nysska tried to look for more foes, tried to listen, but saw and heard nothing. Absently she realized she'd asked the question in the Tongue of Truth.

Kagan moved away, replaced by Asch who, aside from appearing a bit mussed, didn't seem to be hurt in any way. "Yes, that is all of them," Asch said. "Just lie still. This is serious wound, and I do not want to risk pulling knife free out here in dark."

"Grand," Nysska said, and her head went light, and she found herself lying back on something spectacularly warm and soft, and when her eyes focused again she realized Kagan was cradling her head and shoulders in his lap. "That was…really something there…what Singer did…did you see that?"

"Singer takes care of herself," Asch said primly, still examining Nysska's thigh as best she could. "I do not think it cut anything—anything…too important. Your trousers make it hard to see. I get bleeding to slow down, but you lose much blood in short time."

"I'll be fine," Nysska said, not even convincing herself. "Haven't needed them…in a while…but I've got some pretty good…uh…salves. For this kind of thing. In my pack." She shifted, cranking her neck to look down at the knife protruding from her leg, and gasped at the pain as she moved wrong. "I think…I can get the, uh…trousers off…little bastard hit me… right on the seam. Let me have…anybody got a, uh…" The world swam in and out of clarity. "Sharp knife?"

"Here," Singer said, stepping forward. She wiped the blood off one of the knives she'd used to butcher the axeman and held it out hilt-first. "Sharp."

Nysska unbuckled her belt and slid it free, then carefully picked at the leather stitching until the trousers split from her waist down to the knife. "There we go. No…no problem. I'm serious, bring me—my pack, if you…"

Asch darted away, and Nysska heard one of the horses snort and stamp its foot. Another sign of the brigands' thuggish, disorganized natures. Any competent thief would have made off with the horses right at the start.

"Singer," Nysska said, her voice weaker than she would've liked. "I get…the Irsans being like…bears. And the…ones…like Kagan. They're wolves. But you're God-Touched…so what animal…blessed you?"

Singer stared at her for several long moments. As the world swam in and out of focus, Nysska couldn't tell if the hesitation was due to Singer formulating her words, or simply because she didn't want to answer. Finally she said, "Badger," and got out of the way as Asch came back with Nysska's medicine.

20

Nysska felt marginally better by the time the sun came up. The wound was deep enough, and the brigands' weapons filthy enough, that she had used almost the entire pot of what her mother had always called "anti-pus cream." That, along with a generous amount of painkiller in and around the wound, as well as an efficient and surprisingly delicate bit of stitching by Kagan, and she figured she'd be back to more or less normal in a few days.

As long as no one else attacked them, they'd be just fine.

She hoped.

Singer brought her a long stick of wood with a fork at the end, which Nysska cleaned up, fashioned into a serviceable crutch, and made use of to get to her feet.

"Are you sure you should stand?" Asch asked, after swallowing a bite of hardtack from their store of rations. "Blade went deep."

Singer seemed quietly pleased that Nysska was already mobile. Kagan was focused on his own breakfast and offered no comment.

"I'd better be standing, if we want to get to General Cullen's place before the seasons change." Nysska turned in a careful circle, surveying the results of the previous night's skirmish.

The ones she'd killed lay in a heap, covered in lacerations and puncture wounds. The ones Kagan had killed—using a battle axe, along with his fangs and claws—were in much worse shape. Hacked-off limbs and a few severed heads lay scattered about. Over to one side, in a massive, crumpled pile, was the multiply-perforated, remarkably throat-free brute that Singer had taken out all by herself.

"How many were there?" Nysska asked them. "And did any get away?"

Her normally vivacious tone subdued, Asch said, "You kill seven. Kagan kill eight more. Plus that big one that Singer did."

Nysska frowned. "Sixteen? That was it?"

Her expression unreadable, Singer gestured toward a large boulder ten meters outside the camp. "Few more over that way."

Something subtle passed between Singer and Asch. Nysska couldn't decipher it, but instead of trying she stumped over to the great rock. When she saw what waited on the other side, her eyebrows threatened to tangle up with her horns.

Six more brigands lay there, all quite dead, yet none displaying any of the telltale touches of blade or claw or tooth. Instead, sprawled haphazardly as they were, they looked very much like half a dozen marionettes whose strings had been cut mid-dance. Several elbows bent the wrong way, as did a few knees, and round, coin-sized bruises decorated their exposed skin like polka dots. All six sported broken necks.

Nysska returned to the camp, brow furrowed and eyes narrowed as she peered at Asch and Singer. "I know where I was during that fight. And I know where Kagan was. I don't know where you got off to, Singer, until you made that flashy re-entrance—and Asch, I don't know what happened to you at *all*. Would the two of you care to account for your whereabouts?"

Asch cut her eyes toward Singer. "I think what she asks is, 'Who is responsible for six other dead men.'"

Singer kept her silver eyes on the ground, and spoke in her barely-moving-the-lips way that had prevented Nysska from noticing her fangs. "I am bodyguard to Prince Chrysaor. While we are here, I am bodyguard to his wife."

Asch grinned at Nysska, as if that answered the question. Nysska considered saying, "Badger indeed," but instead went with, "Finish whatever breakfast you're having and let's get moving. We need to be far away from here when these bodies are discovered, whether that's by humans or wild animals."

General Cullen's knowledge of the terrain leading to Cliffside proved near-flawless. He had taken an Imperial map and, using a charcoal pencil, drawn a series of landmarks that proved more or less impossible to miss. Nysska had been the one scrambling up trees to make sure they were on the right track, but as even the thought of doing so made her thigh throb, she let Singer do it instead. They made good progress despite a light rain shower that caught them in the afternoon. When Nysska woke the following morning, her leg was already a bit less stiff and painful.

After their cold breakfast, they mounted up and continued on their path through the forest. Cullen had pointed out places on the map where they could ford the rivers lying in their way, and had steered them clear of ravines and canyons. Nysska held a silent hope that no more humans would show up to bar their progress.

When they stopped for a mid-afternoon rest and quick meal, Nysska gingerly dismounted and crutched her way over to where Asch sat on a fallen tree. "Give me a hand, here," she said, and Asch steadied her as she lowered herself to sit beside the young woman. "Thank you. Now. I believe we have a conversation to finish."

Asch looked surprised. Nysska couldn't tell whether it was feigned or not. "Do we?"

"Concerning knowledge, yes. And the procuring of hidden information. I was asking you where one might find such a thing."

Asch spent a few moments chewing a bite of salted meat. "Is it so hard to think? Idea of knowledge lost, then regained?"

Nysska carefully stretched her leg. "My people thrive on knowledge. The knowledge-keepers are the highest of the high in sethyd society. That was one reason we felt Emperor Valco might welcome us, when we fled our homeland after the *Krizo*. The Imperial Colleges hoard information in ways that would make the most learned sethyd proud." She winced, and stopped stretching. "You should see their libraries. The books...the *scrolls*, thousands of them, tens of thousands. I can imagine some tidbit getting lost in such a system, but you make it sound as though your father has people digging in distant caves."

Asch regarded her evenly. "I try to say this properly. Do you ever see something you cannot explain?"

Nysska snorted. She knew it came out rude, but couldn't help it. "Until we learned about your chervoxite, yes."

"Not chervoxite, then. Something you see, and you think, 'I never see that before now. They do not teach me that in school.'"

Nysska was about to shake her head—when the image of a strange structure sprang to mind. A structure she and her team had found in a cave below a mountaintop site called Altamar. How the bizarre, blocky building appeared to have been poured from some kind of melted gray rock...and how it had sat on a broad, tilted table of a different kind of melted rock, black instead of gray, inexplicably painted with faded, criss-crossing yellow lines.

"Maybe," she said.

"In Borealis..." Asch's expression turned wistful. "Humans care more about knowledge than God-Touched do. Much more. We, ah...we have to. God-Touched rule Borealis. They are on top. Most powerful God-Touched use magic to *stay* top."

"The two continents have that much in common," Nysska said drily.

"So if humans want any kind of—any kind of chance... My father's father *does* dig in back of cave when he is young man. And he find something."

Nysska shifted position to look at Asch more squarely. "What did he find?"

"He thinks it is library. It has books—hmm. Maybe I should not tell you this."

"Oh? Afraid you can't trust me?"

Asch's eyes, black as a starless night, peered into Nysska's yellow ones. Searching them. Finally, she said, "You save my life. A *lot*. And...well...I have *thought*. It is crazy thought, but I think maybe I have idea about how to get back to Borealis. But if I make you understand, I have to tell you more. Lot more. I do not know if I have words to."

Nysska became aware of Singer and Kagan watching them as Asch spoke, but Asch waved a dismissive hand. "They already hear everything I say."

Nysska shrugged. "All right, then tell me whatever you're comfortable telling me."

Asch took a long, deep breath and let it out just as slowly. "Books my father's father find—a lot fall apart when he touches them. Most. But some do not. He never see books like these. He does not think any human has—so he gathers them up and takes them back to Sanctum. Where my family lives. ...Where most humans live."

"So what was in the books?"

Asch took a deep breath. "What do you know about how world began?"

Nysska took a moment to try to judge whether or not she was being serious. "Truly? Well…nothing definitive, I suppose. I know what the humans think. The humans here, I mean."

"What about your people?"

"Our…knowledge…of how we began is…imperfect."

"How so?"

"We know the first sethyds awakened underground, and made their way up to the surface. We know the humans were already here. Past that…I don't know that any of us has actual details. That was five hundred years ago."

Asch nodded slowly. "All right. And what do humans think happened?"

Nysska made a languid gesture with one hand. "Most of them are wrapped up in the Great Silver Dragon. The Dragon flew across the land, breathing fire, and dropped his scales on the earth. Except some of them say he breathed fire *directly* on the earth, and they get really irritated with the scalies. Either way, the first humans arose from the scales. Or the fire. And they claimed the land as their own and went about doing human things. You know. Conquering shit."

Asch laughed a little sadly. "Humans as conquerors…that is…hard to see. In my head."

"The word is 'imagine.'"

"Yes—thank you. That is hard to imagine."

"And yet that's the way it is here. So what do the people of your land say about the beginning of the world?"

"God-Touched go on and on about how One God Into Many gave them gift—"

Singer broke in. "Not all of us."

Nysska shook her head. "No, I mean *your* people. The humans of Borealis."

Asch rubbed her face. "This is where my words fail me. Again. Story has many parts. Difficult to say. Is…kind of crazy."

"I'm guessing it has something to do with the books your great-grand-father found?"

"In Borealis, humans believe many things. Some agree with God-Touched. Some do not believe in anything—like your people. But my family…I think I already say—we know that we do not know. That we *cannot* know. We put…" She snapped her fingers a few times, her eyes squeezed shut. "Faith! We put faith in scholars of old. Humans who write old books my father's father find. We try to be like them."

Nysska's eyes narrowed. "What do you mean by, 'of old'?"

Asch sat up straighter. "All right. I say this, and you think I am crazy, but I say it still. There is world before this one."

Nysska frowned. "I don't think you're crazy, but I don't understand."

"It is this world, but everything before is different. People are different. And...there are only humans."

Singer said something quietly to Kagan in the Borealan language, prompting him to let out a single snorting laugh, but when Asch threw the two of them a reproachful look Singer switched back to the Language of Truth. "No, no, go on," she said, sounding mostly sincere.

Asch sighed. "We still do not know enough. Our knowledge is...not finished. We do not know if it is ever finished. But we learn that humans come from another place. In ships that breathe fire. Silver ships."

Nysska's eyes widened. "Wait, wait, wait. Just wait. You're saying the Great Silver Dragon was one of these ships?"

Asch threw her hands up. "I do not know! I never hear of Dragon until face-changers take us and bring us here. But there is more for me to say."

Nysska folded her arms under her breasts and cocked her head to one side. "Oh, by all means, go on."

"Old humans—first humans. They have different kind of magic from... from any other. Not royal blood, like in Borealis. Not runes, either. Magic is locked up inside things. Things that are...that have...many parts..."

"Sorry, you lost me."

Asch sighed. "I know. I know. I do not have proper words. But listen. This does not make any sense to me when I read it. But it does now. With face-changers, and...and with you. The first humans know something bad is going to happen."

Nysska immediately thought of the *Krizo*. "Bad such as what?"

Asch's face wrinkled up. "Bad that make everyone die, bad. Everyone in whole world. They know it is coming—they have few months? Maybe one year? But they know they cannot stop it. Some leave. Not many. Some *try* to stop it, but they cannot. Others...try to figure out how to let some people survive. Few people."

Nysska tried to imagine a *krizo* immense enough to wipe out all of Kainos and Borealis across the ocean. With a dry tongue she asked, "How?"

"Some humans try to...try to *change* themselves. Try to make themselves stronger. More able to survive."

An icy ball formed in the pit of Nysska's stomach.

"Change themselves how? ...Make themselves like animals? Like the, the Irsans, and the Kogari, and the Katorrans?"

"Maybe? We do not have books about that. But I think it makes sense."

The icy ball grew larger. "What *do* you have books about?"

"Some humans say they wanted to make...better humans. Make them strong. Fast. Smart." Asch searched Nysska's face. "Give them new skin to protect them." She took a breath and blew it out slowly. "*Violet* skin."

Nysska surged up and kicked a nearby fallen log so hard it burst apart, which made her wounded leg throb unbearably. "What are you telling me, Asch? What the *fuck* are you saying? You're saying sethyds were, were, some kind of *project*? Built by *humans*? Humans gave us our skin, gave us our *horns*? How are horns supposed to help us survive the 'bad thing'?" She closed her eyes and tried to fill her lungs, but that only made her angrier. "These shit-eating dumb-as-a-stump *humans* are supposed to have created *us*?"

Singer hadn't moved, but Kagan's hand drifted toward the battle axe in his belt. Nysska got no closer to Asch, and did her best to lower her voice. "If we were meant to survive catastrophes, then the humans responsible for—for making us what we are did a fucking *piss-poor* job."

Asch tilted her head. "I do not know. I hear skinshifters say lot of sethyds survive when Crisis hit your homeland. If your homeland is filled with humans instead, do they survive? Do *any* of them survive?"

Nysska buried her face in her hands. "Fuck. Fuck fuck fuck." She glanced down and saw that kicking the fallen log had popped some of Kagan's stitches, as blood was seeping through her bandage.

Kagan spotted it as well, and rumbled a few words as he got up and went to one of the horses. Singer said, "Inconsiderate."

Asch had fallen silent, and Nysska kept her mouth shut as well as she lay down on her bedroll and waited while Kagan stitched her up again. The ball of ice in her stomach felt as if it had fractured and sent frigid needles into all of her organs.

Improved humans.

She'd never heard such bearshit.

And yet...

From nearby, Asch said, "Can we talk more?"

Nysska said, "No," and kept her eyes closed.

21

Seven days later, Nysska walked out of the woods with only a twinge deep in her thigh to remind her of the chaotic and bloody ambush. The approaching soldiers saw her and quickened their pace.

Part of her wanted to laugh—how ridiculous that she, out of the group she had escorted, would be the most normal-looking, the least likely to provoke hostility when hailing a patrol of Cathedral soldiers. But Singer's eyes would have been impossible to explain, Kagan was out of the question entirely, and Asch spoke no Plainish. So Nysska strode out and stood in the middle of the road, the late-morning sunlight glinting off her bronze-inlaid armor, violet skin exposed and one-and-a-half horns held high, and hoped with all her heart that General Cullen's maps were accurate.

The two soldiers sauntered up to her, mounted on Imperially-trained horses, eyeing her with equal parts curiosity and confusion. They looked to be in their mid-forties. The larger of the two, whose piercing blue eyes peered out from under his helmet amid errant strands of yellow hair, said, "Are you supposed to be out here?"

"That depends, Corporal," she said, acknowledging the pattern of bronze strips decorating his collar. "Does this road border the estate of General Boris Cullen?"

The other soldier, who had pure-black eyes and skin so dark it seemed to flash blue highlights in the morning sun, stared hard at her as he spoke. "That depends. Who's asking?"

"Enforcer Nysska Stonegate of the Ninth Crucible," she answered, trying to sound authoritative without any unnecessary challenge.

The dark-eyed soldier dismounted, never taking his eyes off her. "If you'll forgive me, Enforcer, there are protocols we have to follow. Identification measures."

As he approached, slowly and cautiously, Nysska considered backing up—maybe even going for her sword. Instead she stayed put and said, "What sort of measures?"

"Well, in your case, the kind that doesn't take much time but—again, if you'll forgive me—will seem a bit personal." He paused, and she realized what he'd been staring at. "I'm going to need to make sure those horns are attached."

Nysska almost snorted laughter. Instead, locking her eyes on his, she bent forward just enough for him to reach up and take hold. One at a time—the whole one first, then the jagged stump of the broken one. Once he'd finished his verification, the soldier stepped back and bowed with an apologetic air. "Sorry, Enforcer Stonegate. The General was quite specific."

"I'm sure he was. Is he here? On the premises?"

"He is, ma'am, along with the rest of your Crucible, I believe."

"Then if you'll deliver this message to him, I shall be in your debt." She handed the dark-eyed soldier a piece of folded parchment, fastened with an amber seal.

The blue-eyed one said, "Wouldn't you like to come to the house with us?"

Nysska shook her head. "No, I'm going to stay here and wait. So if you boys would be so kind as to move quickly?"

After the dark-eyed soldier mounted up again, the two men moved out of earshot and conferred briefly, which led to the blue-eyed one giving Nysska a short, polite nod as they wheeled their horses and trotted back the way they'd come.

Nysska glanced toward the tree line, saw Asch standing there, mostly hidden behind a tree but peeking out, and made a subtle gesture: *just wait.* The young woman disappeared into the trees again while Nysska stood on the road, trying to ignore the rumbling hunger in her belly. Traveling always gave her a massive appetite.

She wasn't sure how much time had passed—it wasn't yet noon, she knew that much—when she heard a clattering in the distance. The sound grew louder and louder, until a pair of horses hitched to a coach rounded a bend in the road and bore down on her.

Raoul sat high on the driver's bench, the reins in his hands and a grin of relief plastered across his handsome face.

He brought the coach to a stop and bounded down off of it, and to Nysska's immense but not unpleasant surprise he threw his arms around her and almost lifted her off the ground in a bear-like hug. "It is *so* good to see you! Did you all make it? Is anyone hurt? I have some bandages in the coach, and there's a doctor back at the house." Releasing her, he blinked and looked around. "Where is everyone?"

Nysska raised a hand and beckoned, and Asch, Singer, and Kagan emerged from the woods and moved swiftly to the coach.

Raoul opened the door and waved them in. "Inside! Inside! Everyone inside!" He looked back and forth, up and down the road, and even though he was speaking in Plainish, his meaning was unmistakable. The three Borealans clambered in and sat, and Nysska saw that someone had fastened heavy cloth shades across all the windows.

Raoul turned to Nysska. "Do you want to ride in there with them, or up top with me?"

"Let me tell them everything's good, and I'll join you."

He nodded and climbed back up while Nysska went to the still-open door and switched to the Tongue of Truth. "We did it. This is General Cullen's estate. You're safe." As soon as a widely-grinning Asch translated that for Kagan, Nysska added, "Now just sit tight till we get to the house."

She shut the door and made her way up to the driver's bench, the whole coach tilting and creaking under her weight. Raoul snapped the reins, sending them rattling and bumping along the hard-packed dirt road.

The first thing out of Nysska's mouth was, "Is Cam all right?"

Raoul laughed. "Yes! Yes, we're all fine. Once we didn't have to travel with never-before-seen wonders of nature—or with a sethyd, no offense—"

"None taken." The image of the grimy priest in Norwalk loomed large in Nysska's memory.

"Yeah, once we were just three unremarkable humans and a couple of cats, my father brought in practically a whole Cathedral division to escort us."

Nysska frowned. "So a lot of people know where we are?"

"No—he had them peel off, bit by bit, as we got farther and farther from any towns. This place is awfully remote. So now it's just—well, I don't want to call them his 'personal guard,' but, well..."

"They're his personal guard?"

"They might as well be. Soldiers he's served with for years. People he trusts."

"You know one of the ones that found me made me let him feel of my horns?"

Raoul almost choked. "Great Dragon's earwax. Does he still have hands?"

Nysska shrugged. "It was for a good cause. Skinshifter turns himself violet, sticks on a couple of horns, you've got yourself a fake sethyd."

"Well, *that's* a horrifying thought. And of *course* my father had already considered it." Raoul steered the horses onto a different road, slightly narrower than they one they'd been on. "We'll be back at the house in no time." He cut his eyes downward, toward the coach. "How was it? Traveling with them?"

The images that Asch's wild stories had conjured in Nysska's imagination played before her like some kind of demented parade. "It was either informative, in a disturbing way, or I spent a great deal of time listening to utter nonsense. I haven't made up my mind which yet." She paused, wondering how much sound was making its way to the coach's occupants —and then realized it didn't matter as long as they kept speaking in Plainish. "Aside from spinning some pretty fantastical yarns, there's something about Asch. Something she's hiding."

He threw her a sharp look. "Something we need to worry about?"

"Hard to say...but no, I don't think so."

"She gives me the impression that the two things she's good at are talking and being cheerful."

"She is good at those, yes."

Raoul guided the horses onto another road that led into a thick stand of trees, and when they came out the other side Nysska gasped. She said, "Is that the 'house'?"

Raoul chuckled. "That's what we call it, yeah."

"Clearly being one of the Cathedral's most respected generals pays well."

"Oh, this didn't come from military money." He said it matter-of-factly, and when he followed it with, "The Cullens have been wealthy for generations," Nysska could detect no trace of pleasure in the words.

The gray stone manor toward which the coach made its way was twice the size of the Governor's Mansion in Tember, and would have looked more at home in Caulspring than out here in the wilderness. It rose four stories off the ground, with a slate roof that boasted more gables than Nysska cared to count, and dozens upon dozens of windows fitted with clear, smooth glass flashed sunlight and made the whole structure look like something made of pure silver rather than stone. Outbuildings sprawled on both sides, as if the great house had budded offspring and sent them on their way, and one of them—

Nysska squinted. She hadn't noticed before now, because of the house's grandeur.

One of them was…a lighthouse?

"Holy shit, Raoul."

"What?"

"Beyond the house. Is that—"

He regarded her quizzically as her speech trailed off. When it didn't start back up again, he said, "You knew the place was on the ocean. I mean, you saw the map."

"I knew it was *near* the ocean. I didn't realize it was *on top* of the ocean."

He grinned. "Here, I'll take us the back way so you can get a better view."

Raoul had been aiming the coach straight toward the house, but now he guided it to the right, onto a gravel lane that passed through an impeccably maintained ornamental garden and skirted the house's right flank.

As he brought the coach back around, with the great house looming on their left, he said, "There you go," and pointed to the right.

Nysska couldn't help herself. She stood up, balancing with one foot on the back of the bench, and stared with her jaw hanging open.

The accurately-named Cliffside had indeed been built at the edge of a cliff, which dropped to a rocky shore hundreds of meters below them. The view looked as if the world had simply broken and fallen away, tumbling down into a void. Far, far below, at that rocky shoreline, the gray-green ocean lapped at this breach in reality. Its own unknowable reaches stretched away to the horizon, broken only by a double-handful of wide-spaced Buoys.

A salty wind rushed up the cliff face and washed over her, as if the ocean had sensed her presence and seen fit to respond. The truth of what lay out there beyond the Buoy—the *possible* truth, if Asch hadn't lied to her—struck at Nysska like the harshest mocking words.

Come and speak with us, little land-walker, little horn-bearer. Come and find out if your yellow eyes can see, down deep beneath the waves. Come and learn the truth we have kept from your kind for so long.

Her hair had come loose from its braid at some point in the night, and she hadn't bothered putting it back that morning. Now it rose and flowed around her head, the black onyx and cobalt-blue strands waving like the shreds of a ragged battle flag, and a chill struck through her body that made her tremble so hard and so unexpectedly that she sat back down with a heavy thump.

"You all right?" Raoul asked. When she nodded silently, he said, "We're good here—the staff know what to expect." The coach slowed and stopped under a grand portico, and when the pair of three-meter-tall polished wooden doors swung open, General Boris Cullen walked out, followed by Percy and Cam.

Nysska was off the coach in a heartbeat and across the flagstones, grabbing Cam up and spinning her around.

In her ear, Cam whispered, "Careful! The General's watching!"

Nysska set her down, expression carefully neutral, and squeezed her upper arm once before she turned and gave the exact same treatment to Percy. The pale little man squeaked out, "Careful, now! I'll need those ribs at some point!"

Nysska turned him loose and, feeling a soft, furry presence at her ankles, dropped to one knee and gave both Flax and Jax a thorough petting. The big cats purred almost as loudly as a human could talk, but at the sound of the coach creaking, they broke off and dashed past her to sit and stare as the Borealans climbed out.

Nysska turned to General Cullen. He gave her a restrained smile and held out a hand. "No hugs necessary for me, Enforcer, but it is a pleasure to see you safe."

She shook his hand. "Appreciated, sir. As are your cartography skills. The land lay exactly as you indicated." Nysska turned and watched as Asch, Singer, and Kagan approached—and then whipped her head around as frantic barking sounded from inside the house. Rosie the brindle hound came scrambling out onto the portico, tail wagging ferociously, and danced around Nysska as Morrin James followed at a more sedate pace.

Rosie jumped up and put her front paws on Nysska's chest, and

Nysska petted her head and leaned down enough to let the dog lick her face, and then—

Nysska had never seen a dog do a double-take before.

Rosie's gaze locked on Kagan and froze for a long moment. Everyone else had seen this as well, and the whole group fell silent as Rosie dropped down to all fours, padded straight over to Kagan—who stood statue-still, tall as a door and almost as broad—and sat, staring up at him with her big, brown, soulful eyes.

Kagan returned the stare with his silver ones.

Another salt-laced wind blew through…

And Rosie flopped down on her side and rolled onto her back, legs poking up in the air and tongue hanging out, tail wagging.

Kagan knelt and gave her some thorough and, it appeared, expert belly scratches. He said something in his deep, rumbling voice—something that sounded like *"Doh-vra cheff-zhin-ka"*—but Nysska didn't have to speak the Borealan tongue to hear the pleasure in his words.

"Well," Morrin said softly at Nysska's elbow. "That's not something I expected to see. Ever. In my entire life."

Nysska looked down at her. Something had changed, there—something…fundamental. "Did you get…taller?"

Morrin smiled up at her, and the difference grew even more pronounced, despite Nysska's inability to put her finger on exactly what it was. "Nysska…General Cullen is setting up a—a kind of—I guess you'd call it a warehouse? He talked to Overmaster Brinn and got the whole thing cleared!"

Nysska had only ever heard the name *Overmaster Brinn*—the head of the Thaumetallicon, and one of the Emperor's closest advisors—used in hushed, reverent tones. That General Cullen would not only be on good terms with the man, but also held some sway with him, she didn't find at all surprising. "A warehouse of what? For what?"

Morrin put her hand on Nysska's arm and leaned closer, conspiratorial. "It's like a *scent bank*. You know how I told him I could only identify things I'd smelled before? Well, he's bringing me examples of *everything!* His troops are, I mean. Blades of grass, flowers, cooking ingredients, rocks, dyes, bits of dirt, animal hair, *people* hair—we're keeping them all in little glass boxes, and they're all labeled so we know exactly what they are and where they came from!"

Nysska realized what was different about Morrin—what she had now that she'd never possessed before.

Confidence.

"Who is 'we'?"

Morrin clapped her hands together. "Other Scent Sensors! We're cataloguing *everything*, Nysska, or at least as much as we can, so if there's another crime site like Summergray, Scent Sensors can identify things just like how I did with the purple linen. And you won't believe this—*I'm in charge!* Of the other Sensors, I mean. General Cullen made me the head of it! It's going to be a whole Sub-Ministry! And we're going to have scent banks all over the Empire!"

Nysska found herself grinning. "That is *amazing*, Morrin. I'm so happy for you. But does this mean you'll have to leave your Crucible?"

The young woman shrugged. "Yeah? I think so? It's all in the planning stages right now. But I'm going to be in charge! Can you believe that? *Me?*"

Nysska hugged her. "I can absolutely believe it."

General Cullen raised his voice to mass-address level. "Everyone. It's cold out here. Let's go inside and we can all get caught up."

Cam moved close to Nysska as the group filed in. Making sure they weren't anywhere near the General, she whispered, "I was so worried…"

Nysska whispered back, "I made a promise, didn't I?"

Cam's fingers brushed against hers, which had to suffice for the moment.

After explaining to Asch and Singer and Kagan that she was going to recount what happened on their journey, Nysska did just that, laying everything out for the rest of her Crucible and General Cullen and the subtly-but-profoundly-altered Morrin James. She did her best to downplay the severity of the wound to her thigh, but since her mobility wasn't quite back to normal yet, she felt she had to let her team know she'd been taken down a notch or two. She thought Cam did an admirable job of containing her concern, but knew she'd have to let her teammate—and, no doubt, whatever doctor Cullen had present—examine the wound before the evening was over.

Nysska was about to bring up a more serious topic when the doors to the sitting room in which they'd all gathered burst open, and three men wearing chef's attire wheeled in bronze-inlaid wooden carts piled high with fresh-picked mushrooms, roasted winter vegetables, loaves of bread still hot from the ovens, several roasted chickens, and—to Nysska's intense delight—ham that had not been salted to within a millim of its existence. Before General Cullen could give the go-ahead, Nysska's stomach growled so loudly that it echoed off the vaulted ceiling. Her cheeks grew a darker shade of violet as everyone, Borealans included, burst out laughing.

Two plates later, as the chefs rolled in a new cart heaped with various kinds of pastries, Nysska's eyes had grown heavy. She occupied half of a small couch, seated next to Cam, and though the dessert cart called out to her, she set her plate on a small walnut end table and folded her hands over her full belly.

"You look like you could use a nap," Cam said. "We've been eating almost this well the whole time you were traveling, by the way. I might have to request a larger-sized uniform."

A thick brown bear-skin rug lay on the stone floor in front of a massive, roaring fireplace. Nysska regarded it with envy. "You're not wrong about the nap. I could slither down onto that bear skin and sleep for about eighteen hours. Even when I was living with my mother in the wilderness, I at least fashioned us decent beds." She spotted General Cullen on his way to the dessert tray, and with a brief squeeze of Cam's knee said, "Pardon me for a second."

Nysska came around to the other side of the cart. "General. Thank you for this spread. I had begun to forget what real food tasted like."

Cullen cast a quick look toward the Borealans, who had clustered together not far from everyone else, still eating with great gusto. Pitching his voice low, he said, "So it was mostly trail rations? I wondered if that large, hairy fellow over there might not bring an entire deer to the camp-fire each night."

Nysska gave him a lopsided smile. "I'm sure he could have, if we'd had the luxury of building a fire large enough to cook a deer."

He dipped his head. "Good point. So—you walked over here with purpose. Time to start thinking about next steps, then, now that our unusual visitors are safe?"

"Yes, sir."

He looked around the room. "Why don't we give everyone time to finish eating, then we can dig in?"

"Thank you, sir."

It took another half hour, but eventually even Kagan had had his fill, and the chefs returned to wheel the now-mostly-empty carts back to the kitchen. General Cullen called for everyone to gather in a rough circle, rearranging couches and chairs as need be, and Nysska translated for the Borealans. "I'd better sit next to them," Nysska said to Cam. "So I'm not shouting across the room."

"Of course." Cam kept her face neutral as she leaned closer to Nysska's ear. "But you and I have some catching up of our own to do later."

"Don't I know it," Nysska shot back, and rose to take a seat next to Asch. "How do you feel?" she asked the young woman in the Tongue of Truth.

"You need to roll me into nearest bed." Asch patted her belly. "Well... after long, hot bath. If I can get one. That is first good, solid meal any of us have since we are in Borealis. Maybe I like your Empire more now." Asch nodded toward General Cullen. "He is rich, yes?"

That caught Nysska a little off-guard. "Well...yes. Very rich, I would say. Why?"

"I have idea—about how to go home. I think, first, you need to teach me language better. So I do not sound like stupid girl when I talk. Do that, and I tell you all about idea, but it takes...I do not know word. Things that let you do other things. Things you use to build. You buy things, and do things with them."

Nysska arched one eyebrow. "Resources?"

"*Tahk!* Resources, yes! Idea needs lots and lots of resources. It is big and crazy and maybe it does not work at all, but if it does, it will need much resources. And General Cullen is one I talk to about this, yes?"

Nysska said, "I'd say so, yes," as the General clapped his hands together a single time. The resounding *crack* brought all conversation to a halt and focused every eye on him.

"The Cathedral trains its soldiers well," he said, voice echoing. "And quite thoroughly. Following all of its rules and strictures is how I have risen to my current rank. The situation in which we now find ourselves, though—and by 'ourselves,' I'm afraid I mean the entirety of the Empire— defies any procedure I've ever heard or seen written anywhere. As my son put it a few days ago, we are all exploring unmapped land."

Nysska translated quickly and quietly, and appreciated how Cullen paused to let Asch do the same for Singer and Kagan.

"One of the things that does still apply from my military career, however, is the delegation of tasks to those most suited to complete them. Raoul, you've been eyeball-deep in all of this since it began. Why don't you make sure everyone is reading from the same scroll here?"

Nysska couldn't tell whether or not Raoul had been expecting that. His face gave nothing away as he got to his feet, the General taking a seat next to Morrin. To Nysska's growing surprise, she saw General Cullen lean over and say something to Morrin, who flashed an easy smile as she answered him.

Raoul cleared his throat. "I'm just going to sum everything up best I'm able to. The current situation, for which we have no name yet, began with the murder of Runemaster Naveed Olkoff at the Imperial College of Taurus Hill. Something interfered with the functioning of Seer Camble Delakroy's runes and prevented us from apprehending Olkoff's killer in the customary fashion. Fortunately for us Enforcer Nysska Stonegate had joined the Ninth Crucible by then. Using methods to which none of us were accustomed, Nysska guided our Crucible to the discovery of a group of people with the ability to change the pigmentation of their skin to such a degree that they could take on the appearance of someone completely different. Even to the extent of impersonating specific men and women. We decided to call them 'skinshifters.'"

Singer, who seemed to have learned at least that word in Plainish, spat on the floor.

Ignoring that, Raoul went on. "We tracked the movement of a skinshifter known as Lockridge to a place called Altamar, where we found evidence that the skinshifters had used metallurgy to alloy argonium runes with an unknown metal, creating an entirely new division of thaumaturgy. We referred to the results of this as 'blood runes,' because of their reddish color and glow. Anyone with an idea for a better name, please speak up, because I feel a little silly every time I say it." He paused. "No? Blood runes it is, then. One of the properties of blood runes, as we learned first-hand, is that they can re-animate cadavers. These cadavers are undetectable to Sensors—at least until they start rotting, when they become detectable to anyone—and were used to kill Runemaster Olkoff. We discovered that Lockridge had designs on the Governor of Tember, Wendell Anwar, and Nysska raced back there in an attempt to prevent Anwar from coming to harm. Sadly, Lockridge had already killed Anwar and used blood runes to re-animate him, with the intent of having the impostor issue new decrees, presumably benefitting the skinshifters, before his body began to decay. Nysska dispatched Anwar's hostile corpse, then defeated Lockridge in a, to hear her tell it, embarrassingly public skirmish."

With delight in her voice, Morrin said, "So all of that *is* true? The songs aren't lying?"

Percy, who had the blood lynxes in his lap—both of them staring at Kagan—favored Morrin with his typical imp-grin. "Oh, she's every bit the badass you always thought she was."

"Let's try to stay on-topic," Raoul said—but favored Morrin with a quick smile. "Except to say that Nysska is *more* of a badass than the songs let on." He cleared his throat and resumed. "Now we've been made aware that there is another entire land mass across the Salt Ocean, with another, very different empire, and that the skinshifters have learned how to *cross* the ocean. They have also located a source for this metal—the metal which I'm told is called 'chervoxite,' which combines with argonium to form blood runes—and kidnapped our visitors here to force one Prince Chrysaor from Borealis to supply them with enough chervoxite to make thousands upon thousands of blood runes.

"We cannot allow this to happen. One of the other effects the blood runes can have is to imbue an individual with all the strength of a Tarnished One without any of the related mental instability. And just recently, we learned that if you take chervoxite, grind it into dust, and sprinkle it around a crime site, it nullifies the ability of any Sensor to read the site and trace the perpetrator. Or perpetrators."

General Cullen broke in, speaking directly to Nysska. "I've received dozens of reports during your journey here. Other towns, other places, rife with crimes that no Sensor, no Crucible can touch now." He looked around the room. "There is a wave of unrest spreading. The Emperor doesn't want to acknowledge it, especially not publicly, but the Argonium Infantry has been dispatched to quell two territorial border wars in just the last week. What could have happened at Summergray…what I believe was *supposed* to happen…is taking place in dozens of other locations."

Morrin surprised Nysska again by speaking to the group. "As far as the metal dust corrupting the crime sites, we've been working on ways around that. I'll let everyone know as soon as we have something solid."

"So now," Raoul picked back up, "we've taken the skinshifters' hostages away, removing their political leverage—except that the huge shipment of chervoxite may have already arrived on Kainosian soil, not to mention that if Prince Chrysaor doesn't *know* his wife and her companions are safe, they might as well still be in the skinshifters' hands. Therefore…" He counted items off on the fingers of his left hand. "We have to find this shipment of chervoxite. We have to get Princess Asch and Singer and Kagan safely back to Borealis. And we have to do this before the skin-shifters forge enough runes to create an army of...I don't know what to call them. Blood-tarns? We have to stop them from creating this army, because if they do, they'll overrun us in a fucking heartbeat." He glanced around the room, eyes growing sorrowful. "The problem is that we have no idea where the shipment might be, no idea where they're forging these runes or how many they've already finished, and no idea whatsoever how to cross the ocean without getting killed by...whatever's out there."

Once everything had been translated, Asch grabbed Nysska's forearm. "It is that—what I want to talk to General Cullen about. Crossing ocean."

Percy's eyebrows rose. "What'd she say?"

Nysska spoke to the group. "She said she might have an idea about how to get her and her friends back to Borealis." Getting to her feet, she went on. "And I have a suggestion addressing the first two problems...but it's crazy, and no one here is going to like it. *I* don't like it. So it might be best to discuss in a smaller group—one that only includes people who are also crazy, and might end up getting declared enemies of the Empire."

Cam frowned. "What, you're saying your idea to save the Empire might get us branded traitors?"

Nysska nodded. "And hung on forks. Yes."

"Well, you heard the lady," Percy said, his icy blue eyes darting from face to face. "Anybody want to step outside and let the grownups talk?"

Morrin continued her new trend of astonishing Nysska by saying, "*Fuck* no—I've got to hear this."

No one else moved.

Nysska sighed, and translated for the Borealans. None of them moved, either.

"Well, don't keep us waiting," General Cullen said. "What's this grand plan that's going to kill us all?"

Two hours later, after Nysska had talked and talked and answered questions and talked some more, the group decided a break was needed, and General Cullen suggested they all get some rest until time for dinner.

Nysska stepped out of one of Cliffside's lavish restrooms and, not knowing what else to do with herself, headed back toward the sitting room. She had come to think of it as the "war room" at this point, and knew she could either go over the idea that had become a plan a few more times, or perhaps facilitate the talk Asch wanted to have with General Cullen, additional language lessons or not.

She didn't make it back, as a slim, dark-russet arm snaked out of a doorway, a hand with a familiar grip fastened onto her wrist, and Cam hauled her out of the corridor.

Trying not to laugh as Cam closed the door behind her, Nysska turned to take in her new surroundings. The two women stood in what appeared to be an office. Or a small library. Or an office with a library. Thick rugs on the floor stopped just shy of a couple of plush leather chairs in front of a stately polished-wood desk, behind which sat a larger, grander chair, and beyond that a set of glass double doors that led outside. Nysska could hear the faint pounding of the surf far below.

Cam slid into her arms, the runes in her eyes flashing, and pulled Nysska's head down into a hungry kiss. Nysska had barely caught her breath from that when Cam took her hand and led her to one of the leather chairs, where they sank down together, Cam straddling Nysska's hips. Fingers twining into Nysska's hair, Cam's lips left a trail of soft yearning from her horns down to her eyelids, across her cheekbones and to her mouth again. Nysska wrapped Cam in her arms and pulled her tight, and they both laughed at Cam's gasp.

"Careful, now—I know you missed me, but I won't be much good with punctured lungs."

Nysska twisted her neck to look back at the door. "You know we can't *do* anything. Not here, not right now."

Cam kissed her again. "I know. I know. But if I'd had to wait a single second longer to taste your lips again, I might've died."

Nysska made a sound deep in her throat and nuzzled Cam's neck. "Under other circumstances I'd already have your thighs on my shoulders."

Cam groaned, and pressed Nysska's face to her breasts, horns resting on collarbones. "Maybe we could slip away—find somewhere more priv—"

Her words broke off and Nysska's breath clenched in her windpipe at the sound of General Cullen's voice right outside the door. Nysska couldn't understand him at first, the words muffled, but they quickly resolved into, "...thought I saw Enforcer Stonegate duck in here."

The handle turned halfway and paused, and Nysska surged up off the chair, the wound in her thigh flaring in sudden agony. Dragging Cam behind her, Nysska skirted the desk, opened one of the glass doors as quietly as she could manage, and the two of them slipped outside—

Onto a small stone balcony overlooking the ocean.

It wasn't more than five meters wide, and about half that deep, just room for a couple of chairs and a little table suitable for setting a cup of coffee. Precisely the kind of place where General Cullen could step out from his office and relax while he enjoyed the sea view. Looking around in a state approaching desperation, Nysska saw no other balcony anywhere close to theirs, and below them nothing but a sheer drop for several hundred meters.

She closed the glass door, and she and Cam flattened themselves to a wall right next to it.

If General Cullen did so much as take one step out onto the balcony, he would see the two of them, which would lead to a raft of questions about why the pair was sneaking around his office together...which might then lead to suspicions regarding the nature of their relationship. Or, worse, confirmation of suspicions he might already hold.

The General's voice came again, muffled but clear enough to understand: "Would have sworn I saw her come in here. Ah well. I suppose I was mistaken."

The latch to the same glass door she and Cam had come through twisted and released, and Nysska thought her heart might stop, but though the door swung halfway open, no one stepped through it. Cullen's voice reached her ears again, perfectly understandable now. "There. Pleasant enough outside for a breeze." She heard what must have been the chair behind the desk creak as weight settled into it. "Have a seat." Then, after a pause: "Well?"

Raoul's quiet voice carried out onto the balcony. "I'm—not sure where to begin, sir."

"I've seen the confusion plastered across your face every time we've talked. Tell me why."

After a pause, "Surely you know...? Sir?"

Nysska heard the General's chair squeak, then his footsteps. She imagined him pacing back and forth behind his desk. "Son...I've been hard on you. Perhaps too hard. I acknowledge that and—for what it's worth—if I've caused you pain, or...made you feel...small...you have my apologies."

Just at the edge of her hearing, Nysska detected a tiny, sharp intake of air. The kind of minuscule gasp that often precedes a sob.

"I've always stressed the importance of rules, son, I know I have.

Maybe I rang that bell too hard, too many times. But I was always waiting for you to see *past* it."

Half-choked, Raoul said, "You were…what?"

"Dragon's teeth, son, you saw me bend rules growing up! I even broke a few. When they needed breaking. But I swear, once you'd gotten the first half of what I was trying to teach you lodged in that skull of yours, it was like there wasn't room for anything else."

Raoul's voice rose a notch. "Are you saying…all the times you spent *hours* screaming at me…all the times you *humiliated* me. In *public*. That was all *my fault?*"

The chair squeaked again, sharply, and Nysska envisioned General Cullen's weight dropping into it. Cullen heaved a weighty sigh. "No. I should've done things better. I let frustration get the best of me, at your expense, and I can only ask that you forgive me. Or perhaps hope you can, one day. I just wanted you to stop being so damn rigid all the time and see the possibilities around you." The chair squealed as Cullen's weight shifted. "But that's what you *did*, son. With that Dragon-damned Lockridge business. Everything you accomplished at Altamar. You were faced with a situation for which no rules *existed*. And you changed. You adapted. You broke the rules when you had to, and you pulled off a bloody miracle."

Cam tugged on Nysska's arm, and when Nysska lowered her head, Cam breathed into her ear, *"We shouldn't be hearing any of this."*

Nysska shook her head, fervently wishing they could be anyplace else.

Raoul sounded as if he might not know where he was as he spoke. "That's why you were…so different…when we met you at Summergray? That's why you've been so…" An uncomfortable pause. "So *nice* to me?"

"What I am, son, is proud. As I've told you. You made me so Dragon-damned proud that day—the day you and your Crucible undid Lockridge's plans. I knew you were meant to be great. I always knew it. I was just…waiting for you to find your greatness on your own."

"Sir, I—" A chair moved on the stone floor. "Permission to speak freely, sir."

After a pause: "Granted."

Raoul cleared his throat. "Actually…permission to speak as a son, not a Commander."

"Say what you have to say, Raoul."

"Sir…what has been established over twenty-seven years cannot be wiped away with a few kind words."

Nysska heard a note of incredulity in General Cullen's voice. "You're rejecting my apology?"

"I'm glad you approve of the actions my Crucible and I took, sir. One of the things I've always wanted most was to provide distinguished service. So no, I'm not—exactly—rejecting your apology."

"Then what *are* you doing? Exactly?"

"I'm saying, Father...that you've been a right bastard to me my entire fucking life, and if you think I'm going to welcome you with open arms after you spend a few days talking up my military service, you're sorely mistaken."

A silence fell. Stretched out. Nysska dug her fingernails into the palms of her hands.

The General's words came out thin and flat. "I'm glad you feel so comfortable speaking your mind."

"You know what *I* did, all those years you were 'waiting for me to find my own greatness?' I hated you. I wished you were *dead*. And when that didn't work, when you didn't collapse from a heart attack just because I hoped you would, I started to wish *I* could die."

"Son—"

"How many times did I stand on that balcony, the one right behind you, out there with my hands on the rail so tight they cramped, hating myself because I didn't have the guts to jump? How many hours did I spend kicking myself in the teeth because I wasn't brave enough?"

"Raoul—I never—"

"Do you know...when I swear. Just like everyone else—I swear to the Great Silver Dragon. Dragon's bones, Dragon's scales. Dragon save me. But do you know what I think of, when I think of God? That first split second, that fraction of a heartbeat, when the thought of *God* enters my head. I don't see the Great Silver Dragon. I see *you*."

Nysska heard another choking, hitching breath, and couldn't tell who had taken it, Raoul or the General.

"Son—please—"

"I'm glad you're proud of me, Dad. But you want me to forgive you? Maybe you can forgive *me* for not giving a greasy rat shit."

Thunderous footsteps crossed the floor, and the door opened and slammed.

Nysska looked down at Cam, who mouthed, *What do we do?*

She shook her head: *I don't know.*

Nysska almost jumped out of her horns when the chair that had sat behind the stately desk hurtled through the unopened glass door and out over the balcony's edge, the wake of shards behind it flashing and flaring in the sunlight.

Receding footsteps reached them. Slower. Heavier. The office door opened and shut.

Into the silence, Cam murmured, "How long do we stay here?"

Nysska had no idea what to say, so she kept her mouth shut.

22

The setting sun threw half of Caulspring into red-tinged shadow. Nysska sat with Cam, Percy, and the two blood lynxes in a dingy room in an even dingier inn, poring over the tower's layout. She had the parchment spread on an uneven wood-plank table, weighted down with a plate, a coffee cup, and two of her knives.

"It won't get any different, the more you stare at it," Percy offered after a deep swig of ale.

Nysska raised an eyebrow at the mug in his hand. "Your ass is on the line along with the rest of ours."

"It's never *my* ass I'm worried about," Percy said, scratching Jax's chin. The big silver-eyed cat lay in his lap in what appeared to be a fully boneless state, loudly purring. "Relax. I'll be sharp."

Cam stood behind Nysska, hands on her shoulders, and peered at the drawing. Sketched out in charcoal was a fair likeness of the Imperial Archive, where every record the Emperor kept—scratched down by the desk-wearing scribe that followed him everywhere—stayed locked up, preserved, waiting for this or any future head of state to peruse. Cam leaned down and nuzzled Nysska's ear. "Well," she breathed. "As ideas go, you can't say this one isn't bold."

"Bold is one word for it," Percy said between swigs. "Place isn't quite Fort Slade, but it's close."

Nysska's brows drew together. "What is 'Fort Slade'? I've heard the name here and there, but I never got around to asking about it."

Cam kneaded Nysska's trapezius muscles. "It's the Empire's argonium mine. *The* argonium mine."

Nysska leaned into the massage. "What, there's only one?"

"Only one we know about," Percy said between swigs. "Nobody can get there. It's surrounded by, I shit you not, its own dedicated army, including a whole company of Argonium Infantry." He made a vague toasting gesture with the mug. "Bronze may be law and peace and all that shit, but argonium's what makes the Empire run. And they protect the *fuck* out of their investment."

Nysska sighed and leaned over the map again. "Well, then, I'm glad that's not the place we have to break into."

The Archive consisted of a short, blocky tower, sealed away from the rest of the city by a twelve-meter-high brick wall. The wall itself was more of a formality—an announcement of how seriously the Cathedral took the Archive's security. It had four locked gates, but only a single soldier stood watch at each one. Still, Nysska had stealthily made her way around the wall's perimeter, taking note of every angle, and there was no way anyone could scale that wall without being seen by hundreds or even thousands of city-dwellers.

The details inside the wall were less clear. Raoul had done guard duty at the Archive years ago, so they had no way of knowing what might have changed since then.

Each of the four gates in the outer wall, to Raoul's recollection, opened onto a narrow bridge that spanned a fifteen-meter drop down to sharp rocks. The bridges led to the tower itself. There they ended in more locked gates, behind each of which five heavily armed and armored soldiers stood ready to defend any potential incursion, as well as to sound an alarm that would bring two-score more troops within minutes.

The outside of the tower, however, presented an opportunity created by the very wall meant to seal it off from the city. Nysska contemplated it, running risks and consequences in her head for the thousandth time. "Is this insane? Are we insane for considering it? Am I insane for proposing it?"

Cam sat down on a stool across from her. "If not this, then what? We go to the Emperor and tell him what we've found out?"

Percy said, "Yeah, and then he wants to know *how* we found out, and where, and who told us what. And we have to spill every fucking bean about Asch and Miss Silver Eyes and their big hairy friend."

Cam had been nodding at Percy's words, and added, "Plus, how are we supposed to trust Valco when we know he's got runes of his own? He might be doing what he's doing in exchange for the skinshifters sparing his life when they come in and tear the Empire apart."

Nysska sighed. She looked down at Flax, who lay at her feet. "Are you sure about this, too?"

Flax stared Nysska in the eye for a couple of seconds, then rolled over on her back. Nysska smiled as she bent down to scratch blood lynx belly —and almost jumped off her stool when the door swung open.

Raoul wobbled in, smelling of ale and sweat and badly-mixed perfume. He threw off his cloak and sank down onto the room's single, sagging bed.

Nysska said, "Well? Did you get what we need?"

Raoul pulled off his boots. "I did. It only cost me five pitchers of ale and, I have no doubt, a hangover worthy of the Dragon Himself, but yes. The man's name is Benjamyn Hunter, he's married, and he's on the East Gate tomorrow night." He leaned forward and put his face in his hands. "I would give my left nut for some clean water."

Percy stood. "Well, since I'm the only one who looks like an average human *and* can walk in a straight line, allow me to oblige."

"Thank you." Raoul stretched out on the bed. "Hunter has his own place, since he's married. No invading any barracks. I've got the address." He felt of his face with one hand as if it were a foreign object. "I cannot handle booze the way I used to."

Cam picked up a charcoal pencil. "Well, for Dragon's sake, tell me where Hunter lives before you pass out."

Nysska watched Cam and Percy and the two cats silently, and wondered what business she had asking any of them to risk their lives for her.

An hour later, with Raoul safely snoring under Percy's watchful eye in the room at the inn, Nysska and Cam stole through Caulspring's darkest streets and alleyways. No one could know that a sethyd Enforcer and a Sight Sensor were on the prowl, so Cam kept her eyes shut, relying on the clicks of her rings and Nysska's guidance to navigate.

Caulspring lived and breathed at night every bit as much as during the day, if not more. It seemed to Nysska very much like Tember, only on a grander scale. The brothels bigger. The violence of the street-corner robberies more brutal. The desperation of the populace to seek out whatever bit of gaudy joy they could get their hands on nearly palpable.

Corporal Benjamyn Hunter lived on the fourth floor of a red brick building with a central courtyard, and Nysska led Cam up a narrow wooden exterior stairway. Nysska had taken careful note of which windows had lights burning within, and once they made it inside, she went to a door right beside the rooms where Hunter and his wife Ulla lived. There had been no light visible from the outside and, ear pressed to the door for a quick listen, she heard nothing within. The latch turned under her touch. She led Cam through silently and shut the door behind them.

Cam whispered, "Well, this is lucky for us—" but broke off mid-sentence as she clapped a hand over her mouth and nose. "Oh, Dragon fuck me," she hissed, her runes powering up. "No wonder this place is empty. It smells like someone died and rotted while taking a shit. And then the shit died and rotted."

Nysska tried her best to breathe through her mouth. "Well, here's hoping we don't have to stay long."

Cam nodded and turned to the wall shared with Benjamyn Hunter's rooms. She draped her cloak around her head and arms and, leaning against the wall, made a sort of tent with it, so that the brilliant silver thaumaturgical flare would alert no one outside the horrible-smelling flat.

"All right," Cam murmured. "Here we go…"

Nysska moved to her shoulder. "What can you see?"

"Hunter's wife, I'm assuming. And…yeah, they have a child. Hang on." She moved farther down the wall. "Looks like it's an infant. Got a crib… and a name…it's a little girl. Name's Charri. And…" Cam fell silent. A moment later she pushed away from the wall and let her cloak drop back into place, her eyes fading to the simple gleam that granted her average human vision. "I've got what we need." Her face clouded. "It's shitty, and I feel shitty about doing this, but I've got it."

"It won't hurt him for long."

"No…until someone realizes what we've done. Then it'll hurt him in a whole different way."

"Not if we don't get caught. Come on, let's get going."

The following night, once the sun was down and Corporal Hunter had taken up his post at the East Gate, Nysska stood in a shadowed corner thirty meters away. Watching. A heavy leather pack across her back, its contents hot enough to make her sweat even on an evening as cool as this one. She watched as a tiny, dirty, homeless boy—one Raoul had picked by hand that afternoon—came running up to Hunter, breathless, and pushed a slip of paper toward him.

"What's this?" Hunter snapped, making no move to take it.

"It's about Charri," the boy wheezed, and even from that distance, Nysska could see Hunter's face clench. He snatched the paper away and, as the boy dashed across the street and disappeared into an alley, read it by the light of one of the torches ensconced on the wall on either side of the gate.

Hunter's knees came close to buckling. He crumpled the paper in one hand, took an unsteady step, and sprinted away from his post, footfalls pounding, sword rattling in its scabbard.

He hadn't made half a block before he collided with a slightly-built, dark-bearded man, who apologized profusely and made sure Hunter was all right. Hunter swore at him—by then he'd gotten too far away for Nysska to make out the actual words, but the tone was clear—spun free and sped away, headed home.

Nysska knew what the note had said. She'd helped Cam compose it, based on the selection of medicines on Hunter's shelf over the baby's crib.

Come quick. Her lungs. It's bad.

The dark-bearded man crossed the street, impish blue eyes and familiar grin flashing. "Any trouble?" Nysska asked.

"The only trouble will be getting this fucking stain out of my whiskers," Percy said, handing her Hunter's keys. He indicated the pack. "No trouble there?"

"None. Relax. You've done brilliantly."

"Product of a misspent youth." His grin grew wider. "You realize it's impossible to take you seriously right now."

Dry as dust, Nysska said, "What, do you not think the moustache suits me?"

Her disguise was simple enough. Brown body paint hid the violet skin, an oversized brushy moustache covered her lips, pillows inside her dark blue robes turned her lithe frame into that of a tall, plump man, and an oversized Estmani turban decorated with feathers concealed her horns. Only her eyes might have given her away, but the watersight lids turned them green, and she didn't plan on making eye contact with anyone in any case.

As disguises went, she thought, it could have been much worse. The only part she truly minded was how itchy the chervoxite flakes were. Percy and Cam had dusted her with a liberal amount taken from Summergray. If she was really doing this, putting up with a bit of discomfort was a small price to pay for not having the crime site read by some other Sensor.

As Percy stifled laughter, Nysska thumped a hand on his shoulder and crossed the street, her gaze locked to the paving stones directly in front of her. One thing she recognized about cities, whether human or sethyd: assemble a big enough population, and every one of them will become intensely focused on minding their own damn business. Personal interaction was no more welcome here than in Patrinomonto's capital, and since she moved with confidence and purpose, no one opposed her as she fitted the purloined key to the east gate's lock, swung the gate open, and disappeared inside.

If the plan was going to fail, this was the perfect time for it. The time when Nysska was wide-open vulnerable—clearly visible to anyone looking out from the tower.

She ducked into the ink-black shadows of an alcove to the left of the gate and waited.

Nysska could hear pedestrians passing by on the street, just on the other side of the gate. Laughter. A couple deep in a heated argument. The clip-clop of horses' hooves as a coach rattled past.

Nysska's nose wrinkled when she got a whiff of the shit bucket tucked into the alcove's back corner. It smelled almost as bad as the room that shared a wall with Hunter's place.

When she heard no doors opening, no orders barked, Nysska repositioned herself slightly—still in the thickest shadows, but close enough to the edge to get a good look.

The bridge that spanned what she had decided to call the "rock moat" was wide enough for a single human to walk its length, and around ten meters long. It led to the second gate, set in the tower's base—more like a large, heavy door—where a window at eye height would let anyone standing on the other side get a good look at whomever decided to use the bridge to approach.

Unless that someone used the bridge the way Nysska was about to use it.

She shucked the padded robe and peeled off the turban first, folding them and setting them down as far away from the bucket as she could while keeping them out of sight of anyone in the tower. Then she took off the pack, re-fitted it so that it pressed against her chest instead of her back, and slipped over the side of the foot bridge.

The bridge's underside showed her how it had been constructed: stone slabs laid atop a bronze-reinforced wooden frame, just as Raoul had said. With her hands pressing against one side of the frame, feet jammed against the other, and her back flush to the underside of the stones across which a person was meant to tread, Nysska slowly, carefully worked her way sideways, crab-walking from one side of the bridge to the other. Giving the jagged rocks directly below her as baleful a glare as she could muster.

Once she reached the tower it got just the slightest bit easier, at least for a few minutes. A narrow ledge level with the bridge ran around the squat tower's perimeter, and Nysska worked her way out from under the bridge, used the corner formed where it met the tower to gain leverage, and pulled herself upright, flattening against the tower wall.

One mistake, and she'd fall to her death in the rock moat.

On the other hand, thanks to the positioning of the gates and the wall, no one could see her where she clung to the bricks.

She had transferred the pack to her back again as she'd climbed out from under the bridge, and now came the part of the plan about which she was honestly, genuinely nervous. If she lost her grip…if her feet slipped from the ledge…if Raoul's information proved outdated…

Nysska couldn't think about the consequences. Wouldn't *let* herself think about them.

She worked her way out along the ledge until she reached a small, barred window. Nysska pulled a tough length of black rope from a pouch on her belt, passed one end of the rope around one of the bars, and tied it with a single-hand knot her uncle had shown her when he'd taken her rock climbing years ago. Wrapping the rope around her wrist gave her the anchor and leverage point she needed to be able to lean back from the wall, toes firmly planted on the ledge.

Nysska reached over her shoulder, tugged the flap of the pack loose, and whispered, "All right, come on out, but be really *really* careful."

Fluid as a fish in a lake, Flax shimmied out of the pack and perched on

Nysska's shoulders. Percy had worked a heavily-stitched bronze loop into the blood lynx's harness and tied another, much longer length of rope securely to it. Nysska painstakingly pulled the coiled length of rope out of the pack and used the same one-handed knot—reversed, since her left hand was busy keeping them both from falling to their deaths—to tie the end of the longer rope to her own belt.

Flax moved on Nysska's shoulder, and when Nysska turned her head it put her nose-to-nose with the big feline. "Are you still sure you want to do this?" she whispered. "I won't force you. And Percy will kill me if anything happens to you, no question."

To Nysska's amusement—which felt misplaced and inappropriate—Flax nuzzled Nysska's nose with hers, and then looked upward.

Nysska took the big cat in her free hand, braced herself as best she could, and launched Flax toward the tower's roof.

The cat sailed over the top and out of sight, and Nysska hoped with every tiny bit of her soul that Raoul's recollection of the roof being unmanned remained true.

Nysska closed her eyes and envisioned the process she'd undergone, teaching Flax how to tie the rope off to one of the chimneys. The circling, the weaving around and under, the necessity to keep the rope slack so that she could wriggle through a loop. *Why are you worried?* she asked herself. *Flax is smarter than most humans you've met. She's got this.*

A jerk on the rope made her look up, to see a silver-eyed cat head poking over the roof's edge, gazing down at her.

Nysska tugged on the rope. Felt no give. Tugged harder, and harder still, and finally she invoked Atiina's wisdom, swung out from the wall with her full weight, and scaled the tower.

Flax was waiting for her when she slid over the edge. Staying low, Nysska freed the cat from the line, undid the perfectly respectable knot Flax had tied around the nearest chimney, re-coiled the rope, and slipped it back into her pack. "Come on," she whispered. "They're not expecting anybody from this direction, but we still need to be really quiet."

Flax yawned and groomed a paw, but followed after Nysska as she made her way across the roof, crouched low. The door that Raoul had described was there, locked as he said it would be, but the lock was more a formality than an honest security measure. She took the lock itself as a handle to slowly, carefully pull the hasp free from the wooden door. Kneeling, she spoke to Flax again. "All right, you go ahead of me, and if there's some sort of hazard I can't see, push against my shins or something. Got it?"

Flax winked her left eye and sauntered through the door.

It wasn't completely dark inside, as by that point the second moon had risen and silver-blue light filtered through a handful of small, rectangular windows. Still, Nysska knew she couldn't afford to light a torch or a lantern yet, and appreciated Flax's vastly superior night vision. They descended the stone stairwell and stopped at the door to the top level, where the most recent records would have been kept. Nysska opened the door a crack and peered through.

Raoul's descriptions again held up. Nysska had a narrow view of a huge, low-ceilinged room crammed with row after row of shelves, each shelf in turn packed tight with scrolls. She heard nothing. The room held the kind of dead-air, tomblike silence that only came from unoccupied spaces. Noiselessly, she stepped inside and moved from aisle to aisle, staring through the looming shadows, straining to find even the tiniest hint of movement.

There was nothing.

Now comes the tedious part. Nysska had no idea, and neither did Raoul, exactly how the Imperial records were catalogued. If there was some kind of recognizable system, she hoped to be able to use it to narrow down the year and find what she was looking for without any extraordinary effort. If, on the other hand, the Imperial Archivist simply remembered where everything was and had no discernible system, this entire endeavor was most likely pointless.

Nysska pulled a small oil lamp out of her pack, struck a spark to the wick, and started at one corner of the room. The tiny pool of yellow illumination would have been useless at lighting a way for her to navigate some unfamiliar place, and worse than useless in a fight, but it proved near-perfect for showing her the labels on the ends of the scroll cases. *"This is from last year,"* she whispered to Flax, who was winding around her ankles. *"The dead skinshifter said Valco did...whatever he did...five years ago. So that would put the scroll I'm looking for—"*

Flax hissed, and Nysska spun to her right, so that the oil lamp reflected brightly in the watery green eyes of an Imperial Archivist, who stood no more than a meter away. It was the same man she'd seen during her audience with Valco—the Scribe, as she'd thought of him then—now absent his portable writing desk.

Nysska's favorite hook-bladed knife flashed to the man's throat, but he didn't so much as flinch. Instead he just stood there, staring at her with a mixture of sadness and...awe? "What are you doing?" he said, and Nysska would have sworn he sounded on the verge of tears. "Why would you cover up your skin like that?"

Ignoring the knife entirely, he lifted a hand, and his manner seemed so submissive, so *reverent*, that the movement didn't even register to her as a threat. The Archivist's soft fingertips grazed Nysska's cheek. "Your beautiful, beautiful skin...why would you ever hide it?"

Flax had taken a couple of steps back, and now sat, staring up at the tall, pale, gangly man. She didn't seem to understand what was happening any better than Nysska did.

"This makeup...I can only assume it is part of a *disguise*...ugh. Such measures are beneath you, my lady."

Nysska lowered the knife. There didn't seem to be much point to it. "Wh..." She groped for words. "Are you alone here?"

"I am always alone here."

The Archivist wore what appeared to be sleeping clothes—a long, soft cotton nightshirt, matching trousers, and wool socks. Over his shoulder Nysska caught sight of a cot against one of the tower's outside walls, and wondered how she could have missed a sleeping man on her sweep of the room. *Maybe he had so many blankets piled on top of him, and lay so motionless, that I mistook him for a bench?*

Nysska raised the knife again. "I'm looking for a scroll. Something Valco did five years ago. Something to do with the skinshifters."

The Archivist's weak eyes clouded as his brow furrowed, but only for a moment. "Oh—you mean the Gemini."

It was Nysska's turn to frown. She had never heard that word before. "The what?"

"That is their proper name. The Gemini—both singular and plural, I discovered. Of course I will show you. Follow me."

He turned, but Nysska slid in behind him, her arm crossing in front of his shoulders so that the curved blade rested against his larynx. "Do not even think of sounding an alarm."

A tremor made its way through the man's entire body, and a low groan escaped his lips. "I will do whatever you ask of me, Enforcer Stonegate."

Something about the way he said the words caused Nysska's gorge to rise. She stepped back, arm sliding free of him, but tapped the tip of the knife between his shoulder blades. "Fine. You seem to know exactly what I'm looking for. Take me there."

"It's just this way…"

With Flax padding along behind them, Nysska let the Archivist lead her across the room to the far row of shelves, where he went unerringly to one particular scroll case. "Here. This is what you're looking for. The fact that you *are* looking for it means you have specific questions. Trust me, the answers you want can be found within."

Nysska took the case from him. "Flax, if he even acts like he's thinking about running, tear his throat out."

Flax growled, low and deep in her chest, and for the first time the Archivist looked marginally frightened. Nysska popped the case open and took the scroll out. It looked very much like the scrolls she had seen him writing on before—heavy, fine-quality parchment affixed to two highly-polished wooden spindles. She unrolled a bit and read the first few lines.

The Archivist said, "Was I wrong? Is that not what you sought?"

Nysska rolled the words back up and slid the scroll into its case. "I'm taking this with me."

"Of course."

Impatience giving her words a dangerous edge, she said, "Explain yourself." When the man did not immediately respond, she added further harshness. "Why are helping me? Why are you not *afraid*?"

He took a deep breath. "Because I want something from you."

She lifted one eyebrow. "What? What do you want?"

She could tell from his voice that his heart had sped up. "I want you to end me."

Nysska's lips parted silently. She swallowed. "I beg your pardon?"

"My soul. I want you to destroy my soul. I know you can." He took a step toward her. "Please."

"Wh…why? Why would you want that?"

The Archivist's eyes took on an unsettling gleam. "I am not alone, my Lady Demon. There are many of us. We meet in secret, where the ignorant masses cannot see us, cannot touch us. We know the time of humans has come and gone. Now is the age of the Demon. Take your rightful place in the world, my lady. Remove me from the eternal suffering that is human existence. Grant me this mercy. Please. I beg of you."

Nysska blinked. For some reason she didn't understand, her own eyes had begun to water. "I—can't—we can't *destroy souls*. We're not demons. I'm just as much flesh and blood as you are. I just…we just…we only *look* different."

He clasped his hands in front of his face. "I know that isn't true! You can look deep inside us and find our puny human souls and snuff them out! Don't let me be condemned to an eternity of torment! Don't let the Great Silver Dragon bathe me in His flames when I die! Grant me this mercy, Lady Demon. Have mercy! Have mercy, please!"

Nysska's hand flashed out before she fully realized what she was doing. The hilt of her knife struck the Archivist on the hinge of his jaw and he crumpled, eyes rolling back in his head. She caught him before he hit the floor and, cradling his head in her arms, snapped his neck.

Fighting down wave after wave of nausea, Nysska led Flax back up to the roof, which remained just as unpopulated as when they'd arrived. She disliked the thought of leaving the long rope tied around the chimney to mark their presence there, but not nearly as much as she disliked leaving the Archivist's body there among the shelves. Yet there wasn't a damn thing she could do about either one. Rappelling down the side of the tower—with Flax safe in her pack again—Nysska retraced her laborious path.

Climbing back up from the bridge's underside, careful not to make any noise, she saw that Corporal Benjamyn Hunter had returned to his post. The man was shaking, panting, a hand clenched around one of the gate's bars to steady himself. Nysska could only imagine the personal hell he'd been through in the last—twenty-five minutes? Thirty? She wasn't sure how long it had taken to infiltrate the tower. Nysska didn't want to imagine the heart-piercing terror that their message must have instilled in him, growing with every pace as he raced home, but she could scarcely help it.

Still silent, she slipped into her disguise, crept up behind him, reached through the bars of the gate, and dropped his keys back in his pocket. He must have felt the action despite all of Nysska's care, but she had never had anything to do with picking pockets and didn't have Percy around to do the job for her. As Hunter's head began to turn, she reached through the bars in a different spot, grabbed him by the neck, and banged his head against the gate.

Hunter slumped nervelessly to the cobblestone street as Nysska slipped through the gate and sprinted away into the darkest alley she could find.

23

Part of the reason they had chosen the shabby inn was the layout of its roof. When Nysska ducked into another patch of shadows at one end of a short bridge, all she had to do was roll over the side and drop three meters to put her right above their room's window. No one was surprised when she swung in, and Percy closed the shutters immediately behind her.

Raoul started to say something, but Cam brushed past him and threw her arms around Nysska, and then Percy came in with, "Where's Flax? Where's my little girl?" Nysska didn't try to dislodge Cam, but did indicate the pack on her back with one thumb, so that Percy pulled and clawed at the straps until the flap came loose and Flax leapt out into his arms.

Raoul cleared his throat, finally, and Nysska kept one arm around Cam as she turned to face him.

"Any complications?"

Nysska nodded as she unslung the pack and moved to the room's tiny round table. "One. Yes. And it was...weird." In as efficient and dispassionate terms as she could manage, Nysska told them about being surprised by the Archivist, and about how he had begged her to end his life.

"Holy fuck," Percy said from the floor, as Flax and Jax groomed each other's heads in front of him. "He *wanted* you to kill him?"

Nysska pulled the scroll case out of the pack. "Not before he led me to this, though." She opened the case, but Raoul put out a hand.

"Wait, wait, wait. So?"

Nysska untied the emerald-green cord binding the scroll in place. "So? What?"

Cam made a tiny scoffing sound. "So did you kill him?"

Nysska shrugged, maybe a touch too theatrically. "Well I had no *choice*, did I?" As Raoul groaned and clapped a hand to his forehead, Cam's eyes narrowed thoughtfully.

"No," Cam said after a couple of seconds. "You didn't."

Nysska sat and propped her elbows on the table, aiming her words at Raoul. "The man was Scribe to Emperor Valco himself, Raoul. He said he *worshiped* me—and all other sethyds—and, who knows, maybe he did. He kept calling me 'Lady Demon.' Maybe he was babbling because I surprised the piss out of him. Or maybe he came up with all that on the spur of the moment hoping I'd get confused or feel merciful or whatever and decide not to touch him. I don't know. But if I'd left him alive, tell me what would've prevented him from going straight to Valco and telling him who I was and why I was there."

Flax and Jax had gone from grooming to wrestling, and now rolled and thumped about the floor, hissing softly and kicking back legs at each other. Percy kept his eyes on them, but spoke to Nysska. "Sounds to me like you granted him his fucking wish."

Raoul threw his hands up. "Fine. All right. Fine. The place was supposed to be unmanned, and I fucking *hate* it when civilians get killed in shit like this, but...fuck. *Fuck.* All right. What's in the Dragon-damned scroll?"

Nysska scooted the stool over so that she could rest her back against the wall. The cool of the stone felt good through her shirt, and she realized her muscles had kinked up with anxiety. "For what it's worth, I hate it too," she said quietly. "So everybody listen, and tell me if you think breaking the man's neck was worth it." Nysska unrolled the scroll and read aloud, doing her best to enunciate every word as clearly as possible.

"Seventeen August, Fifty-one Thirty-seven. An Imperial mining expedition made a discovery after an earthquake opened a crevasse in the earth at a location eighteen kliks due north of Greenwater and twenty-two kliks due east of Severance."

"I remember that earthquake," Raoul said. "Five years ago? Yeah, that was a big one—cracked a wall at the barracks. Crack's still there, last time I checked."

Cam had an Imperial map spread out on the bed, and tapped a spot on it with one forefinger. "This is it. This is the location." She looked up at Nysska. "There's nothing but forest."

"Nothing but forest on the *map*," Percy said. Then, to Nysska, "So what'd they find?"

Nysska kept reading. *"The expedition had been searching for new sources of copper and decided to see if the newly-opened rent in the earth afforded any advantage. They did not find copper, but what they did find proved to be of sufficient import that word was sent to His Brilliance the Emperor straightaway. This Recorder—"* Nysska looked up from the scroll. "He's talking about himself, there. Capitalized 'Recorder.'" She picked the narrative back up. *"This Recorder was quite surprised to learn of the Emperor's decision to view this discovery himself. Consequently, I packed my belongings and fresh supplies of quills, ink, and parchment, and joined the Emperor's caravan as it headed west."*

Raoul blew a puff of air out of his mouth. "The Emperor left Caulspring? Shit...I can count on one hand how many times that's happened."

Percy chuckled. "Can you? Sounds like Valco could've been stepping out on the fucking regular with nobody the wiser."

Cam touched the back of Nysska's hand. "Please. Go on."

Nysska carefully unrolled the bottom spindle and rolled the top one down. *"Upon arriving at this great open wound inflicted upon the face of Imperial land, the Emperor found—and likewise This Recorder found also—that it was possible to navigate a narrow pathway down into the great rift, moving above a vein of the earth's hot blood far below."* She looked up at the others. "A vein of the earth's hot blood?"

Cam said, "Is he talking about *magma*? How deep is this crevasse?"

Raoul nodded at the scroll.

Nysska cleared her throat. *"The convulsions of the earth had revealed a sort of cave system, in much the same way that carefully excavating an anthill reveals a sidelong view of the tiny tunnels fashioned by the ants."*

When she paused, Cam handed her a mug of ale, and Nysska gratefully took a couple of long sips before continuing.

"At once this Recorder observed an odd phenomenon in these caves. At first it seemed to be naturally occurring, but certain features quickly convinced me otherwise. The caves were all clad in a dull gray metal, in such a fashion as to prove the involvement of craftsmen's hands."

Nysska looked up again, yellow eyes traveling from one face to the next as she waited for those words to sink in. It didn't take long.

"Altamar," Cam breathed. "That weird building we found there—this sounds like—"

Raoul finished her sentence. "Like it was built by the same people."

Percy made a harsh, guttural sound. "Does this mean the canyon's filled with glowing dead fuckers like Altamar was?"

Nysska focused on the scroll. "*One of the captains discovered a large door of weighty proportion that led into a second, much larger section of what the Emperor began to refer to, astutely in this Recorder's estimation, as 'the Anthill.'*"

"Sounds like that door that led to the smelting room," Cam said, but mostly to herself. Jax had tired of wrestling with his sister, and crawled into Cam's lap. She scratched his head absently as everyone listened to Nysska.

"*Once the soldiers determined that no threat was present, His Brilliance the Emperor entered this second section, with this Recorder in tow. There we witnessed an astonishing spectacle. The details of this mind-fraying sight proved equally as hard to describe as they were to understand, but This Recorder shall do his best.*

"*A vast cavern is what we saw, so broad and tall that the light of our lanterns failed to find the far walls at first, and never came close to the ceiling. A cavern, this Recorder calls it, and yet it was no such thing, other than in dimension, for it was clad in the same metal as the tunnels found previously. Present in this unfathomable metal cavern was a kind of sunless garden, reminiscent of the Emperor's vineyards, and yet composed of metal and glass, with vines and bulbs covered in a heavy layer of dust.*"

Percy said, "Fucking metal and glass fucking *what*? Garden? The fuck is he talking about?" He put up his hands and fell silent when Nysska shot him a look over the scroll's top spindle.

"*Once a bit of this dust had been cleared away, revealing the intricacy of the garden's design, the Emperor made the discovery that each bulb held the body of a full-grown man or woman.*"

"Dragon's scaly taint," Raoul said, his eyes haunted. "They found some kind of...mausoleum?"

Nysska's eyes had skipped a few lines ahead, and her brow wrinkled up below her horns. "No. I'm getting to it. *A lantern held high in one regal fist, the Emperor revealed in detail the nearest of the bodies. A young man it was, a pale-skinned lad of well-nourished countenance, and as His Brilliance watched, the man's chest rose and fell. He lived, somehow, there in the garden, and soon Emperor Valco determined that all of the bodies so contained still drew breath."*

Cam had softly gasped. "But *how*? How could any of this be tr—" Cutting her own words short, she shook her head. "No. Forget I said that. The shit we've seen? Keep reading. Please."

Nysska's eyes had stayed fixed on the scroll. *"The vines of the garden drew the attention of His Brilliance, so that he divined their origin, and saw that the place had been marked with a weighty jewel. His Brilliance the Emperor laid fingers upon the jewel, causing a brilliant crimson light within."*

Raoul had sat down on another of the stools and hunched forward, elbows on his knees. "Light within—wait. Is this talking about a Conversation Stone?"

Cam's brow knitted. "Or is it more chervoxite-rune bearshit?"

Crimson light within made Nysska think of the rune-trap orb that had done such horrendous damage to Gower, Lasko, and Boggs, but she decided not to bring that up.

"Upon the exertion of his will, the soldiers observed a great many tiny fires throughout the garden, and scores of unseen lanterns commenced shining. Forthwith, one of the garden's great bulbs blossomed and opened, thereby disgorging its living, breathing occupant.

"Said occupant was seized immediately and brought before the Emperor, who demanded to know who he was, who all of the others so contained might be, and what the purpose was of such an unearthly endeavor. The man babbled as would an imbecile, and the Emperor would have judged him one whose mind functioned insufficiently, until something took place for which this Recorder had no explanation, nor did any other present. The man from the cocoon moaned as if in anguish, and as everyone assembled watched, his face changed."

Percy said, "Ooooohh shit."

Raoul groaned, but offered no words.

Cam reached out and gripped Nysska's wrist. Not to stop her. Certainly not to hurt her. It felt like an earnest attempt to connect to something real.

"The skin rippled and changed color, and in a matter of seconds, though the wretched man still groaned piteously on his knees, his face had transformed into a near-perfect likeness of Emperor Valco's own. This enraged His Brilliance, who immediately ordered the strange man's head struck from his shoulders, and the nearest captain drew his sword and swiftly obliged.

"Even as the strange man's blood spilled on the metal floor, however, more tiny fires lit in the darkness of the cavern, and more and more of the garden blos-

somed. *First one by one, then ten by ten, and soon hundred by hundred, the countless bulbs vomited forth the bizarre men and women held within, and no sooner had their feet touched the cold floor than their skins began to tremble and shimmer and slide from one appearance to another."*

Nysska rolled and unrolled, revealing more of the Archivist's careful scripted hand. *"Filled with the utmost revulsion, and seeing no choice in the matter, His Brilliance the Emperor ordered the soldiers to strike down these abhorrent creatures. Even as the soldiers set about the grisly task, Emperor Valco lifted his voice high, declaring that no such infestation should be permitted to exist on Imperial lands, and that like the lowest cockroach each and every one of the filthy creatures must be crushed.*

"The Emperor's men numbered eighty strong, all of them armed and armored as befitted men of the Cathedral, and since the wretches emerging from the glass cocoons were defenseless, the bloody work progressed apace. Yet even as the soldiers moved through the garden's rows, hewing and slashing the length of the cavern, their blades could not move fast enough. In full retreat, the unholy creatures scuttled away into the cavern's far reaches, screaming and weeping, and only much later did the good men of the Cathedral discover four additional points of egress through which some of the creatures surely escaped.

"Still, hundreds of bodies lay bleeding on the cold gray metal, perhaps as many as a thousand once all was said and done, and the Emperor declared the work good. He ordered the bodies collected and disposed of in the deep, hellish ravine, and ordered a permanent outpost built so that no one else should have access to the strange metal caves or the Dragon-forsaken horrors that had awakened therein. Upon leaving, His Brilliance the Emperor took in the peace of the wilderness and declared the site be named Solace Canyon.

"Naturally the Emperor declared all other face-changing creatures be hunted down and slain with no quarter given."

Nysska set the scroll down.

Cam said, "Is that it?"

Nysska rubbed weary eyes. "The next entry involves a decision on corn tariffs."

Percy rubbed the bridge of his nose. "Fucking...*fuck.* No wonder Lockridge and the rest of his stooges hate the Emperor." To Nysska, he said, "It's a grand fucking wonder Valco didn't try to slaughter all of *your* people the minute you got off the boats."

Nysska shifted her arm so that she could hold Cam's hand. "We weren't defenseless. Or disoriented. Or trapped." She sighed. "Maybe he learned something? Maybe he actually felt bad about it later, and tried to do better when the *Krizo* forced us to ask for his mercy? Or maybe he just saw us as the opposite of the Gemini—as people who'd stand out no matter what, instead of scuttling off and blending in. Who can say?"

Cam's grip on Nysska's wrist grew firmer. "Did you say 'Gemini'?"

"The Scribe said that is what they're properly called. He seemed confident about it. Just the one word, if I understood him correctly—one Gemini, two Gemini. Like fish. Or moose."

"Beats 'skinshifters,'" Percy muttered.

Raoul sat hunched over, elbows on knees, his fingers laced together just below his eyes—which stared, unseeing, into the distance. "So what we've got here is a group of people who were kept underground. Somehow. It sounds like they were waiting. Waiting on something."

"Yeah," Cam said, "but waiting on what?"

Raoul shrugged. "It might not matter. Because in one *profoundly* shortsighted swoop, Valco woke them up, killed a bunch of them—maybe most of them—and sent the rest scattering out into the Empire. With the ability to look like *anyone.* All of them with a raging hard-on to hack Valco's head off."

Nysska gently took her hand out of Cam's. "This...actually fits in with some of the things Asch was trying to tell me."

Raoul lifted his head and focused his eyes. "What things?"

"In the wilderness—her grasp of my language isn't great, and I wasn't sure I understood everything she was saying, but...all right, let me try to get this across in a way that won't make either her or me sound insane." She took a measured breath. "According to her, her family makes a habit of digging up lost knowledge. She, uh...she says they have evidence that there was an age before this one, more or less. And that in that previous age, the world belonged to humans. Just humans. No sethyds. No God-Touched. No seraphic animals. And they were a lot more advanced than we are."

Percy lifted one eyebrow. "Advanced? What'd she mean?"

"She meant, say, the way the most remote Skahna tribes are? Compare them with the Empire, and these ancient humans were that much more sophisticated than we are now. We'd be the Skahna tribes in their eyes."

Cam scowled. It narrowed the silver of her eyes to hard slits. "What's that got to do with this 'Solace Canyon' business?"

"She said these humans figured out that something bad was going to happen. Sounded like something that could kill...everyone. Some kind of apocalypse. And while a few of them tried to stop it, others tried to figure out how to survive it. They tried to *change* some of the humans. Make them stronger and tougher. And—I have to tell you, I don't know if I believe her, I don't know if I want to *try* to believe her, but…shit. Supposedly one of the ways they tried to improve on themselves…resulted in us. In the sethyds. We were supposed to survive. *Designed* to survive."

Cam sat back. Eyes wide now. Quietly, into the dense silence that had descended, she whispered, "The sethyds came up from the steel caves…"

"Now, just—now just hang the fuck on, now!" Percy grunted as he got to his feet. "You're saying these ancient fuckheads *created* your people? To be *better* than humans?" His face twitched on one side, and he rubbed the back of his neck. "Actually that makes a fuck-ton of sense, now that I think about it."

Raoul waved his hands. "I'd heard that nonsense before, about the sethyds coming up from the steel caves, but nobody even knows what that *is!* 'Steel'? What the hell is 'steel'? Does anybody know? Do *you* know, Nysska?"

Nysska shook her head. "No. But unless the Archivist wrote fiction as a second career, it sounds to me like that earthquake opened something up that had been buried. The way that building at Altamar had been buried." She paused. "Maybe the way the sethyds were buried. On Patrinomonto. Until we…until we woke up. So if Asch is right, we might be looking at another attempt the ancient humans made to change some of their fellows. Change them in some way that would let them survive… whatever was coming."

Raoul stood and began pacing. "Too many 'ifs' in all this. *If* the Archivist recorded all this accurately. *If* this is the real reason the skinshifters—I mean, the Gemini—hate the Empire so much. *If* Aschling isn't full of shit."

Nysska scooted her stool around to sit closer to Cam. "True," she said, her tone dark. "But there are some things we do know. We know about that shipment from Borealis. We know if the Gemini get it and forge runes with it, they're going to rip the Empire apart. We know we've got to stop them."

Percy's gaze lingered on Flax and Jax. "And now we know where we can look." He pointed at the map. "Eighteen kliks north of Greenwater and twenty-two kliks east of Severance."

Raoul faced the group. "We ride at first light."

24

Solace Canyon proved to be a hair better than two kliks long, and ran almost perfectly north-south through an otherwise dense forest. Approaching it, Nysska couldn't help thinking of the Ninth's torturous climb up to the top of the falls known as Dragon's Pain, where the former hunting camp known as Altamar had once sat. Scaling a steep mountainside for hour after hour hadn't been pleasant, but she would have done it again gladly if it meant not having to endure the icy rain that pelted them now.

She wasn't sure what the hour was. The rain had come in hard and fast, striking from a low charcoal sky, and as far as Nysska knew the sun might have already set. She had pulled the hood of her cloak down as far as she could and still see where she was going, but wind kept whipping lashes of hard rain straight into her face. It hadn't taken long for it to make its way down the back of her neck and between her breasts. She felt it pooling in her boots.

The horses moved carefully, gingerly, picking their way over the same kind of uneven forest floor that she had covered so much of with the Borealans. The team had spotted the Cathedral outpost at the canyon's southern end—the shallow end, where the land began its descent into the earthquake-revealed depths—and given it a wide, quiet berth as they skirted around to the northwest.

Clouds of steam rose from the canyon. They hadn't gotten close enough yet to peer down into its farthest reaches, but Nysska imagined she could hear the hiss of raindrops striking molten rock.

Raoul called a halt. Nysska followed Percy and Cam as they dismounted, Raoul already on the ground and headed east, and the four of them crept through the black, rain-soaked trees like wraiths. Flax and Jax kept pace, a silver eye flashing now and again from the shadows.

The northern end of the canyon bore many similarities to the sheer rock faces so common around Altamar, the walls not quite vertical but still far too steep to climb. To the south, halfway down the canyon's walls, a dim light shone out, but in the heavy, rain-blotted dark they could make out no details.

"No soldiers around here," Raoul said, just loud enough to be heard over the downpour. "I thought there might be a patrol, at least."

Nysska's yellow eyes glimmered in the depths of her hood. "Depends on whether or not anyone's figured out what scroll we took. With any luck, the Archivist's death will appear to be the purpose for the invasion of the Archives. Not theft."

"When have we ever been lucky about any fucking thing?" Percy asked of no one in particular.

Cam's runes glowed a brighter silver for a moment or two, and Nysska said, "Careful—those things are like a beacon in the dark."

"I know, I know, I'll keep it down. Just wanted to get a look at the canyon walls. There may not be any patrols up here because trying to climb down at this point would be suicide."

Nysska moved forward, poking her head over the canyon's lip until she could see the bottom. Sure enough, a river of magma coursed along the canyon's length, little more than a thread of fiery red at that distance.

"How far down, you reckon?" Percy asked from beside her. "Half a klik? More?"

She murmured, "Let's not find out."

Nysska turned to Raoul, and saw him considering options. She said, "Let me skirt the canyon head and scout along the east side. The less movement we can get away with, the better, and if I can get a good look at what's down there on the western wall, maybe I can spot a decent access point."

Raoul frowned, but nodded. "Be careful of your own eyes. They're not argonium runes, but they stand out."

She gave him a tiny, grim smile, and snapped her watersight lids closed, turning the candleflame yellow a soft green. "How about this?"

He nodded again. "Don't get caught. Or seen. Be a ghost."

Cam gripped her upper arm, and leaned in to put her lips at Nysska's ear. "Come back to me."

Nysska put her hand over Cam's and squeezed it. "Always."

As Nysska turned to move away from Cam, Raoul, and Percy, she stopped at the sight of the two blood lynxes staring at her—both soaked to the skin, water dripping off their whiskers. Flax inclined her head to the north, yawned, and winked.

"No, no," Nysska said. "Both of you stay here. I'm not infiltrating anything, at least not yet. You need to keep the humans safe. Watch out for any soldiers coming this way, and warn Percy if you see any. Got it?"

Flax narrowed her eyes at Nysska, but Jax seemed to take her at face value. He padded over to Percy, rubbed against his ankles for a second, and headed south along the canyon's edge. Nysska knelt in front of Flax, scratched her chin, and smoothed some water off the top of her head. "This is an important job you've got. Understand? Make sure nothing sneaks up on our friends here."

Flax opened her jaws and closed her teeth on one of Nysska's fingers, but exerted no pressure. Nysska looked over at Percy. "Think that means 'be careful'?"

"Who the fuck knows?" Percy said, but smiled at Flax as he said it. "Just come back in one piece."

Nysska left them and threaded her way through the woods up and around the northernmost point of the crevasse. The rain showed no sign of letting up, and even though she cursed it for the chill that had finally begun to creep into her bones, she knew it rendered her task a bit easier. The rainfall would mask any errant sound she might make, and whatever unfortunate Cathedral grunts prowled the canyon's perimeter would be focused more on a dry bed and a hot cup of coffee than on anything creeping through the forest.

She almost ran straight into one such patrol.

The two soldiers had stopped, taking shelter under the overhang of a rock outcropping, and if they both hadn't been facing the other way they no doubt would have seen her when she stepped around it. As it was, she bit off a startled yelp and ducked back out of sight, skirting the outcropping the same way she had the canyon head, and left the patrol behind in the rain.

Redoubling her caution, Nysska finally made it to the crevasse's eastern edge, where she dropped to her belly and wriggled under a massive, dense holly bush, her hood pulled down tight. She was afraid the effort would push the tip of her unbroken horn through the leather and ruin the hood, but it held, and in a few more seconds she reached the canyon's lip.

Solace Canyon fell away below her again, filled with a dense twilight that rendered everything in shades of black and gray. The only actual light poking through the gloom came from a trail of lanterns strung along a narrow wooden platform driven into the crevasse's western wall. The platform stayed level as the rocky floor fell away beneath it, creeping along the wall until it reached a yawning black opening halfway between the magma and the lip.

Over to her left, Nysska spotted a narrow rope bridge—an uncomplicated affair consisting of thick, heavy lengths of hemp rope holding up a walkway of rough wooden planks. She couldn't tell how old it was, but the rope looked far too frayed for her to test it. The bridge began at two massive wooden poles driven into the earth of the canyon's eastern lip, and stretched across to a similar anchor almost directly above what had to be the cave mouth the Archivist had described.

From this vantage point Nysska could see that a blocky wooden structure had been built in that opening, taking up roughly half of its space. She thought it looked like a guardhouse. Not a heavily manned one, though, as only one lantern hung inside a window, and no patrols made their way along the platform. Maybe there wouldn't be any patrols around the entrance, as long as the rain kept up? It certainly gave no signs of stopping. Once it got fully dark...before the second moon rose and filled any gap that showed up in the clouds with its dazzling blue-white light...they might, *might* be able to take advantage of their surroundings.

Nysska backed carefully out from under the holly bush and, melting back into the trees, made her way north.

Crouched at the edge of the canyon, ropes anchored to aged oak trees, the Ninth Crucible waited. None of them looked happy, Nysska thought, but Percy's scowl took on a note she found sour even for him. *Not that he doesn't have a good reason*, she told herself.

From the outpost blocking the canyon's shallow southern entrance, muffled by the rain but still audible, came the screams of many horses followed by near-panicked shouts. Nysska couldn't quite make out the sound of pounding footfalls, but she knew the Cathedral soldiers would be sprinting for the stables.

"Now," Raoul said, and he and Cam rappelled down the face of the canyon, with Nysska following a few seconds later. Nysska knew Flax and Jax would have hidden—right after leaving painful but superficial slashes along the Imperial horses' rumps—and that as soon as their distraction cleared the path, they'd make their way around the edge of the canyon and reunite with Percy.

The wind whipped lash after lash of rain against Nysska's back, driving up under her cloak and somehow finding its way behind the waistband of her trousers, but it was the effect of the water on the rope that concerned her most. They followed proper technique, the ropes passing through smooth metal clips attached to groin harnesses, but all it would take was one slip for someone to lose control. And even a tiny loss of control could get them all killed.

Nysska glanced down and saw the three ropes pooling on the roof of the guardhouse at the tunnel's entrance. Unlike the nerve-wracking circumstances of her invasion of the Archives, this time Percy was there to pull the ropes back up as soon as they reached safety and disconnected. Nysska had no idea how long they would be inside the "metal caves," but she had no doubt that any Cathedral soldier who happened to glance up and see ropes dangling from the canyon's edge would sound an alarm with great gusto.

Nysska descended faster than Raoul and Cam. She touched the roof first, as gently as she could, grateful again for the wind and the rain that would make a wooden structure like this one groan and creak and pop. Raoul and Cam touched down on either side of her. They each disconnected their lines, gave them three tugs, and watched as the ropes slithered back up the face of the canyon. Nysska untied and removed the groin harness and stowed it in her pack, made sure all her blades were in place, and glanced at Raoul and Cam. After a couple of nods and a discreet hand signal, she took a deep breath, got a good grip on the edge of the roof, and swung down through the window into the guardhouse's upper level.

Next to the window, supported by a heavy wooden frame, was the same kind of alarm bell they'd seen at the mine where they found the Borealans and the dying Gemini. A few feet from the bell, slouched in a chair and half asleep, sat a paunchy man wearing an Imperial College robe.

Of course there's a Sensor, Nysska thought in the tenth of a second it took her to draw a heavy-pommeled dagger and cross the floor to him. *Just like at the mine.* The man's eyes popped open, flaring brilliant silver, and he sucked in a breath to shout—but not fast enough to keep the dagger's hilt from connecting with his jaw.

She caught him as he pitched sideways and laid him carefully out on the floor. Behind her, Raoul dropped down and crouched in the window for a moment before stepping fully in, then turned and offered Cam a hand. She came in the same way he had, and batted the offered hand aside with a good-natured half-smile.

Nysska was about to make a further series of gestures, indicating that she was going to take a look through the square hole in the floor three meters behind the Sensor's chair, but before she could do so a deep, rumbling growl rose up through the floor and surrounded them.

Nysska remembered the Third Crucible's tracking animal—the massive gray wolf their Keeper had called "Sickle"—and didn't relish the thought of tangling with another Thaumetallicon-trained animal. She said, "Fucking hell," bounded to the hole and plunged through it.

She didn't think she had ever seen two humans—a pale, golden-haired man and a boney dark-skinned woman with streaks of gray through a black mane—look more surprised than the pair goggling at her. They had been lying down together on a thick pallet in a back corner, but now surged upright, blinking gritty eyes and reaching for weapons.

The massive black wolf in the middle of the floor did not appear surprised in the least. It lunged at Nysska's throat as Cam and Raoul dropped through the hole in the ceiling, and Nysska needed every bit of her reflexes to throw herself backward, so that the wolf's great glistening teeth snapped together on empty air.

"The fuck—" Golden Hair got out before Raoul swarmed him. He had only made it up to one knee at that point, and Raoul came in with his own knee driving straight for the man's nose. The crunching impact snapped Golden Hair's head backward, and Gray Streaks might have drawn her blade to good effect, but the blood from her companion's shattered nose sprayed directly into her face and eyes.

"Don't kill them!" Nysska hissed, as Cam took a two-handed swing and struck Gray Streaks flush on the side of the head with the flat of her longsword's blade. The woman's eyes rolled up in their sockets and she collapsed back onto the pallet.

The wolf, in Nysska's perception, seemed to have transformed into a giant pair of jaws filled with dagger-sized teeth. Those immense jaws snapped at her again and again, faster than they should have been able to move, and as much as Nysska tried to spin and dodge, the animal backed her into a corner.

"I don't want to hurt you," she gritted out, and sent a kick past the enormous teeth. She felt her shin connect with the wolf's ribcage, but though it let out a *whuff*, the blow only seemed to make it angrier. "You're only doing your job!" Wishing she had something like a mace, Nysska tried a similar shot to the one she'd landed on the Sensor upstairs and aimed the pommel of her dagger at the top of the wolf's head, hoping to stun it.

Instead the wolf whipped its head back and around, came forward again and clamped his jaws down on Nysska's forearm.

Pain blinded her.

She'd been stabbed and cut many times, but not even having her thigh skewered by the brigand in the forest had hurt like this. And yet, as her consciousness weaved in and out, she realized the inlaid strips of bronze in the sleeve of her Imperial jacket had kept the wolf's fangs from penetrating.

Instead, it felt as if the animal were crushing her arm flat. Flesh and bones squeezing in a hot, slavering vise.

Just when she thought the agony could grow no worse, the wolf began thrashing his head from side to side—an action designed to snap the necks of smaller prey. Nysska feared her arm was going to come off her body—

Until Raoul smashed a chair over the wolf's head and shoulders.

The wolf flinched, and for half a second the pain in her arm grew even worse, but then the jaws slacked off enough for her to wrench free of their grip. Cam followed right behind Raoul and smashed another chair across the wolf's body, which made it yelp and wobble.

Nysska drew her longsword, flipped it around so that she held it near the tip of the blade, and swung it like a hammer. The hilt cracked against the wolf's skull right over his eyes, and the great shaggy beast gave a pitiful *yip* and collapsed to the floor.

Nysska knelt next to him, made sure he was still breathing, and sighed in relief.

"Harnesses," Nysska said, low and urgent. She couldn't use her right hand, but she shrugged her pack off onto the floor and dug into it with her left. "*Harnesses.* We've got to tie him up."

Cam immediately went into her pack, but Raoul stood for a second, blinking. "That thing almost ripped you in half. *You*. Run a sword through its heart and be done with it."

Nysska stood, glaring down at him. "He's a trained animal! He was doing exactly what his owners taught him to do! If someone got the better of Flax or Jax, would you want them killed?" When Raoul exhaled through his nose and said nothing, Nysska barked, "We muzzle him and tie him up! Same as the rest of these assholes. We're not assassins. Right? Right, Raoul?"

He rolled his eyes, but produced his rappelling harness nonetheless. Soon they had the wolf's muzzle bound tight, then lashed it to the floor by passing the rope between a couple of loose boards and around a joist. The three humans they gagged and hogtied, and cinched a blindfold tight over the Sensor's eyes. Neither Cam nor Nysska was completely sure that would keep him from using his runes, but it seemed like tempting fate not to try.

Nysska turned and headed for the guardhouse's exit, but Cam put out a hand and stopped her. "Hey." She gestured at her own forearm. "How bad is it?"

Nysska peeled off her armored jacket, unbuttoned the cuff of her shirt and pushed the sleeve up, revealing a space between her wrist and elbow that appeared to be nothing but livid bruise. She flexed her right hand, and discovered that she couldn't quite close it into a fist. "Could've been a lot worse. I never thought I'd be this happy to wear the bronze."

Raoul let out a long, low whistle. "I'm stunned the bone's not broken." His eyes tracked up her arm. "How's your shoulder?"

"Sore." Nysska moved experimentally. "Not dislocated. And the feeling's coming back to my hand. I got off lucky." She saw Cam gazing at her, and could only guess at the emotion in the glimmering silver. Anger? Fear? Compassion?

"I'm just glad you're on our side," Cam said finally, and took Nysska's undamaged hand in hers. "Sethyd bones. Makes me jealous."

As Nysska squeezed her hand back, Raoul said, "All right. We're not assassins, but we're not tourists, either. Let's go try to find out what we're dealing with."

At the lip of the canyon, tucked up high in the arms of a pin oak, Percy Bitters waited. He doubted any patrolling soldiers would cast their eyes upward, not when that would get them faces full of driving rain, but he'd chosen his perch carefully for the screen of heavy foliage between him and anyone passing below.

"This sucks Dragon's scaly balls," he whispered to no one. "'Stay up here with the cats, Percy.' 'We can't run the risk of anyone spotting the ropes, Percy.' 'We might need you as backup, Percy.'" He kept his whispers light enough so that the hiss and drum of the rain swallowed them. "As if my kitties didn't save all our asses up at Altamar. As if th—"

Percy broke off when Flax appeared next to him on a branch, having scaled the tree in hurried silence. She looked him in the eye, then turned her head and stared at something below them. Not directly beneath the tree, but back in the thick of the woods—back the way they'd come.

Percy cranked his neck, trying to see what the big cat saw, but the light of the second moon couldn't penetrate the canopy of trees. "What is it?" he asked Flax softly. "What's down there? Is it a patrol? If it's a patrol, you stay put. We don't want them to know we're here."

Movement in the corner of his eye made Percy turn his head, to see Jax on another branch, breathing hard and dripping water. The blood lynxes traded glances, silent communication passing between them, and before he could say another word both cats dashed back down out of the tree and vanished into the rain-soaked darkness.

Percy stayed put for several long seconds, cursing foully under his breath, before he scrambled down the tree trunk and followed them.

The first ten or twelve meters of the cave beyond the guardhouse looked to be just that: a cave. Rough stone floor, walls, and ceiling, no more than a wide crack in the earth, exactly the kind of fissure that an earthquake might open up. But lantern light gleamed through a jagged rent at the cave's far end, and gave Nysska glimpses of a metal surface she'd hoped never to see again.

"Dragon's aching balls," Cam murmured, and Nysska realized she'd brought the power up in her runes as they approached the rent. "It's like Altamar. But...cleaner. No weird mutant moss growing, I don't think. Just lanterns."

"Any people, though?" Raoul asked.

"None close. Right in front of us it's just empty corridor."

Nysska imagined Percy chiming in at that point with one of his smart-ass remarks, and realized how much she missed his presence. Thinking back on the blood-rune-animated corpses they'd encountered at Altamar and the blood lynxes' roles in defeating them, she missed Flax and Jax as well.

"All right, turn your eyes down," Raoul said quietly. "Don't want to alert anyone." He glanced back toward the guardhouse. "At least, not until someone discovers the lookouts back there and starts beating the shit out of that bell."

Cam said, "You're so optimistic," and Raoul signaled Nysska to move forward and take a look.

Nysska approached the jagged gap in the wall silently and peered through, left and right, before turning back to Cam and Raoul. "It's a pretty sparse corridor. Ends in a set of double doors eight or ten meters to the left. To the right it goes on for a good bit longer—a couple of doors along the way on the left—and down at the end I'd say that's where the personnel are. More lanterns there, and I saw some movement. Can't tell how many people."

Raoul frowned. "I hate trying to sneak up on people in an empty hall-way." His eyes flicked toward Cam. "You feel like pulling the same trick you did on Benjamyn Hunter's family? Look through a wall, do some spying?"

Cam shrugged. "We're just making this up as we go along, aren't we?"

Raoul shrugged out of his cloak and put it back on inside out. Drawn tightly around him, it hid the Imperial-issue jacket and trousers. Before either woman could ask, he said, "I'm the only one of us who looks like an average human. Let me go down and see what's through those doors. Maybe we can get close enough for Cam's spy shit to work."

Before either woman could object, he simply stepped through the jagged opening and padded away.

Cam stepped close and pulled Nysska into a tight embrace. She stood on tiptoes so her lips could find Nysska's, and put enough longing into it that Nysska felt a fluttering heat rush from her abdomen into her groin, but before she could do anything about it—such as offer a regretful comment on how this was really not the time nor place—Cam stepped back.

"What was that for?" Nysska managed.

"I don't have words for how crazy all this is," Cam whispered. "It's like we're trying extra hard to get ourselves killed. And if we do get ourselves killed, I want your lips and tongue to be the last things I taste."

Nysska took Cam's hands in hers, heartbeat booming against her ribs. "Cam...do you remember when I told you sethyds didn't have husbands and wives? Not the way humans do?"

Cam nodded. "The bonded brother and sister pair raise the children. The seed donors aren't part of the family."

Nysska squeezed her hands a little tighter. "They don't *have* to be part of the family, no. But any romantic partner can stay, if both parties want that. It's...not uncommon for a couple to—to commit. Commit to each other."

Cam's breathing quickened. "Is that so?"

"And yes, you're right, this is crazy. But I've never loved anyone —*anyone*—the way I love you. I—"

Raoul stepped back through the opening and beckoned to them. "Come on," he said softly. "And try not to make any noise."

Nysska made a tiny, rasping sound deep in her throat, just loud enough for Cam to hear. Cam brought one of Nysska's hands up to her lips and kissed her knuckles, then followed Raoul into the corridor and to the right.

He led them past the first of two doors set into the left-hand wall and, with no hesitation, pushed the second one open and ducked inside. Nysska stepped through right after Cam—Raoul had lit a lantern, and held it high now, shining its meager light on their surroundings—and found herself in a square room about five meters by eight, thick with dust. She saw boot prints from where Raoul had explored the room's perimeter, marked out on the dust-covered floor as clearly as if they'd been painted there.

At her side, Cam whispered, "What am I seeing?"

Nysska took the place for a storage room. She just couldn't figure out what had been stored there. Two thirds of the floor space was taken up with crumbled, regularly-spaced piles of...something she couldn't even begin to identify. Perhaps glass and...some kind of wood? Plus corroded metal and scraps of what might have been fabric. Nysska thought she could see a wheel of some kind in one of the piles—black, the size of her palm.

Answering Cam, Raoul spread his hands. "Not a clue. But we're not here to pick through someone else's garbage." He moved closer. "I took a look around the corner at the end of the hall. It's just a little foyer-type area, but there's a much larger place to the left." He pointed into a far corner. "If I'm judging correctly, it's right on the other side of that wall. So I'll keep watch at the door, Cam, and you take a look?"

Cam nodded and headed for the corner. Nysska went with Raoul, sliding her longsword out of its scabbard. He glanced up at her, but didn't say anything, and Nysska divided her attention between listening for anything moving on the other side of the door and trying to watch Cam across the room.

Her argonium runes flared brilliant silver, and a couple of seconds later Nysska heard Cam whisper, *"Dragon's fiery bowels."* Cam stayed there, moving her head back and forth, up and down, for a full minute before she left the corner and came back to the door, eyes a soft silver again.

Cam whispered, "I couldn't see the whole room, because it's fucking huge, but you remember that smelting equipment we found at Altamar? Well, there's a lot more of it in there, and it's a lot bigger, and they've got wagons piled high with red rocks that don't look like any kind of stone I've ever seen before."

Nysska breathed the name. "Chervoxite."

Raoul's scowl deepened in the lantern light. "This is where they brought it all."

"I guess that makes sense," Nysska said, more to herself than to Cam or Raoul. "They know this place...it's got the magma as a ready-made heat source...infiltrate the army that's already keeping people away, and you've got rock-solid privacy."

Cam went on. "Yeah, speaking of magma. One whole wall is gone, basically, and there's this flow of actual, Dragon-honest molten rock. It comes down in this—I'm trying my best to do it justice here—it comes out of the ceiling and falls maybe two or three meters, flows horizontally another four or five meters, and then drops again, below the floor. And they've got some of the smelting equipment set up so that it diverts some of the magma. As you said. Heat source."

Raoul's eyes had unfocused, and he chewed the cuticle on one thumb. "How many men are in there?"

"Not just men. Women, too. I counted about a dozen, but I couldn't see the whole space, so there may be more. And I'm pretty sure I saw one of their faces change when he stopped to take a break."

"A whole rabbit warren filled with Gemini," Nysska said. "This is where they brought all the ore. Where they're forging the metal to make the blood runes."

Raoul put a hand on the back of his neck. "This can't be everything, though. They've got to have somewhere to do the fine work. The delicate work. The Empire's argonium mine sends metal to the Imperial Colleges, and the runemasters forge the runes there. Not in the mine itself."

Nysska's yellow eyes flashed. "We'd better see what's at the other end of the hall, then, hadn't we?"

25

As busy as the chamber at the far end of the metal corridor was, with all its workers and the clangs and hisses of the smelting equipment, so the space they entered now lay as quiet as... Nysska absently cast about for a comparison. The bottom of a well? A childless home? *No,* she realized. *A mausoleum.*

The massive door wasn't precisely the same design as the one at Altamar that had kept out the blood-rune-animated corpses, but was similar enough that Nysska knew how much strength it would take to move it on its thigh-thick hinges. The door stood open just enough to allow an upright body to slip through into the darkness on the other side —darkness which had clearly been cut in the past, since a number of lanterns sat on the floor beside it—and Nysska went first. She paused for several long moments, straining her ears for any hint that they might not be alone. When she found none, she lit one of the lanterns and held it high, its golden dome of illumination pushing the darkness away.

She heard Cam's footsteps behind her, then Raoul's, and silver radiance joined the lantern light as Cam sucked in a sharp breath.

From right behind her, Raoul said, "What...are we...looking at?"

Nysska hadn't blinked yet. "This is what the Archivist was talking about. This is his 'garden.'"

The chamber seemed impossibly huge. Not like the cavern at Altamar —though the floor beneath their feet did appear to be the same kind of melted-and-poured stone they had encountered there. This was no cavern at all. The metal walls on either side of them stretched away, out of sight, and though Nysska held the lantern high over her head, she couldn't see even a hint of the ceiling.

What was perfectly clear, though, were the endless rows of metal racks. Nysska decided she couldn't blame the Archivist for calling it a garden, since it did look a bit like some bizarre metallic orchard or vineyard, with square, slender, dull gray tree trunks sprouting from the melted-stone floor and marching away into the dark. These metal trees bore no leaves, though, nor fruit.

Instead the bulbs sprouting from the trunks were all made of glass.

Insane glass...*gourds*, was the best Nysska could come up with for them. She took a few steps down the closest aisle. These were no tree trunks, any more than the chamber in which they stood was a cavern. These were nothing more than metal racks, though a metal she couldn't identify. Horizontal beams had been affixed between them, stabilizing them, and beyond that there were *platforms* bolted between each upright. Platforms where people were meant to walk. Accessible, she saw, thanks to crumbling metal stairs set at regular intervals.

Nysska's mind accepted all of this, creating new niches and alcoves in her brain to accommodate this alien knowledge, and as it did, she also came to accept what she hadn't wanted to.

Each of those glass gourds, hung from the metal uprights, was just big enough to hold a full-grown human.

Most of them had been broken—smashed, or cracked, or damaged to one degree or another—but Nysska went to the closest one and ran her hand along the dust-covered surface until she found what she suspected she would: a seam. Her fingertips traced that seam back to the next inevitable discovery, which lay at the spot where the gourd met the thick metal post.

A hinge.

The silver of Cam's runes grew brighter, and she spoke at Nysska's elbow. "How? How is anyone supposed to, to, to *wake up* inside one of these? I don't..." The silver flickered as she blinked rapidly. "I don't understand. Any of this."

Raoul joined them. "Neither do I. But if it's true, if there were men and women inside these things, and Valco woke them up and slaughtered them..." He turned in a slow circle. "How many of them were there? How many of them did his men kill?"

Nysska shifted the lantern, letting its illumination fall on a cluster of what looked like heavy ropes encased in smooth black leather. "Look at this—one of these ropes connects to each of these—" She glanced at Cam and Raoul over her shoulder. "I've been thinking of them as 'gourds.'"

Raoul shrugged, and Cam said, "Sure."

Nysska shifted the lantern again. "One rope leads to each gourd. But they all come down to the floor, and run…" She pointed off into the darkness, away from the door. "That direction. So. Who wants to see where they lead?"

Raoul cast a look back at the door. "No one seems to come in here, judging by the dust. I guess we'd better try to figure out…" He made a gesture with both hands, vague and hinting at futility. "As much as we can."

Nysska thought she might know what they were looking at here, in this vast chamber, but she kept the thought to herself. *Just for a bit longer,* she said silently. *Just till I can figure out how to put it into words.*

Once Raoul had grabbed a lantern from outside the massive door, the three of them slowly, carefully made their way deeper into the vast chamber.

They had been walking for several minutes when Raoul spoke up. "I don't know how many rows of these things there are in here. But I've counted forty-three posts on this row alone so far, with eight gourds per post. That's…three hundred forty-four gourds. If there are twenty rows of these things, that means at *least*…uh…okay, I'm rounding, but we're talking about between six and seven thousand Gemini."

Cam's silver eyes flashed in the lantern light. "Right, but how many of them did Valco's men kill? The scroll didn't say he had more than a hundred troops, did it? Six thousand versus a hundred? Why didn't the Gemini overwhelm the soldiers?"

Nysska paused by one of the gourds and held her lantern close. "Look at this." She drew her sword and slid it through a splintered hole in the glass. "We don't know how fast they woke up. If the soldiers made their way through the chamber, killing the Gemini when they were still asleep, it would've been fish in a barrel."

Raoul growled low in his throat. "I'm trying to imagine. I'm in one of these things, and I've been asleep for Dragon only knows how long, and the first thing I know when I wake up is that men with swords are killing everyone. I might panic. I might…what'd the scroll say? Scurry away like cockroaches?"

They came to the end of the row, and Nysska's lantern showed her what looked like a far wall, off in the shadows. Maybe a door as well.

"So, how many was that?" Cam asked.

Raoul did a bit of silent calculation on his fingers. "There are five hundred gourds on this row. Wait here, I'll be right back."

As Raoul made his way along the rows' ends, Nysska followed the leather-encased ropes and came to an object the sight of which made her belly tighten. "The Archivist said they followed the vines of the garden to a 'weighty jewel.'"

Cam moved past her, silver light playing across the thing's surfaces. "For an Imperial Archivist, the man's powers of description were kind of shit."

It might have been called a pulpit, had the pulpit been three times as wide as normal and curved into a half-circle. "That's got to be the red jewel he was talking about."

Gleaming in the lantern light, a round, smooth, ruby-red dome sat in the center of the "pulpit," amid an array of holes that may have once held other jewel-like objects.

Cam tapped the red half-globe with a fingernail.

Nysska reached in and did the same, then ran a fingertip across it. "It's not glass. I don't know what it *is*, but it isn't glass. It's nothing like that rune-trap orb from the mine, either." She peered out at the endless rows of racks and glass gourds. "So Valco did something with this thing, and all the Gemini out there started waking up."

Raoul's lantern drew closer, but as he approached them he didn't slow down. "Stay right where you are," he said, walking swiftly past.

Cam turned to face Nysska. "I still don't understand any of this. Why would the Gemini have been sleeping in those things? Why would *anyone* sleep in those things? What's the point? Why would this group of people no one's ever heard of come down into this place no one's ever heard of, find this...whatever this is, and think, *Hey, why don't we all climb into these things and take a nap?* Especially if there was a chance somebody would stumble across them." Cam's forehead knitted. "Wait a minute. The mining expedition found them, and then sent word to Valco, and then he came all the way out here. And, what, the Gemini stayed in the gourds all that time? How? They would've starved to death, wouldn't they?"

Raoul came back. "There are twenty rows. Five hundred gourds per row. One Gemini per gourd, we're looking at—"

"Ten thousand people," Nysska finished. Then, before she had fully considered the wisdom of it, she added, "A breeding population."

Raoul shot a quick, visibly puzzled look at Cam before returning to Nysska. "Excuse me?"

Nysska took a long, deep breath and let it out slowly. "All the things Princess Aschling told me on the way to Cliffside…"

"Right." Cam tilted her head slightly to one side. "Ancient humans making sethyds, all of that. What about it?"

"Well…if you're going to—I don't know what the term for it would be. If you're going to *make* a new kind of people…you'd have to make enough that they could continue. Reproduce. Make new little Gemini."

Cam held a hand up. "Wait. Hold on. How long ago was this supposed to be? This other era?"

"Back before humans started recording history. So…five thousand years. At least."

The silver in Cam's eyes pulsed. "And you're thinking the people in these gourds were—were asleep in there? What—for *five thousand years?*"

Nysska shrugged. "I don't know. Maybe. Maybe they were. Maybe the ancient humans figured out how to put them in there for…for safekeeping. But then the earthquake happened, and opened the caves up, and Valco's miners stumbled in and had not a clue what they'd found."

Raoul shook his head. "Too much. That's too much. I can't—my head won't—I can't put all that in my brain right now." He pointed at the wall. "The Archivist said some of the Gemini escaped. Right? And I want to know if there are other ways out of here. So let's take a look, and maybe not worry about what happened in the distant past. Not for now, anyway."

Nysska trailed after Raoul as he marched toward what turned out to be one of two doors, but Cam caught up with her and took Nysska's hand in hers. "Is it all true?" she asked softly, keeping her voice out of Raoul's earshot. "Does Asch really know about things like that? What I mean is… do you believe her?"

Nysska looked down at Cam, deep into her eyes. She found that she didn't want to say anything at all. She only wanted to take in Cam's beauty, appreciate the features of the woman she loved, accept the aching perfection of her face. "You're aware of what people say about the origins of the sethyds. How we climbed up from the steel caves."

"Well…yes…"

Nysska's eyes tracked around them. "I know we've all been thinking it.

To one degree or another. What if that's what this is? What if we're standing in a steel cave? What if these ancient humans were *desperate* to survive—and sethyds and Gemini turn out to be just two of their attempts? What if we end up finding steel caves all over the place?"

A door squealed on its hinges, and Raoul swore. "Well, they might have gotten out this way before, but it's not happening again." He stepped aside and let them see the wall of rocks and dirt clogging what might have been a hallway.

Nysska left a wordless, frowning Cam and moved in for a closer look as Raoul went to the other door.

"We might be able to dig through here," she said, leaning close. "I can't tell how thick this fall is, but I feel cool air coming through a couple of cracks." She tried to move one of the stones, but it was wedged in tight. "Maybe if we had time. And the proper tools. Any luck with the other one?"

Raoul came back. "No. Same story."

Cam waved a hand around. "So that's it for this place. Giant room, no exits. What do we do now?"

"What we came for, I'd say," Nysska answered. "We get rid of all that fucking ore from Borealis."

Raoul grunted. "Too right. Let's go."

26

Nysska learned, immediately and to her pronounced displeasure, the vast difference between listening to Cam describe a room and actually setting foot in it.

They had to push through two sets of heavy swinging doors to gain access to what she'd decided to call "the Smelting Chamber," and as soon as the second set opened the heat struck Nysska in the face as though someone were trying to smother her with a steaming-hot wet blanket. *Steaming is right,* she thought, taking note of the condensation running down the walls. The floor under her feet shined slick, and the air assaulted her nose with equal parts body odor and the acrid, jarring scent of molten metal and rock.

The chamber was much smaller than the vast space where the Gemini had slept and awakened and died, but it was still easily as big as the Governor's Mansion back in Tember. Every bit of it glowed with orange-red light, either reflected off the thousands of puddles and billions of droplets of water or lit directly by lanterns and torches and the sluggish, deadly flow of magma that took up the far wall. Cam had seen clearly. The molten rock dropped out of a crevice just below the ceiling, flowed along the floor for a few more meters, and disappeared into a four-meter-wide pit near the far wall. Hellish light glared up from the pit's depths.

Smelting and metal-working equipment took up the entire wall to Nysska's left. As Cam had described, the Gemini had diverted a bit of the magma flow and used it to heat a pair of giant bronze cauldrons—near which sat a stack of argonium ingots. *Where did they get it in quantities like this? How much would one of those ingots be* worth?

She followed the path of labor down the wall from the cauldron. The forms on the floor into which the mixed molten argonium and chervoxite would be poured. The racks where the new ingots cooled. The broad, sturdy bronze tables where smiths with heavy hammers would beat the ingots into sheets...sheets that would then no doubt be sent to whatever kind of twisted, profane version of Imperial Runemasters the Gemini had in their employ. There to be forged into blood runes, or ground into the powder that rendered Imperial Sensors all but useless.

But that was all the aftermath. The tinkering, the fine-tuning. Nysska's real target lay in a series of six bronze-reinforced wooden wagons, linked together by bronze bars attaching the front of one to the back of the next, stretched across the floor—a floor which seemed to dip ever so slightly toward the magma-filled pit. Wooden chocks were wedged under the wheels of the one closest to the pit, drawing Nysska's eye.

Each wagon, with the exception of the one closest to the cauldrons, was piled high with chervoxite, the ore dully gleaming crimson.

"Where is everyone?" Cam murmured. "This place was crawling with workers less than an hour ago."

Nysska took a tentative step forward and stopped at the sight of a shadow flickering across the floor. The wall opposite the smelting equipment turned a corner near the magma pit, twelve meters from where she stood, and beyond it someone moved. "There's another part of the room—down there."

Drawing their swords, the three of them padded the length of the Smelting Chamber. As they moved, Nysska saw a stream of ruby-red blood emerge from around the corner and move with the tilt of the floor toward the magma pit.

At roughly the same time, she heard Cam gasp, whirled around—and slowly laid her sword on the floor in front of her.

"Where'd you go?" Percy breathed, hustling after the blood lynxes. He'd bragged on more than one occasion about how well he could track the two felines, and while that remained true, he'd also never tried to do it in the dark in the rain in unfamiliar territory.

Percy caught a whiff of cat piss that told him he was headed in the right direction, darted around a massive oak tree, and almost tripped over Jax. The big cat stood, statue-still, a meter behind his sister, both of them staring into a patch of impenetrable darkness beneath the spreading branches of a cluster of maple trees.

Percy knelt next to Jax. The blood lynx twitched, startled, when Percy ran a light hand down his spine, but his stare never wavered. "What is it, boy?" Percy whispered. "What d'you see in there?"

Something shifted in the darkness.

Something *huge*.

Percy almost lost control of his own bladder when a stray beam of moonlight caught a pair of silver eyes...then another. And another.

The man holding a dagger at Nysska's throat was barely tall enough to do it properly. She felt sure she could disarm him and drive the dagger into his heart before he even realized what was happening...but neither Raoul nor Cam were that fast, and the men holding daggers to *their* throats kept Nysska still.

"Praise be to the Great Silver Dragon," the knifeman whispered in Nysska's ear, flooding her with the kind of breath that only comes from a mouthful of rotting teeth. She could hear the smile in his voice. "Move slowly, or we'll open you all up."

The men marched Nysska, Cam, and Raoul around the corner, into a second chamber filled with death.

None of the men wore any kind of uniform, but of the two dozen present, she easily picked out eight soldiers. Five of those reminded her strongly of Darlo, the Argonium Infantryman who'd moonlighted for the spoiled noble man-child Sergei Benitoff. All of them moved and spoke in deference to a tall man with iron-gray hair, fitted with priest's robes and an immaculate Dragon-wing harness. He had pale skin and eyes so light blue they were almost clear, along with square, corn-yellow teeth that displayed themselves one by one as his weathered face split open in a humorless grin.

Beyond the priest lay the Gemini metalworkers. Nysska recognized wounds inflicted by swords. On the battlefield, a killing stroke was enough—deal the damage and move on to the next target. The Dragon-worshippers had taken their time with these deaths. The Gemini's bodies looked like chum to be slopped over the side of a fishing boat.

"There's the one we have to thank for this," the priest said, his voice high-pitched and raspy. "We were just about to come looking for you. Repay you for the good deed of leading us to these unholy scum." He spread his arms, and Nysska saw the wicked-edged jet-black dagger in his hand. "I imagine you feel right at home in a place like this, don't you, demon? Isn't this the kind of place from whence you and all your filthy brethren crawled all those centuries ago?"

"Are you two all right?" Nysska asked.

She cast her voice toward Cam and Raoul, but the knifeman at her ear barked, "Shut up!" and pressed the blade into her throat hard enough to draw a thin line of blood.

The priest sheathed his dagger, chest puffed, and swept toward her, the hem of his robes fluttering against the floor and his polished wings glimmering with magma-red light. "You think you can pollute our lands," he grated out when he came within a meter of her. He was shorter than she'd first thought, and having to tilt his head to look up at her appeared to be adding salt into whatever wound he imagined he bore. "You and your unholy ilk. You can see how we dealt with those face-crawling freaks. We'll do the same to you...and then we're going to dump your blasphemous corpses into that pit, along with all other evidence that you ever existed."

The priest drew even closer, almost nose to nose with her, and had opened his mouth to say something else when a heavy-shafted arrow entered his right eye, passed all the way through his skull, and drove deep into the chest of a Dragon-worshipper behind him.

Nysska had never thought much about the way it would sound if the world were to come to an end, but the explosion of screams, lacerating flesh, and breaking bones that slammed through the chamber seemed appropriate for an apocalypse.

In one motion she took the dagger out of the knifeman's hand, spun, and used the momentum to plant the blade in his chest, sliding in between a couple of ribs just to one side of the breastbone so that it lodged in his heart.

Feet pounded everywhere as the screaming grew louder, and repeated flashing glimpses came to her of runes beneath skin alight with silver flames, but Nysska couldn't focus on anything but dragging the dagger away from Cam's throat. The Dragon-worshipper who'd held Cam at knife-point had gone slack-jawed, staring at the brutal chaos unfolding around them, and might have come to his senses if he'd had another second or two.

Nysska gave him no time at all. Closing one hand around the fist gripping the dagger, she dragged it away from Cam and crushed it at the same time, and before the pain could register on the man's face she slammed her own head into his. Nysska's right horn crunched into his skull, and she pulled the dagger loose from his nerveless grip as his body collapsed.

Raoul had already taken advantage of the situation, gripping his own knifeman's wrist with both hands, and threw the Dragon-worshipper over his hip so that the man landed in a pained heap at Raoul's feet. Raoul twisted the dagger free and slashed the man's throat.

"Nysska, what is this," Cam said, pressing herself to Nysska's side. "What *is* this?"

Nysska knew what it was—knew the source of the arrow that had slain the priest and begun the chaos—but she couldn't bring herself to put voice to it.

Five midnight-blue specters of death moved through the chamber. Too fast to comprehend fully, almost too fast to see at all, flickering ghosts with blades for hands and heads crowned with proud black horns. Eyes of yellow, and orange, and deep shimmering ruby red. Nysska pulled Cam and Raoul back into the farthest corner. "They are *araneoj*," she said. "My brother's people."

"Holy hell," Raoul breathed, and Cam began to cry.

Five sethyds in midnight-blue leather armor, each armed with one short blade and one longer than any Imperial longsword, swept through the crowd of Dragon-worshippers very like farmers harvesting wheat, weapons reaping swiftly, efficiently. Mercilessly.

The regular men—the farmers, the miners, the devout who'd answered the priest's call and left their fields straightaway—fell and died so quickly that Nysska wondered if they even felt much beyond the fear they'd brought with them.

The five that she'd picked out as Argonium Infantrymen were a different story.

They suffered.

Nysska had fought and killed one Infantryman—Darlo, Benitoff's lackey—in hand-to-hand combat, and it had taken very nearly everything she had not to shatter under the horrendously amplified strength the Touch runes provided. The Infantrymen facing the *araneoj* wore armor beneath their peasants' clothing and had filled their hands with bronze as soon as the priest had fallen.

It made no difference. Nysska watched as the elite sethyd soldiers took the Infantrymen apart, bit by bit, piece by piece. Long and short blades alike seeking out the gaps in the armor, the gaps in the techniques, the lack of speed and skill that made them no match for Patrinomonto's deadliest.

Nysska realized the sethyd fighting closest to her was Gerrit himself. He caught her watching and gave her a flame-eyed wink as his long blade darted in and severed all the tendons on the back of an Infantryman's hand. Gerrit speared the soldier's other arm through the bicep with the long blade, drove it through until he came close enough, then thrust his short sword up through the solar plexus and into the heart.

When the Infantryman fell to the floor with a pitiful clanking rattle, a silence fell. Nysska pulled Cam around behind her as the *araneoj* assembled, facing the three members of the Ninth Crucible.

Gerrit casually wiped his blades free of blood before sheathing them. "All right, you three," he said, in a manner casual yet allowing no room for disobedience. "Come on."

The other four *araneoj* had stowed their weapons as well. Now they simply stood, staring, waiting for Nysska, Cam, and Raoul to comply.

"Come on where?" Nysska asked, as carefully as she could.

Gerrit pointed out to the main chamber. "Out there. I want to make sure I understand everything I'm seeing."

Silently, the *araneoj* surrounding them, they left the butchered Gemini and the slaughtered Dragon-worshippers and moved back out into the Smelting Chamber proper. Nysska traded glances with Cam and Raoul. Neither of them appeared to have any idea what to do, and looked to her for guidance. She wished she had a good way to tell them that they were all about to die.

27

"Maybe if we split up," Raoul murmured, almost too softly for Nysska to hear, turning away from the sethyds and barely moving his lips. "Bolt for the door in three different directions. They can't catch all of us."

"Yes, they can," Nysska murmured back. "They are *araneoj*. Spiders. They are...the elite among the elite in the sethyd military."

"I could take them off guard," Cam whispered. "Bring my runes up to full. And if you gave them one of your battle screams, we—"

"I do not know how much my sister has told you about us," Gerrit called out. "But part of *araneo* training is the development and control of every sense. I can hear every word you're saying. Just as any one of us could shut our ears to Nysska's annoying little squeals."

To Nysska's horror, Raoul stooped and swept up a fallen sword. "Ah-rah-nay-oy? Sounds like bearshit to me." He lifted the sword, both hands on the hilt, and planted his feet. "I've been trained by the Cathedral my entire life."

Nysska wanted to hiss, *What the fuck are you doing, drop the fucking sword,* but a split-second, wild-eyed glance over his shoulder conveyed the message. *Run,* he meant them to understand. *When I do this, run.*

She didn't get the chance to say anything at all. The sethyd closest to Raoul moved in a violet-and-blue blur, and in a terrifying simultaneous impact of metal on metal and flesh on flesh, sent Raoul's sword sailing across the room. It clattered hollowly on the floor as Raoul gasped and staggered.

His left arm *folded* halfway between wrist and elbow. Cam shrieked and caught him, and then Nysska was there as well, supporting him as they lowered him to the floor.

"Oh, fuck, fuck fuck fuck," Cam whispered, trying to examine the arm.

"We've got to straighten it out and bind it," Nysska said, aware of how Gerrit and his fellow Mountain Bulls simply stood and watched in quiet amusement. "I don't think we've got anything to make a splint, but if we wrap some belts around it, maybe keep it immobile like that—"

"Don't bother," Raoul gritted through lips gone gray. "Not like I'm going to have time to let it heal." Sweat coated his face. "Least he went for the other arm. Now I've got a matching pair." His eyelids fluttered, and Nysska vividly re-lived the fracturing of Raoul's right arm at the hands of one of the blood rune corpses at Altamar.

"You can't have this ore," Nysska called out, getting to her feet. "That's what you're here for, isn't it? You saw what Lockridge did, and now you want the blood runes for yourselves. It's not enough that any sethyd is three times stronger than the strongest human. Faster than their fastest."

"Smarter than their smartest," Gerrit added with a smirk.

Nysska went on. "No, you want to take this new kind of thaumaturgy and run roughshod over the entire continent. Well, I'm—"

She broke off.

Trying her absolute hardest not to let her eyes betray her, as she looked past Gerrit—

At *Flax*, who had just darted into the Smelting Chamber. The blood lynx stayed at the rear of the chamber, silent, but as Nysska almost ruptured a vessel trying to focus with her peripheral vision, Flax lifted one paw and gave Nysska an unmistakable signal.

Wait.

"Yes?" Gerrit said. "You are what?"

Nysska swallowed, and dropped her eyes to her sword on the floor a few meters away. "I'm not about to just stand here and let you kill me— kill the three of us—without a fight."

Gerrit sighed. "There will be no fight, Nysska. I would have thought our handling of the Dragon-lovers back there would have disabused you of any notion so foolish."

"I'm not talking about a free-for-all. I'm talking about you and me. One on one. *Frato kontraux fratino.*"

Gerrit's incredulity turned to unvarnished derision. "Brother against sister? Proving what? How profoundly I outmatch you, in the fleeting moments before your death?"

Nysska never took her eyes off her brother as she stepped out, away from Cam and Raoul, hoping with all her heart that neither of them had seen Flax. "Proving, I would guess, that you've never told any of your little spider friends how I used to beat the shit out of you on a regular basis."

A few eyebrows raised among the sethyds—in sharp contrast to Gerrit's abrupt scowl. "What are you *talking* about? The *araneoj* recruited me the same year as the Temple of Atiina came for you. Lying does not become you, Nysska."

She gave him her brassiest grin. "Oh, now who's lying? Mother had to make me let you up off the ground at least once a day." One of the Mountain Bulls chuckled softly, giving Nysska courage. "I'm willing to bet all your fearsome training is no match for my natural talent." She spread her arms. "Why don't we find out? As you said, it will change nothing. So why not indulge me? At worst, I give you the ass-whipping you deserve, and then your friends gang up and kill me. At best, you get to shut my mouth once and for all."

Gerrit shook his head. "I asked you to find out who was responsible for Summergray. We've been watching you—except for that annoying week you seem to have spent traipsing through the wilderness—yet I can't tell if you've discovered the culprit or not. Tell me now and we'll give your friends a quick, painless death. Or don't. You've seen us fight. We'd love a chance to show you how we *persuade*."

Nysska opened her mouth to speak—

But stopped at the bone-jarring sound of something like a landslide, echoing off the metal walls.

The floor trembled, followed by a roar that sent spiking pain into her eardrums, and seconds later the doors to the Smelting Chamber exploded out of their frame.

The biggest great gray bear Nysska had ever seen or even heard of catapulted into the chamber.

The bear roared again, its immense body like a fur-covered hillside as it rose to its hind legs, the top of its head brushing the ceiling, and Nysska felt as if she were in the presence of some kind of merciless forest deity.

The red-orange light flashed and danced in the bear's eyes—eyes of the purest solid silver, like those of the blood lynxes. Eyes behind which a vast, fearsome intelligence gleamed.

Another great gray bear came charging into the chamber behind the first one—

Then a third, with Percy clinging to its back as if it were some kind of wild horse.

"There's the fuckers!" Percy bellowed. "The ones in the dark blue leather!"

With that, the Smelting Chamber became something new.

When Nysska was a tiny girl, a tree grew outside her family's home. Old it was, a towering oak, an immutable wooden sentinel. She imagined its roots reaching down a klik or more, its grasp on the land unbreakable, while its branches often disappeared among the scudding clouds. Her mother's mother had built a treehouse, high up in its boughs, accessible by way of a ladder made of bronze pegs hammered into the wood. Nysska spent hours in that treehouse, far above her town, watching the miners come and go as they hauled coal up from the depths, knowing the boards beneath her feet were as strong in the tree's embrace as the house of stone where she and her brother slept.

Until the day the hurricane came.

Every sethyd in Fajrosxtono took shelter in the mine as the air outside grew teeth and sought their deaths.

When Nysska and her mother and brother came back to their house, the great oak tree was gone. Not just broken, but ripped up, roots and all, and cast half a klik away, as if it had been the flimsiest of playthings.

The *araneoj* were the oak when they killed the Gemini and took apart the Dragon-worshippers.

The great gray bears were the hurricane.

The first bear lunged for the closest sethyd, and the Spider danced to one side, blade screaming through a deadly arc aimed for the massive beast's neck—but the bear *anticipated the blow*, its colossal body moving almost too fast for Nysska to see, and the dagger-long claws found the Spider's arm before the blade had done more than scratch skin. Blood sprayed straight up, spattering across the ceiling, and the Spider staggered backward with the shredded ruin of his arm held high, sword clanging to the floor.

Two of the remaining four Spiders tried to flank the second bear, tried to divide its attention, but the first beast abandoned the sethyd with the mangled arm and flung itself jaws-first back into the fray. The nearer Spider realized what was coming a fraction of a second too late, turning just as the bear reached him, and the bear did what bears do, jaws sideways, crunching down on the sethyd's chin. The Spider screamed and gurgled and died, the lower half of his face torn away.

The other Spider, who had tried to help his cohort with the flanking maneuver, drove his sword deep into the second bear's shoulder. If the beast felt any pain it failed to show it. Instead it reared upright, tearing the sword free from the Spider's grip, and swept the sethyd up with both paws, crushing him against its chest. Nysska heard the wet snapping of ribs as the Spider's body went limp, but the bear seemed to tend toward thoroughness. It closed its massive jaws around the sethyd's skull and ripped his head off his shoulders.

Nysska thought ten seconds might have passed since the bears' arrival. Maybe fifteen.

The remaining two Spiders—Gerrit and a sethyd with horns like a bull's—had backed up, closer to the wagons loaded with chervoxite. Bull-horns broke to the right, and might have skirted all three of the beasts as he sprinted for the door, but just as he evaded the closest bear's swiping claws Jax launched himself with a screech straight into the sethyd's face.

Nysska gasped—she knew if the Spider got his hands on the cat, he'd kill him in a heartbeat—but Jax leapt clear as quickly as he'd come, digging into the Spider's cheeks with his back legs for purchase. Bull-horns' hands flew to his face, and he didn't see Flax as she threw herself against his shins, so that he tripped and came down on the points of his elbows.

A bear's immense paw planted itself in the middle of the Spider's back and crushed him like an egg.

Nysska had spread her arms wide, keeping herself in front of Raoul and Cam as the great gray bears swept through the *araneoj*, and now she pivoted, following the third bear as it hurled itself full-speed toward Gerrit.

Gerrit leapt high in the air, tucked his legs and spun, and his blade carved a wicked channel across the bear's back as he passed. The bear roared, and its entire body weight slammed at full speed into the chervoxite wagons—

Which popped the chocks free from the front wagon's wheels.

Gerrit screamed, *"Ne!"* Which confirmed Nysska's guess about his desire for the ore.

As the bear righted itself, coming around to face him, Gerrit danced in and plunged his sword into the great beast's neck halfway to the hilt. The bear bellowed, body thrashing, but Gerrit hung onto the blade, working it deeper, sawing through muscle and bone.

Until the bear spun, pinned him against the nearest wall, and bit his right arm off.

Gerrit's remaining hand let go of the sword. His knees buckled, but not quite enough to send him to the floor. He backed up, staring at the spurting stump, and almost tripped over the drained body of the first Spider to die there in front of the pit.

The chervoxite wagons rolled toward the edge. Slowly at first, but with steadily greater speed, and when the first one tipped over the edge, Nysska saw something inside Gerrit die.

The three great gray bears encircled him. Watching. As if they knew all the fight had left him—that he was now little more than a curiosity.

Gerrit pushed between them and ran, staggering, for the exit, and the massive seraphic creatures watched him go. One of them turned instead to the wounded bear, gripped the pommel of Gerrit's sword in its jaws, and carefully pulled it from his friend's neck. The wounded one dipped its head in an unmistakable gesture of thanks as, beyond it, the final cart of the chervoxite wagon train clattered and clanged over the edge and sank into the magma.

Nysska turned to Cam and Raoul, as Percy and the blood lynxes joined them, her eyes cutting toward the door through which Gerrit had disappeared. "I've got to go after him."

"Why?" Percy shot back. "Fucker's got his arm off! He's already dead!"

Nysska shook her head. "No. The bleeding will be slowing down by now. I've seen sethyds survive worse wounds than that." She took in the three great gray bears, who had swung around and were now watching her with unreadable lights in their silver eyes. "They're not going to maul *us* now, are they?"

Percy grinned. "Not hardly. The kitties and I have an understanding with them, but *you*—they're mighty fucking impressed with you, Nysska. Something about dismantling bear traps, I think? They were drawing pictures in the dirt, so it was hard to tell for certain."

Cam came forward and put a hand on Nysska's chest. "Go. Deal with him. We'll take care of Raoul's arm."

"Yes, please," Raoul said faintly, his lips gray.

Nysska ran full-tilt out of the Smelting Chamber, following her brother's blood trail.

It led her down the corridor, past the entrance from the canyon, and into the vast artificial cavern where Emperor Valco's "garden" lay—a broad red ribbon at first, then narrowing, soon leaving only fat crimson drops in Gerrit's wake. Nysska took precious seconds to light a lantern, fearing Gerrit would appear from around a corner as she did it, but the blood trail led her straight across the floor and down one of the aisles.

A few seconds into her pursuit Nysska noticed traces of dirt and small rocks where there had been none before. Even as the blood trail diminished, the rock and soil grew thicker, until it led to one of the doors at the chamber's far end that had been blocked and inaccessible earlier in the night. *There's the landslide I heard,* Nysska thought, passing the stony debris left scattered by the great gray bears' entrance. Percy owed her an extensive explanation, she decided.

The blood trail led through the door, down a short corridor, and up a flight of carved stone stairs, where a broad door set flush with the earth had been thrown wide. Nysska took the stairs three at a time and emerged into a bitter cold night. She noted the mounds of earth cast aside where the bears had dug the buried doors open—but much more important, the rain had stopped, and the drops of Gerrit's blood led away through the darkness.

Something large moved off to her left, and Nysska's heart almost leapt up out of her throat. Her hand flew to her sword—the near-panic growing worse when she realized she'd left it behind in the Smelting Chamber—and she tore a dagger loose from its sheath on her thigh before she realized what had made the sound.

"Oh—hey there, horses," she said, and the Imperial mounts tethered to a sturdy sapling whickered at her. "Percy left you here, huh?"

Her own mount bobbed its head, and Nysska's eyes narrowed.

Nysska tracked the fat drops of ruby red across the forest floor, heading north parallel to the canyon, her breath visible in long plumes from her nostrils. The lantern swung from her belt, extinguished. Unnecessary under the light of the second moon. She had seen two places so far where Gerrit had collapsed, yet dragged himself back upright and continued. The blood loss had almost stopped. If he got proper treatment she had no doubt he'd survive, but right now he *had* to be weak as a kitten.

Nysska pushed out of the woods onto the bare strip of land at the canyon's edge and froze.

The rope-and-plank bridge stretched away in front of her.

Halfway across, facing her, stood a man with dragon's wings.

The man held Gerrit tight, the point of a dagger resting against his larynx. She saw Gerrit trembling, teeth bared and eyes flashing in impotent fury.

Nysska didn't know the Church of the Great Silver Dragon's ranking system. She had seen plenty of priests, but the man holding her brother at knife-point had to be something higher up the food chain. His flawlessly polished wings were enormous and ornate, and instead of white he wore robes of a deep blood-red. The mirror-surfaced, paper-thin tin sent the moonlight flashing off his wings like glimmering silver fire.

"That's far enough," the man called out. His voice boomed and echoed from the canyon's walls. Nysska squinted. Beyond him, on the other side of the bridge, a small army of Dragon-worshippers had gathered, all of them staring at her.

"Who the fuck are you supposed to be?" Nysska said, matching his volume.

"I am Arch-Pastor Kelmaine Polidori. Servant of the Great Silver Dragon. Leader of the Dragon's North Central Clutch. And your time has come to an end, sethyd." Polidori was a big man, tall and broad, his head slick-bald but with ash-gray sideburns flaring from his jaws.

Nysska hefted the broad-bladed headsman's axe she had taken from the harness on her horse's saddle. She had never been trained in how to fight with an axe, but it was a good bit better than nothing. When the axe head caught the moonlight she heard a faint gasp from the crowd on the far side of the canyon. "'Sethyd' now, is it?"

"Throw down that axe and come with us," Polidori said. He took a step backward, dragging Gerrit with him. "Or I shall carve the life out of this wretch and fling him into the chasm."

"Why do you want me alive? Surely you'd rather see *both* of us plummet to our deaths."

"You will be tried. Tried and found lacking in the eyes of the Great Silver Dragon. Punished in accordance with His will. That fate awaits all sethyds now."

Nysska had to force herself not to grind her teeth. "All right, but —*why?* I know you hate us, but we've never done *anything* to your fucking church!"

Polidori's mouth stretched in a grin devoid of humor or goodwill. "The ground your feet cover...the food in your stomachs...the air in your lungs. None of it belongs to you. You take and take from us, you take from the Dragon, and expect us to do nothing?" He hitched Gerrit tighter to him. "Everything we do is for the people of Kainos. And for the Great Silver Dragon above."

For the people of Kainos.

Nysska felt the world tilt and yaw around her—

As connections in her mind clicked into place.

"That's…that's what Nikolai Petrovich said. Right before he died."

Polidori glared at her.

Voice rising, Nysska cried out, "You? *You?* We kept trying to put the blame on the Gemini, but the whole thing was *you!* The Church!"

Polidori spat over the side. "We know the truth now, sethyd. You and your kind are no supernatural creatures. What you are is *filth.* Unworthy to live among humans. Unworthy to live, full stop. I will not rest—none of the Dragon's children will rest—until you and all your people are brought low. If I have to use one kind of vermin to drown out another, as the Dragon's blood flows through my veins, so I shall, as the wretches at Summergray learned! Now throw down that axe!"

Nysska took a great breath.

Deep enough to propel her voice across the canyon.

Deep enough to ring Polidori's skull like a bell.

"From now on," she bellowed, "You will address me as *Demon!*"

The headsman's axe flew high over her head, and in two graceful, deadly arcs Nysska sliced through the ropes anchoring the bridge to the canyon's lip.

Arch-Pastor Kelmaine Polidori's wings did not allow him to fly.

She watched as Polidori and Gerrit fell. Since the rain had stopped, she had the clearest of views as they bounced and caromed off the canyon walls and finally disappeared into the fire-bright thread far below. Two tiny impacts, like a pair of pebbles disappearing beneath the surface of a river. Neither one ever screamed.

Nysska lifted her eyes and stared across the canyon at the gathered Dragon-worshippers. She couldn't tell how many there were.

Only that they looked *terrified.*

Nysska propped her axe on one shoulder, turned and disappeared into the forest's darkness.

28

Nysska leaned against the stone railing of the lighthouse and stared out at the darkening sea. Behind her the sun was still setting, painting the western sky in spectacular reds and oranges and golds, but Nysska preferred to gaze eastward at the water instead. There were still a couple of boats down there, tiny at this distance. Chasing one last cast of the net before stars filled the sky and the fish left the surface for deeper waters.

Salt air filled her nostrils. She drank it in, savored it, relishing the taste that took her back to her homeland. In many ways, Patrinomonto and Kainos couldn't have been more different, but the ocean smelled the same. If she closed her eyes, she could imagine the scent of her uncle's cooking, drifting out from the kitchen. The happy grunts and woofs Springer always made as he danced around her. The games she used to play with Gerrit...

"Ah-ha!" Asch said from her seat on the cold stone floor. Nysska turned to look down at the circle of papers surrounding the young woman, each held in place by a stone, corners flapping in the chill evening breeze. Asch made a mark on one of them and grinned up at Nysska. "You see why I like to come all way up here?"

Nysska turned and half-leaned, half-sat against the railing. "Because cold air makes your brain work better?"

"No!" Asch laughed. "Uh...well...maybe. But no! Is because no people are here. No questions." She made a motion near her ear with one hand that looked like a duck quacking. "Talk talk talk! I do not think well with so much talking."

Nysska decided not to comment on how much Asch herself talked as she crouched and looked over the papers. "So you think this..." She gestured at the assembled pages. "Can actually work?"

Asch grinned and shrugged. "Works on paper. Works in my head. Hot air goes up, yes? Trap hot air like so...wind blows that way..." She pointed out to sea. "General Cullen says he can get me things I need. Try to make it work." She gathered up the papers and stood and stretched. "This tower is good! We can use it as place for flying ship to..." Asch frowned. "To grab onto."

The sethyds had a term—*sagxa nescio*. It meant, more or less, "wise ignorance," and applied to people who did not know that a thing was impossible, so that in their ignorance, they accomplished the thing anyway. Nysska couldn't decide whether Asch was truly brilliant, could actually construct such a flying craft, and only sounded daffy because of the language barrier...or was just daffy, and about to waste a tremendous amount of time and money. She thought she was leaning toward that first option.

"And you think you can put this thing together and fly it east. Carrying you and Singer and Kagan. All the way across the ocean to Borealis, through the sky."

Asch's perpetually sunny disposition slipped a notch as her face darkened. "We will fly home, or we will die. Maybe I will see my husband again. Maybe... Those Who Dwell Beneath Waves will watch our ship fall into water, and come and eat us. I hope we make it back to Borealis. But I know we cannot stay here."

Nysska nodded. That much was certainly true. The conditions at Cliffside were a damn sight better than those in the cell deep inside the mine, but it was no less a prison, at least for Singer and Kagan. Nysska shuddered to think what the public reaction would be to either of them, and couldn't decide which the Imperial citizens would loathe and fear more. It seemed to be an evening for indecision.

"I go down to talk to General," Asch said, her grin having returned in full force. "You come with me?"

"No, I'll stay up here for a few more minutes. See you at dinner."

"All right!" Asch squeezed Nysska's upper arm and stepped inside the tower's glass enclosure, disappearing down the spiraling stone steps.

Nysska turned and leaned on the railing again. She was a little surprised the two boats were still out there—it was just about to get actually dark—but they were both well on the safe side of the Buoys, so what business was it of hers? Maybe they weren't fishing boats at all. Maybe they were people who simply enjoyed being on the water.

Still. Their presence bothered her. One of the reasons they had chosen Raoul's childhood home as their site of safe retreat was its isolation. Asch could hardly attempt to build a secret flying vessel if citizens could just show up and gawk at it.

Familiar footsteps on the stairs made her turn, smiling. Cam stepped out onto the balcony, and Nysska opened her arms. "Come to me."

Cam licked her lips and moved into Nysska's embrace, and Nysska found her mouth and worshiped it with her own lips and tongue. When the kiss broke, Cam laid her head on Nysska's chest and said, "It's cold up here."

Nysska wrapped her cloak around Cam and held her tight. "Better?"

"Better."

The first few stars peeked through at the eastern horizon. Nysska's eyes traced a path from the brightest star, down and closer, along the ocean's surface, to the waves that crashed against the face of the sheer cliff a hundred meters below. "Have you come to let me know how fucked I am?"

Cam's back stiffened under Nysska's touch. "I don't know how far the ramifications of all this go, or how far they're going to go. The Church of the Great Silver Dragon hiring out mass assassinations? Members of the Argonium Infantry working with them? Secret white runes on the Emperor? What does any of it even *mean*?"

Cam had been functioning as Nysska's eyes and ears for the last week, sitting in on some meetings, eavesdropping on others, and outright spying on at least two. Meetings from which Nysska had been pointedly excluded, as General Cullen, the Thaumetallicon's Overmaster Brinn, and a personal representative of Emperor Valco had all tried to decide how to proceed.

Nysska knew the facts in evidence. The destroyed shipment of chervoxite. The involvement of the *araneoj*. The culpability of the Church, or at least of one of its Clutches. What no one but their immediate group knew of, on the other hand, was the existence of Singer and Kagan. The visitors might have seen Princess Aschling skulking about, but she looked like nothing special on the surface and easily passed as part of the estate's cleaning staff.

Nysska stepped back from Cam, swept the cloak from her own shoulders, and bundled it around the smaller woman. Side by side, they stared out at the graying sea.

"Does it feel as though some kind of era has just come to an end?" Nysska asked quietly.

"What do you mean?"

"It's just…I kept secrets. I kept Gerrit from you. All of you."

"And we know why. Dragon's tits, Nysska, he was holding your mother hostage. If ever there were going to be mitigating circumstances, this is it."

Nysska sighed. "I just can't imagine I'll be allowed to continue as Enforcer of the Ninth Crucible. For that matter, I can't imagine I'll be allowed to keep my Imperial citizenship. Be lucky if I don't end up on a fork in the middle of Caulspring."

"It won't be that bad."

"Won't it?" Nysska straightened up and stretched, arms over her head. "I deceived you all. I played a part in destroying several tons of ore that might have given the Empire the edge it needed to weather whatever storm gets thrown at it."

"That wasn't you, sweetheart. I don't think you can be blamed for the actions of a seraphic bear." She paused. "And let's not discount that rune-trap thing you brought back from the mine. If the Imperial College can figure out how it works, shit, they might give you a medal."

Nysska put her hands on the railing. "Part of me thinks I need to hide out until Asch's crazy flying thing is ready to go, and then stow away. Try my luck in Borealis. Pretty sure I've worn out my welcome here."

Her eyes narrowed. Had she just seen a flash of movement on the deck of one of those boats?

Cam said, "Look, no, I don't know how it's all going to pan out, all right? But one thing I'm sure of is—"

Something happened.

Nysska wasn't sure what it was—she'd been standing at the railing, but then, for some reason, her back thumped against the rock wall behind her. The runes in her eyes flaring bright, Cam said, "Nysska?"

In the silver light, Nysska looked down and saw the shaft of a thick, heavy arrow protruding from her chest, and it made sense—that was why her shoulder blades had struck the wall, because the impact of the arrow had driven her backward, and that cold, detached section of her brain kept working, working as the heat drained out of her limbs, out of her stomach, out of her heart. She knew the arrowhead must be lodged in the stone, that was why she was still upright.

"Nysska! *Nysska!*"

Cam's voice seemed to grow louder and softer at the same time, how was that possible, the horror and pain Cam poured into her name growing and growing yet coming from somewhere so far away. Nysska's brain kept working, though she felt it begin to hitch and sway, thoughts buckling, even as a sound reached her ears. Carried on the salt-laden wind. The deep, thrumming *twung* of an Argonium Infantry bowstring.

Nysska moved then, the shaft slipping through her—no—she slipped along the shaft, along the polished black wood that had invaded her body, all the way to the fletching, and the feathers hurt worst of all as she slid free—

The railing ground against her waist as she pitched forward, Cam's hands reaching for her, grabbing at her, too weak to stop her as Nysska's body left all of its light and heat and life behind, trailing in her wake as she fell.

The last thing Nysska heard was her beloved's fading scream before the crashing waves took her.

TO BE CONTINUED

ACKNOWLEDGMENTS

Writing is often described as a solitary activity, but I couldn't have done this without some truly superlative people. Huge thanks go out to Stewart Vernon, Beth Denton, Kimberly Phelps, Richard Plemons, Dirk Griffin, Dino Hicks, Whitney Danielle Roden, Nancy Terselic, Zach and Sarah Caylor, Angelina Vaquera-Linke, Clay Gilbert, Michelle Miller, Charles C. Collins, Haris Orkin, Robyn Jipp, Michelle Deems Brice, Waseem Aftab, Austin Barclay, James Barry, and Clint McInnes. Y'all are awesome.

ABOUT THE AUTHOR

Dan Jolley began writing professionally at age 19. Starting out in comic books, Dan has worked for major publishers such as DC (*Firestorm*), Marvel (*Dr. Strange*), Dark Horse (*Aliens*), and Image (*G.I. Joe*). He soon branched out into licensed-property novels (*Star Trek*), film novelizations (*Iron Man*), and original novels, including the science-fiction/superhero *Gray Widow Trilogy*.

Dan began writing for video games in 2007, and has contributed storylines, characters, and dialogue to titles such as *Transformers: War for Cybertron*, *Prototype 2*, and *Dying Light*, among others.

His latest work includes *The Storm*, a mystery-thriller inspired by actual events in Dan's hometown, and the best-selling Audible Original audiobook *House of Teeth*.

Dan lives with his wife Tracy in northwest Georgia. Readers can learn more about him on his website, www.danjolley.com.

ALSO BY DAN JOLLEY

ADULT FICTION
The Gray Widow Trilogy:
Gray Widow's Walk
Gray Widow's Web
Gray Widow's War

YOUNG ADULT BOOKS
The Alex Unlimited Trilogy:
The Vosarak Code
Split-Second Sight
True Chemistry

MIDDLE-GRADE BOOKS
The Five Elements Trilogy:
The Emerald Tablet
The Shadow City
The Crimson Serpent

House of Teeth (Audible Original audiobook)

FRIENDS OF FALSTAFF

Thank You to All our Falstaff Books Patrons, who get extra digital content each month! To be featured here and see what other great rewards we offer, go to www.patreon.com/falstaffbooks.

PATRONS

Dino Hicks
John Hooks
John Kilgallon
Larissa Lichty
Travis & Casey Schilling
Staci-Leigh Santore
Sheryl R. Hayes
Scott Norris
Samuel Montgomery-Blinn
Junkle

www.ingramcontent.com/pod-product-compliance
Lightning Source LLC
Chambersburg PA
CBHW050149120726
47903CB00002B/548